THE
RIGHTEOUS
SPY

THE
RIGHTEOUS
SPY

MERLE NYGATE

VERVE BOOKS

THE RIGHTEOUS SPY

First published in the UK in 2018
by Verve Publishing, an imprint of
Oldcastle Books Ltd,
Harpenden, UK
vervebooks.co.uk

Editors: Clare Quinlivan & Katherine Sunderland

This is a work of fiction. Names, characters, places, and incidents either
are the product of the author's imagination or are used fictitiously,
and any resemblance to actual persons, living or dead, businesses, companies,
events or locales is entirely coincidental.

ISBN
978-0-85730-800-9 (print)
978-0-85730-801-6 (epub)

4 6 8 10 9 7 5 3

Printed and bound in Great Britain by Clays Ltd, Elcograf S.p.A.

To
DN and WG
Always

PART 1 – THE CHOSEN

But God chose what is foolish in the world to shame the wise; God chose what is weak in the world to shame the strong.

1 Corinthians 1:27

For you are a people holy to the Lord your God and the Lord has chosen you to be a people for his treasured possession, out of all the peoples who are on the face of the earth.

Psalm 50:15

This day have I perfected your religion for you and completed My favour upon you and have chosen for you Islam as your religion.

Quran 5:3

1

Palestinian Territories – Present Day

Soon.

I know it'll be soon because when we finished prayers this morning Abu Muhunnad's eyes were shiny; and I don't think it was irritation caused by dust and the wind that blows sand from the south.

It was not as if it was anything he said, I just had the sense that he wasn't listening when I told him about my fast, at least not as intently as he usually does. I was describing the verse I'm reading and instead of commenting, he just nodded. That's when I saw his eyes glitter with tears.

I'm okay. Really, I am.

I wanted to say that to Abu Muhunnad this morning. I wanted him to know and be certain that I am truly filled with joy and grateful for the opportunity, *inshallah*. It's as if everything I've done in my twenty-seven years has led me to this point, this place, this precise moment in time where, finally, I am going to make a difference.

2

Tel Aviv, Israel – The Same Day

Seventy kilometres away – as the drone flies – Eli Amiram made his way to the bus stop for his morning commute. Even though he'd strolled only a short distance, from apartment to bus stop, by the time Eli arrived at the shelter he was sweating. His shirt grazed his damp neck and he could smell shower soap, deodorant and his own perspiration. The middle of May and at 7am, the temperature was already hitting 28 degrees. But the heat in isolation was nothing. Humidity was the killer; the wet, dense air that trapped him in its steaming strait-jacket. Eli leaned against the side of the metal bus shelter and narrowed his eyes. He tried to imagine grey London streets underfoot, grey clouds above and what it might feel like to inhale, if only for a second, cool air that hadn't been artificially refrigerated. It was too bad Gal had driven north to see her mother. Otherwise, he'd have been in the car looking out, not on the street, sweating like an animal.

Half a metre away a woman was shrieking into her cell phone. Eli closed his eyes. He stroked the top of his shaved head and felt the new growth on his skull. He supposed it could have been worse; at least the *Khamsim* was over. As far as Eli was concerned, a hard blue sky and 90 per cent humidity was a distinct improvement.

After a few more seconds of being bombarded by the woman's conversation Eli opened his eyes to assess the source of the voice. What he saw was a fleshy face with faded blonde hair brushed back into a bun. He knew the type. The pitch of the woman's voice was bad enough, but her heavily accented Hebrew set Eli's teeth on edge. It was like listening to Stockhausen's Helicopter String Quartet.

The bus screeched to a halt and Eli peeled his back away from the bus shelter and let the grandmother lumber ahead of him. Hauling herself aboard she found a seat halfway down the aisle. Eli made his way to an empty seat at the back of the bus; it was well away from the grandmother but next to a *dati*. Sliding down, Eli glanced over at the grey side burns, wispy beard and pallid skin.

The bus jolted forward and Eli's head jerked back against the headrest. He felt a finger nudging his ribs. Turning, Eli caught a blast of a gastric disorder from the man's mouth.

'You speak English?' the old man said with an American accent. 'Or Yiddish?' His tone was peremptory and he didn't wait for an answer. 'Is this Rosh Pinna Street? Is this the corner of Rosh Pinna and Ariel?'

'Next stop,' Eli said.

'You'll tell me when we get there?'

'Of course, it'll be a pleasure.' Aware that he'd used the right idiom Eli was still irritated with himself because he always struggled with the precision and physical placement of an English accent. The focus wasn't around the lips and vestibule of the mouth like French, neither was it located near the hard palate and throat like Arabic. It sat somewhere around the middle, just before the soft palate and it bugged him that he hadn't got it. Even after years of study.

Five minutes later, when Eli was still trying to select an appropriate expression to practise on the American, they were at Rosh Pinna Street. Eli stood to let the man out.

'Take your time, sir,' Eli said. 'There's no rush, no rush at all.' Shit. He'd done it again. Rolled the 'r'. As he sat down, Eli grimaced trying to achieve the oral position for a non-rolling 'r'.

That was when he noticed a new passenger, a woman, step into the body of the bus.

Eli stared. In dark blue jeans and flowing green top, skeletal shoulders sat atop a lumpy waist and an ugly hat shaded her face. But it wasn't the absence of any aesthetic that made the base of Eli's neck prick as if an elastic band had flicked against his flesh; it was her expression – she was terrified.

Eli glanced across the aisle at a soldier to see if his combat receptors had kicked in but the kid was more interested in the horse-faced girl by his side. No back-up there.

Up ahead, the woman was hauling a black and white shopping trolley down the aisle. Judging by her strained expression the load was heavy. Eli stood up to get a better look at her.

Was she ill?

Beneath heavy make-up the woman was pouring sweat. She was drenched. A slick of moisture dewed her upper lip and the armpits of the blouse were almost black. Okay, it was hot outside and okay, she'd dragged a loaded shopping trolley to the bus stop, but there was something wrong with her. Between thick eyebrows there was a deep frown crease and her eyes flicked around the bus, not settling, not making contact.

Eli reached into his pocket for his cell phone. He glanced down and fingered the button to call the emergency services. Was he overreacting? Up ahead he saw the woman's lips were moving and her hand was clenched around the handle of the shopper.

She'd found a seat. Right in the middle of the bus. Right where a device would cause the maximum damage. She sat down and Eli got a good view of her back and the narrow profile of her shoulders atop the billowing green top. Her waist was out of proportion to the rest of her body and she was holding on to that damn shopper as if her future depended on it.

'*Slicha*, excuse me,' Eli slid out from his seat and shoved aside a kid standing in the aisle reading his phone.

Ahead, the woman was still clutching the shopper and positioning it with both hands. Not one. Struggling to keep it upright. Eli was two metres away from her and closing in when a man, an office worker in a white shirt, stepped into the aisle and blocked Eli's way.

In one hand he had a paper cup of coffee and he was reaching to take a linen jacket off the seat hook with the other. Using the flat of his hand against the man's chest, Eli pushed him back into his seat. The coffee went flying as the office worker lost his balance and fell on top of another man reading a newspaper.

'What the fuck!'

Eli didn't look back.

The bus grunted to a halt and the brakes squealed. The doors hissed open. Eli reached the woman and wrenched the shopper from her grip. He glimpsed the fear in her eyes. Behind him people stood about to get off. Eli blocked them. He ripped open the Velcro cover of the shopper and dove inside. He pulled out a nightdress and a toilet bag and tossed them across the floor of the bus where they skittered under the seats.

'What's going on? What's happening, why can't we get off?' Sharp and anxious voices. Voices close to panic. Meanwhile, Eli plunged his hand deeper into the shopper again and again but found only softness; no wire, no block, no bomb. In his peripheral vision Eli saw the soldier boy holding back the passengers.

'What's happening? Is there something wrong?' Eli heard from the crowd of commuters.

'*Bitachon*, security,' Eli said. 'Everything's under control.'

Now on his feet Eli dragged off the woman's hat. Tear tracks striated the make-up on her face.

'Are you out of your mind? What do you think you're doing?'

That voice, that awful accent, it was the grandmother sitting right next to the girl Eli had just assaulted.

'I had reason to believe –' Eli tried to make his voice sound authoritative hoping that a firm tone would camouflage his cock-up.

Her face was red and one of her dockworker's arms was around the girl's skinny shoulders.

'Didn't the good Lord give you eyes in your stupid big head? The girl's sick, she's going to the hospital and she's frightened to death.'

'Lady, we all have to be vigilant and aware of security at all times. D'you understand? Okay, I made a mistake, I apologise, but I was acting in the best interest of everybody.'

There were rumblings from the other passengers. They were divided. Eli saw the man with a coffee stain across his white shirt; he nodded at Eli. He got it. He understood. But the grandmother didn't.

'What kind of idiot are you?'

He hissed, 'The kind of idiot who is trying to protect you from being blown to pieces. Do you have a problem with that?'

'*Maspeek*, enough, please,' whispered the girl through tears. 'It's okay, I'm okay.'

'Lady, I'm sorry, I made a bad mistake,' Eli grabbed a handful of clothes from the floor and dumped them on the girl's lap. Then, since the soldier boy was still holding back the rest of the passengers, Eli scrambled down the steps on to the street.

He walked the rest of the way to the Office.

3

King Solomon Street, Tel Aviv – Ten Minutes Later

Eli stepped through a set of automatic doors into the blessed chill of the downtown mall. It was a relief. The incident on the bus was unfortunate but defensible. Eli strode past the small café where the gym bunnies hung out. As usual, he pulled in his gut. Next, he passed a branch of Bank Leumi and a small supermarket with a metal turnstile and cliffs of cut-price vodka. Finally, Eli reached the northwest corner of the mall and a scuffed metal door that bore no sign. As he did every office day, Eli curled his right hand around the vertical handle and contacted the fingertip recognition keypad. Hand in position he looked around the mall, checking to see if there was anyone nearby. It was unnecessary as there were cameras everywhere but it was procedure. It's what you did; it's what you were trained to do.

Periodically refurbished and updated, this particular Mossad facility was located in a building within another building. It had its own generators, electronics and water supplies, communications, cryptography and the rest of the technical tricks department. While Eli visually swept the mall, his vital signs were being monitored, fed into the computer system, compared to a set of algorithms and minutely measured to see whether he was unusually stressed or unusually unresponsive.

The door clicked open and Eli slid into the first security section where he handed in his home cell phone to the staff behind the desk and had a further retinal identification check.

As always, Eli was struck by how quiet it was when the door to the mall shut behind him. It wasn't just a door – it was a boundary; like walking from the beach into the sea to take that first breath through the snorkel into another world. Here the atmosphere was sterile; the only colour was the lights from the bank of monitors against the white wall; the only sound, apart from human voices, was the hush and hum of electronics. Beyond the reinforced door, the mall shrieked with its discordant colours, tinny music and neon pleas to purchase.

Eli assumed his easy, affable, professional face. The one he used in the field, when he didn't want to share his thoughts.

'Good morning one and all,' Eli said.

'Morning Eli,' Ze'ev, a curly haired blond boy didn't look up from the machine that was scanning Eli. 'See the game last night? Disaster.'

'There's only one team worth talking about; Maccabi Tel Aviv is and always has been the best.'

Ze'ev glanced away from the scanner to roll his eyes while a young woman stepped out from behind the desk and ran a second, hand scanner over Eli who stood with his legs apart and arms above his head.

Pronounced clean, Eli made his way through two more double doors to the lift and the second-floor canteen.

The canteen was modern with pale wood, stainless steel and deftly placed mirrors to give the illusion of light even though the space was enclosed by metres of blast-proof concrete. There were a few windows in Mossad's central Tel Aviv building, but those were on the upper floors where department heads had their offices, not in the 24-hour canteen where everybody ate, from the cleaners to intelligence analysts to signal collectors, to the tech geeks, to the shrinks. The single canteen was a nod to the dim memory of kibbutz life where the cow-shed worker sat next to the nursery nurse who sat next to the kibbutz administrator.

Pushing the wooden door open, Eli caught the scent of fresh coffee. He also spotted Rafi sitting on one of the blue plastic chairs right near the coffee station.

Eli joined the queue at the pastry station for a Bulgarian cheese *boureka* and kept his back to Rafi to avoid eye contact. It had been four short weeks since Rafi had been let loose on the mid-Africa desk; and already he'd created something of a stir in the office. Maybe it was his leather biking jacket and white tee shirts but apparently the girls in Collections had coined a name for Rafi: 'movie star'. Eli wondered if they had a name for him too. Best not to think too hard about that.

The server gave Eli the hot pastry wrapped in greaseproof paper. Walking towards the coffee station, Eli kept his eyes locked straight ahead as if he was lost in some meditative thought.

'Eli, my main man,' Rafi called over in mid-Atlantic English. '*A'hlan*,' he continued in street Arabic, and finally in Hebrew, 'Eli, sit for a moment, great to see you. So, tell me, what's going on with Red Cap? I just read the London signal in the summary. Looks pretty serious to me. For this to happen two weeks after the passport fiasco in London...'

Using an outstretched leg, Rafi pushed out one of the blue chairs. It was an invitation to sit down; Eli remained standing and with deliberation helped himself to the coffee at the dispenser.

'Patience, Rafi,' Eli said. 'As Tolstoy said, the two most powerful warriors are patience and time.'

4

The Office, Tel Aviv – Thirty Minutes Later

By the time that Eli stepped into the meeting room he'd worked out both tactics and strategy for dealing with Red Cap.

It was no big deal. Just a manifestation of the perennial problem with agents: you might even say it was 'the nature of the beast'. Pondering the provenance of the English idiom, Eli settled himself in his usual chair with his back against the wall. In keeping with the organisation's current culture, there was no magisterial boardroom table down the middle of the meeting room and no refreshments either. Just a few Ikea side tables stacked for convenience and you brought in your own coffee.

While Eli waited for Yuval to arrive he massaged his eyebrows with thumb and middle finger. In spite of Rafi's gleeful anticipation that the Red Cap fallout would spatter in his direction, Eli was sanguine. He was not about to get wound up by this new guy's attempt at dramatisation and disruption.

Eli checked his watch and on cue, 0800, Yuval marched into the room. About the same height as Eli, or perhaps a little shorter, Yuval was dark. In the field he passed himself off, with some success, as Spanish. Thick black hair flopped over his forehead and he repeatedly and impatiently pushed back the fringe with one of his small nail-bitten hands.

In the style of a platoon leader briefing his squad, Yuval picked up the remote control and activated the screens. The logo and motto of Mossad came up and the representatives of the fourteen operational desks sat up to attention. There were no preliminaries, no chit-chat, no social niceties. Yuval was direct and interrogatory. Each day at 0800 and ten seconds for the last three months, he'd circumnavigated the room in the same order, starting with *aleph* – for Africa.

'The situation is like this,' Yuval started. 'We have a special operation underway in Nairobi,' Yuval punched out the words while his eyes pecked at his audience. 'The target has now been located and identified. There's been subsequent verification by two independent witnesses. We're only waiting for the prime minister's authorisation before we go. Rafi, this is your desk, do you have anything to add?'

Rafi stood up and took charge of the remote control and an image of a thick-set, suntanned man with unnaturally white teeth appeared on the screen. He was crinkling his eyes against bright sun and in the background there was blurred blue sea.

'This is Klondyke,' Rafi said. 'An ex-pat, ex-army British major with homes in Barbados and Switzerland. Founder member of an organisation called 91, dedicated anti-Semite, racist, colonialist, funder of any racist group, political or otherwise, who happen to have their feedbags out, and all-round good guy. For a day job he is the main supplier of military spares to Al Shabab and Hamas's long-time go-to man for quality detonators. Recently he's been looking to trade up and invest in laser technology which, on top of everything else, makes him a target.'

Then Rafi reeled off the resources that had been made available for the operation, the estimated time of completion, the training hours the squad had completed and the three fall-back plans.

Eli was uncomfortably impressed. He uncrossed his legs and leaned forward, elbows on knees. All the facts and figures tripped off Rafi's tongue and as he held the floor Yuval's head bobbed in tiny movements of comprehension and approval.

Rafi went on, 'As discussed on Friday and signed off, the tactical decision is for the squad to use a location five K from the contact point.'

'Are they going to rehearse access in situ?' Yuval said.

The subtext in the simple question was clear. No mistakes would be tolerated.

Rafi said, 'No. They've done timed rehearsals at the country club but nothing in situ.'

The country club was the facility to the north of Tel Aviv where the special operations section was based. There were hangars of equipment, fake sets that looked like streets in different cities, flight and car simulators, not to mention the gyms, swimming pools and a prime stretch of beach for the squad to lounge about on between ops.

Yuval frowned, 'Why not?'

'I thought about it, Yuval,' Rafi said. 'But if the squad rehearses in situ the risk increases exponentially. The op area has a population density of 450 per kilometre. The Nairobi police may be corrupt but they're not totally inept.'

Eli had another moment of chagrin. Rafi not only knew his stuff but he was ready to stand his ground with the new boss.

Rafi went on, 'It will take twelve minutes maximum to get from contact point to swamp. It's a decent road, unlike some in the area. The team will be in and out in two hours.'

On cue a satellite image of the road appeared on one of the screens. On another there was a ground view image. On the third, the route from the contact point and on the fourth screen some joker had projected a still of a crocodile. Jaw open; conical white teeth; teeth primed to rip apart human flesh. Eli saw Yuval's black brows twitch into a frown.

'Okay.' Yuval recovered and did one of his bird-like nods. 'Klondyke disappears into the crocodile swamp. No questions and no comeback – just the way we like it. Good work, Rafi. Next, Cana-da, home of the Mounties.'

Yuval moved swiftly around the room getting updates throughout the world, Far East and Australia, the US and finally, Eli's desk, Western Europe.

Yuval checked the diving watch that dwarfed his hands and sped up his delivery, 'So, the situation is like this. Red Cap, an asset in GCHQ for the last fifteen years, has refused to work with his third new case officer, Gidon. Eli, what's your plan?'

Eli stood up. He didn't bother to take possession of the remote control because he hadn't had time to upload any images. And after all, everybody knew what GCHQ looked like. He brushed his hand across his head. 'We have two choices. One, we bring Red Cap over here, give him a nice dinner, say thank you very much and retire him; or two, we find someone he will work with. Yes, his product is consistently good and no, we don't have anyone else in GCHQ at his level but...'

Eli paused for effect. 'Red Cap has never become the agent of influence we always hoped he would be. What's more, the older he gets the less likely it is that he'll ever get a job that involves policy-making. And that's because he's unpredictable. Fifteen years ago he walked into the London embassy because he was passed over for promotion. He has no Jewish connections, no friends, no family, no nothing but he wanted to do the thing that would make being passed over more tolerable for him. But, bottom line, there is a reason why Red Cap didn't get promoted then or now. It's the exact same reason he came to us and didn't go to the SVR. He's unpredictable.'

'All agents are unpredictable. That's part of their charm.' Yuval said.

'Yuval, I'm the first person to agree with you. That's exactly what I say to the kids in training. Agents are liars, losers, fuck-ups, we all know that, but there's a fine line between being unpredictable and being unmanageable.'

'No agent is unmanageable, Eli. It's just a question of finding the right handler. It's like dating, sometimes it works, sometimes it doesn't. You know that as well as anyone. In truth, better than anyone. You concentrate on Red Cap. Start thinking about how to manage him because we've got no one else in GCHQ and no one else to help us keep tabs on 91.'

'But we can't control him,' Eli said. 'He's an accident waiting to happen.'

'Who says?'

Eli waved a sheet of paper in Yuval's direction. 'This is the experts' report after Red Cap's last debrief. That's when he got drunk and smashed a glass coffee table in the safe house. The experts say he has an undiagnosed personality disorder and paranoid narcissism.'

'The experts' was the catch-all expression used for the psychologists, psychiatrists and assorted brain-suckers that were an integral part of the organisation. The CIA and FBI loved their polygraphs, the Brits relied on regular vetting panels, and Mossad had their shrinks; platoons, brigades, whole armies of them.

'Experts,' Yuval waved the piece of paper away, not deigning to read it. 'They've got a name for everything. Red Cap has a drink or two and an accident. So what?' He checked his watch, 'Eli, we're out of time. We're gonna park this for the minute and you and Rafi will meet back here in thirty minutes. After I've spoken to the prime minister and got the Nairobi green light.'

Papers were moved and chairs shuffled back as everybody who was seated stood up to go. But Yuval wasn't quite done. With one of his stubby fingers he stabbed at the wall screens where the crocodile had been displayed in colour-saturated glory. 'Rafi, that was unacceptable. It is not a moment for humour and you know why: a killing must be pure.'

On the way out of the meeting Eli found himself walking beside Rafi who seemed quite undiminished by Yuval's growl about the crocodile.

'Can I buy you a coffee?' Rafi said. 'We've got some time before we go see Yuval.'

'Sorry, I've got a few things to do,' Eli said.

Rafi put his hand on Eli's shoulder. The weight was uncomfortable.

'Eli, come on,' Rafi said. 'Just a coffee, we've got some stuff to talk about before we have the meeting.' The big man shifted from foot to foot, he was smiling. 'I've got some information you might find interesting.'

'What's that then?' Eli said.

'Come and grab a coffee and I'll tell you.'

'Stop behaving like a kid with a secret. If you want to tell me something then do it,' Eli said.

'Okay.' Rafi took his hand away. Eli looked up at him. At that moment, Eli thought just how easy it would be to hit Rafi somewhere between his hazel eyes or, as an alternative, aim for Rafi's Adam's apple at the precise point where a sharp punch might, if Eli were accurate, kill him.

'Get on with it,' Eli said.

'We're going to London,' Rafi grinned. 'That's why Yuval wants to see the both of us. And it's going to be big.'

'London?' Eli said. 'It's not your account, you've only ever worked there as a bag boy; you don't know anything about the place, the politics, the culture. Why on earth would they want you in London?'

'I imagine it's because I have special skills.'

'You?' Eli snorted.

'I also have a connection there who might be useful.'

5

The Office, Tel Aviv – Thirty Minutes Later

Yuval stood with his back to the blank screens in the meeting room addressing Eli and Rafi. It felt like being back in the army or on the three-year Mossad training course when you were given assignments to complete and then got graded.

'This operation in the UK is the beginning of the most significant initiative since 1948 when the state of Israel was founded,' Yuval said.

Eli was accustomed to a certain level of hubris when a new operation was mooted but this statement went well beyond standard introductions. Keeping his expression grave, Eli nodded and waited with considerable interest for what was to come.

'The PM and the cabinet believe that now is the time for us to be accepted as a major power player, not just in the region, but in world politics. After all, if North Korea can be considered as such, why not Israel?'

Eli caught Rafi's expression; he was frowning.

'It's not as crazy as it sounds,' Yuval said. 'The prime minister sees a unique opportunity and whatever we may feel about him, he's shrewd. The situation is like this: the US is faltering under Trump; the EU is riven with dissent; Russia, for all its posturing, is falling apart economically behind the scenes. The war in Iraq is over, in Syria the war is coming to an end and when the superpowers have left the arena, there'll be a power vacuum. We need to be ready to fill it by building our alliances not with America but with our friends in the region. To do that we need better intelligence, and that's what we're going to do even if we have to be a little more creative than usual and push ourselves.'

'And the UK is where this is going to start?' Rafi said.

'Exactly, it's where we begin. Instead of having to be grateful for any crumbs of product the Americans and British throw our way, the first operation in the strategy will make us appear to be pivotal to the security of the UK and thus more significant in the region. How?'

Yuval paused for effect before he answered his own question, 'We're going to stop a terrorist attack.'

Eli rubbed his scalp, 'Nice idea, Yuval, but how can that be guaranteed? We don't have the resources to infiltrate UK groups and even if we did we'd be tripping over MI5 which would make us even less popular than we already are.'

'Very simple, Eli. The way to guarantee that we stop a terrorist attack is... by running the terrorist,' Yuval said with simple pride.

'I see,' Eli frowned. The content of the morning meeting was disturbing to say the least.

In terms of his intelligence career Eli considered himself to be a simple man; a meat and two vegetables man; not an experimental gourmet who mixed incompatible foods for the novelty. Simple was good. Simple was safe. Simple worked. You made the contact; gathered operational information; developed the source; made the pitch and then you ran the source; extracting best quality product possible while keeping the source fit and healthy. Simple.

Yuval went on, 'You two are pivotal to this operation's success. I picked you, Rafi, because of your operational experience, and you, Eli, for your track record as the best agent runner in the organisation.'

Eli stood up and walked around the room, 'So, the idea is that we do a false flag operation on a suicide bomber and then feed the intel to the British so they can stop it? It's certainly original.'

Original sounded better than unlikely.

'And the so-called terrorist has actually been recruited?' Rafi said. 'You're saying *Shabak* infiltrated a Hamas cell at that level? Impressive.'

'Yeah, they're full of themselves. Another reason for us to follow through and get some glory. We can't be seen to let the plodders in *Shabak* look smarter than Mossad,' Yuval said.

Plodding sounded fine to Eli at that moment even though he'd never been tempted by the internal security service, *Shabak*; there was too much bureaucracy.

Yuval was still speaking, 'We're calling the operation Sweetbait – cute eh? What is also attractive is that we won't need to use London's resources which is just as well as there are going to be some changes there.'

Changes? This was news to Eli; it could only mean that Gidon was going to be fired which would leave the head of London station job vacant. Rafi seemed to have missed the allusion.

'I have connections in London,' Rafi said. 'From way back but I'm sure I could reconnect. She used to work for us when I was in London; Alon was her *katsa* and her code name was Trainer.'

'Ah, the legendary Alon,' Yuval said. 'A good man indeed, and I read about Trainer in the archives. Highly respected; skilled apparently – but it won't be necessary.'

From across the room Eli watched Rafi nod, accepting the decision like the good soldier he was.

Eli held up his hand, 'Yuval, I'm happy to go to London; happy to deal with Red Cap; bring him back in, clean up Gidon's mess, but the type of operation you're planning...'

Yuval interrupted, 'I need a spy runner, understood? I need *the* spy runner.'

'Eli, it'll be fine,' Rafi said. 'We complement each other; Yuval has thought of everything.'

'Don't brown-nose me, Rafi,' Yuval said. 'Eli is the lead; you are number two. What's more, the success or failure of this operation rests jointly on your shoulders. In other words, if one of you screws up the other one will be equally responsible. You'll find the reading material in your mailboxes and travel will send you your documents for London.'

6

Old Street, London – A Week Later

'I'm from *London Finance*,' Petra said. 'Here to interview Andrew Canadell.'

She stood in the all-white reception area while the man behind the desk, who looked as if he'd used pumice stone to shave, wrote out a visitor's badge and slipped it into a plastic sleeve.

'There you are, Miss, if you just take a seat, I'll tell them you're here.'

It hadn't been hard getting the interview. Not when Petra had said that *London Finance* was doing a series about leading CEOs. The PR department had leapt at the opportunity to give Canadell a four-page spread in the independent journal.

Five minutes later Petra was shepherded to the twentieth floor and was sitting in Canadell's office overlooking London. The room smelt of wood polish and subdued wealth. Across the desk, Canadell sat framed by a floor-to-ceiling window with the Shard in the background.

Petra glanced down at the list of questions she'd prepared for the CEO; there was nothing too extreme on the list. Nothing that might make Canadell baulk at what she was saying or end the interview.

'Before you took over Gomax Pharmaceuticals you worked in the drinks industry,' Petra said. 'How do you feel your expertise has transferred?'

Canadell leaned back in his chair, his face was florid and his shirt collar was too small. In another life Petra could have seen him in a Hogarth etching with a wig askew. In this life he tugged a yellow patterned tie over his white shirt as if the strip of fabric would conceal his gut. On the left lapel of his suit Petra saw an enamel badge and noted the design of both tie and badge in her notes. The tie was a gift from someone he liked but who didn't know him well; it was too bright and too cheap. The badge was more complex; Petra clicked her camera pen to support her notes.

'Good question,' Canadell said. 'There are certainly transferable skills and indeed, these are both people businesses. I value...'

Petra nodded, smiling with demure respect and memorised the room. She divided it into sections and noted the artefacts and objects. Later on these would be analysed to consider what they might say about Canadell and the report she produced would be sent to his business competitors. Behind him, on a small side table there was the ubiquitous family portrait, with what looked like wife number two – or perhaps even three. There was also a portrait of a school-age child on the desk. From what Petra could see, the CEO's wife was not quintessentially Anglo-Saxon; she had dark hair and high cheekbones. Perhaps Slavic; perhaps Native American. That might prove to be interesting, but so far, in this particular interview there were slim pickings. Not much to interest Canadell's business competitor who had commissioned the report.

To the right of Canadell, on a wood-panelled wall there was a further display of photographs. They showed Canadell posing with various politicians across the political and historical spectrum. There were also pictures of him with the most accessible royal as well as a series at various sporting events. But, Petra noted, no horse racing so possibly no gambling.

Closer, Canadell's colossus of a desk was clear; yet mighty though the desk might be, it was functional. Tidy. Precise. Two laptops were open and as he spoke, he kept glancing in their direction.

'And I see you're a Londoner and support the culture of the capital in many ways,' Petra said.

'Yes, yes, we recently initiated a programme to take young people to opera rehearsals. Although we may have missed it for this season.'

'Why's that?' Petra said, smiling with great understanding.

'Timing,' he shifted in his seat, as if he was trying to get comfortable on the deep padded leather.

That was interesting. What was it about the question that made Canadell display an anxiety tell? Was it personal or professional?

'Of course,' Petra said. 'These programmes have to be organised so far in advance. But you must be keen to continue, having done so much good with these initiatives.'

Canadell nodded, 'We have. So many young people helped. So many young lives enhanced by the power of music. It makes me very proud.'

'I can see that. Who is involved? Would I be able to speak to someone from the charity and get a quote? I think it's something that people would find fascinating.'

In answer, Canadell pushed the desk so that his chair shifted back, 'Of course,' he said. Of course not, he meant.

Yes, there were inconsistencies about Canadell. He looked like a rugby player gone to seed. At a guess, Canadell was using the opera charity for either personal reasons or financial; in other words, the usual: sex or money. Meanwhile, her part was coming to an end.

Petra uncrossed her legs, leaned forward and switched off the Zoom audio recorder. 'Thank you for your time,' she said. 'I'm very grateful. I'll send the copy to your PR department and will wait for your approval.'

Canadell nodded, but he wasn't listening; he was looking at his laptop and frowning.

Petra stood up and walked around the desk to shake hands with Canadell. She was able to see the screen; it was a live update of the Hang Seng. 'It's been great to meet you,' she said.

Glancing at her watch, she made a note of the time to feed into her report. The geeks back at the office might be able to work out what was disturbing Canadell. There couldn't be that many options on the Hang Seng screen at that particular time. And her role was over; she'd write up both the article and the private report. The article would contain the superficial information about Canadell; the do-gooding CEO that would appear in *London Finance*. And her report, the one commissioned by Canadell's business competitor that contained detailed thoughts and recommendations for further action, would go to her employers, the security company.

7

Palestinian Territories – Two Weeks Later

Today I was moved to an amazing room, the walls are purple and painted with verses from the Koran and green birds. It's so beautiful. The birds are painted in shades of turquoise, lapis lazuli and emerald. They represent the flock that carries the souls of martyrs to Allah and soon, *inshallah*, they will bear my soul to *Jannah*.

I stroke the wings of a bird and feel paint and plaster under my fingertips. I'd be lying if I said that I'm not thinking about what I'm leaving behind. Sometimes I ache in my stomach when I hear the children laughing as they knock around a ball in the dusty courtyard outside. But in *Jannah* the children won't have been displaced; they won't know poverty and disease, they won't have been bombed and cut down and injured and mutilated. They won't be like the broken babies I nursed at the hospital, day after day after day.

Would it be different if I had my own children? Of course it would. For one thing, if I were a mother the Martyrs Committee wouldn't have accepted me. Neither would I have been chosen if I were the sole support for my own mother who will, when the time comes, receive a good pension and be honoured.

Knowing what I'm doing for my mother makes me so happy. At last she'll have a reason to be proud of me – her divorced and barren daughter. At last she'll be able to talk of me with pride because I'll be the one keeping her secure and in comfort for all of her days.

For a moment I remember how we used to have picnics on the beach in Gaza. In summer we stayed indoors during the day hiding from the heat. But when it got dark and a few degrees cooler we'd come outside and bundle into my uncle's rickety pick-up truck, the car with the blue number plates that identified us. Once we got to the beach we'd settle ourselves on sand still warm from the day and eat the kibbe, tehina and tabbouleh that my mother and her sisters had made. Sometimes I'd sit with my feet in the cool sea eating watermel-on, seeing just how far I could spit the seeds into the darkness. And then we'd sing the whole way home as the truck rattled and rumbled through the night.

I always tried to sit near the back of the pick-up so I could feel the night air cool my arms. Usually I'd have the sleeping weight of one of the little ones on my knee. If I was lucky it would be Amira, holding her tight, holding her safe, holding her close to my heart. If I was less lucky it would be my little brother Wasim who was like a puppy, always looking around, squirming to get out of my arms and lean out of the back of the open pick-up.

'*Kun Hadhira*,' my mother's voice would be shrill with fear from the depths of the truck. 'Be careful.' A lot easier said than done with a metre of slithering, squirming, laughing little boy on your lap who wanted to see and be, and howl at the moon with the sheer joy of life.

I swallow hard thinking of that time. That good time in the past.

Outside the window I can hear the sound of the wind, like the distant roar of the sea and then a clatter of a metal pot that hasn't been secured. It must be rolling around outside. The window is spattered with shapes like little sandy clouds and the sky beyond is yellow, murky, dark. Sadly, it's not simply the sand and the heat that's the problem in *Khamsim* weather, it's the pollution. Poor *Mawmia* – her asthma will be torturing her. I can see her fingering and clutching her inhaler in her gnarled arthritic hands, frightened to put it down, frightened not to have it close by, frightened that she will suffocate. I always made sure there was a spare inhaler in the kitchen dresser drawer – I hope she remembers – or that someone else does.

The door opens and Abu Muhunnad stands framed, as if in a picture, ready to come in.

It must be time.

'*Salaam alechem*. May we enter?'

'*Marhaba. Al'afw*.'

Behind Abu Muhunnad there's another man. I haven't seen him before. He's younger and paler and harder-faced beneath his beard and behind his glasses.

Abu Muhunnad moves towards the single chair and the new man stands slightly behind him. I feel like he's examining me and feel uncomfortable.

But Abu Muhunnad's voice is warm and soothing, 'We have something important to discuss with you.'

Of course I'm nervous but I also feel a surge of exultation and relief. At last the waiting is over. I sit on the edge of the bed upright, feet together, trying to breathe slowly.

'I am blessed,' I manage to say. 'And honoured to have been chosen.'

Abu Muhunnad's hands are folded across his black clad belly. 'My child, we're here to tell you that you're not going on the mission that we have been training you to accomplish.'

What is this? For a few seconds I wonder if I have heard wrongly, misunderstood what Abu Muhunnad is saying. Not going? That can't be right.

I massage my forehead as if the action will help me to absorb the information. Perhaps this is some final test to see if I've got the faith to complete my mission or whether at the last moment I will fail. I must convince Abu Muhunnad and the other man.

'I'm ready Abu. I've memorised the map of the target. I know the bus stops on the corner of Dizengoff and Ester Halmalka. I know the café is two hundred metres away on the right-hand side. I know there are two orange trees in front of it. I've got a copy of *American Vogue* to carry to show I'm interested in fashion. And I know I must sit exactly in the middle of the café to make the maximum impact.'

'We know; we know you're well prepared; indeed, you're perfectly prepared. We could ask for no more in your dedication, but you're not going to the café.'

'Why?'

'Because it's our decision,' the other man says.

I smooth the bed cover with my hand and find a small thread that I tug between my nails.

'Am I not pious enough?' I say.

I'm still uncertain whether this is a test and I have to prove my commitment and obedience. Maybe I've failed and all along there's been someone else training, someone ready to go for the same target who is more righteous. That must be it. Looking at Abu Muhunnad's face and then the cold expression on the face of the stranger I know that's the truth. Someone else had been chosen.

I press my lips together to stop myself crying. There's nothing I can do, I'll be returning to my mother where I will help her wash and dress and be the comfort of her old age. My sister will visit with my nieces and nephews and I'll continue to be the failure.

'I understand,' I say. 'It is the will of Allah.'

I raise my eyes and catch a glance between the man and Abu Muhunnad.

'*Habibti.*' Abu Muhunnad leans forward and places both hands on his knees. 'It's because you're both pious and brave that you will not complete this mission. You see, there's something else for you to do that's far more important and more dangerous; something that only a special daughter can do for the glory of Allah and the destruction of his enemies. You are going to London.'

That night I don't sleep. I lie on the bed listening to the wind and thinking about what Abu Muhunnad said. I am going to London. Can it be true?

Abu Muhunnad gave me a phone with a European number. He said it was safe and wouldn't be scanned by the Jews. I was going to use it so that I could call my mother when it was too late to change anything; call her to hear her voice for the last time. If I'm going to London, will I still be able to call her? Maybe the commander will take the phone. What shall I do? In the dark of the room I look at my phone – I'm sure Allah would forgive me if I call my brother Wasim and tell him that I am doing God's work and that he has to make sure that my mother has a supply of asthma drugs. And to say goodbye.

I text a message to him.

I am going away. Look after *Mawmia*. See she has spare inhalers.

Now I can sleep. I close my eyes and begin to drift off. On the bedside table the phone vibrates. I answer it.

'Where are you?' Wasim says. 'What are you talking about going away? Who said you could?'

Always the same, my brother, just like he was when he was a kid, asking questions, demanding answers.

'I can't tell you more but you must promise to look after *Mawmia*.'

'What, are you going on vacation with our sisters?'

'No,' I say. 'Wasim, it's secret. I'm not coming back.'

I'm now sorry I texted him. Even more so when he says, 'What do you mean, you're not coming back? Sister, I may be your younger brother but I am still the head of the family, I'm your guardian.'

'I'm going to be *shaheeda*,' I say.

There is silence at the other end of the phone. I hear his breath close to the microphone.

'What? What did you just say? Are you crazy?' Wasim says.

'I shouldn't have told you. I'm sorry, forget it.'

'It's too late now, how did you... who's guiding you, Sahar?'

'Abu Muhunnad,'

'Never heard of him. What's his full name and family? Where does he come from?'

'Brother, you haven't been here for a year; things change and people change. You don't know everybody anymore and what's more, you don't know what it's like living here.'

'That's not the point. I'm your guardian, I'm responsible for you, Sahar; I'm responsible for the family. Nobody told me.'

'I'm fine and I'm being looked after. I can't say any more than that.'

'I'm going to find out what's going on. I'll call you again. Soon.'

8

Swiss Cottage, London – The Same Day

It was good being back in London and interesting too. Eli sat opposite Gidon in the Singaporean restaurant; ostensibly he was there to get an update on Red Cap but Eli had an additional agenda; he wanted to find out just how close Gidon was to being sent home.

'I've had such a lousy run of luck,' Gidon paused with a spoonful of hot soup halfway to his mouth. He sounded more like a washed-up gambler bewailing his lack of success on the slot machines than a station manager with two decades of intelligence experience.

'First the passports get left in a phone box by the idiot bag boy and then your man Red Cap goes mad – both in the same month. God knows, I could have handled one crisis; but two, so close to each other? Can't be done. And what's killing me, is that neither of those incidents were my fault.' Gidon swallowed the soup and coughed over the chilli.

As ever, Eli contained his thoughts: he didn't say that if Gidon had run a tighter ship, better procedures would have been in place and passports might not have been left in a Sainsbury's carrier bag in a phone box. Neither did he say that Gidon had completely mishandled a valued asset whose most recent intelligence had given them the tools to target Klondyke. Without Red Cap's product, Klondyke would have been helicoptering to his golf club instead of transiting a crocodile's digestive track. But explaining all of this to Gidon was pointless. What would it achieve? Nothing. Eli would just be grinding yesterday's man's face down in the dirt.

'How's your laksa?' Eli said.

'Good. Delicious in fact. I didn't know about this place and I've lived here for three years.'

There was silence at the table. Gidon broke it, 'So, what are you working on? You seem to be here mob-handed.'

'You know I can't say,' Eli smiled at the freckled face and creased forehead across the table.

'Come on. I know I'm last year's flavour, but I'm still head of London station – at least I am for the moment.'

'Gidon, drop it.'

'What's the new guy like?' Gidon said, still anxious to be 'in' with the news.

'Different.'

Gidon attempted to pour more wine into Eli's still full glass and then refilled his own. 'D'you remember those morning meetings we used to have with Avigdor? The discussions and debates? Now, that man was a leader; a philosopher, a man of intellect and culture.'

'Like I said, Yuval is different,' Eli said.

In terms of discovering what had driven Red Cap to trash the safe house, the evening was a washout. All Gidon did was reprise the contents of the contact report. However, by the time Eli returned to the serviced apartment it was clear that Gidon was more than halfway out of the door and the job of head of London station would be vacant soon.

The next morning Eli was able to observe just how different Yuval's leadership style was to Avigdor's. They were sitting in the safe room at the embassy in Palace Gardens crowding round one end of the big table since it was only the three of them: Yuval, Rafi and Eli. A folder with a printout lay on the table but it was being shunned as if it contained a virus. They had already received the report in their overnight mailbox and it didn't make happy reading; it was a transcript of Sweetbait's conversation with her brother.

'So, the situation is like this,' Yuval said. 'We have a problem; we need a solution. Ideas please.'

Eli laid down the croissant he was eating on the paper plate, 'We can't move until we've got a lot more information about Sweetbait's brother. If he's well connected he might make waves.'

'So what?' Yuval said. 'So, he thinks it's not Hamas but some other group. Or maybe it is Hamas but for once they've got an operation that's so water-tight no one knows about it. I don't think we should fixate.' Yuval said.

'I agree,' Rafi said. He picked up the plastic glass that contained an inch of a kale and kiwi fruit smoothie. He tossed the drink to the back of his throat and then threw the empty container in the direction of the bin in the corner. The glass plopped in but some drops of green liquid spattered the cream plaster.

'It'll be a total mess if he turns up in the UK,' Eli said trying not to sound as negative as he felt, trying to find a solution to the problem. 'But he won't be able to find her if we take away her phone.'

'That won't work. We take her phone, she uses a phone box,' Yuval said working his lips with concentration. 'We change the sim card and block international calls but we still have the same problem.'

'Okay, if we're going to do this we need someone in the school,' Eli said. 'We need someone in the school to be her friend and mentor, who's there round the clock. Someone who, if push comes to shove, can get Sweetbait away from the brother if he turns up.'

'Good, I like that. Rafi see who might make a good student. Maybe one of our youngsters – a boy. No, better a girl. That's what the experts say.'

Rafi opened the laptop in front of him and with his big hands started to access the organisation's database. The tap-tap of his fingers filled the room.

'I thought you didn't believe in the experts' reports,' Eli said.

Yuval didn't look up. 'It depends on the expert.' He pulled another laptop towards him, pecked at some keys with his two index fingers and then started to read the screen. 'No, no, that's not going to work. The experts say she is shy with men and... here...' he pointed at the screen and read out: "Unlikely to be influenced by a woman of her own age or peer group." Have we got anyone older who could be a student?'

Rafi looked up from his screen. 'What about Trainer?'

9

Thames End Village, Surrey – Later that Day

Petra had had an easy day. After a morning meeting in town with a fashion designer who suspected her husband of adultery, Petra had gone home, hung up her corporate suit in the floor-to-ceiling wardrobe and replaced the work costume with her running gear. It would be good to get in some exercise before she sat at the computer and wrote up the proposal. Good to get some fresh air in her lungs after central London's scent of sour petrol. Strapping her iPhone on to her upper arm, Petra let herself out of the two-up, two-down cottage and walked briskly towards the bridle path, picking up speed as she went. As she broke into a jog Petra saw a neighbour, Sandie, in her garden, leaning over her rabbit hutch, cooing. Petra waved but didn't stop.

Through the common, down the path by the trees, Petra pounded the uneven ground, inhaling the damp evening air and lengthening her stride. Her mind drifted back to the fashion designer and her own recommendations for surveillance; in this case, money was no object but the prospective client didn't look as if she'd be happy with a detailed report that would prove her fears; it was often the way. Working for the private security company paid well but gathering intelligence for the high-end divorces was always unpleasant. At least corporate intelligence clients never cried when they read the report.

After her run Petra sat on a bench by the pond and waited for her heart rate to return to sixty beats per minute. By now it was dusk and she could see the roofline of her cottage against the sky and the porch light that would come on automatically. Time to go home; Petra stood up and started walking across the green.

Silhouetted against her porch light, she noted a figure passing her house. It was a man, roughly 1.75 metres with a solid build. When he'd gone ten metres beyond her house he reached a side road that fed into the lane, paused, swivelled and scanned, before turning back and walking back the way that he had come. To Petra it was obvious what he was doing; some people never get over the need to check for snipers.

Petra gazed up and down the road to see if there was a car. Nothing. It must be tucked out of sight. Quickening her pace, the grass underfoot made no noise. A car passed, its headlights strafed the darkness and the green and Petra saw the man pause at her house where he unlatched the gate that opened on to the path to her cottage.

Petra rose on to her toes and sprinted the last few yards across the green and the road to her cottage. At the exact same moment as she stretched out to tap the man on the shoulder, he turned.

'I thought you weren't back till next week,' Petra said.

'I wrapped it up faster than I thought.' Matt smiled.

Petra brushed his cheek as she went past and opened the door. He smelt of work: sweat, travel and heat. Inside, in the light of the hallway, she saw dust in the creases of his suntanned forehead; the whites of his blue eyes were red and the smile was weary.

'Why don't you have a shower?' Petra said. 'Then I'll order in something to eat.'

'You have no idea how good that sounds.'

Matt climbed the stairs looking older than his forty-five years.

Petra called up after him. 'There's a clean robe on the bathroom door. Use that.'

Turning into the sitting room Petra went to the dining room where she'd left her laptop. She started the report aware that in the thirty minutes it took her to collate her notes, Matt would still be upstairs, but now he'd be fast asleep on her bed.

Matt left a little after 10am the next day. He said he had an evening flight to a colder climate and needed to get kitted up for the trip. Petra had no reason to doubt the truth of what Matt said, nor any desire to ask. That's not how their relationship worked.

'I don't know how long this one's going to take,' Matt said. 'That's why I came by last night. I wouldn't have just turned up otherwise.'

'Don't worry about it.' Petra slopped boiling water into two mugs and carried them over to the kitchen table.

'Sometimes I wish I'd never learnt Kazakh,' Matt said. 'I'm so tired, I feel like I've heard everything ten times before and I've eaten enough *Besparmak* to last a lifetime.'

Whatever Matt may have said about feeling tired, he looked fresh this morning; sleep had smoothed the creases in his brow and the dust of the steppes had been washed away. Petra took his rough hand in her own. 'For what it's worth I'm fed up with work at the moment, sometimes it seems so pointless.'

'Why don't we both pack it in?'

'Because we'd get bored. And then get bored with each other.' Petra let go of Matt's hand. 'Anyway, I like how we are. I don't want it any other way. What would we do? Open a bar in some godawful beach resort and think about our glory days? Maybe I'll take some time off and come visit you. How long are you going to be there?'

'The initial contract is two months. It's an oil company who are researching new fields and need security for their geologists. I might get back here and there but that's what the contract said, two months. Why don't you come out at the end? If you've never been there it's fascinating.'

'Maybe,' Petra finished her tea and carried her cup to the sink. 'Come on, let's go upstairs and I'll help you pack.'

Moving back to the kitchen table she wrapped her arms round his head and pulled him into her body.

After Matt left, Petra wrote the proposal. It took longer than she expected because she kept researching Kazakhstan. As Matt had said, it did look fascinating; certainly more fascinating than the fashion designer's crumbling marriage. The day slipped away with Petra dipping in and out of her proposal and into the history and culture of the country. Only at 5pm did Petra realise that not only was she hungry but that she'd also invited Sandie, her neighbour, to come around for a glass of wine.

Petra was standing over the bowl of guacamole when the landline phone rang. It was rarely used these days. Most people used her mobile and Petra had even thought of disconnecting it and indeed, might have, if she hadn't been aware of the security advantages of maintaining a landline.

The phone was cream; a classic 1970s style rotary dial phone she'd bought on a whim. The ringtone had a mechanical peal that made her smile with its repeated trill. It reminded her of Hitchcock films.

Petra reached for the receiver and held it to her ear.

'Hi,' she said.

'Petra? Is that you?'

'Who are you?'

'It's Rafi, Rafi Shomer,' his voice was deep, accented. 'I'm in London and it's been a long time and I thought –'

'What the fuck do you want?'

10

The Israeli Embassy, Palace Gardens, London – The Next Day

'What did she say?' Yuval said.

'What the fuck do you want?' Rafi said in English.

Eli snorted, 'So much for your good connection.'

Yuval frowned but stayed focused on Rafi. 'How did she sound? Did you get another meeting or do we have to try another approach?'

'I'm seeing her tomorrow.'

They were back in the safe room at the embassy and Rafi was drinking another one of his health drinks. 'I'm seeing her tomorrow,' Rafi repeated. 'I'd have preferred tonight but she was busy.'

'It's better tomorrow; it gives us more time to plan,' Yuval said. 'We cannot afford her saying no when you make the pitch, understood? That means I don't want you charging in there like a bull.'

'Relax, Yuval, I'm not an idiot. I know what we need to do. Credit me with some operational experience.'

Eli said, 'That's exactly the problem, you don't have the appropriate experience. You're not in special operations now, Rafi; there's no car to blow up or body to dump in a crocodile swamp. This is different. This is agent-running and requires subtlety and flexibility; qualities you lack and experience you simply don't have.'

'But Rafi has the connection,' Yuval said. 'And Trainer can help us; she is uniquely qualified. So, let's be absolutely clear about the situation and our objectives.' Yuval held his fingers curved over the table, as if it was a keyboard and he was about to type. 'We've had bad luck and good luck. The good luck is that the school is hiring. What's more, according to the file, Trainer has a teaching qualification that can be checked out. And she has the security clearance that any school will insist upon which can also be checked out.'

'Okay, that I understand,' Eli said. 'Let's assume that we persuade her to do it; and she wants to go back in the field after all this time. How much do we tell her?'

'Need to know – as little as possible,' Yuval said. 'She's British. Using Trainer edges us into the forbidden zone of using Jewish nationals in operations against a host nation. Although, technically, since we're stopping the attack, it could be argued...'

'Yeah, and it could be argued the other way,' Eli shook his head.

'Point taken. But need to know protects her. All we say is that Sweetbait has a brother and we don't want him getting to her. Simple. When does an agent ever know the full story?'

'I don't like it, I don't like it at all,' Eli pushed the buff file across the desk towards Yuval. 'I don't like using Trainer; I don't like using Rafi's connection to her; and I particularly don't like the appearance of this brother. I'm sorry to piss on your parade Yuval but I consider the combination of these volatile factors to be cause for a re-evaluation.'

'I can set your mind at rest on at least one element,' Yuval said. 'It just came in from *Shabak*. The brother's a nobody. An uncle in America sponsored him and he's now studying engineering in Kansas. He's in his first year.'

'Kansas?' Rafi said.

'It's in the Midwest. Made famous by *The Wizard of Oz*,' Eli said.

Yuval said, 'In his 18-year-old mind, the boy is head of the family but Sweetbait isn't going to listen to him. Yes, we need Trainer, but she's back-up; she's our insurance. We get her into the school, we monitor any contact with the brother and then we deal with it. Right, let's talk about Red Cap. What's your plan, Eli?'

Eli briefly summarised the sparse comments Gidon had made about the agent during dinner and then described how he was going to re-establish contact with the errant agent. Once they'd met, Eli would re-recruit him, which was, when push came to shove, what it amounted to: bringing Red Cap back in.

In contrast to Sweetbait, Yuval was pleasantly hands-off. He listened to Eli's plan, made a couple of helpful suggestions about the methodology, asked about the time frame and then, glancing at his watch, stood up.

'Okay, we're out of time. I have to get across Kensington Park for lunch with the Right Honourable Oliver Zachary Milne – our illustrious friend at MI6.'

Yuval rolled down his shirtsleeves and shrugged himself into a crumpled linen jacket. From a pocket he took out a tie that didn't match and arranged it around his collar in a semblance of a knot. 'I am expecting the usual two courses of arrogant platitudes but I think in the not-too-distant future Her Majesty's Government will be a little less casual about our contribution to the "war on international terror".' The last expression was spoken in Yuval's strongly accented English. He went on, 'And how pleasant that will be.'

Eli stood up and eased the chair he'd been sitting on under the cherry wood table. 'Does that bother you? Do you care what the Brits say or how they say it?'

Yuval fiddled with his tie while he considered the question. Finally he said, 'In truth, no. I don't. Some of the English I like personally. They're intelligent and they understand war. They've been serving officers so we have that in common. The older generation were in Northern Ireland, so we share the experience and the problems of doing the job. God knows, we gave them enough problems during the mandate. So this isn't personal – it never is; but they have something we want. That's what the Sweetbait operation is about. We might have drones over Gaza watching Hamas pick their noses but we can't compete with GCHQ and NSA – at the moment. Somehow, and we don't know exactly how, they're getting raw data from the Qatar Embassy; with the Hamas European HQ based in the embassy, it would be invaluable to us if the British would share and they will only do that if they have no other option.'

Yuval said no more but walked out of the room leaving a half-drunk coffee and a crumbed paper plate on the table. Eli picked up both and carried them to the bin hesitating for a moment as if considering what to do with the liquid. Then he replaced the cup on the table.

'I know you don't like me,' Rafi said. 'But you heard what Yuval said; we've got to work together for the success of the operation, the organisation, and our careers.'

'I'll bear that in mind,' Eli said. 'Meanwhile, I have to prepare to reactivate Red Cap.'

Rafi uncurled his height from the chair and ambled towards Eli. He sat on the edge of the table while Eli gathered up his file and tablet. 'What unit were you in when you were called up?'

'Military intelligence. Why do you want to know?'

'I was in *hayehida*, the unit, but before that, in my first week of basic training I got into a fight with another kid. As it happens, he was a Brit. He'd got himself into some trouble in the UK, car stealing, shop lifting or something, and his folks bundled him off to the relatives in *Eretz Yisroel* before he could be caught. He was a real punk and a dirty fighter – liked knives. But I gave him a good thumping.'

'I'm sure you did and it's lovely that you feel able to share this touching incident from your past.' Eli was at the door of the room about to key in the code for the exit lock on the panel.

'Wait, it's important, Eli. Listen to me for a minute,' Rafi said. 'So, after they pulled us apart and the medics patched us up we get hauled in front of the platoon leader. He gave us the usual crap about brotherhood and honour and the punishment was for us to be hand-cuffed together while we dug out the trenches for the latrines. So, there we were, in the desert, me and this kid I tried to kill, 40 degrees, dying in the heat, trying to work out a way of doing it. Eli, ever tried to dig a hole with one hand handcuffed? You can't do it.'

The door swung open. But Rafi wasn't done; he put his hand on Eli's shoulder and went on, 'That guy became my best friend. He was my best man at both weddings, I trust him with my life and I respect him. It's a beautiful thing.'

Eli looked over his shoulder at Rafi, 'Don't worry, that's never going to happen to you and me, no matter how much shit we have to dig.'

11

Thames End Village Station, Surrey – The Next Day

Petra picked up the giveaway paper from the train seat next to her and scanned the headlines. It was all inconsequential chatter; not unlike the copy she wrote in her fake corporate journalism.

Why this particular journey into London should be different from any other commute was a puzzle to Petra. Yet so it was. During the entire journey into London she felt flashes of déjà vu. She found herself checking the exits and studying her fellow commuters in a way she hadn't done for years. Much as she tried to focus on the newspaper, her phone, and the changing view outside the window, she felt a familiar and forgotten sense of detachment. She might be on a train with commuters going about their daily business yet she existed in a parallel world: the secret world. For some reason, it was pleasing.

The arrangement was to meet Rafi at one of the old rendezvous; the lounge of a run-down Edwardian hotel in Bayswater. Over the phone Rafi had used the code name for the sprawling building with its quiet corners and bored waiters, '*Sofsof*' he'd said and asked Petra if she remembered where it was. Of course, she did. She remembered all the location code names.

Petra also knew that Rafi was going to ask her to do a job. There was no other reason for him to get in touch with her in spite of what he'd said about being in London and wanting to talk about old times. Yet she'd played along; it was part of the game. She wondered whether he still worked for the Office or had gone off to set up something on his own; that was often the way and indeed, the mixed bag of colleagues at her current employers included several ex-spooks who were supplementing their pension in the private security sector.

Petra held no animosity towards Rafi; it had never been a big love thing. Truth to tell, she didn't remember much about it. But the job might prove to be interesting; it might even be worth doing.

As she climbed the stairs to the hotel's automatic doors, Petra checked her reflection in the glass. It was distorted, shadowed, her black-clad legs looked squat, her hair looked darker, and her features contorted in the warp of the glass. It was an illusion.

The hotel's automatic doors hushed open and she stepped into the air-controlled environment. The place had been done up since the old days and it was unrecognisable; almost as unrecognisable as her reflection had been. The pokey corners and pastel colours of the past had been replaced by a grey slate floor and an acid-lime mural behind the reception desk. Petra strode towards the hotel lounge where Rafi would be waiting. Arranged on a low, lime sofa, his long legs were jack-knifed under him and when Petra stood over him, he stood up with powerful flexibility and kissed her on both cheeks. His dark beard was soft.

Holding her at arm's length he looked her over. 'You look great, you haven't changed,' he said. 'If anything...' he let the compliment evaporate leaving the contrail to disperse into the atmosphere.

'So do you, very dashing with the pirate beard,' Petra said unmoved. 'How long are you in London?'

'Oh, that depends on a few things. Coffee?' Rafi said.

'Lovely.'

'Would you like anything to eat? Maybe some cake or even lunch?'

'No thank you,' Petra glanced at her watch. 'I'm meeting a friend.'

'Of course, busy lady,' Rafi ordered coffee and a cafetière promptly appeared on a tray.

'So, what are you doing these days?' Rafi said.

'I work for a corporate investigations and risk consulting firm.'

'You mean private security? What everyone thinks they'll do after we get our pensions. What's it like? Interesting?'

'Not especially. Most of the time I pretend to be a business journalist and interview CEOs whose competitors want intelligence, or worse, I do high end divorce work. Proving to some rich but miserable person that their suspicions are correct.'

'What about the teaching?' Rafi said. 'When you left didn't you train to be a teacher? I know that's what you said you were going to do.'

'That was years ago,' Petra picked up the coffee and sipped the bitter liquid. 'Years and years. Anyway, what are you up to – or shouldn't I ask?'

'Yes, I'm still at the Office; different, how do you say, sections. But still there and different from when we first met.'

'Ah yes,' Petra said. 'The bag boy – coming to meetings to drop off and pick up the documents. I remember that.'

He smiled. 'Like you said, a long time ago. So, I must ask, why did you stop teaching? You were so keen to do it; wasn't your father a teacher?'

'Have you been looking at my file Rafi, or maybe you've never forgotten a single moment that we spent together?'

'I remember,' Rafi gave Petra the full brown-eyed stroke. 'And I always thought you would make a great teacher. I'd have thought you'd have been head of a school by now. What happened? Didn't you like it?'

'I lasted an entire year until I decided that it wasn't for me. All I do now is some weekends with the kids where I live. Circuit training, gymnastics on the green, yoga, that sort of thing.'

Rafi looked thoughtful. 'For that you must be authorised?'

'Of course, it's called a DBS check. You have to show you haven't got a criminal record – I'm sure there's something similar in Israel. Anyway, what do you care?'

Rafi shifted around on his chair. It was the exact same physical tic that Petra had seen when she'd interviewed Canadell. The physical manifestation of discomfort; Rafi really should learn how to control his body language. The tell indicated that whatever he was going to say next was important; Petra leaned back in the low chair and waited.

'Don't you ever miss the work?' Rafi said.

'Let me think about that for a minute. Staying in crap hotels, standing out in the rain, lying to my friends and family about what I'm doing. No, I don't miss the work.'

He smiled, 'Come on, it wasn't all bad, was it?'

Petra surveyed Rafi, and deliberately didn't respond to the question. He would have to fill the silence. She wondered how long it was going to take before he came out with the pitch; and she was curious about what it was.

'You know, they still talk about you,' Rafi said. 'Talk about that lecture you gave to the new recruits about fieldwork. You're famous.'

Even though Petra was curious about the job, this transparent attempt to flatter her before making the pitch jarred. It reminded her of other unpleasant aspects of the work; when she didn't know who was telling the truth or who was lying, and the constant sense of distrust and paranoia. Maybe this was a closed chapter in her life and it would be better not to go back and open that book.

'You were the best,' Rafi went on. 'A natural; the word is intuitive I think, isn't it?'

'It's very kind of you to say so.' Petra stood up and positioned her shoulder bag ready to go. 'Thanks for coffee, Rafi, great to see you but I need to go. Give my regards to Tel Aviv. How is Alon by the way?'

'Dead.'

'Oh, I'm sorry to hear that.' She meant it. 'Cigarettes?'

Rafi nodded.

Petra sat down again, 'When?'

'Three months ago.'

'I wish I'd known,' was all Petra said. She felt winded. 'How long was he ill?'

'I don't know. I didn't know him so well because he wasn't involved in my section, but someone I'd like you to meet did know him. When did you last hear from him?'

Petra didn't answer. After a moment she said, 'You asked if the work was all bad. No, it wasn't all bad. The work taught me a lot; sometimes I even felt I was making a difference. So, if you'd like to tell me why you're here and exactly what this job is, then maybe we can talk about it.'

12

Heathrow Airport, London – Two Days Later

I'm so tired after the journey yet I'm too frightened to close my eyes in case I don't find the man who's going to meet me. Whatever I feel like, my orders were to stay in this seating area in the arrivals hall and that's what I'm going to do.

It ought to be impossible for me to even think of sleeping, here, on this hard chair, in the middle of the airport. There are so many people. Next to me a mother comforts her child. His eyes are red and she rocks him back and forth. Opposite a fat man in a black suit perches on the edge of the chair, legs wide, suit fabric stretching. He's barking into his cell phone and is pretty angry about something.

Of all the things I thought about I never imagined how hard it would be leaving home.

I wasn't allowed to say goodbye to anyone. Abu Muhunnad said that I'd already said goodbye when I volunteered. Of course, he didn't know I'd spoken to Wasim; how could I tell him? He'd be so disappointed in me. Abu *is* right and I can't let moments of weakness and sentimentality divert me from what I must do. I'm strong – at least, stronger than the old men who sit in the cafés at home, sucking on their *nargilahs*. There they sit, all the day long, drinking coffee, smoking *shisha*, wagging their fingers, bravely spitting *after* the occupiers pass by – and all the while they quietly cash the cheques that their children send from Kuwait and Jordan, Canada and Australia. Our bitter export: scientists, doctors, pilots, engineers – like my brother. Our diaspora spread on the four winds across the globe; I could have joined them; I could have been one of that army of despair; ashamed of where we come from, angry about what we've become. Using our talents to run their hospitals, teach at their universities and build their oil refineries. We're the hired help, serving the people who twist their lips and wring their hands because of our misfortune, because of the homes we've lost. For all that they despise us because we're homeless. Meanwhile, all that's left of the so-called government are the corrupt who grab whatever crumbs the occupiers toss their way.

I watch my hand cross the notebook writing these words. I don't know what I'm going to do with these pages but now that I'm alone and Abu Muhunnad is behind me and my mother is lost to me I feel as if I need a witness to my actions. I need a friend. Is that weakness? Shouldn't Allah be enough?

In my pocket my phone vibrates; there's a message on WhatsApp, from my little brother.

> **WHERE are you sister? I demand to know where you are and who is with you. I've spoken to my friends and they know nothing about you. This is important!!!**

I tap into my phone:
Don't worry. I'm okay.

I turn off the phone and pocket it before Wasim can call me. It's just as well because a man's approaching me with purpose, as if he recognises me. I sit up.

'Sahar?'

'Yes.'

'Taxi to London?'

The man has dark hair and a pinched, pale face. His eyes dart around with wariness and remind me of our street dogs.

'No,' I say, and with care I repeat in English the phrases I've learned. 'I order taxi take me to Bristol Hotel. Thank you.'

'Which Hotel Bristol?' he says.

'The one near the park,' I complete the exchange correctly. He smiles. His bottom teeth are stained. He takes my suitcase and starts walking through the milling mass of people.

'How was your flight?' he says. He doesn't seem to expect an answer. He says something about the weather, he is making conversation. We pass two policemen with guns pointing down and handguns in their belts; they stride with the power of the armed, it's the same gait we see when the occupiers strut down our streets. Fearful, I stumble.

'Easy does it,' the driver says. But I see he's seen the police and is walking faster. 'I hope you brought some warm clothes.'

He says more but I don't understand what he's saying although I know what he's doing. We do that at home. All the time. Talk but expect to be overheard.

By now we are outside the terminal building, crossing the road towards the car park. It *is* cold. The driver didn't exaggerate. I shudder as the wind slices through the thin fabric of my raincoat. I pull the belt around my waist tighter as if that will warm me. The driver doesn't notice; he's intent on getting me to the car on the second floor where he uses a remote key to open a blue Mercedes.

'I like these cases with wheels,' the driver pushes the case so fast I have to trot to keep up. He keeps talking; I understand a word here and there, 'wife' and 'Spain'. He opens the trunk of the car and loads in my case, softly he mutters to me, 'Nearly there, love.'

I slide into the back of the car and the engine thrums to life. The GPS lights up and directs us on to grey asphalt, through a tunnel to a roundabout with a huge model plane and on to the grey road. Outside everything is grey. That is my first and abiding impression of this country. Grey. Inside the car, the driver has lapsed into silence. I may as well be invisible. Maybe I am.

Ten minutes later we leave the stream of cars and drive into a gas station. The driver pulls up and gets out of the car. He leans through the open window back into the car. 'The ladies is round the side.'

I struggle to open the door. I am unfamiliar with the handle and the man opens it for me. I walk past racks of newspapers, stunted flowers and bins of bright-coloured sacks. I try to make out the letters, the Roman alphabet; I try to concentrate on what the words are.

Around the corner I find the toilet. There are two cubicles. A tap is dripping into a sink that's blocked with soapy water. I don't know what to do now. I look at myself in the mirror; I see the shadow of hair on my upper lip and my wide, dark eyes. I look scared. I swallow and take a deep breath.

The door swings open and a young woman comes in. She has a short jacket and a baseball cap on her head. And jeans like mine. And trainers like mine. She tugs off the cap and her dark hair falls down to her shoulders. Like mine.

She smiles and puts her fingers to her lips. She shrugs off her jacket. It's leather, black and white like a bowling jacket I once saw on TV. I start to undo the belt of my coat with my cold fingers, tugging ineffectually at the knot I made. She can see my problem and after a couple of seconds helps me. I feel her hair brush my face and I can smell her perfume. Her fingers are more certain than mine and she unties the knot. Then she slips the coat off of my shoulders and puts it on her own. I slide my arms into her jacket. It's warm from her body even though it's way too big for me. Then she helps me pile my hair into the baseball cap and nudges me towards the door. 'White car, by air pump,' she says. 'Ford Fiesta. *Bittawfiq*, good luck. May God go with you.'

As soon as I get out into the forecourt I see the car. A man is concealed as he kneels to fill the tyres. He straightens up and I walk towards him.

13

M40 Motorway – Four Days Later

Eli leaned back in the car seat and wriggled trying to reach a point just below his shoulder blade that itched. The M40 stretched ahead and outside, on the escarpment by the motorway, tufty sheep dotted the slope, growing fat and woolly on the rich green grass. A truck in the inner lane indicated right giving Eli the chance to nose his car into the outside lane before shifting back to where he was. How pleasant it was to be driving in a country where people used indicators before changing lanes. How novel. Checking the clock on the dashboard, Eli calculated that he was forty minutes away from his destination: Cheltenham. He was going to find Red Cap. Find him and if necessary recruit him again, shepherd him back to the flock where he would be gently sheared.

This was the work that Eli excelled in; it required mental acuity unlike Rafi's brand of action-man expertise. Eli remembered the very first time he'd actually seen Rafi Shomer; before then he'd heard a little about him, but their paths hadn't actually crossed until about a year ago. It was at the 'country club'. There to give a talk to the new recruits on the history of intelligence services, law and ethics, Eli was sitting outside one of the teaching hangars enjoying the February sunshine waiting for the recruits inside to finish the previous session. Squatting with his back against the wall, he was just arranging his notes when the throaty rumble of a Harley Davidson stormed his ears. Like a teenage heart-throb, Rafi appeared, straddling the machine in his black leathers. With a flourish he pulled up, stirring the sand right in front of where Eli was crouched. Maybe he didn't notice Eli; he certainly didn't acknowledge him. He kicked down the side stand and swung his leg over the saddle as if it was a warhorse.

Just then the recruits came onto the hangar for their ten-minute break before Eli's lecture.

'How's the top team?' Rafi strode towards the group fist and arm raised in greeting. The recruits looked up and there was almost a collective sigh of appreciation and admiration. Moments later, Rafi was right among them, high fiving, hugging, kissing. It was like watching a sports star meet a group of ecstatic fans. Watching on, Eli was bemused; as far as he was aware all that Rafi had done was deliver the modules on detonators and illegal entry; that hardly merited this inappropriate level of hero worship.

After a few moments Eli moved towards the training hangar to set up his laptop to deliver the talk. As Eli skirted the group he felt as if he was invisible. One of the kids had got Rafi a coffee, a few were smoking and Rafi seemed to be regaling the group with some thoroughly entertaining story.

Once inside the hangar Eli exchanged a few words with the previous trainer who had just finished the session on surveillance, then Eli connected his laptop, ran through the slides and waited for the recruits to come in. And waited. After fifteen minutes he was still sitting there on his own. Wondering just how long he was supposed to sit there, Eli saw the group still gathered around Rafi but now closer to the beach, away from the administrative buildings. Eli stood watching, his arms folded, waiting. At long last one of the recruits looked up, noticed him and there were nudges followed by a scurry back to class.

Yes, it was only a small moment; the recruits were late back to class because they were talking to another trainer but still the incident piqued Eli. It offended him in a way he couldn't rationalise. He knew he wasn't universally popular and his modules with the focus on economics, geopolitics, not to mention ethics and law, were hard for some of the less intellectual recruits who wanted to focus on the more exciting modules. But it was important. Eli felt that Rafi had deliberately devalued his module; devalued him in some way.

Being in different operational areas meant that Eli had been able to avoid Rafi – until now. At least Rafi had zero involvement in Red Cap and Eli would keep it that way.

Eli returned his attention to the road ahead. Making contact with Red Cap would be done correctly; a team of watchers had been in Cheltenham all week checking to see if Red Cap was clean. He was. Eli had also done a couple of dummy runs from the hire car location to make sure that it wasn't being watched. It wasn't. Yet he still checked his mirrors and monitored the traffic flow as he had been taught; watching the cars coming on and off the slip roads; looking for any patterns that might indicate a tail. More than correct procedure, it was habit; like brushing his teeth – Eli didn't even think about it.

Now assured that Red Cap was living at home in his Edwardian semi-detached, commuting to work and behaving as he normally did – without any change in his patterns of behaviour – all that was left for Eli to do was hope. First, that Red Cap would agree to meet him and also that the agent remembered the operational procedures.

On the second point, there was little doubt in Eli's mind. Of course Red Cap would remember the contact points and security checks; he'd stipulated them when he originally made contact. Within days of establishing his credentials – in the form of a flow chart showing the internal hierarchy of his GCHQ department – Red Cap had laid out how he wanted to work. He detailed primary places for contact and also secondary, as well as the emergency methods that would be used if necessary. He stipulated what was known in the jargon as vinyl tradecraft; that meant no digital, no signals, no phones. Just the old methods, the safe methods that nobody expected any more: the dead letter drops; the secret ink and the chalk. That was how he wanted to do it and that's how it was done. The agent had also stipulated the payment arrangements; the man was a total professional.

Arriving at the B&B in Cheltenham, Eli eased the car between two white pillars that fronted the suburban house. The pillars were incongruous for a 1940s house; even more so were the lion heads atop each monolith but the connecting high white wall served his purpose; Eli's car was masked from passers-by.

The young woman who opened the front door muttered something about the owner being away. After following her into a dark sitting room, she stood over Eli as he filled in the dog-eared guest book. He smelt cigarettes and cooked food on her.

'I'd like to pay cash in advance,' Eli said. 'I'm probably going to leave early tomorrow morning so I don't want to disturb you.'

'Fine,' the young woman took a pad from her apron pocket and scrawled a receipt that Eli tucked into his wallet.

Eli signed in as G Sobers. It was an affectation, a work tic that he'd never shared with anyone, never wanted to, never needed to. If he was on a job where there was no need for a fake passport – and God bless the United Kingdom for not introducing ID cards – each time Eli had to give a name, he used the name of a legendary cricketer.

As usual, Eli used one of his chosen addresses when he filled in the guest registration form. This one was a serviced office rental near Regent's Park where turnover was high. Junk mail and flyers would be routinely trashed.

As soon as Eli had been shown to his bedroom, he showered and dressed again, changing shoes and socks and pocketing what he would need. It was a short walk from the B&B to the municipal cemetery, one of the three 'post boxes' that Red Cap used. It was a pleasant place with trees and benches to rest, somewhere you could imagine lingering, meditating on the impermanence of life. How different it was to home. Eli thought about Alon's funeral. It had taken place in one of the new vertical cemeteries in Israel. The building looked like a high-rise car park but was jam-packed with decaying bodies laid to rest in pods of earth. With the way real estate prices were rocketing, there'd soon be more multi-storey buildings of the dead.

At the far end of this British cemetery a funeral was in progress and a group of people had gathered around a grave, their heads bowed, while a cleric spoke. Eli lingered until the funeral party had dispersed and unobserved, he could make his way to the designated tombstone. Andrew Macpherson's final resting place was under an elm tree. For a moment Eli looked at the inscription and wondered who Andrew Macpherson with his grieving wife, children and grandchildren had been. Then he slipped his hand into his pocket, withdrew the yellow stick of chalk and drew two parallel lines on the left-hand side of the tombstone.

14

The Six Horseshoes Pub, Cheltenham – The Next Day

'You've lost weight, Derek,' Eli placed the tray down on the scarred brown wood table with care. He didn't want to spill his burden of bitter, double whisky, two packets of crisps and a lager shandy.

'You've lost hair,' Red Cap said reaching for the whisky. He tossed it to the back of his throat with practised pleasure. 'When did you go for the full monty?' Red Cap used his fingers to brush back his own lank locks that were streaked with grease and grey.

'When I couldn't fake it any more,' Eli said raising his voice above jeers of the crowd at the other end of the pub. A middle-aged comedian stepped off the makeshift stage and slunk away. The audience's bloodlust satisfied, the decibel level dropped as the next comedian, a tall dreadlocked black man, strode into the comedy arena. Ignoring the drama Eli went on, 'There comes a point when some of us have to give in to baldness, embrace it, if you will.'

Across the table Eli noticed that Red Cap's eyes were watering, maybe it was in response to the hit of alcohol. The agent wiped away the moisture with thumb and finger before he spoke. 'How long has it been? How's business? Booming?'

A grin cracked the raddled face. Red Cap had never had movie star looks but now he looked ill. In the weak light of the fake candle, Eli could see Red Cap's tweed jacket hanging off him, and a stained and frayed cuff visible at the end of the sleeve. He looked like an unemployed teacher who'd been sacked for touching up little girls rather than a deputy departmental head at GCHQ.

'I don't know how long it's been – twelve years?' Eli raised his voice above the cheers and whoops of the open mic comedy session at the far end of the dingy pub.

Red Cap ignored the question, 'Are you here to rap me over the knuckles, bribe me or fire me?'

'Derek, that's what I love about you. No bullshit. Cut to the chase. Straight to the heart of the matter. You could be an Israeli – a Sabra – especially if you ask me how much I'm earning and how often I have sex with my wife. By the way, great location.'

On stage the comedian, such as he was, was delving into a bag that contained different hats. Each hat stimulated a different voice and a different gag. The comic sweated and struggled to project his voice over the baying crowd. A recording device would never be able to isolate an individual conversation. It was a perfect location for a meet.

'Thanks,' Red Cap said. 'It's nice to have one's skills appreciated.'

Eli sipped his lager shandy to give him a moment to consider his best approach. Decided, he placed the glass down on the table, leaned back in the chair and smiled. 'If you're saying you don't feel appreciated by us I apologise unreservedly. What you do for us has immeasurable value and you have my word that it is appreciated at the highest level.'

'Really? Is that why my last case officer had the IQ of an amoeba? I get enough of that at work. And that last meeting I had with him... he had no idea what I was talking about. What's the point of having a debrief with someone who doesn't seem to have even a passing knowledge of current communication technology?'

Just as Eli had thought, Gidon hadn't done his preparation.

'Of course, you're right,' Eli said. 'That was a mistake; he should have been supported by –'

Red Cap interrupted, 'And then there was the one before – a woman. Don't get me wrong, I'm no woman hater but missy had about as much idea of appropriate security as my Aunt Fanny. She called me *at home.* How the hell did that happen?'

Eli swallowed, 'It was thought to be an emergency and she thought your wife would be at her weekly meeting. How is she by the way? How is Carole?' Eli needed to divert Red Cap. Calm him and draw him away from his justifiable complaints.

Red Cap didn't answer.

'Is Carole okay?' Eli said.

Red Cap shook his head as if his neck was struggling with the burden of his head. 'She still tries to hide it so I suppose that's a good thing but she stopped going to the meetings a good year ago.' He glanced at his watch before he went on. 'So it's now 7.30pm – that means she'll be comatose. Lying on the sofa, mouth open, an empty bottle of vodka by her side. Some days she doesn't get dressed at all and often, when she does, that's only to go to the GP who does bugger all in my opinion.'

'I'm sorry,' Eli said. 'Really sorry, what can I say?' He stroked the top of his head and felt the stubble.

Red Cap said, 'I've been cutting back lately but I'm going to have another whisky if it's all the same to you.'

Eli stood up, 'Let me get it.'

At the bar Eli mused over what he'd just heard. For Red Cap to unburden himself with such uncharacteristic openness the situation must be bad. Besides the undeniable fact that Red Cap had been mis-handled by two case officers, his wife's deterioration raised further operational issues. Among them was the question of whether she knew about Red Cap's work. He was unstable enough without the additional problem of an alcoholic wife who knew her husband was working for Mossad. Red Cap wouldn't be the first agent whose an-gry wife had phoned a home security service. The event was so com-mon it was a cliché. They even had an expression for it: *lichporkaki* – angry shit-dropping bird.

With a second whisky coursing around Red Cap's bloodstream, the agent unpacked the rest of the miserable baggage associated with his wife. Phantom illnesses, public tantrums and binge buying to the point that an entire room of their house was piled with unpacked goods she'd bought online.

Eli listened, brain working, as he nodded with sympathy and sipped at his lager between handfuls of crisps.

'I blame myself,' Red Cap said. 'I haven't been much of a husband.'

'Derek, a psychological illness is not your fault. That would be like saying that if, God forbid, Carole had cancer that would also be your fault. You see my point?'

Red Cap didn't answer. He just shook his head from side to side. Eli went on, 'You know we can find someone, someone good, we can find the best shrink there is. We can find someone who specialises in her illness.'

'Thanks, she won't go. Says there's no point.'

There was silence between the two men. Only the noise from the stage, the clamour from the audience stamping their feet, whistling; shouting bouncing sound all around them. The comedian took another bow.

'Does Carole know?' Eli gestured with his fingers towards Red Cap and back to himself. The agent glanced away before he said, 'No... I don't think so.'

Like hell she doesn't know.

'How's work?' Eli said to give himself a chance to regroup.

'Usual crap. Overworked. Underpaid. Management politics. Brown-nosers getting promoted over people with competence and – just to make things even more pleasant – a bunch of Yanks installing a new data science tool. They're wandering around the building like John fucking Wayne.' Red Cap had leapt on the life raft of a change of subject and paddled away as if he might sink.

'Tell me more,' Eli said.

Red Cap smiled his vulpine grin, 'Actually, I thought that's why you were here, why you'd got in touch after all this time. By the way, that guy I read about who disappeared in Kenya on a family safari holiday. Was that you?'

'You know I couldn't tell you, even if it were the case.' Eli said.

'I gave your woman the MI5 file on him – I'd probably get ten years inside just for that. The man *was* a total shit, but when I saw the news items I thought, do I want his blood on my hands? Is that right, Benny?'

Eli sighed. 'Only you can decide. You know what these people want, Derek. The Holocaust deniers, the white supremacists, the world-class haters. Nothing's changed. They want to kill anyone who's not like them. Yes, the Jews are somewhere near the top of the list, but it's a helluva long list. Gays, Mexicans, immigrants, Moslems, Gypsies. It starts with conspiracy theories and ends with institutionalised murder. That's why we need you so badly and your access to the 91 group.'

'Then you're going to love the new American product. They're tracing the Russian money that's going into the far right so it's everything the Yanks have been gathering on their home-grown racist groups; all the rifle clubs, Ku Klux Klan, Aryan Nations, Neo Nazis, Charlottesville demonstrators – you say it, they've got it. All the membership contact details, all the arms caches.'

Eli leaned forward across the table, 'That could be very interesting to one of our sections.'

'There's something else going on but I can't give you more than an overview. I can't get access without being conspicuous, but there's talk about installing RATs in all the target embassies as opposed to the problems of hardwiring.'

Eli knew better than to ask what a Remote Administration Tool was; that's what Gidon would probably have done. Malware that was remotely exploited on to target embassy computers had so far eluded them. If the British had not only developed the malware, but also installed it, in the Qatar Embassy they would be able to listen and see meetings in the embassy between Hamas, Iranian visitors, and anybody else who passed near the computers.

'And that's even more interesting,' Eli said.

Two hours later Eli was back at the B&B standing over the toilet bowl while he pissed away what felt like an ocean of beer but was in fact the three pints of lager he'd drunk on an empty stomach. Empty apart from the packets of crisps that had made him thirsty for more beer. Eli needed to eat something before he manoeuvred the car out of the car park past the lion-topped pillars, never mind driving on the 'wrong' side of the road to the motorway. He meandered back into the bedroom and sank down on the side of the bed. There, he wrenched open the plastic tub of pasta salad he'd bought from the all-night shop at the service station. Using the teaspoon from the in-room facilities he shovelled up the food and thought about his contact report.

He needed to get something in the first paragraph stating that Red Cap was once again fully operational – in spite of incompetent handling by two case officers, including Gidon. Should he use the word 'incompetent'? Maybe not. Maybe that was too strong. But he ought to still make the point that the problems with Red Cap would never have occurred if a superior agent runner – such as himself – had been the handler. Eli burped and closed the plastic container on the salad. It was only half eaten but he'd had more than enough of the rubbery gloop. He wiped his fingers on one of the tissues in the box by the side of the bed and picked up his Moleskine notebook and pen. On a fresh page he made a few marks that were incomprehensible to anybody else but would serve as the basis of his report.

He decided to skip the first paragraph about other case officers' incompetence. That wouldn't win him any friends and Gidon was in enough trouble without any more help. He'd just quote what Red Cap had said somewhere in the body of the text, but he'd start with a summary of Red Cap's current health and domestic issues. Both of which were undeniably problematic. By the side of the hieroglyph that stood for Red Cap's wife, Eli scrawled a question mark and an exclamation mark.

Of course the woman knew. That sideways glance of Red Cap's had said it all. And then there was the way he'd thrown in the gold nugget about the American product. Whether Red Cap had told his wife or she'd somehow found out about him was irrelevant. The situation was that an alcoholic with behavioural problems knew that her GCHQ employee husband was committing treason.

Eli sighed and pinched his lower lip together. If he was going to put that in his report – and he had to – he needed to come up with some sort of recommendation for further action.

Given the woman's condition and unpredictability the best course of action would be to retire Red Cap. But that was without taking into account the tantalising hint of American product being dangled within reach. This was the sort of intelligence the *Tsafririm* section that kept an eye on Jewish communities would die for. The product was even more alluring because spying on the Americans was a sin of biblical proportions. They weren't even allowed to use American cover stories in their legends and God forbid they should use an American passport in a covert operation. It was an issue of extraordinary sensitivity exacerbated by that shmock Pollard.

Eli had heard the full disgraceful story from Alon, who'd been in Washington at the time. Pollard, a US naval intelligence officer had thrown himself at the Israeli Embassy in Washington like the last virgin of a dying race; he'd begged to give information, pleaded to be heard. Of course, the product had been top-grade, Alon had said, it was irresistible. But Pollard's runners got greedy and pushed too hard. End result, Pollard gets caught and the resulting scandal seriously damaged relationships and damaged relationships meant damaged American support. It was a salutary tale.

Eli stretched out on the lumpy mattress and closed his eyes. Going in via the back door – as it were – getting the product via the British might not be so bad. And Red Cap was a pro – not some James Bond fantasist like Pollard. Admittedly, Red Cap might have problems with his wife, but they weren't insurmountable and who's to say that she knew for certain? Maybe she only suspected that Red Cap was helping them – and, if it came down to it, would people actually believe her? She was hardly a reliable witness.

The bed creaked as Eli stood up and padded towards the bathroom where he had to piss again. Feeling lighter, he stripped off and stepped into the shower. The tepid water pinged off of his body and as he squeezed the tiny bottle of soap and lathered up, he began to feel more alert. Afterwards he towelled himself off with harsh pressure, pulled clothes on to his damp body and quit the B&B. He needed to get back to London and file his report recommending maintaining Red Cap and accessing the high-grade Yank product. If Red Cap's new product was half as good as it sounded, Eli would be perfectly placed to get London station.

15

West Kensington, London – The Next Day

Being freelance had huge advantages; Petra was able to tell the private security company that she wasn't available for assignments until further notice. This meant she could spend the three days after meeting Rafi thinking: about her father, about Alon, and about the past. She emptied the old shoebox that contained Papa's memorabilia, passports, birth, death and marriage certificates on to the carpet and sat cross-legged, grasping for what was gone.

The age-stained documents smelt of decay and tears. Among them, tucked between crinkled paper there was a single black and white photograph; two boys holding hands with a woman wearing a coat and hat. She walked towards the camera smiling with the stubborn determination of someone on a holiday they couldn't afford. In the background there were beach huts and other passers-by. One of the boys carried a bucket, the other a spade. The grinning kid with the bucket had tousled dark hair; his shirt was half undone, and half tucked in. The other boy was distracted by something out of frame and despite the holiday setting his expression was troubled.

Petra had taken the photograph out of the box and slipped it into her iPhone wallet. Now she carried it with her when she went to meet Rafi and his colleague.

She spotted them as soon as she walked into the long, low hotel lounge in West Kensington. It was an anodyne space, more a gallery than a lounge, with chairs to one side leading to a dining room at the far end. There, by a colourful board advertising the business breakfast special, a hopeful maître d' eyed the empty space.

But he surveyed the lounge in vain; it was empty apart from an older woman resting on a sofa with a big bag by her swollen feet and

– as far away from anybody else as possible – the Israelis. There were two of them, Rafi and a man with a shaved head, hunched around a low table, heads forward conspiratorially, coffee on the tray. Petra strode over to them and Rafi stood up.

'Hi, good to see you. What would you like?' he said.

'Just another cup, please,' Petra said without sitting.

The other guy stood up. He was shorter than Rafi, only about five-foot-nine but he had fine grey eyes with heavy lids. He held out his hand to shake hers. 'I'm Benny,' he said.

'Nice name,' Petra said.

He smiled. It was a warm smile. 'One of my favourites. Thank you for coming. Thank you for agreeing to help us.'

His English was almost perfect.

'I haven't agreed to help you, I've agreed to talk to you. By the way, are you British?' Petra said. 'Or have you studied here?'

'Studied and worked.'

'Benny is one of our best people,' Rafi said. 'How many languages have you got? Eight is it? Or more?

'Don't exaggerate,' the Israeli calling himself Benny said.

Another cup arrived and there was some small talk about traffic, weather and caffeine before Benny sat straighter, stroked his skull and said, 'I understand that Rafi has given you the bare bones of the story.'

Petra nodded.

'To flesh it out – a young woman we're interested in is attending a short course at an English language school near Oxford,' Benny said. 'As luck would have it there is a vacancy for a tutor. We want you to apply for the summer job. The target will be living at the school which is a boarding school during term time, the type of place the British aristocracy go to. So, you will live at the school.'

'Hold on, all Rafi told me was that there's someone you want me to babysit,' Petra said. 'He said nothing about teaching.'

Benny said, 'Is that a problem?'

'Yes, I'm not a teacher and my experience, such as it is, was with children up to the age of 11. All I do now is some voluntary athletics with kids. It's not teaching English as a foreign language which is a specific skill.'

Benny appeared to be unfazed. 'Not perfect, I agree,' he said. 'But more importantly you have what you call the DBS check, and it's current.'

'Disclosure and Barring Service? Yes... it's current. But it's in my name, my real name. I can't transfer it to a cover name.'

Rafi broke in, 'You *will* be using your real name.'

'I don't understand,' Petra said.

'That's why we need you,' Rafi said. 'And only you. You have a teaching qualification and the DBS. We will provide you with more recent references.'

'And you have the operational experience,' Benny said. His voice was warm and encouraging and she recognised it as the carrot moment; the pep talk to send you over the top; the soft sell to con you into buying what you don't want; the professional manipulation.

'We have a problem,' Benny said. 'The young woman we're interested in has a brother. We want to be certain – or as certain as we can be – that he doesn't come to visit her. If he does, we need to know instantly.'

Benny broke off as a businessman in a blue suit ambled slowly past, his eyes fixed on the dining room. The maître d' bobbed up and pushed a menu into his hand which the businessman studied.

'Much as I'd like to help there are a couple of elements I don't like about this. To start with, you're talking about a six-week residential in a professional role where I have zero experience. It's one thing to tell a target you're a fund manager or a doctor or a travel agent. It's another thing to actually do the job. Also, even if I could be convincing in that role, I'm not happy about using my own name.'

Benny nodded then glanced at Rafi before he spoke. He sounded grave, 'The fact is that the girl has some very dangerous connections; there is a threat to the United Kingdom. We are monitoring that threat and we want you to help us find the connections and that includes the brother.'

'I see,' Petra said.

'That's why we need someone with operational experience and your particular skill-set. You will need to be alert at all times. It's extremely important that we have eyes on her that we can rely on.'

There was silence around the table. Petra was aware of the two men watching her, waiting for her to agree.

'Give me five minutes to think about it,' she said.

Jolting herself to her feet, Petra marched away from the two men who returned to their hunched position over the low round table. As she walked towards the stairs that led to the reception area and out into the street, she checked her phone. The photograph was tucked into the leather cover and it was still there. Safe.

Glancing around the lobby through the doors into the street beyond the grey drop-off parking area and the humming traffic, she thought how easy it would be to just walk through the doors and go home. Why not? They couldn't do anything about it. There was no reason in the world for her to stay and get involved with the lies, deceit and paranoia again. Yet she recognised with clarity that she was the best person for the job.

Petra found a seat in a corner of the lobby and slumped into it. Then she looked at the photograph.

The boy with his head turned away from the camera was her father; the teacher she'd tried to emulate and failed; the kind man who never spoke of the past. There was no doubt in her mind that he would have approved of her taking part in an operation to protect the UK. He loved England for the home it gave him and the foster parents who took him in when his own were murdered. And Alon, the tousled boy in the photograph who had shared her father's journey; shared his food with him, his boots with him. And shared his loss. Not brothers bonded by blood, but by grief and survival.

Unlike Papa who would shake his head, look away and then change the subject when she asked why she had no grandparents like the other children, Alon was different; he told her. Happy to talk about the past, he'd stab the air with his perennial cigarette, and tell her all the stories that her father denied her.

And however grim the story of loneliness, danger and privation might be, Alon always spoke with a casual shrug as if dismissing the pain, 'Everybody in Israel has got a story of survival,' he'd often say. 'Everybody. Everybody has a story about decisions that were right or wrong. Of getting on the train to occupied Germany where work was promised, or waiting for the Russians to come. Of running away from Turkey after the Thrace pogroms and finding it more dangerous in the British Mandate of Palestine.'

'Right decisions and wrong decisions,' Alon had said the last time they'd met when she told him that after five years she was resigning. She remembered him stirring the tiny cup of coffee in the Hippopotamus Restaurant in Paris.

'It's okay,' he said. 'We all need to stop running. It's what I said to your father when I told him I was going to fight the British Mandate for independence. We argued. He didn't agree with me. He said the UK was our refuge.' Alon had picked up the spoon and stabbed the air. 'I told your father I was fighting for the chance to stop running. You know what "sabra" means?'

'It's the prickly fruit, the national fruit, sweet on the inside and —'

'It means – to rest. To stop running.'

Petra tucked the photo back in the phone cover and put it away. Her wrong decision had been not to keep in touch with the man who'd looked after her father in the displaced persons camp after the war. Her right decision would be to keep faith with him and keep the UK safe.

Turning away from the door to the street, Petra walked to the stairs that led to the hotel lounge.

16

West Kensington, London – Thirty Seconds Later

Eli watched Petra and Rafi walk down the narrow lounge and disappear from sight. As soon as they'd disappeared, the man in the blue suit who'd been drinking coffee at the end of the lounge ambled over to Eli. He sat down on one of the empty chairs; Yuval, the man in the blue suit, poured coffee from the cold cafetière into Rafi's empty cup and tossed the liquid to the back of his throat. He wiped the back of his hand across his mouth and grimaced at the taste. Then he took the directional mic out of his ear and dropped it into a small box that was in his pocket.

'She looks okay,' Yuval said. 'At least from where I was sitting. The connection with Alon is useful. Did you really visit him on the *moshav* as you told her?'

'As a matter of fact, I did,' Eli said.

'Good,' Yuval said. 'What do you think? Can she do it?'

'For sure. She's smart, maybe she's too smart but she's convincing and she's experienced.'

Yuval nodded; he sounded thoughtful. 'I noticed that you didn't help them make a plan for the job interview. Why?'

'*Auftragstaktik*,' Eli said using the German word. 'Mission command. It's best for flexibility. Trainer and Rafi know they need to get her into the language school so they have the target and the time frame. It's better if they develop their own plan.'

'You wouldn't be setting Rafi up to trip over? You wouldn't do that would you?' Yuval said.

Eli considered the question, 'I think we need to see how Rafi behaves in the field. As I've said, he may know his way around a detonator and can hotwire any car, but he's not experienced at agent run-

ning. That's not a criticism; it's a fact. And if he's not up to this particular job, it would be better for the operation to find out sooner
rather than later.'

'Agreed, he hasn't got the experience and he certainly isn't the
agent runner you are, but we give him a chance.'

'That's exactly what we're doing,' Eli said. 'If he gets Trainer into
the school, fine. If he doesn't then I should run her; I'll get her into the school. In fact, there's a good argument that if I ran Trainer it
would make the operation more cohesive.'

'You haven't got the time,' Yuval said with finality. 'You can't be
in two places at once.'

Yuval stood up and tugged the edges of the crumpled jacket towards the middle but made no attempt to do it up. 'Ready?'

Eli patted the pocket of his linen jacket, 'I've got my tie.'

'Good. Be alert. It will be a complicated meeting. I want you to
take note of all their reactions while I make the pitch.'

Yuval extracted a neat package out of the plastic bag by his side.
He ripped open the tissue and revealed a black silk tie with a pink
diagonal line. 'Like it?' Yuval said. 'My wife bought it for me – she
had to tell the shopkeeper I went to school here. You know why? It's
a Westminster school tie – that's where all the famous British spies
go.'

Eli stood up and waved to the serving staff for the bill. 'Ah, the
old school tie,' he said. 'Perhaps we should all get them. That and a
Yale class ring and SVR-issue rubber sole shoes so we'll all look the
same because we are all the same. Come, Yuval, let's bait the line.'

On the Number 9 bus to The Travellers Club in Pall Mall, Eli and
Yuval talked about British architecture, military history and soccer.
It was procedure not to have operational conversations on public
transport.

At 12.30 the bus stopped almost outside the door of The Travellers Club and seconds later the two men climbed the steps to the massive front door. The door swung open and they gave their names to a man who looked like a retired adjutant.

'We're here to see Mr Milne,' Yuval said stroking his Westminster school tie.

'He's expecting you, Sir. David will show you through to the library.'

Yuval and Eli followed a slight man up a mahogany staircase and on the upper landing they were shown into the empty library. Alone in the room, Eli listened to the tired tick of a clock on the mantelpiece while Yuval drifted over to the windows and examined the glass. He tapped the surface with approval.

'Good grade. The same as we use at HQ; it'll stop a bullet among other things.'

'Why would a library within a club need it?' Eli was studying a black bust set in an intricately carved hollow in the wall. 'Who are they expecting?'

'Preparation,' Yuval muttered. 'Good practice. I love that about the Brits. They used this place when they brokered the deal with the Libyans in 2003. And there were plenty of people who would quite happily have shot that deal apart including Tsar Putin.'

'These clubs are a really useful resource. We could do with something like this.'

'We've got Cyprus – but then so has everyone else.' Yuval said.

'Good morning, Yuval,' a soft voice interrupted the two men. 'Lovely to see you again.' Eli turned to see a medium-sized man in a fine worsted suit of charcoal. Very much the slick technocrat, Milne wore a crisp white shirt, tortoiseshell glasses and an open, easy smile. Only his shoes betrayed him; they gleamed and when Milne approached Yuval he used long, strong steps – army parade ground steps.

The MI6 man shook Yuval's hand and then noticed the tie. For a moment Milne looked perplexed. 'Really?' he said.

Yuval grinned, 'Just trying to fit in.' He rolled the 'r'.

Milne threw back his head and barked a laugh. 'Very funny,' he said. But when he straightened his head Eli caught a glint in Milne's eyes.

'Permit me to introduce Eli Amiram,' Yuval said. 'My deputy and the acting liaison officer between our services.'

'How do you do,' Eli said.

'How do you do,' Milne replied. 'I'm delighted to meet you and by the way, your accent is remarkable.'

'Thank you. You're very kind.'

'May I offer you gentlemen an aperitif before lunch? The club serves a more than passable Pink Gin.'

'You know I don't drink,' Yuval said.

'I'm ever hopeful,' Milne said. 'Eli you must join me for something, I insist. Pen Hardy, our American friend is as dry as the Mojave Desert. He makes me feel like an alcoholic when I have even a single glass of wine. And the cellar here is justifiably famous. There's everything from Chateau Petrus to Dom Perignon.'

'In that case I would love a glass of sherry before lunch – your recommendation,' Eli said.

'Splendid,' Milne rubbed his hands together. His fingers were long and manicured; the muscles were strong. It occurred to Eli that they were the type of hands that could strangle if the necessity arose.

The drinks duly arrived and Eli was sipping a dry fino when Pen Hardy, the American representative of the CIA joined them. He was about 40, tall, black, athletic and business-like. He declined refreshment and was keen to sit down for lunch in the coffee room where he ordered one course, still water and repeatedly glanced at his watch. Very much the senior partner in the proceedings, Pen seemed keen to make that point.

In huge bites, Pen wolfed down his meal and then spoke. 'I know Milne has already tackled you about the passport fiasco. While that didn't directly impact on my government's activities, it was still a breach of the relationship between your government and UK/USA. This isn't the first time that you've been caught using NATO citizens' passports for your targeted assassinations with the end result that we get dragged into your dirty business. Let me stress, this doesn't sit well with the current administration.'

Yuval looked abashed, even stricken. Eli was impressed.

Hardy went on, 'The message I have from our government is that you cannot expect us to supply you with intelligence related to your specific interests when as far as we can see you are not adhering to previously acknowledged and mandated agreements.'

'Pen, this is why I have come to London,' Yuval said. 'And this is why the previous liaison officer has been immediately replaced by my colleague Eli. This incident with the passports was a serious lapse of judgement; we have already initiated an investigation to try to find out how this could have happened and to make sure it never happens again.'

'I repeat, this isn't an isolated incident,' Pen said.

Yuval ignored the argument; he went on, 'To show you... to demonstrate our regret... we will... I have been instructed to advise you of all of our most up-to-date product.'

Milne swallowed the morsel of cheese on the biscuit and raised the small glass of port to his lips.

'That would be most appreciated,' Milne said, still holding the glass and not drinking.

Eli kept his own expression neutral by glancing at one of the mighty chandeliers in the middle of the room and then back to Milne. The muscles around Milne's eyebrows contracted imperceptibly and Pen Hardy leaned forward in his chair to concentrate all the better on what Yuval had to say.

'The situation is like this,' Yuval said. 'As you are of course aware we have significant coverage from our drones over Gaza and the Territories. Over the last month, we have seen increased chatter. And, from what we've picked up and analysed, we believe that a new Hamas group is planning an initiative.'

Interest in both the American and British eyes visibly dimmed. As far as Milne and Pen were concerned Hamas was regional, only good for motivating disaffected kids into knifing civilians far far away from British or American citizens. In other words, the mighty UK/USA didn't give a damn.

'Do go on,' Milne said as he carved another shaving of cheese from the block on his plate.

'That is it,' Yuval said. 'Chatter. So far. We think Al Qaeda may be collaborating with Hamas.'

'Unlikely bedfellows,' Milne said. 'Well, we'd very much like you to keep us appraised of any future developments, wouldn't we, Pen?' The American wasn't listening; he was checking his phone for messages. There was obviously something important because he stood up from the table and strode across the carpet towards the door.

'Shall we get the bill?' Milne wiggled a finger in the direction of an attentive waiter and only then glanced in the direction of Eli and Yuval. 'Or would anyone like anything else?'

Yuval puffed out his chest, 'As I said, we believe that there is a new initiative in the area but to be certain we need more raw data for our matrix. We'd like the product you're collecting from the Qatar Embassy in both London and Washington.'

There was silence at the table.

'I beg your pardon,' Milne said.

'The Qatar Embassy; Hamas works out of there.'

Milne's expression was rigid, 'Let me be absolutely clear about this, Her Majesty's Government does not spy on accredited diplomats to the Court of St James's.'

'Really?' Yuval said. 'How about so-called second secretaries working under diplomatic cover? Do you spy on them? It's common knowledge that Hamas's European desk is run out of the Qatar Embassy in London. They've been there for thirty odd years; they even have their own parking space.'

'Very well; let's say, for the sake of an entirely hypothetical argument, that we would be so discourteous as to collect data from an ally who also happens to be a billion dollar investor in our infrastructure. In that implausible situation, our analysts would pick up on potential threats.'

'This is where you are completely wrong,' Yuval said, a finger poised on the white table cloth and he pressed down as he made his point. 'You can do all the potential searches through the raw data for key words and combinations but your analysts simply don't have the language skills that ours do. Arabic is a beautiful and complex language with huge variations in content across the regions. But if someone speaking Hassaniya Arabic can't understand Najdi, how are your analysts going to pick up references?'

'And your analysts can?' Milne said.

'We have a head start. Arabic is our second language and kids start learning at 10. Oliver, I don't have to remind you that the CIA's lack of language skills was a factor in 9/11. That's history.' Yuval went on, 'It's very simple; if you give us the raw data from the Qatar Embassy we can feed back the results to you. If you don't, we can't.'

Milne shook his head, 'Even if we did have that raw data you're talking about, it's never going to happen and in the meantime you haven't got anything concrete with which to tempt us – have you?'

Pen came back to the table at the same time as the waiter who presented the bill in a leather folder. Without missing a beat Milne said, 'As I said, and I am sure Pen agrees, when you have something concrete, let us know. In the meantime, do not embarrass either Her Majesty's Government or our allies.'

On the way back to Kensington Eli and Yuval didn't discuss the lunch meeting – even in the most general terms. They kept their conversation strictly to London musicals, theatre, restaurants, the exchange rate and football. All the same, Eli could see Yuval struggling to restrain his body language, fighting to damp down the spring in his step and the smile on his face. But as soon as the door to the safe room at the embassy was shut behind them, Yuval ripped off the Westminster tie, tossed it on the table and fell back into the leather chair.

'That went well,' Yuval grabbed one of the laptops on the table and flipped open the lid. 'So, the situation is that I need to write this up before I go to the airport. And you need to see whether I missed anything, anything at all. What are your headlines?'

Eli ran through the sequence of events in chronological order – what was said, how it was said, the associated body language, psychological attitude – while Yuval made rapid notes on the laptop pecking at the keys with lightning speed. He interrupted Eli's account every so often and double-checked a comment here and there.

At last the lid of the computer was down again, 'I'll send you my draft,' Yuval said. 'If anything's not right let me know.'

'Certainly,' Eli said.

Yuval tidied the laptop away and was preparing to leave the room, but just before he did he picked up the discarded Westminster tie from the table. With mock solemnity he handed the black and pink fabric to Eli. 'You're in charge now – this is your badge of office. Keep Red Cap in line, monitor our watchers just in case he is at risk, and let me know if Trainer has got herself into the school. And if Rafi does fuck up, you can run Trainer.'

'Shall I send Milne a note thanking him for lunch?' Eli said. 'It would be polite.'

'No. Let him think we're pissed. Let him think we're licking our wounds. As Napoleon said, "Never interrupt your enemy when they're making a mistake".'

'Are they the enemy?' Eli said.

'No, not at all. We're all in the same business, they just happen to have different interests to ours – at the moment.'

17

M25 Motorway – Two Days Later

Petra noted that Rafi was a bad driver. She also realised that when they were lovers, back in the day, she'd never been in a car when he was driving. If she had, she wouldn't be in one now. Rafi's lane changing, acceleration and braking bore scant relationship to the traffic flow. And when the torrent of cars on the M25 slowed down to a crawl around Heathrow, Rafi fiddled with the audio controls on the grey Ford Focus as if he had some sort of palsy. Finally he tapped his hands on the steering wheel and frowned.

'Are we in a hurry?' Petra said.

'No.'

'Then why the hell are you driving so fast *and* so badly?'

'Sorry, I wasn't concentrating.'

'Are you worrying about whether we're clean? Did you see the guy in the blue suit at the hotel?'

Rafi frowned, 'Guy in the blue suit?'

'Five-foot-eight, dark, heavy fringe, blue suit, mid-40s, slightly overweight; he walked past, talked to the man outside the dining room, then sat down and ordered a coffee,' Petra said.

Rafi appeared to be thinking and he spoke slowly, 'Outside the dining room and ordered a coffee?' And then he speeded up. 'No, no, I didn't see anyone or at least I didn't notice anyone.'

Petra sighed. 'Rafi, you're lying. I saw Benny react when Blue Suit walked past. What's more you shifted in your seat and then ignored him. One of ours, I presume, or are you going to keep denying it?'

Rafi shrugged. 'Like I said, you're a natural.'

'If you're not worrying about Blue Suit, you're worrying about the job.' Petra said. 'Why?'

Rafi took one hand off of the steering wheel and massaged his beard, 'I won't deny it. I've got a lot of experience in other areas, but this is the biggest operation I've done of this type, and... well, some people are putting me down. You know the politics.'

'What, they're saying you're not good enough? Is that it?'

'Not experienced enough. So I'll be relying on you.' He glanced over at her, taking his eyes off the windscreen.

'If you're relying on me try to concentrate on your driving,' Petra said.

He slowed down and Petra stretched her long legs into the footwell, 'Good,' she said. 'So, now that I've got an interview and submitted my accreditation what else do I need to know?'

'You will be seeing Deanna Morgan, principal of the Clock Tower English Language School. She is in partnership with her husband who also works part-time in the PR business; mainly aeronautics and engineering. The language school has been running for five years. They are trying to specialise in secure, upmarket language courses. That's why it's located at the fancy private school during the holidays.'

'Public school,' Petra said.

'No, it's a private school.'

'That's what we call a public school,' Petra said. Rafi frowned.

'Never mind,' Petra went on. 'We know where this woman lives and we know where she works?'

'Yes, the business is registered to the house.'

'I'd like to do a drive-by this evening to get a sense of the place and the surroundings. See what we can gauge from the external factors.'

Rafi looked over at Petra and smiled. She ignored him and went on, 'Say we check in to wherever we're staying, do a drive-by and then get something to eat? Do you need to liaise with anybody else?'

'No back-up, no watchers,' Rafi smiled once more but this time he kept his eyes on the road. 'I like the dress by the way. You've got great legs.'

'Fuck off,' Petra said.

'I was giving you a compliment. Why are you so sensitive?'

'Because I'm here to do a job. Anyway, I want to ask you about something that Benny said. Why is this woman a threat to UK security? Is that true or is it bullshit?'

'I can't give you all the details. You know the rules as well as I do.'

'Come on, we're old friends, how can you expect me to be your point woman if I don't know the details?'

Rafi was tight-lipped and for once seemed to be focusing on the road ahead. Petra went on, 'For goodness sake Rafi, if you give me more information I'll know what I'm supposed to be looking out for. For all I know the girl could be working with the Russians. Is she?'

'The problem is the brother which is why you're there – but it's complicated, much more complicated than I can explain at the moment. I promise you, when I can, I'll explain.'

'Complicated and you'll explain,' Petra said. 'Okay... So, tell me, how old is this Deanna Morgan?'

A white van hooted at Rafi who, having slowed down, was still hogging the centre lane. He put his foot down and veered right, into the fast lane and shot past a bunch of cars before cutting in front of a blue Clio and resuming his middle-lane location.

'How old is she? Coming up to fifty,' Rafi said. 'Her husband is a few years older, second marriage for him, no kids. Like I said, he works in PR, high tech.'

Petra started to formulate a plan based on the information. Maybe she'd talk about the benefits of being child-free. Maybe talk about wanting to relocate to Oxford and the job would be a trial period. That could work. People feel validated if they think someone wants to be like them; live like them; live where they do. Deep in a reverie, Petra visualised operational information as directional arrows – all different ways into the target. Some were dead ends, some were circular; some made direct contact. It was just a question of choosing the right arrow. Petra wound a lock of dark hair around her fingers as she mulled over the best way to connect emotionally with the principal of the school.

'You're married aren't you?' she said absently. 'Second wife, several children you dote on, and you're probably still fooling around.'

'How do you know?'

She ignored the question: 'Okay, what if I tell Deanna Morgan that I'm thinking of moving to Oxford – but before I rent out my place I want to try it by taking a summer job. I quite like that. I think I'll also say there's a relationship in my life of some sort. Just so that she doesn't feel threatened if her husband is actively involved in the language school business; also she'll know that I'm not going to be dating while I'm there. Also, if I need to bring someone else into the operation at some stage we have that option. What do you think, Rafi? It's pretty unoriginal in terms of cover stories but it'll work.'

'Yes,' Rafi said. 'I have three children and two wives. One current. You?'

'Me? Oh, it's complicated, but I promise you, Rafi, when I can, I'll explain.'

18

Summertown, Oxford – The Next Day

In the morning, Petra went for a run before breakfast. Even at 7am it was hot, humid and cloudy – storm weather. Back at the hotel Petra showered, washed her hair and dressed in her costume. For that's what she thought of the blue and white print skirt she'd bought in a charity shop. It was a costume that she would don for the part she was about to play. The only difference in what she was about to do was that the audience of one, Deanna Morgan, would be on stage with her.

As soon as Deanna opened the door to the basement home office, Petra knew that her print skirt and pumps had been the right choice. It echoed Deanna Morgan's style, a woman who on first sight would have passed for the leggy girl about town she'd probably once been.

'Please excuse the chaos,' Deanna said. 'This is always the most difficult time of year. There's so much to do.'

Turning, Deanna led the way through the small hall into a sunlit room at the back of the house. French windows looked out on to a courtyard garden and Deanna sat at a desk with her back to the view.

The small basement room was a mess. Walls were covered with shelves of files and year planners with coloured marks that had been smudged and then amended. On the desk, besides a bulging box file, there were dog biscuits, a single shoelace, a tape measure, and a buff paper file with 'applicants' scrawled in bold black letters.

It was hard to say whether the woman was inefficient or whether the mess indicated money issues; in other words, she couldn't afford to hire a secretary to deal with the administration.

Petra studied Deanna as she pulled the buff file towards her with her manicured sun-spotted hands. The manicure was professional, indicated by the regularity of the nail shapes; glancing down Petra recognised that Deanna's dirndl skirt was from an upmarket high street chain and the pumps on her feet were new. If the school was running at a loss, if finances were tight, the principal wasn't taking the hit.

Deanna extracted Petra's application form and looked up, smiling, 'You have an impressive CV,' she said.

'Thank you, it's very kind of you to see me.'

'I'm sorry this is such short notice but the teacher who has been with me for the last five years suddenly decided she didn't want to do it this year.'

'I'm sorry to hear that,' Petra said.

'I think it's for the best.' Deanna returned her attention to Petra's CV. 'I see you coach young people on a voluntary athletics programme.'

'I enjoy it and it's a chance to give back something. Some of the kids need to do something away from home and computer screens.'

'I'm sure,' Deanna looked up and fixed Petra with her pale eyes. 'Now, much of what you might be doing is in the area of pastoral care.'

'You mean making sure the students are comfortable in their environment?'

'Exactly. But it can be a little more complicated. To be frank, last year we had more than our fair share of students with acute homesickness and in one particular case, well... let's call them behavioural issues.' Deanna grimaced. 'Sex and drugs.'

'I'm sorry to hear that,' Petra frowned in sympathy and crossed her ankles. The action was also an attempt to ease the weight of the Spaniel lying across her feet.

'They're young people away from home. It's par for the course.' Deanna noticed the dog, 'Please push him off, Freddie can be insistent.'

'He's lovely,' Petra leaned down and tickled the dog behind his ears.

Dogs and children – bitter enemies of the actor were beloved friends of the spy. On stage or in front of a camera, animals and children sucked the attention of the audience. Yet in the shadow world, where the fourth wall became a mirror, an animal or child was a bonus. Petra remembered exploiting it because being seen to be attentive to an animal or child would make her seem like a nice person, a kind person and an honest person. Would it work on Deanna; would cooing over her dog appeal to her?

Petra said, 'We had a dog like Freddie when I was young. Great character and so intelligent.'

'I'm biased but I do agree,' Deanna said without warmth. 'Now, where were we?'

'The pastoral care and behavioural issues.'

'Thank you, Petra; my brain is a sieve at the moment. I've got so much to do before we go away for the weekend.'

'Lovely, I just had a weekend with my boyfriend in Wales. It's so refreshing to get away.'

'Yes, but I've got so much to do. Now let's see,' Deanna placed a pair of reading glasses on her nose and peered at Petra's form. 'As I said, your qualifications are most impressive. And you write articles for the business press which will be good for some of the students who might go on to study here.'

'Thank you.'

Petra, I think you'd be absolutely perfect. In fact, I think your experience with younger children would be a positive advantage.'

Petra smiled, waiting for the inevitable job offer and preparing her gracious words of thanks.

Still seated in her chair, Deanna dived into the folder again. She tugged at another piece of paper and looked at Petra over her reading glasses. 'Now, I'm going to be absolutely frank with you. There's another good candidate: a man. He has a strong sports background which might work well with the young men, because it's the young men who... who were the problem last year.' Deanna took her glasses off and sucked on one of the arms as if there was jam on the end. Withdrawing her plastic dummy she said, 'You are both strong candidates so what I propose doing is making the decision after the weekend and when I receive your references. Is that acceptable, Petra?'

'Of course, and I would certainly like to add that besides athletics I have trained in martial arts in the past although I didn't put it on the CV as I didn't think it was appropriate.'

Deanna had shuffled up the folder and stood up. If Petra said any more it would weaken her position as a desirable candidate; she would seem desperate or worse, argumentative.

Petra eyed the folder. Could she lean across the desk and knock it to the floor? Find out who the other applicant was?

No, not with Deanna watching her so closely.

'I'll look forward to hearing from you, thank you for seeing me,' Petra smiled as she stood up. 'Where are you off to tonight?'

'France, on the eight o'clock shuttle,' Deanna said.

'Have a wonderful weekend away.'

Petra found Rafi sitting at the back of the Prêt à Manger drinking a smoothie and reading the sports pages of a free newspaper. Petra sat down on the opposite chair. He raised the plastic tumbler, 'You should try one of these. They're good.'

'No thanks,' she said.

'How did it go? When do you start?'

'I messed up; I wasn't offered the job.'

'Okay,' Rafi shrugged. He stood up. 'Let me get the coffee. You want something with it?'

She shook her head, 'Just a latte.'

Soon, armed with her coffee and a fruit salad for himself Rafi placed both containers on the table and resumed his seat opposite Petra. Elbows on the table, he rested his chin on his hands. 'Let's start from the beginning.'

Petra relayed the meeting in chronological order. There was only one omission: her overconfidence and her certainty that the job was hers. That was something she preferred to process alone.

'Okay,' Rafi said. 'The problem is that if the other guy's references are better than yours –'

'I don't get the job. I know that; so we need to find another way of getting to the girl. There's got to be something I can do. What if I go back to Deanna and tell her some hard luck story like... how badly I need the job? Debts to pay off, sick mother, appeal to her compassion, something like that?'

Rafi pushed the drink aside. 'It will put you in a weak position. Let's think; what do we know about the other applicant?'

'Only that he's sporty and his details are in the folder that I couldn't get a look at. If only the wretched woman had offered me a coffee I could have pushed it over the desk but she didn't. There's got to be something we can do.'

Taking a pen from inside his light jacket he started to draw on the corner of the newspaper.

'Tell me about the layout in the office,' he said.

'Why?' she said.

He went on, 'You said there's a file on Deanna's desk with the other guy's details in it. You said the house will be empty because they're going on holiday tonight. So we find out who this guy is.'

'Then what? Oh... I see what you're thinking. Okay... Do you need to clear it with someone?'

In answer Rafi stood up and looked at his watch. 'I'll be back in, say, three hours. I'm taking the car. You go to the hotel, make a scale drawing of the office, then have a rest this afternoon. It may be a late night.'

19

Summertown, Oxford – Nine Hours Later

The street was still damp from the storm. The day had surrendered to a mizzle and on the bush outside the car window rain drops decked the leaves like drops of mercury. Inside the car Petra and Rafi sat in silence. They could have been a couple out on a date; a couple who had stopped to make a phone call, check an address or have a row. During their preparation they'd decided that their cover story would be the row. It would easily explain why they were in the area if they were stopped by police, neighbour or community officer. A row was attractive because no one likes to get involved in a domestic between adults.

Petra inhaled deeply and observed the tight sensation in her gut; it might be uncomfortable but she was aware that she liked this sensation. Even yearned for it.

'Are we ready?' she said.

'As ready as we'll ever be,' Rafi looked at her and smiled. She could see that he was as primed as she was.

'Then let's get on with it.'

In synchronisation, they opened the doors and stepped out of the car. Petra reached on to the back seat and pulled out the bunch of flowers and the bottle of wine while Rafi took a black rucksack. Still only dusk at 9 pm this was the kind of street where people went to bed early, where curious curtains twitched and helpful neighbours kept an eye on holidaymakers' homes.

Petra and Rafi strolled past Deanna's house chatting softly to each other. Pausing to find something in her handbag, Petra rooted around in the depths muttering about finding the address. Meanwhile, Rafi, in his role as the dutiful date, held the wine and the flowers. While she searched, apparently in vain, apologising for the loss, they both had the opportunity to study the closed windows that spelt empty house and the security light visible in a room beyond the hall.

There was no one on the street. They walked on fifty more metres then turned and walked back. Now certain they were unobserved, when they drew abreast of the house, Rafi peeled off and Petra saw his silhouette slide into the darkness and disappear down the basement steps. Alone, Petra walked back to the car.

As soon as she was settled into the driver's seat she called Rafi using the disposable phone he'd bought earlier. He answered instantly, 'Hey.' He sounded breathless as if he'd just climbed over a wall.

'Am I seeing you tonight?' Petra said using the safety word code.

'For sure, looking forward to it. I'm just getting everything organised, here,' Rafi said. 'And then I'd like to spend the night with you.'

'Fuck off,' but she was smiling. 'I don't want to spend the night with you so don't get any ideas.'

Tunelessly, Rafi droned, 'Let's spend the night together.'

'And you can't sing either. Night or day,' Petra said. 'Let's get this straight, I'm not that desperate Rafi, and you're not that charming.' During each speech Petra checked the wing mirrors and swivelled round to make sure that she hadn't missed anything.

'I could be, I could be very charming if you give me a chance. Tonight could be ours.' Rafi's voice sounded as if he was moving around. He must have disabled the alarm and was inside. Presumably he was inside the office.

A light went on in a house across the street and a hand drew the curtains shut. Petra was still, waiting to see if anyone peered out or there was further movement. No, it was quiet. No twitching curtain, no curious face at the window.

'You know, I never realised until now just how little I have in common with you,' Petra said. 'I don't even know how we ever managed more than one night together. But then I suppose I didn't think about it at the time. It was just fun and sex.'

'A night of passion,' Petra heard the excitement in his voice. He must have found the file and was photographing the application form. 'Seriously, was that it?' Rafi said. 'Was that all it was for you? I remember when we met; you were so different Petra, so different from any girl I'd ever met. Was it really nothing for you?'

'Can't remember. A few nights all those years ago. Another time and place. Great sex but...'

'That's a start. Let's work on that tonight,' Rafi said. 'Two minutes.'

Petra glanced into the left wing mirror and started. She swivelled round. A short shape had come into view. Petra said, 'Better in daylight.'

There was a pause at the other end of the phone. When Rafi spoke there was tension in his voice. 'Daylight?'

'Yeah.'

The shape was drawing closer. It was a woman and a dog.

'Okay, if you say so,' Rafi said.

The woman was walking past the car. She was small, just over five-foot, square, wearing shorts, trainers and a fluorescent cagoule. But the dog was the real problem. It looked like Freddie, the Spaniel that had been sitting on her feet earlier that day.

'Yeah, definitely daylight,' Petra said.

Holding the phone in her left hand Petra wound down the window on the car. She had no idea what she was going to do. The only certainty was that if the dog and the woman were heading towards Deanna's house, they'd walk straight into Rafi.

'Excuse me,' Petra called out. 'Excuse me, sorry to trouble you but... Winchester Gardens? Am I anywhere near there? I took a right and now the satnav's not getting a signal.'

'Let me think... now, if you go straight and take the second right past the house with the Wellingtonia, and then left, that should bring you out to the main road,' the woman said.

Petra gesticulated with her hands as if she was trying to memorise a complex set of instructions. 'You said, straight and then, sorry, so sorry, would you mind saying that again?'

The woman repeated it twice and still there was no sign of Rafi coming out of the house. Either Petra waited and made herself look suspicious or she drove off and waited for Rafi around the corner. There was nothing else she could do without inviting unwanted interest.

'Thanks,' Petra said. The phone was in her lap and the line was still open so at least Rafi would have time to prepare if he was still in there.

'Well, I'll be getting along too,' the woman said. 'Come along, Freddie.'

There was a tap on the window of the passenger side and Petra turned. Rafi walked around to her side and Petra felt a rush of relief. 'I've found out where Winchester Gardens is.' Rafi pulled open the door and tossed his black rucksack on the seat. 'We're a long way away.' He loomed over the dog sitter and smiled at her.

'So, it seems. This lady has been kind enough to help with directions. Apparently, we need to get to the main road.'

'Exactly – what a great dog,' Rafi said. 'Doesn't he look just like Benny! Same markings, same look in his eyes as if he's so clever. Good boy.'

Rafi knelt on the ground and tickled the dog behind its ears, looking as if he might linger there all night, as if there was no hurry in the world.

'You know I always wanted a dog like this,' he said to the woman. 'My girlfriend won't let me have one. Don't you think that's cruel?'

'Why don't you get in the car?' Petra said.

Rafi looked up at her, and then Petra saw him wink at the dog sitter trying to include her in this fake lover's tiff. What was the matter with him? Why was he dragging it out?

'If you don't get in the car we're going to be even later than we already are,' Petra said.

'Only if you promise that tonight's gonna be a good night...'

Petra pressed the ignition and slipped the car into gear and Rafi opened the door and sat in the passenger seat beside her.

'What the fuck were you playing at?' Petra said when they were moving off.

'Relax, you never used to be so uptight. It was little bit of *keyf*,' Rafi said. 'Fun. We were out of there. We've got everything we need and no one's the wiser.'

'And if that woman with the dog remembers the nice young couple she chatted to, then what?'

'Then nothing. Take it easy, Petra. We're on top of this.'

'What if you left something behind, moved something and then she remembers you?' Petra said.

'Do you know how much plumbing I've done in my career? I've lost count of the number of locations I've broken into and if there's one thing I know about it's how to get in and out and not leave a trace. Relax, okay?'

Petra gripped the steering wheel and her knuckles turned white. Unperturbed Rafi went on, 'We do some work on his social media accounts, or what looks like his social media accounts. When the school checks him out he isn't the best candidate. Maybe they make some pictures of him drunk at a stag night; maybe some comments about young boys. You know the sort of thing that would disturb a private language school. All in all – terrific job. And let me just say, you were great.'

'Don't try to change the subject and don't patronise me.' Petra flicked the indicator and pushed into the moving lane of traffic. She flashed a tight smile at the driver she'd forced out of the way and a heavy-set man scowled back in response.

Rafi covered Petra's hand with his own. She snatched it away.

'Get off.'

'I'm not patronising,' Rafi said. 'Please don't think that. You gave me all the time I needed to finish up and get out of there. Like I said, it was as near a perfect job as it could be, and I'm sorry if I stressed you by talking to the woman with the dog.'

'You didn't stress me, you pissed me off.'

The traffic was stationery and Petra tried to change lanes again. This time no one would let her out and by the time she had righted herself in her original lane the bonnet of the car was in a box junction. She looked in the mirror to see if she could reverse. She couldn't. So, she pushed forward and jammed the car in between a Fiat and a Mini. The traffic moved, Petra shoved the car into gear to get ahead of the Mini and as she accelerated she heard the sound of metal scraping metal.

'Oh shit,' she gesticulated to the Mini driver who was glaring and pointed ahead to a bus stop.

'That's what happens when you don't concentrate. You'd better pull in and we'll exchange details,' Rafi said. 'The hire car company will sort it out.'

'I told you not to patronise me, didn't I?'

'I'm not – you just drove into another car.'

Petra had shifted into the left-hand lane and she was getting closer to the bus stop. Up ahead, the Mini was parked but the driver hadn't yet got out. Petra spotted a turning on the left, before the bus stop.

When Petra was abreast of the turning, she wrenched the steering wheel around and slammed her foot down. The car sprung forward, thunked over a speed bump and in her peripheral vision Petra had the satisfaction of seeing Rafi grab the ceiling handle.

'Are you crazy?' he said.

'Didn't you say the hire car company would sort it out?'

The road was downhill and with a screech of brakes, Petra threw the car around the corner and shimmied between two rows of parked cars.

With his free hand, Rafi studied the map on his phone, 'Okay, if you drive up on to the pavement and go down that road, take a sharp left, it looks like there's a way through.'

The rush surged inside of Petra, 'Now where?'

'A hundred metres, turn right.'

Petra swerved to avoid a pedestrian who dodged out of the way between two cars; then she slammed her foot on the accelerator loving how her body was forced back in the seat.

'Nice,' Rafi said. 'Take a left after that red car.'

The brakes screeched as she turned and a warning light flashed on the dashboard.

'Now right, fifty metres,' Rafi said. 'That gets us to the roundabout, then we're on the main road out of town.'

They didn't speak again until they were two streets away and then Petra beat out a staccato rap on the steering wheel.

'Wow, that was good.' Petra's heart was pounding and her skin tingled.

'That's how I remember you. You haven't changed.'

'Neither have you,' she said as she put her hand on his thigh. She was burning with an intensity she hadn't felt for years. 'Never did a cold beer taste so good... or a man so sweet.'

'What?'

'It doesn't matter,' she moved her finger up his thigh. 'One night only, Rafi, okay?'

Part 2 – THE RIGHTEOUS

Whoever works righteousness benefits his own soul
    Quran 41:46

The eyes of the Lord are on the righteous, and his ears are attentive to their cry.
    Psalms 34:15

20

Watlingford Public School, Oxfordshire – One Week Later

I'm awake before dawn and in the quiet of the new day I make my morning prayers. I imagine the glow of the sun over the white buildings, the hazy heat and the soothing call of the muezzin. Here, there is only birdsong to break the silence beyond the walls of my room. Here, there's barely enough space to lay down my mat between bed and desk. Here, I'm alone.

My room is like a cell with one exception: the window is not barred. It's high, wide, and through it I see fields of green grass; the colour is so intense it looks fake. I'm blessed that the window faces east as the sun rises as I pray for guidance and strength.

Afterwards I sit at the pale wood desk. Above my head there are bookshelves. This is a place to read and study, a place to look out of the window and it's here that I write in my book.

I know I shouldn't be writing down my thoughts but I've got to get them out of my head otherwise the fears go round and round. Maybe I'll take this book with me when it's time and it'll be destroyed. Or maybe I'll find a way to send it to Wasim, so he understands and isn't angry. I can't decide and I don't have to, at least not yet.

Last night as I lay in this unfamiliar bed I had a fresh fear to chase away my sleep. What if something's happened to my contact? I've heard nothing since I was dropped at the bed and breakfast a week ago with my suitcase full of new clothes, a train ticket to Oxford and an envelope of cash. Not one word. What am I supposed to do? How long do I wait? I did exactly what was asked of me. I played the tourist, I visited museums, went to Madame Tussauds, the London Eye. It was so strange wandering around with nothing to do.

101

And London wasn't at all what I expected; wherever I went I heard different languages, it's like the whole world is here.

I'm also worried about Wasim. He called again last night and I answered the phone trying to get him to understand that I know what I am doing.

'Tell me where you are,' he said. 'I'm your guardian, Sahar. That makes me responsible for you; and it dishonours me if you don't trust me.'

'I'm in Britain, okay?' I said. 'That's all I can tell you.'

'Britain? Where in Britain? We've got friends there; people who will look after you, visit you.'

'Wasim, you're being stupid and should know better than to ask me; now, please, wait for me to call you.'

'No, I'm not doing that; I'm coming to find you.'

'You can't do that. I'm not going to tell you where I am. I'm okay, please do not come.'

'Too late, sister. I've already made arrangements. I'm coming to Birmingham, it's in the middle and I'm going to find you and take you home.'

He's such a fool; he can only find me if I choose to be found.

And I lied to him. I kept saying I was okay when the truth is that I'm sick with anxiety because no one has made contact. On top of that I'm very uncomfortable in this strange place.

I go to the dining room and collect some bread and eggs from a cafeteria-style bar. It's like the hospital where I used to work, although the food is quite different. No salad. No hummus. No white cheese. Shiny pork sits in a pool of fat next to yellow egg and grey porridge. I take jam and toast.

Afterwards, I stack my tray and find the corridor to the class. The floors are scuffed from a thousand absent feet and the walls hold echoes of voices far away. The classroom, when I find it, is empty. I sit with my back to the window facing the door.

'Is this... it is right... am I?' Another student comes into the room. She is Chinese, I think. I don't know.

'Yes,' I say. She pulls out a chair and sits down near the door. Two boys of about eighteen stroll into the room. I don't recognise their language. They are white, fair, so alike they could be brothers. Perhaps they are. One shows the other something on his phone. They laugh. It's not a kind sound; I lower my eyes. Next into the room comes a black boy with round glasses. Tall and skinny, his wrists creep out of the sleeves of the white shirt. He sits near me but does not say anything. I am uncomfortable but I have no reason to fear him or them.

Sitting there in silence I remember delivering my first baby. It was during an air raid. The taped-up windows shuddered as the sound waves from the explosions made dust rise and air shimmer. Yet the new baby came easily, with joy. The mother, oblivious to the chaos outside, was concentrating on giving life in the midst of death. I cut the cord and still wet, slippery like a fish, covered with vernix and blood, I wrapped him in a clean towel to present to his mother. I helped her make a life, save a life, make another soldier, to do God's work *inshallah*.

The classroom is nearly full. I have to move closer to the skinny black boy to make room for a girl who smells of cigarettes. She has wild dark hair and a tattoo on her hand between thumb and index finger. It is like a spider. She thrusts out that hand towards me.

'Aneeta,' she shakes my hand. 'Espagnole.'

'Aneeta,' I reply, smiling back the greeting.

She laughs showing white teeth and the wadge of gum she's chewing. She points to herself and says, 'Aneeta.' And then points to me, her eyebrows raised in question.

I understand. 'Sahar,' I say.

'Good morning, everyone,' two women come into the room. 'I hope you are all rested and refreshed from your journeys. Some of you didn't get here until late last night and have come a long way.' The woman who speaks is tall and fair, English; she's like someone I saw once in a very old film. The other woman is darker; she smiles at us. At all of us.

The fair woman continues, 'I'm Deanna Morgan, owner of the Clock Tower Language School.' She speaks clearly and slowly. I can understand quite a lot of what she says and fill in the words I don't understand. 'I would like to introduce you to Petra. She will be your main tutor. If you have any problems, any worries or there is anything you need, please talk to either Petra or myself. We want you all to have a wonderful time during these weeks and learn a lot of our language in our beautiful country.'

The women exchange a couple of words and then we're left alone with Petra. She sits on the desk. She's wearing a black and red striped tee shirt, a black linen skirt and black sandals. Her face is long, chin square, smile open and friendly; she looks like a woman who's never known anxiety or fear. With her hands on either side of her body, resting on the desk, she swings her legs like a child and says, 'Welcome. You are new here and far from home. I am new. This is the first time I teach English to foreign students. As you know, all the conversation is in English, we talk English, tell stories in English, tell jokes in English. When you do not understand – and there will be words you do not understand – tell me. Okay?'

Everyone nods.

'Understood?' she says. Everyone nods again.

Her big smile covers all of us like a warm blanket. 'I can see this is going to be a piece of cake.'

There are frowns. 'Piece of cake is an expression which means easy,' Petra says. 'This is going to be easy. Right, what I would like to do now is go around the class one by one and for you all to tell us your name, tell us where you come from, which country, and tell us one sentence about what you want. It might be anything. It might even be a piece of cake.'

She starts on the other side of the room with Li from China, who wants to improve her English so she can go to university and study medicine. The two boys who are still playing with their phones come from Russia; they both say they want a piece of cake.

'And so you shall,' Petra says. 'Lots of it.' She smiles but there is a coolness in her voice.

'How about you?' she says, her voice warm again directed at the black boy with the round glasses.

'I am Mfoniso,' he says.

'Where do you come from Mfoniso?'

'I come from Nigeria,' he speaks slowly as if the words are stuck in his mouth and have to be extracted one at a time.

'Good. Very good. What do you want Mfoniso?'

'I want... I want... English.'

'Well done. Very good,' Petra says.

It is Aneeta's turn. She takes her chewing gum out of her mouth and sticks it on to the corner of her spiral book. 'I am Aneeta.'

'Hello, Aneeta, where do you come from?'

'I come from Espagne.'

'Very good. You come from Spain,' Petra corrects.

'Spain,' Aneeta repeats.

'Excellent,' Petra says. 'You have a nice accent. What do you want Aneeta?'

The girl sits up straight, tosses her hair back, places her hands on her hips in a parody, as if she is a beauty pageant contestant. She says, 'I want world peace.'

Everyone laughs. Even the Russian boys. 'Very good, Aneeta,' Petra says. 'When you can make jokes in another language, you have got it. Now, how about you?' She looks at me. She smiles; she is warm. I sit up straight. 'I am Sahar,' I say. 'I am from Palestine. I too want peace.'

21

Herzylia, Israel – The Same Time

Palestine. Islamic Art and Archaeology of Palestine. Eli flicked through the book on Gal's side of the bed.

'This looks interesting,' he said. 'Not your usual choice of bed-time reading. Have you taken up with an archaeologist since I've been in London?'

'*Ma?*' Gal said. 'What?' She came into the bedroom carrying a tray of food and drink. In her white towelling bathrobe she was alluring.

'What did you say? I didn't hear you. Eli, move over and clear a space.'

Eli took the tray from her. On it was a platter of the smoked delicacies Eli had brought back from London: smoked salmon, cod's roe, halibut. They picnicked on the white bed, in the cool grey room with the aircon on and the blinds down. Beyond the windows was the constant hum of traffic on the *Kvish Hahof,* the beach road that never stopped – except once a year, on Yom Kippur.

'When are you going back to London?' Gal said. 'It seems as if I haven't seen you since you got here.'

'That's why I asked whether you'd taken up with an archaeologist. If you had have how could I blame you?'

She followed his gaze. 'Oh, the book. It's fascinating. One of my patients' parents recommended it to me. You'd like it, it's scholarly. In the meantime, I was thinking the same thing, wondering what you're getting up to.'

'Just the job,' Eli said. 'But it is going well.'

Eli's two days in Tel Aviv had been spent with a team of communication and encryption experts, not just from the Office; they'd also drafted in a couple of professors from The Weizmann Institute.

Step by step, they explained to Eli how the data science tool worked in relation to the American product Red Cap was passing on and when Eli thought his head was about to burst, the experts talked to him about RATS and malware, exploitation and reverse software engineering and how crucial it was for Red Cap to find out how the British had managed to get their malware on to the Qatar Embassy computers.

It would have been easier and more efficient if Red Cap could have spoken directly to the experts but his operational terms were only to meet with his *katsa*, in this case, Eli. This demand was even more understandable given the agent's recent experiences and it was no bad thing for Eli; it was evident that he was the nucleus of the operation; as such no one could oust him.

Walking through the corridors to the briefing rooms, Eli felt enveloped in a warm cloud of respect, admiration and even envy. That's what came of being the goose that was single-handedly bringing in Red Cap's golden intelligence eggs. He was even sought out by Nathan, head of *Tsafririm*, the unit charged with protecting Jews at risk in other countries. The short, grisly-haired man who was wearing a *kippah* pumped Eli's hand and clapped him on the shoulder saying that the work he was doing combatting 91 had been blessed and what they expected to come from Red Cap was beyond measure. 'Evil shall indeed perish guided by the righteous,' Nathan said.

'If you say so,' Eli said.

Yuval was in Washington, in and out of his own meetings with seven hours difference, so they'd only managed one brief conversation to discuss Rafi's report of the break-in. It appeared that the stupid bastard had bought a couple of pay-as-you-go cell phones to use as operational comms and then broken into the home office of the language school owner.

Eli couldn't have been happier.

Since the break-in was unauthorised and had put the entire operation at risk, the buzz round the Office was that an inquiry was being mooted. Eli was optimistic; an inquiry would bring Rafi back home, if not in disgrace, certainly chastened and at the very least, Eli would be running Trainer. According to the gossip, it seemed that the only mitigating point in Rafi's favour was that he hadn't actually been caught red-handed by a British bobby. A pity.

With all the drama going on at the Office Eli had only managed this one evening at home with Gal and as luck would have it, Doron was back from the army. The joy of seeing his son was tempered by the lad spending a total of forty minutes in the apartment, divided between unloading his kit into the laundry basket, eating straight from the fridge, and showering. The twenty-year-old submitted to only the merest hug from his father before dashing out of the door leaving behind a cloud of cologne.

'Is Doron seeing someone?' Eli leaned back in the pillows.

'Don't ask me. So long as he's happy and safe, I don't care who he's seeing. He looks okay doesn't he?' She had a worried crease between her brows.

'He looks great.'

'You know how hard they push them. And where they send them...'

'He looks great,' Eli repeated.

Gal understood. Another reason to love her.

'How have *you* been?' Gal said as she snuggled into Eli's arms. 'Do you have any idea when you'll be back?'

'Perhaps a month and then we can take a vacation? Or... How would you like three years in London?'

'London?' Gal pulled away and looked at him. 'What are you talking about?'

'Things are going so well that I could be in line for head of London station.' The aircon hummed around the room and Gal lifted the tray off of the white bed and placed it on the side table.

'What about Doron? He's still got three months to go in the army. I couldn't leave him.'

'You could stay here till he's out and then... well, I know he wants to travel when he's finished but he might like to go to university in the UK. He might like it there. Might meet someone.'

Gal sat down back on the bed and pulled her legs up under her, wrapping her arms around them and resting her chin on her knees. 'What about us? What would we do then?'

'Who knows? I can't think about that now.'

'What I mean is, are we going to grow old here? While you've been away and Doron was in the army, I was thinking and trying not to think. And then thinking again. Are we going to sit here and watch Doron's kids go to the army? Watch him being as frightened as we are? As I am?'

He took one of the hands clasped around her knees. He held it between his own and looked into her clear eyes, 'Now is the best chance I will ever have of moving up quickly. If I do that, come back here for a couple of years, then get Washington, well... I could get the top job. And then... then I could make a difference. Gal, the job gives us a lot of power. We can change things for the better. We can initiate behind-the-scenes conversations with the neighbours; Iran, Saudi, Syria, Hamas, Hizbollah. We can influence the prime minister. That can't be done living somewhere else, that can't be done being a security consultant for some fancy company in America or the UK. Living in Florida or LA or London with all the other people who have given up on what our parents and grandparents hoped for. Gal, I've got to do my best – for all of us.'

'I know,' she said. She nestled closer to him. Eli held her to him and stole his hand into her robe.

'What about Rafi?' Gal said. 'Would he be your deputy?'

'No. Why do you ask?' Eli's exploring hand had stopped.

'I saw his wife in Ramat Hasharon a couple of days ago. She'd just picked up their youngest from *gan*, kindergarten; you can't believe how cute that little girl is.'

'Oh yeah,' Eli said.

'Anyway, Hannah said Rafi is in London with you. Said you're working on some huge thing.'

Eli shook his head, 'Thank God you don't go round telling everyone what I do and how well it's going.'

'It's not her fault,' Gal said with reason. 'She's only repeating what her husband said.'

'He's an idiot.'

'That's not what she thinks.' Gal said. 'She thinks he's God's gift to the organisation, Israel, and humanity.'

Eli grunted. He was not going to tell Gal that instead of getting to be deputy of London station Rafi was more likely to find himself in front of a disciplinary panel. And that at long last justice had prevailed. And the reason why Eli would not tell Gal was because he did things properly and by the book. Unlike Rafi.

He was a type.

It was Eli's father's job that took the family all over the world and gave Eli and his sister both language skills and a sophisticated set of cultural reference points. Early exposure to the diplomatic and academic circuit meant that he could recognise if it was Ozawa or Gergiev conducting within the opening three bars of a recital. As a teenager he'd met leading musicians, artists, scientists and politicians at embassy functions where he'd learnt good manners and how to talk to people. His father wanted his education to be eclectic. But these opportunities came at a price; it made Eli an outsider and the constant shifts in country and school were miserable.

Before coming back to Israel to do his national service, Eli had been to school in five different countries but there was one constant: at every single school, whether it was in the UK, France, the Far East or Timbuktu, there was always a guy like Rafi.

Eli remembered arriving in Paris for his time at the American School; he was 11 years old. Only the week before he'd been in non-winter Singapore and the January cold was shocking. It was his first day and during the afternoon there was a sports period supervised by a shaved head athletics teacher who looked like a Nazi. The class was trooped out to the athletics fields for a soccer session and after a series of exercises which involved jumping up and down in the freezing mud the children were lined up in front of two boys. Selected by the teacher the two team captains were clones of each other in that they were taller, smarter and certainly cooler than the rest of the children in the line-up.

One by one the captains picked their teams; 'Cooper, Kucek, Elkin.' The chosen skittered to stand behind the captain who had picked them and the line around those left grew smaller.

'Blears, Amato, Davis.'

And still neither of the captains picked Eli. Finally, Steve, the captain of the blue team, a handsome boy with the smile of someone who had no shred of doubt about his future success finally shrugged and nodded for Eli to join his team. It wasn't about not being chosen that irritated Eli, it was the shrug and nod; that gesture of supremacy, as if being the captain of the soccer team really mattered.

Yet for everyone else on the team, Steve was the boy they most wanted to be, the boy to be close to, the boy who got the girls, won the prizes, the boy who could do no wrong; a hero – like Rafi.

'What's the matter?' Gal was kissing the side of his face and running her hand down his chest towards his crotch. 'Mmm?' she said. 'You've tensed up, and not in a good way.'

'Nothing. Nothing at all.' He pulled her towards him.

22

The Israeli Embassy, Palace Gardens, London – The Next Day

During the entire journey from Heathrow airport to the meeting in central London Eli finessed his reasoning; it was imperative that he immediately take over running Trainer. Besides the break-in, under Rafi's influence – possibly even led by him – Trainer had nearly caused another incident by leaving the scene of a traffic accident. How could this dangerous state of affairs be allowed to continue? With Rafi involved they were racing towards a major diplomatic incident even before the operation was underway.

Eli was satisfied; his arguments were incontrovertible.

And by being the senior officer on both Red Cap *and* Sweetbait, his promotion to head of London station was about as close to a sure thing as anything ever could be.

An hour later, still revelling in a cosy quilt of righteousness, Eli pushed through the side door of the embassy. He went past the security checks to the dedicated lift to the top-floor safe room. Once in the lift he made final preparations; he altered his expression. He wanted to appear to be stern yet still sympathetic. Or as sympathetic as anyone could be to someone whose career was going down the toilet because of their consummate arrogance and innate stupidity. However, after Eli stepped out into the lobby between elevator and safe room and the guard opened the door for him, the first thing he heard was laughter.

Unexpected.

Urit, one of the London analysts was sliding her laptop into its sleeve. She breezed past Eli with a friendly smile. He was left alone in the room with Rafi and Yuval.

For someone who was about to be the subject of an internal investigation that would, at the very least, see the end of his immediate promotion prospects, Rafi looked remarkably relaxed. His long legs were stretched out in front of him, crossed at the ankles and he was wearing a football shirt. By contrast Eli felt overdressed and unshaven in his plane-crumpled jacket.

Eli sat down on Urit's empty chair. First he addressed Yuval, 'How was Washington?'

'*Ein baayot*,' he said. 'No problem.'

'And I don't need to ask how Oxford was,' Eli said to Rafi. 'I read the report.'

There was no response.

Eli went on, 'Reads like James Bond; all that was missing was the helicopter, speedboat and the part where the intelligence officer fucks the agent.'

'Thanks,' Rafi smirked.

'You didn't? Please tell me you didn't fuck Trainer on top of everything else,' Eli said.

Rafi looked neither embarrassed nor abashed and didn't give the slightest hint that he was in trouble.

'Hasn't he been recalled?' Eli said to Yuval.

'The interview will take place here, in London.'

'Why?'

'Operational reasons,' Rafi said. 'We're in the middle of a complex operation and I have to be here – I'm needed.'

Rafi's head was back and he was smiling. Eli got a clear view of Rafi's throat, below his beard; his Adam's apple. Eli's hands clenched and he spoke with care, or as much care as he was capable of, given that he wanted to lash out with his fists at the bigger man.

'Forgive me, but I thought the purpose of this meeting was a handover. I would take over Trainer while Rafi heads home. My mistake. But I must ask: even allowing for Rafi fucking Trainer – which as we all know always ends badly in James Bond – I was under the impression that plumbing jobs need to be authorised.'

'Eli, stop being a pompous ass,' Yuval said.

'I'm serious – putting Trainer in a position where she could have been arrested was irresponsible at best and certainly negligent. And then there was the traffic incident.'

'Nothing happened. And it was a break-in, that's all,' Rafi said. 'It would have taken too long to get a plumbing team here and I handled it.'

'And you didn't even attempt to think of another option,' Eli said.

'Such as?'

'Such as getting Trainer to phone the woman at the school after the interview and coming up with a story why she'd do the job without the salary. Such as... Trainer wanted the job experience and had an educational grant from some research centre. Or something. The woman would have bitten Trainer's hand off. Qualified staff for no salary? It's irresistible for any company. Why didn't you do that, Rafi? Use your brain for a change.'

Yuval spread out his small hands over the polished table, as if he was stretching out the tendons and muscles. 'Eli, the situation is like this... It's the first rule of intelligence. It worked. Yes, Rafi did his own plumbing; yes, Trainer assisted; yes, she had a small accident with the car – but it worked. Rafi came out with the necessary information to proceed with Sweetbait – and that's all that matters.'

'So is that the message we want to send to new recruits? It's all DIY and hope for the best?'

'*Auftragstaktik* – mission command,' Rafi said. 'You said it yourself: make the plan, get Trainer into the school any way I can. And that's what I did. What's the problem?' Rafi picked up a paper cup in his big hands and gulped back the contents.

'And what about Trainer,' Eli said. 'You may have done your own plumbing, unnecessary though it was, but now that you've fucked her how are you going to contain that situation without damaging the operation? Trainer has all the potential to blow you and Sweetbait out of the sky.'

Rafi said, 'Why is this a problem? She's an adult. She knows I'm married and it will not affect the mission except... in a good way. And it was her idea anyway. Eli, come on. You're being ridiculous and looking for things to obsess about. You remind me of my grandfather. He was always moaning and my grandmother was always saying, '*Quien mucho pensa, no se la fada Yersalaim.*' Do you know what that means, Eli? Is Ladino one of your many languages?'

Rafi didn't wait for Eli to answer, 'Whoever thinks too much will never find Jerusalem. And you, brother, think too much.'

Eli looked at Yuval for support and saw none coming, 'Enough,' Yuval said. 'As far as I'm concerned I don't care if Rafi fucks an orangutan so long as it doesn't affect the operation. I need both of you so you can get off your high horse, Eli, and join the rest of us. The interrogator is coming next week to give Rafi the bollocking he richly deserves and you will remain the lead in this operation. Is that understood?'

Eli scowled in response. Yuval continued, 'In the meantime, we have a bigger problem than your ego. Sweetbait's brother is here.'

23

Paddington, London – Three Days Later

Although they knew Wasim was in the Birmingham area, getting his exact location took a few days and gave Eli the opportunity to quietly work through his fury at Rafi's undisciplined behaviour and arrogance. During the daily meetings he wrote and rewrote his resignation in his head, fantasised about Yuval's expression and, finally, realised that the only person who would be damaged by him walking away was himself. And anybody he was trying to help. After all, he was the best spy runner in the organisation.

That day Eli was under additional pressure. At last they had an address for Sweetbait's brother but before driving to Birmingham for a first look at Wasim, Eli had to debrief and rebrief Red Cap with the questions he'd brought back from Israel. This tight schedule, not to mention the prospect of the side trip with Rafi, was making him anxious. No, Eli would never admit to that. Constrained – that was all. The meeting with Red Cap could be achieved in three hours if it all went smoothly.

Sitting in the corner of the tourist hotel in Paddington, Eli glanced at his watch; he eyed a young tourist who was apparently studying his phone. The boy looked up and through black rimmed specs nodded. It was the signal that Red Cap was on the way. Good. Unlike some agents, Red Cap was punctual. Unlike some agents, Red Cap remembered the locations. Thank God for that. Finishing the last of an overstuffed wrap, Eli drained the glass of water and prepared himself mentally.

'It's a dance,' Eli was fond of saying when he lectured on the training courses. 'A tango if you like. It's not jigging around, Dad dancing or club dancing. Running an agent is a dance of seduction.'

That's what Eli said to the fresh-faced recruits and that's what it needed to be. After all, what was bringing Red Cap to him? It certainly wasn't the money. It was the love. Eli signalled for the bill, not wanting to waste any more time when Red Cap did come down the stairs into the basement lounge of the shabby hotel.

The kid in the corner held two fingers behind his phone and nodded. Two minutes before Red Cap completed his journey from Paddington Station to this shabby hotel on a summer Saturday morning. The agent had been watched from the moment he left his house in Cheltenham, to the station, and now here. And there would be more support between the hotel and the safe house. A big operation attracted budget and interest. Everyone wanted to be part of it and Eli was using the resources for security to make sure that nothing went wrong.

Eli saw the kid with the glasses stiffen and then saw a figure in his peripheral vision stepping into the basement lounge.

Red Cap's weekend get-up was no different from his everyday wear. In fact, as far as Eli could see, the agent was wearing the same frayed shirt and rancid schoolmaster's tweed jacket he'd worn the last time they'd met. In daylight, or what passed for daylight in the basement lounge, Red Cap looked worse than ever. The drinker's rash on his skin was redder, his jowls drooped further, and the whites of his eyes were jaundice yellow.

Eli stood up and stretched out his hand, 'Looking good, Derek.'

They shook hands and Eli noticed a tremor in Red Cap's left arm. Somehow they needed to get the guy to have a health check. It wouldn't do for him to end up in A&E yapping on morphine or, worse, making a deathbed confession. But persuading him to have a health check would have to wait for the next meeting. For now, Eli had a tight schedule; he needed to meet Rafi and drive to Birmingham.

'How was the journey?' Eli said. Two women burdened with shopping bags came into the lounge and sat on the other side of the room near the bar. The one with the red wiry hair held her thumb and index finger together forming an 'O'. It meant Red Cap was clean.

'Fine,' Red Cap said, 'the journey was fine, for once the trains were running on time and no delays. They usually choose to do maintenance at the weekend, but today...'

Red Cap was about to collapse his skeletal legs into the olive-coloured chair. Before he could, Eli said, 'Thanks for your customary punctuality. We have a lot to get through in a short time; would you mind having a coffee somewhere quieter?'

Red Cap raised an eyebrow, 'Sounds marvellous.'

Eli gestured towards the stairs and ushered Red Cap up them. Together they left the hotel and walked down the road dodging thundering traffic and inhaling dust-filled air. Over the noise Red Cap drawled on about the Pakistani cricket test. Eli shared his thoughts on the outcome, all the while trying to pick up the pace so that they could reach the safe house and get started.

Once they were off the main road and down a quieter avenue of Edwardian houses that had been converted to flats, Eli had the key ready to use. He opened a blue door and they moved into a dark hall with black and white tiles and steep stairs rising to the first-floor accommodation. The stairs creaked as they went up.

'Nice place you've got,' Red Cap said indicating a patch of damp on the wood chip painted wall.

'Thanks, kind of you to say so.'

Upstairs it was the usual set-up; a mix of second-hand junk, not deemed good enough to be shipped back home in a container by outgoing diplomatic staff, some mismatched Ikea furniture and a few throws to disguise the frayed fabric and cushions to cover sinking springs.

There was a smell of emptiness, sweat and fear typical of safe houses. Also typical was that the fridge and kitchen in the dingy flat were well stocked.

Yes, everything was as Eli had specified on the requisition form. On a small round table by the window in the kitchen someone had laid out a platter of smoked salmon, a basket of different breads, cold roast beef, horseradish sauce, a selection of cheeses, a bowl of fruit and a plate of pastries.

Less pleasing was the view from the window. It was at the back of the house and overlooked the dustbins. Through the sash window with its chipped paint, Eli glimpsed a rat scavenging among the scattered debris in the walled area. Eli reached up and pulled down the roller blind.

On the scarred wooden worktop by the hob was a kettle, a thermos of coffee and a selection of cold drinks. But no alcohol. Eli had requested the alcohol should not be immediately visible. He didn't know whether Red Cap was drinking or not; but what Eli wanted to avoid was Red Cap getting drunk before he'd given him the new set of questions.

However, during the walk to the safe house Eli smelt a sour scent coming off Red Cap; the agent had been bingeing. So Eli changed his mind; better to open the bottle of whisky and delay the hangover. It was the best chance of working Red Cap in the available time.

'Beer and a chaser?' Eli said reaching down to the stacked cupboard to the left of the fridge. 'I've got some whisky I think you might like.' Eli placed the ten-year-old single malt on the tray that already held two supermarket glasses bloomed from overuse in the dishwasher. 'Sorry about the glassware.'

'It's what's in it that counts,' Red Cap said. He looked as if he was holding himself back from grabbing the glass as Eli reached into the fridge for a couple of bottles of beer.

'Taste it, Derek, tell me what you think.'

With apparent relief Red Cap reached for the glass and took a mouthful. He nodded with a pretence at appreciation before he knocked back the rest of the glass. Eli refilled it. He would have to move quickly, not just to get to the meeting with Trainer.

'How's your wife,' Eli said. 'The offer still holds.'

'What offer? The one where we time travel?' Red Cap gulped the second drink back and smiled a softer smile that suggested he was feeling mellow. It was a look Eli recognised, the stage where Red Cap was great company: erudite, intelligent, perceptive.

'You remember,' Eli said sipping at the single malt, feeling the burn at the back of his throat. 'We talked about getting some specialist help for your wife.'

'*You* talked about it. I didn't. Don't worry, we're both on a one-way ticket to hell.'

'I'm not worried, you look okay,' Eli made his voice light and re-assuring, 'but we have resources, Derek. Resources that you should take advantage of.'

'Highest doctor-to-patient ratio in the world? Is that it, Benny?' Red Cap poured himself another three fingers of whisky and looked over the top of his glass at Eli.

'Something like that. I'm not going to nag you anymore but I'd like to help if I can.'

'I believe you would.'

There was an awkward silence at the table. Eli filled it by taking out his Moleskine notebook and pen from his inner jacket. They were props; the flat was wired for sound and sight but if physical notes were taken it gave the illusion that Red Cap was being listened to, concentrated upon, respected and believed. 'So, let's get going. I have some questions for you.'

Red Cap felt inside his tweed jacket and extracted a USB chip; he placed it on the table and nudged it forward with his index finger. His nail was ragged.

'That's it, Benny, all the latest on the data science tool that's analysing the American far right, who's funding them and how – it's my parting gift.'

'Parting gift? What are you talking about?' Eli looked up and met Red Cap's rheumy eyes.

'I wanted to tell you face to face. I might have just not turned up, but somehow it didn't feel right – although I did think about it,' Red Cap smiled that disarming expression that showed the man he once had been. 'I wouldn't have started again if it hadn't been you; you do know that, don't you?'

'And I appreciate that. Believe me. But...' Eli laid down his pen and pushed the pad and the chip aside. 'What's going on?'

For a second, Eli was back on the training course, looking down at the eager young faces, each convinced that they were the real deal, all with conviction that all the dirty stuff they were about to do was meaningful, was safeguarding their heritage, their future, their children, their parents' and grandparents' memories. And Eli was giving them as many of the tricks of the trade as possible. Among the smoke and mirrors, the rabbits pulled from hats and the disappearing ladies, was the absolute certainty that at some point in the course of the handler-agent relationship, every agent has a crisis. For some of them it was the first time they passed over information. For others it was the moment they realised that behind the false flag of a multi-national company, a news agency or a friendly intelligence agency that it would do no harm to help – they were dealing with Israel. And for some, like Red Cap, it was personal.

When the crisis came sometimes they threw up; cried, wept, threatened, even begged. That was the hardest: begging and pleading. To see someone that you had developed over months, maybe even years, disintegrate into helpless tears was hard. When that happened, the most important action was to let them recover alone for a moment so as not to allow them to lose face. The handler had to judge the appropriate action for the situation; like the tango dancer, the handler always had to lead. In keeping with his singular nature, Red Cap's crisis had taken none of these forms. Wreck of a man he may be, anti-establishment and angry, but he was still British to the core and was in control of his emotions and the crisis.

Eli poured another shot into Red Cap's glass and refilled his own.

'Talk to me, Derek. Let's forget about all this, tell me what's going on.'

'I told you, I've had enough and I want to wrap everything up.'

'Why now? Nothing happens in the summer; it's the best time of year. Why don't you wait a few months, say September for example, and then stop?'

'It's getting to me, Benny. I thought I could handle it, but I can't.'

Eli said, 'Is it home or work or something else.'

'I'm not going to bother you with all this; suffice to say, I need to stop. Now.'

Eli stroked his scalp, 'You're not bothering me, Derek. Just tell me why; maybe I can help in some way.'

Red Cap shrugged, 'I'm not sleeping and when I do, I have nightmares. During the day I have palpitations and I feel sick all the time.'

'So, let me get you in to see a doctor, a good doctor. Derek, all you need is a decent doctor.'

The agent grinned ruefully, 'You mean a shrink. I could check into the same place as my wife.'

'Whatever you want, whenever you want, I mean that. But don't walk now, Derek, we're right in the middle of the job; you're a professional.'

'Don't try to manipulate me, Benny, and stop sounding like a used-car salesman. Let's end this well.'

Eli poured himself a drink and sipped at it. The agent was right; this was the downside of working with someone who knew the process. 'Point taken. I apologise if that's what it looked like.'

Red Cap said, 'To do right, we must respect other people – my father told me that. He was a vicar.'

Eli looked at Red Cap eye to eye. He spoke slowly, 'I want to do right and I do respect you. Derek, I've got some questions I brought from back home, they're about the RAT in the Qatar Embassy.'

'I told you, it's not my department. It would look suspicious if I was interested. Everybody just does their own job and then goes home.'

'Look, if you can get the answers, even some of the answers, I promise we'll call it a day.'

Red Cap was still and held eye contact, 'And would that be doing right?'

'In the long term, yes.' Eli said.

Red Cap picked up his glass and without drinking, placed it on the table between them. He spoke slowly, 'I never told you why I came to Palace Green and Kensington Palace Gardens when I volunteered.'

'Our embassy was closer to the tube than the Russian Embassy?' Eli said.

'No, it was a deliberate choice. I'd thought about it for years before I did it. It was because of Mrs Stein.'

The agent's smile lifted the lined skin over his cheek bones.

'Mrs Stein?'

'My music teacher. My dear father had aspirations for me, perhaps wanting me to fulfil his own thwarted ambitions. Who knows? Anyway, on a Wednesday night when he and my mother met parishioners for tea and cake, I went to Mrs Stein for dinner and a music lesson.'

Red Cap narrowed his eyes; he was looking beyond Benny at the wall as if he could see something there. 'Our piano was in the front room and on top of it was a lamp with a coloured glass lampshade – faux Tiffany I believe. But it was the only colour in the house; everything else was dark wood, brown, beige, magnolia, but no colour. Funny the things that one remembers.'

'Was Mrs Stein a member of your father's congregation?' Eli said.

The question brought Red Cap back to the room. 'Hardly. She was one of your lot. They lived five doors away. She was quite beautiful. At least I thought so, and she was younger than my mother or she seemed to be; she was certainly merrier. I haven't thought about her for such a long time; she had lots of red hair that was probably dyed and I was fascinated by how she secured it on top of her head – with a pencil, or a knitting needle, or a chop stick, or anything else she could find. When I got there, she was never ready so I'd sit at the table in the kitchen with the twins in their high chairs while she simultaneously fed them and prepared whatever had to go into the pot or oven before we had our lesson. I absolutely loved it, Benny. The radio would be on and she might sing or do a dance to get the twins to eat their pulped-up mush. And she used to get me to sing along. It was something I could never imagine happening in our house; the only songs my dear mother ever sang were hymns and never at home. Sometimes Mrs Stein's mother was there, and the old lady knew music hall songs like "Abdul Abulbul Amir". D'you know that song?'

Eli shook his head and Red Cap started to sway in his seat. His rasped voice began, '*The sons of the prophet are brave men and bold, they're quite unaccustomed to fear...*' The tune dissolved into a hacking cough that Red Cap soothed with a gulp of whisky. At last he cleared his throat, recovered even though his face was flushed when he looked up.

'So, that was Mrs Stein,' Red Cap said swallowing. 'And why I came to you and not the Russians. But my terrible guilt, which I confess for the first time to you, my friend, is that I wanted Mrs Stein to be my mother. With all my heart I yearned for that woman, I fantasised about her taking me to school, tucking me up in bed when I was sick, singing me a song instead of the sad woman waiting for me in our colourless house. Was that a betrayal, Benny? Was that my first secret betrayal and the reason I'm here with you?'

'Of course, it wasn't,' Eli lied because that's what you did with agents. 'I wanted my uncle to be my father.' Another lie.

'What happened to your uncle?'

'Got himself killed in a commando raid in Syria. My father never got over it.'

But sometimes, like a snake, truth slithers out of the lie.

It must have been the whisky, Eli thought afterwards: he was ten – sitting by his father's side on the bed in his parents' room. *Abba* was holding a small box on his knee and ever curious, Eli watched his father open the blue box with the gold Star of David on it. Nestled on pale blue silk was Uncle Danny's posthumous medal. It was the only time Eli saw his father weep, the only time the suave, witty, erudite man broke down. Holding the medal in his hand, *Abba's* shoulders shook and he sobbed.

Eli shut his notebook and smoothed down the leather to indicate that the private part of his life was closed.

For a moment or two there was an awkward silence between the two men. At last Red Cap broke it. 'A little while ago you said you'd try to give me anything I want if I kept going; if I tried to get the RAT. Is that still a firm offer?'

'Within reason,' Eli said.

'Then drink with me now, Benny. Just for once, let's forget about all this; the questions; the answers; the people behind you with the questions – and the people behind me. Let's find somewhere where we can watch the cricket test together; like friends. And drink together – like friends.'

24

Birmingham, Three Days Later

Three days. Three whole days with Rafi and they were no closer to making contact with Wasim than they had been when they'd arrived in this miserable corner of Birmingham. It was frustrating; no matter how much time Eli spent studying the image they had of Wasim that had been lifted from the University of Kansas's website, the reality remained elusive. And if Wasim continued to stay in the flat above the laundrette, there was little they could do, short of knocking on the door and inviting themselves in for a cup of tea.

To compound the misery of the stakeout the weather had turned bad. Squally, blustery wind and quite unseasonal according to the incessant and obsessive commentary in the shops and cafés where they passed the day trying to be as grey and unmemorable as the ubiquitous clouds.

Their favourite watch spot was a corner shop with a few tables for punters to have a coffee and a microwaved bap. Here they could sit on plastic chairs and watch the traffic rumble past the entrance to the flat. The view was partially obscured by a bus stop but at least inside the café/shop they were dry. They took turns being the eyeball which meant doing a circuit around the block, going into different shops and checking to see if there was any activity from the flat. It was stupefyingly boring work.

Rafi came into the café and sat down opposite Eli. He shrugged off his jacket and rain dripped on to the grimy floor. He seemed unfazed, even relaxed, even enjoying himself.

'We know he's in there,' Rafi said. 'Now it's just a question of waiting for him to come out. Listen, he wants to see his sister, so he can't stay in there forever. When he comes out we'll get a look at him, make a contact. You'll do your spy runner magic and everything will be *achla*. So, relax, Eli. Enjoy the moment.'

The moment Eli was currently enjoying was a rebellion in his oesophagus; acid reflux from the fat in the bacon bap he'd just eaten. He didn't answer, just pushed his chair back and got to his feet reaching for his jacket which was still damp; it was his turn to do a pass.

Rafi hadn't finished, 'You know what your problem is, Eli?'

'I'm sure you're about to tell me.'

'Seriously, man, you don't know how to pace yourself and as I've said to you before, you think too much. You should try meditation.'

'That's him.'

Over Rafi's shoulder, Eli had just seen a gangly young man on the other side of the road. Even in a hoodie and baseball cap there was no doubt in Eli's mind that it was Wasim; he'd spent long enough staring at the kid's image to have memorised the wide brow and etched frown, the bushy hair and narrow chin. He was standing by the bus stop, knees slightly bent, taking the weight from one to the other as if there was elastic in them. Apparently nervous, his head was turning as the traffic hurtled past, he was eyeing the island in the middle of the road to see if he could get to it. Rafi had stood up.

'Wait,' Eli raised his hand. 'Let's just see which way he goes when he gets across.'

Standing in the rain, the boy hunched further inside his hoodie, he seemed impatient to cross. A gap appeared and he scuttled towards the island and then dashed across, like a foal, all legs and not quite co-ordinated. Safely on the same side of the pavement as the café, the boy paused again, shifting from foot to foot, a trait Eli was already starting to recognise as being particular to Wasim. It looked as if the boy was uncertain of where he was going but then he made a decision.

'Oh shit – he's coming this way,' Eli said. 'He's coming in here.'

Rafi sat down, turned back to face Eli and picked up the laminated menu. They both concentrated on avoiding eye contact and merely glanced up as Wasim came into the shop and broached the aisles of food clearly looking for something in particular.

'We've got to get to him before he goes back in the house,' Rafi said. 'Who knows when he's going to come out again.'

'No. If he's come out once, he'll come out again,' Eli said.

By now the boy was at the till; he had a carton of milk, a carton of juice, some beans and tomatoes. He passed over some money and then waited for change. Closer, he looked younger than 18; thin, below average height, wiry dark hair and a shadow of beard on his chin. He looked like a kid you'd see on any campus, anywhere, even down to the thick-framed glasses that were now speckled with rain.

Just then, a man came into the shop; he abruptly turned away from the boy, avoiding his ten to two: the dangerous area in front of Wasim. Eli did a double-take; the man had positioned himself precisely at three – at right angles to the side of the boy, out of his range of vision; it was exactly like watching a playback of a training film, without the commentary. The man had cropped red hair, a beard; solid built, tough, arms hanging free, as if ready to respond and his eyes were alert.

'Problem,' Eli said.

'What?' Rafi said.

Then a blond woman came into the shop, middle-aged, straggly hair, a hollow-eyed expression from too many late nights working and too many parties making up for it. Wasim was still at the till packing his food into a plastic bag and the woman hung back, with casual skill, at the magazine rack, finding her position and, once again, precisely avoiding the boy's ten to two. With her back to Wasim she leafed through *Hello*, frowned, and then picked up another magazine as if that might be better. The woman ignored the man with the red hair who was working the aisles but she just couldn't help herself; she just had to snatch a look towards the till and Wasim.

'Give me the menu,' Eli said. 'We have a big problem. Unless I'm very much mistaken, the house across the road is under surveillance by our friends at MI5.'

There was nothing they could do. For another thirty minutes the two men sat in the Birmingham café and drank another pot of tea even though Wasim had gone and so had his watchers.

'We may as well see how many there are,' Eli said.

Using the hire car they cruised past the house and competed to see how quickly they could spot the rest of the surveillance team who were spread in a classic pattern around the house. The red-headed man was at a bus stop fifty yards down the road; blondie was in the launderette under the flat with a bag of washing – a nice touch they thought – and there was a moon-faced kid selling *The Big Issue* next to the bus stop. In total there was an additional five other watchers and when Eli and Rafi saw the shift change at 8pm they knew that the notion of making an unseen contact with the boy was absurd.

'What the hell are we going to do?' Rafi said for once apparently pessimistic. 'We know the boy's here but we can't get close to him.'

'We can't stick around here that's for sure. I say we go back to London, discuss it with Yuval, and think of some other way to make contact with the boy. In the meantime we have to hope that he's not arrested and that he doesn't go visit his sister.'

25

M40 Motorway – The Same Day

Petra flicked her car into sports mode, put her foot down, and felt the car lurch forward as she reached ninety miles per hour. At five in the morning the M40 was an empty ribbon, curling up the hill between the chalky Chiltern escarpment before High Wycombe.

This weekend would be the first break she'd had away from the school since the language course had started. She needed the time away from the school for several reasons, both operational and emotional — although it pained her to admit it even if only to herself. Being in the field was far more tiring than she remembered; the constant concentration, playing the role, extracting information, trying to observe and memorise nuance that may or may not be important made her head ache. Making it worse was using her real name. This singularity made it impossible to detach. There was no barrier between who she really was and what she was doing.

Petra saw the sign for the M25 and relaxed her shoulders; she was nearly home. Besides this chance to wind down, it would also be the first time she'd seen Matt. It had been easy to tell him on a shaky Skype call that she'd got an interesting summer gig; it would be complicated if he saw her at the school with Deanna and the students. Matt was no fool; he'd instantly smell the sulphur of espionage.

Home. By 6.30am Petra was shoving her front door against the stack of post that had wedged it shut. Successfully inside she knelt to gather up the paper on the mat. Between front door and kitchen she glanced up and experienced the house with the fresh eyes of a stranger. She encountered her home as someone else might. Her first impression was smell. A bad smell. Above her some lilies in the vase on the hall table had shrivelled, one or two petals had dropped on to the floor and lay twisted into shapes of agony. Before doing anything else, Petra needed to get rid of the decomposing flowers and the stinking water. That done she rinsed her hands and powered up the Sonos to get some music flowing around the house.

'That's better,' she said aloud. The intermezzo from *Fedora* drifted down the stairs and around the house. It slid and shimmied off the walls. The set of Petra's shoulders softened and she wondered what time Matt would get back.

Matt was aware that she was Jewish and that her father was a refugee, but he knew none of the details. There was no need for him to know. No need to describe the bitter day in 2001 when she'd buried her father and met Alon; no need to relate how the stranger at the service had choked up with tears and introduced himself as the other little boy in the photograph.

It was the same for Matt. He hadn't told her what he'd done in Iraq during Desert Fox; never said how he'd got the wound on his arm or, later, how he got the wound of his first marriage. When they'd met as inductees at the investigations firm he'd quoted: 'The past is another country.' She'd readily agreed – she hadn't told him about her work in the past and there was no reason for her to tell him about it now. Shortly after they'd joined the firm their work paths diverted; Matt had been seconded to the Risk department and used his army skills in some of the more inhospitable areas of the world keeping corporate clients safe. She sometimes wondered how long he'd be happy doing the same job but they didn't have those sorts of conversations; their time together was to enjoy.

While the kettle boiled, Petra leafed through the envelopes, opening anything that wasn't immediately obvious and putting the paper into piles. A flyer slipped between her hands and drifted down to the table. It was an A5 sheet with balloons, smileys and text in different colours. 'Street Party' it announced.

Petra looked at her watch and checked the date. Then she went to the window at the front of the cottage and spotted Bob, a neighbour from three houses down. The old guy was standing on the green in a blue cashmere sweater giving instructions to a gangly lad standing atop a pick-up truck. Bob was gesticulating, telling the kid to get the bollards off the back of the pick-up truck.

Grabbing her car keys, Petra dashed out of the front door to move her car before it got blocked in. And on cue, as if she'd been waiting, Sandie, from next door, came out on to the street.

'You're back! That's wonderful. I'm so pleased you could make it. We're going to have such a great time.'

26

Thames End Village, Surrey – Same Day

Four hours later there was still no sign of Matt but the street party was in full swing. A band had set up on the mini-roundabout at the far end of the close. There were keyboards, drums, stacked amps and Jeff, a building society manager, was at the heart of it. The band was belting out 70s and 80s covers. They were competing with a Punch and Judy show and the clatter and clamour of the local kids. If the scene had been in black and white it could have been old newsreel – apart from the proud parents taking photos on their phones.

'Have a sausage roll?' Sandie thrust a paper plate of pastry and what looked like sausage at Petra. 'They're going fast so I thought I'd better save you a couple.'

'Thanks.'

'How's the teaching job going?' Sandie was swaying from side to side in time to the music. 'I must come and visit you while you're there. Where is it exactly?'

'That would be great,' Petra slid away from the question. 'I'd love that. How are Kurtz and Rollo? I must come and see them before I go back.'

'They're both well. I was worried about Kurtz but I've got this new vet and we've made some changes to his diet,' Sandie looked abashed. 'They may only be rabbits – '

'Rabbits?' A voice interrupted the women. 'Are you ladies talking about rabbits?'

Petra turned and saw Bob the neighbour at her elbow with a small boy in tow.

'Hi Bob, and who is this young man?' Sandie said.

'This, ladies, is my grandson, Callum,' Bob said with rooster pride. 'Callum this is Sandie and Petra, what do you say?'

'How do you do?' the toddler said.

'It kills me,' Bob said. 'It totally kills me. Probably hasn't learnt to read a word at that fancy prep school he goes to but when he opens his mouth he sounds like the royal family.'

Petra said to the wide-eyed boy. 'How do you do Callum? It's very nice to meet you.'

The boy smiled shyly.

'He's down for the weekend,' Bob said. 'And he wanted to meet the lady with the rabbits.'

Sandie took her cue, 'Would you like to come and see my rabbits, Callum?'

The kid looked up at Bob, who nodded. 'And if you're good, Sandie might let you feed them some carrot.'

Petra watched Bob's face as Sandie and Callum disappeared towards her cottage. The craggy features of the older man softened as he watched his grandson's stumbling gait.

On the mini-roundabout the band launched into an enthusiastic cover of 'Nothing's Gonna Stop Us Now'; two middle-aged women started to jig around, glasses held aloft, sadly shimmying under grey summer clouds.

'How's business?' Petra said to get Bob pre-empting questions.

'Ticking over.'

A small-scale property developer he bought one property at a time, renovated it and sold. It seemed as if the whole purpose for him was the chance to do battle with the planning authorities, contractors and estate agents and Bob was always ready to talk about how he knew best.

His latest deal was in Tilton, a nearby village; the flat was empty, but Bob couldn't and wouldn't start the work until the plans had been signed off by the council.

'I know better than that; if I do, then they'll have me over a barrel,' Bob said. 'I reckon they do it deliberately, they haven't got anything better to think about down at the town hall.'

Petra felt her phone vibrate and answered the undisclosed number, 'Matt, where are you?'

'Who's Matt? Should I be jealous?' It was Rafi on the phone.

'No. What do you want?'

Aware that Bob was listening Petra moved away.

'We need you back at the school. That relative of our friend may be visiting sooner rather than later. Can you get back first thing tomorrow?'

'It's not great,' Petra said. 'Okay, I'll think of something.'

Petra ended the call and pocketed the phone. Bob's eyebrows were raised so Petra glanced down at her watch and she looked over Bob's shoulder giving as clear an indication as possible that the conversation was over; she was looking for someone else to talk to. That's when she saw Sandie. Stumbling, red-faced. She was carrying Bob's grandson. The kid's face was blue. Petra sprinted towards Sandie.

'I tried to... I tried to...' Sandie said breathlessly. 'He's choking.'

'Give him to me. And call an ambulance.'

The boy was limp in Petra's arms. Being as gentle as possible she knelt down behind him and placed her arms under his. With one fist she felt for the space between ribs and naval. His blue tee shirt was damp and his hair was brushing her chin. This was the key moment. She needed to find the right spot otherwise she might damage his ribs or, worse, press down on his heart. Meanwhile Bob had rumbled up; he loured over Petra red-faced and terrified. By his side, Sandie stood ringing her hands.

'Okay Callum,' Petra said making her voice calmer than she felt.

With her arms looped under the kid's armpits and around his small body, Petra grasped her fist with her other hand and took a deep breath before she pulled sharply inwards. Once. Nothing.

Twice. Three times. The sweat poured down her arms and face. She didn't dare look up at Bob. Four times. One last pull and the kid coughed. A lump of carrot came out of his mouth along with stomach bile over his tee shirt and Petra's hands.

'Okay, love, you're all right,' she said. He breathed in deeply, a rasping breath.

'Sandie, call a bloody ambulance, will you?'

'Callum, boy, my boy,' Bob was trembling as he struggled to kneel down and take the boy in his arms. The party around them had stopped, only the band continued unaware of the drama that was being played out.

'He's okay,' Petra said, suddenly choked up herself, her face still in the boy's hair. Calming herself she looked up, cleared her throat to swallow the emotion, 'He's okay, Bob, but it's important he's checked over.'

Bob garbled. 'Thank you, thank you.' Tears coursed down his face.

'It's just first aid, Bob. Anybody who's done a basic course would know what to do. When the ambulance gets here they'll check Callum's heart function and then you can forget about it and tell him to chew in future.'

'I owe you,' Bob said. 'Just remember that, I mean it.'

Petra gently nudged Bob and Callum towards a tree in the shade and waited with them until the green-clad paramedics bundled out of the ambulance. The kid had just disappeared into the ambulance for the heart function tests when she was conscious of someone at her elbow and turned.

'That was well done,' Matt said. He was wearing a crumpled grey suit and the pale blue shirt made him look more tanned. 'I got here just as you were doing the abdomen thrusts. I watched you. Perfect position, rhythm and from what I could see pressure. You're a helluva girl, Petra, but now, I think you deserve a drink.'

Matt hung his crumpled jacket on the branch of a tree and rolled up his sleeves. After downing a beer, he led Petra out on to the dance area in front of the band. Dancing with energy if not grace Matt moved around the circle of shy onlookers dragging them on to the makeshift dance floor until the road echoed to a roar as all ages belted out the chorus to 'Hi Ho Silver Lining' arms raised, fists clenched. Beneath the sweat, the laughter, the matey claps on the back, Petra sensed his need to slough off whatever he'd seen and whatever he'd done when he was away.

When it was dark they slunk off back to her cottage without saying goodbye to anyone and walked side by side, good companions, along the quiet street.

'Do you ever wonder what's the point of it all?' Matt slipped his arm around her and squeezed her waist; she smelt the beer on him.

'Make the world a better place?'

'Well, it's not working is it?'

'We've still got to try,' Petra said.

They were at her door and while she shuffled in her bag looking for the key she was aware that even drunk, Matt was checking her house for signs of a clandestine entry. She let him in first and while he checked all the rooms she put the kettle on.

Matt made love like he danced. With energy but not much grace. Yet it was good; he hugged her like a bear with a cub and when he went to sleep she stroked a strand of fair hair off his forehead. After watching him for a while she left him to snore and went into the spare room to slip between cool sheets where she could think about the job ahead and how trying was the point of it all. That's why she was doing it. If she saved one life then it would be worth it; she would have done something that would have made her father proud.

Lying awake, listening to Matt snore through the thin walls of the cottage, Petra visualised the contents of her workbag that was now packed and positioned by the front door so she could steal out without waking Matt. Inside the bag was some tech she'd taken out of her safe; it was good to be prepared for any eventuality and with the knowledge that Sahar's brother might be visiting, it seemed a sound precaution.

Petra's safe was a concealed compartment within a shelf in her wardrobe; building and painting the chipboard design had taken an entire weekend. But Petra was proud of her work; she was confident that a team would have little chance of finding the safe because it was bespoke; the design wouldn't be in anybody's manual. The wardrobe width compartment was big enough for cash, papers, a spare passport, sim cards, two spare phones and tracking devices, several of which were concealed in Shakespeare commemorative coins.

These coins were now in Petra's work bag; they might come in useful. Or not. Meanwhile, she needed to grab a couple of hours sleep before driving to Oxford. As Petra closed her eyes, she felt a sense of relief that she wouldn't have to lie to Matt about where she was going at 2am because she wouldn't be there when he woke up.

Petra turned over, pummelled the pillow into a more comfortable shape. She liked the relationship, the sense of detachment and respect. Why did it have to be any more than that? She didn't want to be dependent on a man and she didn't want a man to be dependent on her. It would be like a claw tearing at her equanimity; her sense of self. That's why she never shared a bed with Matt; sex was one thing but spooning, love whispers, stupid names and the besotted clutching of lovers seeking solace and intimacy to stave away fears of uncertain future was quite another.

Rolling on her back Petra glanced at her watch. She really needed to get some sleep and now wasn't the time to think about Matt; it was the time to work out what she'd do if the brother appeared. First impressions of Sahar were of a petite young woman with wiry dark hair and worried eyes. Sahar seemed anxious to please which ought to make manipulating her easier. But becoming a trusted mentor took time and the brother might be on his way.

Shifting on the bed once again, Petra thought about Bob's grandchild and the moment when she'd held the child safe and secure, smelt his hair, felt his heart beating and wanted to weep. Yes, she'd wanted to weep.

Her reaction disturbed her.

27

Pall Mall, London – The Next Day

On the way to The Travellers Club Eli broke protocol and discussed business on the street. Once again, he broached the subject of Red Cap's retirement; and, once again, Yuval was intransigent. The problem, the unsolvable problem, was success. As Yuval put it, not only was Red Cap's American product valuable but the prospect of any intelligence about the Qatari RAT was too good to miss. Thanks to Eli's handling, the agent was finally under control; it would be like cutting your dick off before a sure thing.

'He's not stable,' Eli insisted. They were walking down from Piccadilly towards Pall Mall, dodging the tourists with cameras and the scurrying people on the pavement. 'I can't be sure what he's going to do and the pressure from his wife is making him unpredictable.'

'You need to run him at the very least until we finish Sweetbait and the British give us their raw data from the RAT; in the meantime, we cannot afford him breaking down, getting caught or making some scene that may implicate us. After Sweetbait it will be a different story; our relationship with the British will be secured because we saved them from an attack and we'll be able to ride out the storm if he does expose us.'

Yuval touched Eli's elbow pausing him in his stride. 'We're talking weeks, Eli, a month at most. That's all. You can manage that. If anyone can, anybody in the whole organisation can, you can.'

Eli said nothing.

They were standing by the side of the road waiting for the lights to change.

'Eli, the situation is like this: you keep Red Cap active; we work Sweetbait. And you get London station. You know that don't you?'

'You'll back that all the way to the top? I know I'm not the popular choice.'

'I've already put it forward and discussed it with *Menume*, the big boss.'

The green man icon flashed and a woman struggled across the road with a wheelchair that carried an old lady. Eli assisted her to get back on the pavement.

'Thank you,' the woman said. 'It's very kind of you.'

'My pleasure,' Eli said and turned back to Yuval who was looking at him with a bemused expression.

'Why did you do that?'

'I don't know. It's something Red Cap said to me about doing right. Come on, let's go,' Eli said to Yuval. 'Let's get on with it.'

Ten minutes later Eli, Yuval and MI6's Milne were sitting in the library at The Travellers Club. Whether by design or coincidence, the room was deserted. The three men sat on leather seats around a low table that seemed to have been created for low conversations, although there could be little doubt that the conversation was being recorded. On the wall by the leather bound books, Eli noted the white humidity monitor fixed to the oak panelling. If that's what it was.

Gathering intelligence through such devices as the monitor and analysing it were two entirely different disciplines. It was like a car and gasoline; one was no good without the other. That was one of the great Friday morning meeting conversations back home; the out-of-hours chat about the problem of too much intelligence product and not enough analysis; or not enough intelligence and too much analysis. It was one of the challenges of the business.

Eli thought it would be interesting to share views on this subject with Milne and Pen. Indeed, if all went well and Eli became head of

London station the intelligence/analysis conundrum might well be one of the conversations they would share, perhaps over a sandwich lunch at the 'Wedding Cake' at Vauxhall, perhaps over pink gins, perhaps even at Lord's or the Proms or the Royal Academy summer exhibition – when Eli got to be head of London station. Because Eli genuinely liked and respected Milne even while he was planning to deceive him.

Eli shifted in his seat, consciously positioning himself to have open body language. He was tickled to see Milne mirror his position. That movement was a little too fast. He should have waited, made it look more natural. Milne seemed uneasy.

'No Pen?' Eli said after the refreshments had been provided.

'No Pen,' Milne said. 'He's gone home.'

'Gone home or been sent home?' Yuval said.

Milne's mouth twitched, 'I don't think there's very much difference, do you?'

'That rather depends on the circumstances,' Eli said. 'Was it the end of his term?'

Milne pushed the coffee away from him as if he didn't like the taste. Or maybe he just didn't like the company. After a pause he said, 'Things are in a state of flux at Langley at the moment and no one knows what's going to happen next. The last time I saw Pen he was talking about the great purge.'

'That bad?' Eli said.

Milne nodded, 'It wouldn't be the first time there's been a cull in the Company. I will, of course, send feedback directly through our Washington liaison but for the moment we're waiting to see who they will send in Pen's place.'

'Understood,' Eli said starting to get to his feet, 'In that case would you like to reschedule for when we have a replacement for Pen? Because I can't see you being able to authorise access to raw data we believe you're collecting from the Qatar Embassy in the UK without US agreement. Or am I wrong?'

'Sit down, please,' Milne said. 'It's simple as I explained to you the last time we met. If we did have raw intelligence – and your arguments about the quality of your analysts compared to our own is convincing – you still don't have any product to trade. It's a one-way deal; we give, you take and if we ever do give, you take too much.'

'That's not true,' Yuval pointed his finger. 'We gave you the laptop airplane bomb plot and in return you compromised our agent. If there is a one-way deal, it goes in your direction.'

'That was the Americans, it was nothing to do with us,' Milne said. 'And you know it. And you can't blame the Company either. We're all the servants of our administrations, more's the pity.'

Milne sounded tetchy. Unusually tetchy. Quite unlike the last time they'd met when he'd been all smooth and dismissive diplomacy. Whatever the circumstances of Pen's sudden disappearance it must have had some knock-on effect to Milne's sphere of influence. Maybe he was now tainted and fighting his own internal battles.

Eli decided to play the cards differently.

'Okay, what if we do have something to trade?' Eli said.

'Go on.' Milne's mouth was tight. The MI6 man neither trusted nor believed what he was about to hear.

Eli took a deep breathe, 'A Hamas splinter group backed by Al Qaeda is planning an operation in Britain, in the British Home Counties. We can't be absolutely precise because, without raw intelligence from a European source such as the Qatar Embassy –'

Milne interrupted, 'You have raised this point before, Eli. Just the facts please.'

'It is still at the planning stage according to our HUMINT but they are planning something that's high profile with subsequent loss of life. And the target is definitely in the Home Counties. What's more we have an address in Birmingham where we believe the cell is located.'

'Birmingham? I see.' Milne picked up the white damask napkin and unnecessarily dabbed at his lips. He went on, 'If you would be kind enough to give me the details I will be most grateful even though, thus far, I am not convinced. Hamas and Al Qaeda co-operating would be unusual to say the least. Are you certain?'

Yuval broke in, 'No, we are not certain. The point you miss is that we cannot be precise about Hamas's operations in Europe without the intelligence you're *not* gathering from the Qatar Embassy.'

'You did well,' Yuval said. 'Milne is sharp. But you did well. He's one of those brainy Brits, well educated, with vision and experience. They're a new generation. Seasoned by Northern Ireland and hardened by 7/7, Afghanistan, Iraq; the class war and Cold War disasters are ancient history.'

They were waiting for the bomb-proof door of the safe room at the embassy to swing open.

'Update Rafi, I'll go see if the kit we're waiting for is in the bag; then you have to call Sweetbait's brother and tell him to get out of the house. Do you want to run through it again?'

'I'm pretty sure I'm okay. If you want to update Rafi I'll get the diplomatic bag,' Eli said.

'They won't let you sign for it.' Yuval slapped Eli on the back. 'Not yet anyway.' The inference was clear and Eli felt warmed by it.

Yuval disappeared towards the lift leaving Eli to listen to the clunk of bolts sliding back and the hiss of hydraulics as the door opened. Rafi was sitting alone in the room, on his usual seat in the corner, tapping away at a laptop.

'*Ma yesh*?' Rafi said looking up. 'What have you got?'

Eli shrugged off his jacket and dropped it on a chair. He helped himself to one of the bottles of water in the fridge at one end of the room and ripped off the top. 'It went okay,' he said.

'Only okay?' Rafi said. He was drinking one of his health shots that for some reason were always green. This one was obviously particularly potent. It was in a small plastic pot and Rafi grimaced after he necked it.

'Does it help keep your dick up?' Eli said.

Rafi's smile was indulgent, 'Sure. You should try it sometime.'

'I don't need to,' Eli said. 'I'm neither a performing rabbit nor the office whore.'

Rafi laughed. 'Which? Rabbit or whore. Be reasonable, man; I can't be both.'

'Fuck off.'

'What's more, I've got to tell you, Eli, this hostility of yours is not healthy. You might want to talk to your wife about it. She's a psychologist isn't she?'

'Child psychologist,' Eli growled.

'Need I say more?'

Eli flipped open one of the laptops and started pecking at the keyboard, opening a document and starting his contact report.

But Rafi wouldn't let it go, 'So, it went okay? The Brits and the Yanks know we have something valuable but don't know what? And they also know they'll have to pay for it?'

Eli stopped typing. 'Exactly. Except Pen, the CIA liaison wasn't there because he's been recalled and I told Milne that there's a terrorist cell in Birmingham. But we can't be certain without their raw data.'

Rafi nodded, 'Wow, big gamble.'

'We had nothing to lose. We know MI5 is already watching the house so this makes us look good.'

'What about Sweetbait's brother? Now you've told MI6 that even we know there's a terrorist cell in Birmingham they'll have Five breaking the doors down.'

'I'm dealing with that next,' Eli said.

'Can I stay and listen?'

'No.'

28

The Israeli Embassy, Palace Gardens, London – Fifteen Minutes Later

Eli sat square on the chair in the safe room at the embassy with his notes in front of him and a pad. Adjusting the headset, putting the bottle of water within reach, he gave Michael, the comms guy the thumbs up to make sure the recording equipment and encryption equipment were tested and ready.

Then he heard the number being dialled and the trill of the ringing tone filled his ears.

The boy answered on the second ring; he sounded American.

'Wasim,' Eli said taking control of the call. He pitched his voice low, from the gut, sounding stern and authoritative, gruff. In Arabic Eli said, 'Can you speak safely?'

'Yes, who is this?'

'I am a friend who has your family's interests at heart. I am calling about a family member. You know who I am talking about don't you?'

'Who are you? What is going on with Sa –'

Eli interrupted, 'Don't say the name. Do not speak it. You want our enemies to hear you?'

'I must know who you are. My... that person you talk about... she told me she is to be *shaheeda*, but no one I have talked to back home has heard about it.'

'Because this is so important,' Eli hissed. 'It is secret you fool. You speak to anyone, it becomes more dangerous. Do not talk on the phone.'

'Why? This is a new phone, I just bought it. WhatsApp is secure.'

Eli laughed. 'No it's not. That is why I call you on another system. WhatsApp has never been secure; the big lie is that it is. That's how they listen to us. We are deceived if we use that system, they are cunning. Now listen carefully, brother, we have little time before this call is picked up – you understand? We know who you are; we have spoken to friends of your commander. They say you are an honourable young man; a fighter. You are in danger.'

'What?' The boy's voice cracked with anxiety. He sounded younger than 18.

'You must leave the house immediately. Don't tell the people you are with that you are going or why. Do you understand? Go to the coach station and take the first bus to London, to Victoria. Someone will meet you there.'

'My sister?'

'No. She is involved in something very great and very secret. It will be an honour for your family and for you as head of the family,' Eli said. 'But you must go quickly. There will be a man at the Victoria bus station who will be carrying a green book and a red bag. Understood?'

'Yes.'

'God be with you.'

Eli ended the call and gave Michael the thumbs up. That ought to do it; the boy had sounded impressed, frightened and excited. Eli hoped it would be enough to get him out of the house and once he got picked up in London, they ought to be able to keep him quiet at least until the end of the operation.

Taking the headset off, Eli realised his face was covered with sweat.

29

Watlingford Public School, Oxfordshire – The Next Day

Today's a good day. I'm sitting in my room writing and I'm happy. I've decided what I'm going to do with this journal when the time comes. I'm going to find a way to give it to my brother, Wasim. So these pages are for you, most cherished and favourite brother.

As well as being happy, I'm also relieved. Today I met my contact. After weeks of thinking I'm alone and forgotten, there was a message on my phone. It was an icon, a bear; it meant that I should miss the morning class and go to meet my contact.

Getting Aneeta to go to the class without me was really difficult, even though I said I'd been sick all night. She fussed. 'Maybe you go see doctor,' she said. 'I get breakfast for you and you stay in bed. I tell Petra to call doctor. It is no good to have this pain again so soon.'

I held her hands between my own. Her nails are painted black and they shine like oil.

'I'm okay,' I said. 'I come to class this afternoon. This morning I sleep.'

'I come back in the break to see you,' Aneeta said.

'Please no. It will disturb.' I patted her hands. I squeezed her hands. 'Aneeta, I promise I am okay. I eat lunch with you.'

'Are you sure, Sahar? I am your sister here.'

'I promise. Go, you will be late.'

She stood up and seemed hesitant. One of the Russian boys stuck his head around the door. 'Ready, Aneeta?'

He really likes her. But he doesn't want his friend to know. He's the gentler of the two boys but simply on appearance, you can't tell them apart. Aneeta looked at him and then at me.

'I will come for you at 12.'

Thanks to God she left. I made myself wait five minutes in case she'd forgotten something and then I dressed. The corridor outside the sleeping cubicles was empty. The cleaners were working in the boys' area so I was able to walk quickly towards the exit, unobserved. I carried a ring binder in case I met anyone. I thought of that. On my own. It was all planned; if anybody asked I'd say that I was on the way to class.

You would have been proud of me, Wasim.

I was prepared.

Before I left home, Abu Muhunnad explained to me that if I couldn't make the first contact for some reason, I must be at the second location two and a half hours later.

As I walked to the meeting place I felt my heart beat against my ribs. I recited the ninety-nine names of Allah to calm myself. It worked. I stepped to the rhythm of the words.

I walked on the grey path towards the tennis courts. Beyond them I saw the walled vegetable garden. I held my folder more tightly ready to be challenged but when I stepped through the brick arch into the garden there was only a gardener weeding one of the beds. I sat on a bench and opened my work folder seeing the words that I'm studying in front of me. The verbs. I repeated them under my breath.

My instruction was to wait for fifteen minutes. This is a peaceful spot but I was far too nervous to enjoy it.

I smelt man sweat before I heard, '*Marhaba.*'

It was the gardener. Imagine.

'Follow me to the herb border,' he said. 'I will pretend to explain to you what is being grown here. You will want to know the words in English and Arabic.'

He sounded as if he came from Djebdah, the north. I wondered if he knew our cousins who live there; do you remember them Wasim? They came to visit us when we lived in the house near the hospital?

This man, with the Djebdah accent, wasn't tall, but he was strong, you could tell, his head was shaved and his eyes were grey. You'd like him I'm sure.

'We're very pleased with everything you've done,' he said. 'You're a noble and most blessed *shaheed al hay*. You've been chosen by Allah because he's seen in you all that's good and I'm humbled and honoured to be your guide and mentor during these final days.'

I was blushing; I could feel how warm my ears were.

'My name is Abu Marwan al Djebdahi,' he said. He told me that the next time we met it would be during one of the student outings and I should separate from the group and he would meet me.

Then he walked towards the wheelbarrow and wheeled it out of the walled garden leaving me breathless, excited and bathed in certainty. Wasim, dearest little brother, believe me, I'm blessed. My actions will change the world, I will help people and I will be *shaheed*. It is written. God is great.

30

Bayswater, London – The Next Day

Summoned to London for a meeting Petra had begged an afternoon off to visit her ailing fictive godfather; Deanna hadn't been happy but she'd agreed. Sitting in the Bayswater hotel lounge, Petra unfolded a piece of paper and handed it to Benny. Newly shaved, with a white shirt, he seemed younger than she remembered him from the first meeting and his eyes were a clearer seascape grey. He scanned the single sheet that contained all the details of the cultural programme that the language school organised for the students. 'Thank you,' Benny said. 'Seen this Rafi?'

'Yes.'

'Looks like Petra has some nice cultural experiences lined up,' Benny read. 'A trip to Bath; an evening at the Sheldonian Theatre; punting on the river. And the Air Tattoo.' Benny looked up from the sheet of paper. 'The school uses private transportation?'

'Yes, there's a driver with a minibus who is contracted to the school for the summer,' Petra said.

'The same driver every time?'

'Yes.'

'Okay. And the target?' Benny said. 'What do you make of her?'

Petra said, 'She had another morning off school yesterday. Didn't turn up for class; Aneeta, that's the Spanish girl, said it was stomach pains. But Sahar seemed okay at lunchtime.'

Benny seemed unperturbed. He repeated: 'What do you make of her? Do you like her?'

Petra leaned across the table. 'She's... diligent, serious, kind to the other students and tries to help the weaker ones in class. Modest. You know, I think you should get someone else in if her brother is around. Maybe some watchers. I'm constrained. I can sit with her, talk to her, give her homework, extra lessons, hot cocoa in the evening, but I can't leave the group during lessons. Believe me I tried. Yesterday when Sahar didn't turn up to class I was just about to go and check and Deanna was outside the door. I told her I was worried because the girl hadn't shown up and she told me to wait till lunchtime and give the girl some privacy. What Deanna meant was, don't leave the group otherwise they'll start complaining. Just to make it even more difficult, the classroom is a fifteen minute walk from the dorms.'

'That is a problem,' Benny said. 'So, you don't think the girl's sick? You think she's duplicitous.'

'No. Not exactly,' Petra felt flustered as if she hadn't prepared for the meeting. 'Like I said, there's a problem. I'm here, sitting with you and I don't know what she's doing or who she's talking to. Her brother could have turned up at the school.'

'Okay, we'll think about that. But you thought she was okay yesterday afternoon after she was absent from class in the morning? Not moody or under the weather.'

'Definitely; she seemed happy so if there is some sort of health thing going on it's variable.'

'Thank you,' Benny said. 'That's extremely helpful. Does she talk about her family at all? Has she said anything about her brother?'

'No. Nothing at all.'

'Good.'

Benny stroked his skull and seemed to be in thought. Rafi opened his mouth to speak but Benny raised his hand to silence him. 'You know, Petra,' Benny said. 'I think it's much more important that you monitor the girl's moods than risk breaking your cover by trying to follow her around. We worked very hard to get you into the school and it is a unique position. It would be too bad if you upset this... Deanna, is it?... and we have no one on the inside.'

'There is that. Deanna does walk up and down outside the class,' Petra said.

'We'll put our heads together and work out some better surveillance,' Benny said. 'Don't worry. Meanwhile, Rafi can drive you back to the school – he's not busy. If you've got time he can take you out for dinner.'

An hour later, Rafi and Petra were sitting opposite each other in a country pub. It was a random choice; the first pub they passed at 7pm. In the car Petra had continued to ruminate about Sahar. She was aware that she had deflected Benny's question about liking Sahar but wasn't sure why. It was a standard operational inquiry; it was hard to work an agent if you despised them, only the sociopaths in the organisation could do it. You had to have some empathy to engage with a target. Of course she liked Sahar.

That was all there was to it.

'Where's Sahar's brother?' Petra said scoping the chalked board of specials, the horse and hound prints on the wall, and the bar of reclaimed wood with a shiny copper top.

'What?' Across the table Rafi was focusing on the menu.

'The brother? The reason I'm at the school. Why did Benny say we should take our time getting back to the school.'

'Because we know where the girl's brother is at the moment. And he's quite safe,' Rafi said. 'Needless to say, you're not supposed to know that; we want you at the school until all the ends are tied up because Benny is a neurotic.'

'The English expression is belt and braces. Double security.'

'Neurotic is more accurate,' Rafi said still reading the menu. 'What's goujons?' He pronounced it wrongly: 'Gowjons'.

She didn't bother to correct him. She didn't look up. 'Fried fish in breadcrumbs.'

'Is it good?' he said.

'No idea, I'm not the chef.' She looked up and indicated the busy room, the full tables and the bustle of people in the real world. 'Judging by the number of people in here, I'd guess they're good enough.'

'Then that's what I'll have,' Rafi said. 'How about you?'

'I'll have the same, and a large glass of white wine.'

The waitress brought their food and Petra toyed with the battered fish.

Rafi said, 'You seem distracted.'

'A little. Tell me about Benny,' she said.

'What about him?' Rafi was eating his goujons and limp salad with gusto.

'Anything. I'm curious. He's the lead in the operation, isn't he? What's he like to work for?'

Rafi paused, fork in the air. 'Benny is... let's just say Benny is one of a kind. Unique. Special.'

'Sounds like you don't like him,' Petra said.

'It's more the other way around. He doesn't like me.'

'Why?'

'Ask him. No don't. He would deny it.' Rafi drank some of his lime and soda and went on, 'You see Benny is sophisticated. He wouldn't have to ask you to explain things on the menu. He would know. He would make it, he would know the chef, he would ask where the goujon came from. Me, I'm from a *moshav*, a farming community. But Benny was educated in Europe and America. His father was a big deal in the foreign service and his uncle died in a military operation that changed the course of the war in 1967. So you see as far as Benny is concerned, he is something very special.'

'Are you envious?' Petra said.

'Me? No, of course not. I'm just trying to explain to you. This is how it is. You go to the art gallery for some opening in Tel Aviv – you see Benny and his wife. You go to an avant-garde film by a new

Israeli director, guess who's there? The Israeli Philharmonic at Caesaria; a restaurant opening; a charity evening at the Dan. Petra, you know the expression *mi va mi*?'

'Who's who?'

'Yeah – that's where you'll find him and his wife. With all the big assholes. Now me, I'm different. I like to be at home: on the beach, hummus, some olives, a beer. I'm a simple man just trying to do my job to the best of my ability. And Benny doesn't think I'm good enough to do it.'

He wiped his mouth with a paper napkin, scrunched it into a ball and tossed it on to his empty plate.

'Yeah, he's trying to screw me; trying to get me off the operation. Says he doesn't like my approach. More likely he doesn't like my accent. To him I'm *chackh chackh*.'

'And I suppose he's *voos voos*?'

'Yeah, the elite. Like you: Anglo Saxon, German, European.'

'I thought all that was history.'

Rafi rolled his eyes.

'Where did your family come from?' Petra said.

'My father from Greece and my mother from Yemen. My mother's parents had never seen a flushing toilet. They never got over the magic of modern plumbing. You?'

'British and Austrian. My father was in a displaced persons camp at the end of the war. That's where he met Alon who was also orphaned.'

'Of course. That's your connection isn't it?' Rafi quaffed the pint of lime and soda and wiped his mouth with the back of his hand. 'Anyway, Benny is going to get me fired. It's his life's work. It's why he's been put on this earth. He's not thinking about the operation; he's thinking about his career. That's why I need you watching my back, Petra. So that we can get the job done and make a difference.'

'Do you think he's clean?' Petra said.

'What do you mean?'

Petra waved to the serving staff and gestured for the bill. She said, 'He wouldn't be the first intelligence officer in the world to go wrong.'

'Not Benny. He's too much of an asshole to break the rules.'

31

West London – The Same Evening

Wasim was at that age where he talked before he thought and acted without any restraint. Like a pinball he bounced off the arguments and then flipped up around the board again and again and again.

'I hear you, commander, but I still want to see my sister.'

'I understand and I am sorry, but it would endanger the mission and everything we are going to achieve, *inshallah*,' Eli leaned across the table between them and poured out another cup of coffee from the jug. Irritation. Yes, that's what Eli was feeling and it was an entirely inappropriate emotion for any agent runner. Worse, Eli realised he was more irritated with himself than the kid.

Maybe he was too old to get into the head of an 18-year-old, maybe they should have brought in one of the new guys in Mossad to connect with the boy. Or maybe it was just this particular target and it was only a question of finding the right angle and he'd be able to work his way in. Keep going. Keep repeating and maybe it would sink in. The boy hadn't touched his coffee; the pinball flipped around the board and pinged again.

'If I can just see her then I will feel that I have done my duty as her guardian and head of the family. Is that so difficult for you to understand? You know where she is and what she is doing, but I don't. It's a matter of honour – of doing the right thing.'

'Oh yes, *habibti*, we are all of the same belief and want to do what is right. I am aware of your responsibility but in this case you must pass it to me; I am her guide, I am now responsible for her.'

Across the table Wasim folded his arms. Eli smiled and ploughed on, 'Tell me about Kansas and your studies? It must be very interesting to be studying engineering now with all the new technology, new materials and there will be many opportunities when you qualify. We'll need qualified engineers, people like you, to rebuild our country after the occupation is over.'

No reply. Given Wasim's intractability, the notion of slipping in any questions about who his Hamas contacts in the Occupied Territories might be was about as likely as Elvis being alive and in Tel Aviv. That meant no brownie points with *Shabak* who wanted some payback for their role in Sweetbait. It was bad enough dealing with the complexities of the operation itself without having to service another client at the same time. Meanwhile, the boy sulked. Instead of meeting Eli's gaze, Wasim tugged at the wispy hair on his chin and looked towards the window.

They were using a safe house in Ladbroke Grove; it was on the first floor of a Victorian conversion and in the next-door flat a couple were monitoring and acting as remote babysitters. The situation was far from ideal and the fiction that Wasim had been rescued by a secret Hamas cell could unravel at any moment but there were no other options – at least none that wouldn't lead to an internal inquiry which was why the boy had to be convinced and he had to co-operate.

Eli stood and walked towards the small kitchen where he ran some water just for something to do. 'Wasim, you must trust us, you have seen what we have done; we saved you from being arrested by the British. Did that mean nothing; did it not show you that we want to help you and your family? It is a hard truth but if you'd been arrested you would not be able to go back to Kansas, even if you were in the house because they were just friends of friends. The Americans won't let you back in and your career will be over. Please, let us help you, Wasim. Go back to America and do what's right.'

Eli was talking to the taps, washing up the coffee cups, drying them, rinsing the sink of the grounds from the pot and wiping down the surfaces.

A noise from the room made him turn. The kid was at the window, his long leg halfway out and then the other leg shifted and he disappeared from the first floor window.

'Daylight,' Eli said running to the window. 'DAYLIGHT,' he repeated hoping that the listeners next door weren't on a break or distracted for any reason. 'Kid's jumped out the window.'

Reaching the window, Eli looked down; Wasim was on the ground five metres down, he was dragging himself up using a wheelie bin but even from above Eli could see that the boy had hurt himself. His arm was hanging at an odd angle.

'WASIM!' Eli shouted. But the kid was already limping out of the service area. Eli headed to the front door of the flat and clattered down the stairs two at a time. Outside he legged it around the corner and was in time to see Wasim stumbling along the main road, trying to thread his way through the traffic. A car swerved around the boy but he got to the other side amid hooting and fist waving from angry drivers. Helplessly Eli waved from the other side before plunging across the road and dodging cars. On the other side Eli picked up speed and the kid was slowing, his legs flailing as if the rubber inside was loose. In one final burst of speed, Eli caught up with Wasim and reaching out grabbed him, aiming for the arm that he guessed was broken. Wasim's scream of pain was heartrending and conspicuous, but at least the bastard stopped.

32

Westbourne Grove, London – The Next Day

Eli was on his third coffee of the day; one more and he would get jittery. Even though the botz coffee he'd brought from the embassy commissary had less caffeine than arabica, there was still enough to wire him up like a beachside café at Purim. He was sitting in the safe house waiting for Red Cap to come out of the toilet and from the sound of the concealed microphone that fed into Eli's earpiece, the agent had been retching.

The last twenty-four hours had been no picnic. On the upside, Eli had stopped Wasim from running into the arms of the nearest British cop; the kid was now back in a new safe house tucked up in bed and sedated. Getting him there had been exhausting to say the least. Since they could hardly take the boy to A&E they'd had to get the embassy doctor to reset the arm and check the boy over. However, Menachem, the embassy doctor was more used to issuing sick notes for staff and giving vaccinations than doing anything useful. When they told Menachem what he had to do he looked as if they were asking him to sell the kid's body parts. In the face of such obstruction Rafi had been all for resetting the arm themselves and on reflection Eli was bitterly sorry that he had disagreed and insisted on doing it properly and using the professional. Some professional.

In contrast the prospect of a meeting with Red Cap seemed like an island of tranquillity after bobbing around in stormy waters.

On the scarred wooden table in front of him Eli had already laid out a platter of smoked turkey sandwiches. He looked at them with distaste. Smoked turkey was ersatz bacon and the latest initiative from the apparatchik in logistics. The pen-pushing dweeb had lately got religion and was flexing his devotional muscle; smoked turkey was to be exchanged for bacon in operations that were not false flag. Ridiculous. Yet it was one fight that Eli couldn't be bothered to tackle; there was no point rolling up his sleeves when some asshole was measuring the skirts of interns in the Knesset to make sure they were modest. On the other hand, it wasn't as if a genuine bacon sandwich was going to cure Red Cap's problems anytime soon.

When Red Cap finally came back into the room his white sweating face and damp mouth confirmed the sounds from the toilet.

'Derek, for God's sake,' Eli said. 'You've got to look after yourself. Come on, sit down, what would you like? A coffee, maybe some water with a B-complex, a sandwich? Have you eaten today?'

'Good heavens, Benny, you're turning into a Jewish mother before my eyes.' Red Cap wiped a gob of spittle from the side of his mouth and collapsed into the chair like a bag of bones. 'How about a drink?'

'No, not at this time of the morning and not in your state either.'

'Just kidding, but it might do you some good, Benny. Shake you up a bit, stop you being such a stuffed shirt.' Red Cap laughed; the laugh turned into a phlegmy cough that crackled and threw up more matter that he struggled to swallow down. To give him a chance to compose himself Eli left the table and busied himself in the tiny kitchen. He put on the kettle and made some black tea in a glass, cutting a slice of lemon and placing some sugar cubes on a saucer. He brought the steaming drink back into the room and placed it in front of Red Cap.

'Try that,' Eli said. 'My grandfather used to drink the tea through the sugar cube.'

Red Cap eyed the amber liquid in the glass, then looked at Eli, eyes still watery from the coughing fit. The agent's knuckles were dark against the skin of his skeletal hands and they trembled as he dropped the cubes into the hot liquid, stirred and sipped. Once again he cleared his throat but now he looked more at ease; the spark was back in his eyes. 'I'll skip the drinking through the sugar cube part,' he said with his customary languor. 'A little too Russian for my taste. But presumably that's your background, the Pale, the greater Russian Republic. Unless you're trying to tell me in the gentlest possible way that you're an ancient KGB man and this is all false flag. That would be upsetting to say the least.'

'How could it be false flag when you walked into the embassy all those years ago?'

'Benny, my good man, these days who can be sure of anything?'

'True.'

Red Cap fished in his pocket and pushed the USB stick across the table.

Eli said, 'We could have done this in a brush past, you know. This does increase the risk.'

'I know but I wanted to see you,' Red Cap said.

'I'm flattered. Any particular reason?' Eli pocketed the stick.

'I think I'm being followed.'

'Where and when?' Eli concealed his irritation; if a team of watchers couldn't cover an agent without being made then they should be packed off on the next flight home and chucked straight back into retraining.

'Just here and there,' Red Cap said. 'And on odd days. Not necessarily when I'm travelling into central London. I have spotted your people now and then: the geek with the rucksack, the chain store shoppers, the map-reading tourists. But this seemed different – they had a different rhythm, if you know what I mean.'

Another fucking problem. MI5 checking or FSB scouting.

'I'll look into it,' Eli forced his voice to sound calm, matter of fact, 'I'll see if my guys changed any of the team which would account for a different signature.' If MI5 were doing random checks or the Russians were scouting for talent, it could be another disaster.

Red Cap tugged at his collar as if it was sticking into his flesh, 'Maybe I'm just being paranoid.'

'Goes with the territory,' Eli said.

Red Cap nodded.

Paranoia. Trust issues. Over-the-shoulder glances. That land of shape and shadows, where dear friend might be traitorous enemy and distrusted connection might be true friend. Was Red Cap suffering from agent-paranoia – *shpyon-cop* as they called it – or had he actually seen something?

On the one hand Red Cap was a professional so his sensate interpretation of events should be heeded. But at the same time, he was a man under stress and paranoia was part of his daily diet. No matter how reasonable Red Cap sounded in his description of a different signature, it was more likely that his overall mental state and compromised health were creating the sense of being watched. That's what Eli told himself. Because if Red Cap was being followed by MI5 or any other interested party, then protocol demanded contact be stopped until the risk was assessed.

Eli sipped at his coffee and made a show of finding his pen and notebook to give himself more time to think. It was a gamble and Eli didn't like gambling but Red Cap wouldn't be the first agent to think that the woman standing behind him in the supermarket queue was a honey trap, the homeless beggar was MI5 street surveillance or a wrong phone number was a home check. If they all jumped at every single bleep, bump and squeak in the night and shut down all active operations – including Sweetbait – then they'd never get anything done.

For the moment, Eli would assuage Red Cap's fears, order another team of watchers on to him and, most importantly, dampen down his own rising paranoia. A second team of watchers would establish whether or not it was *shpyon-cop* or a real threat.

'How's Carole?' Eli said.

Red Cap shook his head. 'That's the second reason I wanted to see you. I've thought about it Benny, and I'd like to take you up on your kind offer to find someone to help her. I don't know how you'll do it –'

'You leave that to us,' Eli said. 'We'll think of something, don't worry.'

'She's worse, much worse, she passes out in the afternoon and then she paces at night. All night. But the new development is that she can't get up in the morning. Can't get out of bed. It's as if she's actually paralysed. And... she's threatening me.'

'Threatening what?' For all his years of experience handling agents Eli was conscious of his heart rate increasing.

'Benny, she knows. And now she's threatening to tell people. That's the other reason why I wanted to meet with you, to tell you.'

'Okay...' Eli stroked the top of his skull. He forced his voice to sound calm. 'You did right to call the meeting. So when you say threatening to tell people, which people? Is she being specific?'

'Yes and no, she does it when she's drunk, it's a part of her ranting and raging. She says she'll write to my boss, phone them, tell the neighbours, put a sign outside the house, saying I'm a traitor. Mostly it doesn't make sense.'

'Does that mean when she's sober she does make sense? I think we need to get her into some sort of rehabilitation programme as soon as possible. It sounds as if she's clinically depressed.'

'I agree. Part of the rant is about being a failure and the terrible mistake she made marrying me among all the other disasters in her life. Somehow, Benny, I can't blame her.'

Eli touched the agent on the forearm, 'Ignore the content of what she is saying. If she's clinically depressed there's no logic in it.'

'Are you married? I've never asked you. In all these years I've never asked. Do you really know what it's like, Benny?'

Eli paused: to lie or to tell the truth? To say he is widowed, divorced, gay or single, or to say, yes, I know what it's like to be married. I am as you are, I share that experience with you; we are alike. We are all alike when it comes to our humanity.

'Yes, I am married,' Eli paused. 'We have one son who is in the army. I fear for both his life and for his soul. Even if he does come home in one piece, I fear that what he's seen and done will destroy his humanity. I fear that he won't be able to shrug it off, that he might get into drugs, or that he'll be prey for our religious bigots who seek out the vulnerable, to give them certainties in a way that no one else can. And I fear that if that happens, my wife will never, ever forgive me.'

Eli lowered his eyes to the scarred table. A ring mark on the stained beech showed where his coffee glass had sat. Eli was shocked at himself, yet oddly relieved. And he was grateful that Red Cap was silent.

At last Eli spoke, 'Sorry, Derek, I don't know where that came from. My apologies. I must be more stressed than I realised. We've got a lot going on at the moment.'

Still Red Cap said nothing and Eli avoided his gaze.

'Okay, I'll tell you what we're going to do,' Eli said. 'We're going to look into this surveillance issue. Meantime, I'll organise a detox programme for Carole that will include psychiatric help. Today's Saturday; I'll get something in place by midweek, okay?'

Now Eli looked up; he met Red Cap's eyes which were compassionate in his raddled face. 'Okay, that's a plan,' Red Cap said and then added: 'Looks like we're both in fucking trouble.'

33

Stall Street, Bath – Two Days Later

'Okay, people,' Petra said. 'You have two hours to do some shopping before meeting back here for the afternoon tour of Regency Bath. Please try to not be late and if you have any problems, call me or text. Please make sure you all have my number in your favourites.'

She was standing outside the Roman Baths with the group around her as well as Deanna, Deanna's husband Rod and the dog. Today, they were mob-handed because this particular cultural trip, an hour and a half's coach ride from the school, was fraught with potential. Lost students; accidents; not to mention the opportunities for drug buys and illicit drinking.

'Reputation,' Deanna had said on the drive to Bath, her brown spotted hand clinging to Petra's forearm. 'I know this was supposed to be your half-day off but it would have been absolutely impossible to do this without you. One upset parent, one article in the local paper, Petra, that's all it would take to ruin our reputation and the business could close down. We're entirely at the mercy of these students' hormones and high spirits.'

That afternoon Petra was supposed to have met Rafi but because of Deanna's insistence that she go on the excursion, she had to cancel. There was also the unspoken quid pro quo of Petra's afternoon off to go to the dentist two days before; Deanna was making a point. Petra hoped Rafi got the text message but it couldn't be helped, not if Petra was supposed to be keeping her job at the school as Benny had insisted.

It was too bad that she couldn't meet Rafi to talk things through because ever since the last meeting Petra had ruminated about the operation and her sense that something wasn't right. She'd lain awake at night analysing all the information she had and remembering what Alon used to say: 'We are paid to make assumptions.'

She pictured Alon sitting at Abu Hassan's in Jaffa at the end of one of her debrief trips to Israel. They'd sit outside under the sunshade blocking out the blue sky. Alon used the fork to gesticulate more than he used it to eat. He talked about HUMINT versus SIGINT claiming that no amount of surveillance and analysis would ever replace working with agents. Though dead, he was so clear to her she could almost hear his tobacco-coated voice, 'When you're working with people, you make assumptions based on fragments of information that even you may not be aware of but which you call a feeling or intuition or a hunch. Don't ignore it, Petra.'

And now in Bath, Petra scanned the group and couldn't ignore a sense of unease. Sahar stood at the edge, a little to one side. The girl was studying her phone, presumably to confirm that she did have Petra's number. Or was there something else?

'Any questions?' Petra said watching Sahar. Yes, there *was* something different about her today. Maybe it was the way she was standing, maybe it was the careful way she had arranged her hijab over her shoulders. What might Petra assume about her? It was a guess not grounded in any fact but there was a distinct sense of anticipation about the girl.

Her first thought was to call Rafi and leave a message for him to call her; in the meantime she would have to handle it herself.

Petra straightened up and waved the map in the air. 'Has everyone got the map I gave out?'

Aneeta and Sergei were exchanging glances. Chances are they would try to separate themselves from the others so that they could pursue their romance; that would make it easier for Sahar to do whatever it was that was energising her.

'In that case, we will see you back here two hours from now at 2.30.'

The group dispersed and Petra turned to Deanna and Rod, 'Would you mind very much if I have a quick walk round Bath before I come back here to wait for the group? I need to buy a couple of things.'

'Of course,' Deanna said. 'How inconsiderate of me. We're just going to take Freddie for a stroll around Sydney Gardens and we'll be back here. Take your time.'

Petra was already striding off. Minutes later she was walking down St Christopher's, dodging tourists and the clusters of people perched on chairs outside the pastry shop.

Ahead Petra could see Sahar. She was walking with purpose, her slight figure demure in a long sleeved white shirt and ankle-length skirt. At the top of Northumberland Place Sahar paused. Petra ducked behind a display of summer scarves and peered over the rack to watch; Sahar reached into her rucksack; Sahar pulled out some paper; Sahar looked at her map. Then she walked under the arch and disappeared.

Fuck.

Petra broke into a jog aware that this was a textbook surveillance error; if Sahar turned back then the girl would know she was being tailed. Procedure be damned. Now sprinting Petra reached the end of Northumberland Place. There Petra looked right, then left, raking the crowds, trying to grab a glimpse of Sahar but the girl was gone.

Which way to go? Right or left?

Decision made, Petra's pace was steady, certain; she checked herself, glimpsed her reflection in shop windows, saw long legs, long stride and long jacket. She glanced into the open doors of shops as she passed.

Nothing. Keep moving.

And then Petra got lucky. Or accurate. Visually, she divided the space ahead of her into quadrants and scanned. Three-quarters of the way along the arcade she saw Sahar. Captured in a shaft of light from the glass roof, her beige hijab glinted gold. And more, there was a man by her side who seemed to be hurrying Sahar along. Maybe it was Sahar's brother and he wasn't as safe as Rafi had presumed. Or worse, some other contact they knew nothing about.

Two hundred metres away: Sahar and the man. The man carried a sports bag. Below average height, one metre sixty-eight, bald, stocky. They walked fast.

He looked like someone she knew. The man with Sahar looked like someone Petra knew. Someone familiar. Something about the way his free hand, the one that wasn't carrying the sports bag, touched the top of his shaved head.

Yes, of course, the man with Sahar looked just like Benny.

34

Abingdon, Oxfordshire – The Next Day

'What happened then?' Rafi said.

They were sitting in the car park at Wickes looking like any other couple who might be debating the relative merits of installing an induction hob over a gas range. A family in the next car were loading up a Ford Galaxy with flat-packs. Nearby, strapped into a pram, a toddler was yowling.

'Let's go somewhere quieter.' Rafi pressed the ignition on the car and started to nose it out of the car park.

'Rafi, it was Benny. I'm sure of it – '

'Just give me the facts,' Rafi interrupted, frowning as he pushed into the traffic going towards the city centre.

'As soon as I caught up with them, I was careful, I kept my distance and it wasn't difficult because although he was hurrying her, he had a bag in one hand – heavy, looked like a sports bag.'

'Describe it.'

'Black, rectangle, I wasn't close enough to see any branding, I don't think there was any.'

'Okay,' Rafi tapped the steering wheel. 'Did he hold it with the left hand or the right?'

Petra pulled up the image in her mind. She wanted to be sure. 'Left,' she said. 'Definitely left.'

'What happened next?'

'They turned into a side street and I saw them go into a flat above a shop. He had a key. Here, here's the address.' She shoved a piece of paper into his hand that was resting on the steering wheel.

Petra went on, 'I took up a position, six doors down on the opposite side of the road. It wasn't easy, the café was jam-packed and I couldn't get a table near the door and I wasn't going to sit outside in case they saw me.'

'Good call, Petra,' he said.

The car was picking up speed on the outskirts of Oxford and they were cruising past the Holiday Inn on the Abingdon road. At the roundabout Rafi did a full circle and then drove into the hotel car park.

'Where are we going?'

'I think we deserve a drink.'

'That's not like you,' Petra said.

The lobby of the hotel was bursting with mid-level management in corporate wear; they all seemed to be either trying to check in or check out. It was hard to tell in the maelstrom. Near the front desk a sign welcomed the Sagential Insurance Sales Conference and the Harthand Health Analytics Away Day.

On the fringes of the two groups, overburdened hotel staff with fixed smiles, pushed trolleys, carried bags, and tried to avoid eye contact. It took a few moments for Rafi and Petra to find the lounge and even longer to find two seats together.

'Rafi, we're never going to get served and I need to get back to the school,' Petra said glancing around at the two waiters who were labouring with trays held high as they tried to service the thirsty crowd.

'Leave it to me.' Rafi stood up. Petra watched him approach a waiter from the side and then block his path. From her position on a low sofa, she saw Rafi's smile, some words exchanged and a red note slipped into the waiter's hand. Rafi returned to Petra satisfied.

'Five minutes,' he said.

And within five minutes the harassed waiter returned. Rafi slipped him another note and received something in exchange. Then Rafi nodded to Petra who got up and followed him.

'Where are we going?' Petra said as they left the hubbub of the bar.

'I asked him to find a meeting room where we could have a drink and a conversation for an hour without people treading on us. It's a conference, they're used to it.'

'So you said you were in insurance?'

'Sure. You think he cares?'

Petra followed Rafi to the lift. On the second floor of the hotel they trod down a carpeted corridor and then Rafi stopped outside a door. Before Petra could comment, he produced a door key, slipped it into the slot and pushed the door open.

'It was the best he could do,' Rafi said. 'There were no meeting rooms available.'

Petra followed Rafi into the standard upmarket hotel bedroom; neutral carpet, oversize headboard, and a flat screen TV. Everything was standard – except for the bottle of champagne in the silver bucket.

Petra stopped in the middle of the room. 'What? What the fuck is this, Rafi?'

'I thought it would be nice –'

'What would be nice? I've got to get back to school before Deanna looks for me.'

'Understood. Forgive me. I just couldn't think of any other way of getting a room here or any other drink than champagne. That's the only wine I know. We don't even have to drink it – although it is open.'

'This is serious. I saw Benny,' Petra said.

Rafi settled himself down on the single armchair by the small table. The only place left for Petra to sit was the bed – she sat down.

'Very well,' he said. 'Let's stick to business. Start from the beginning. Everything, from the moment you left the school in the bus, arriving at Bath, the trip round the Roman Baths and so on. I want to know everything you saw and everything you heard.'

She narrowed her eyes as she tried to peer closer into her memory, to see what Sahar was doing at any particular moment. Every so often Rafi would ask a question; where was someone standing, did they use left or right hand? He took out a map of Bath and she showed him her route, the precise point where she lost Sahar, found her and then saw the man who looked like Benny.

'And he massaged his scalp,' Petra said. 'He does it in meetings.'

'And the bag he was carrying, did he hold it in the left hand or right? This is important.'

Petra narrowed her eyes. 'Left, definitely left.'

'You're sure. Absolutely sure?'

She nodded, 'You asked me in the car – why is it important?'

'Because the man you saw can't possibly have been Benny. Much as I would like to be able to say otherwise.'

'What?'

'Benny is a complete asshole, believe me, but besides anything else, he has a hand injury. It happened on an operation; his hand got stuck in a car door, broke all the bones and he can't use the hand for weight. So unless that bag was completely empty, Benny wouldn't be able to lift it.'

'Really?'

'Petra, how close were you?'

'Maybe one hundred and fifty feet.'

'I figure Benny looks like any short, bald guy at that distance.'

'What about the head stroking?'

Rafi shook his head. 'Coincidence. And you're hyper-alert. We have to look over our shoulders, all the time. That's what we do. Okay?'

'Okay,' she said.

Petra was aware that Rafi's eyes were scanning her face. She kept her face relaxed and studied him as he stood up and poured out some champagne.

'We might as well,' he said. Turning back to her he held a glass towards her. Now intrigued, Petra accepted the flute and waited for Rafi's pitch.

'You read me like a book,' he said. 'And like it or not... there's something between us.'

'Sure, there is,' Petra said smoothly. 'The operation, sex, and some history. What of it?'

'The history – it's important. I trust you. And you trust me. It's important in our work that we trust each other and I want to keep it that way. This is a very complicated operation, much more than you realise. As I told you, there's a lot of politics going on and Benny really doesn't like me. But I can tell you one thing – one thing for sure, the guy you saw wasn't Benny.'

'So, who was it, then? Sahar's brother? Some other guy?'

'I don't know. That's what we've got to find out,' Rafi said.

Petra sipped her champagne and smiled, 'Of course, you're right. You can rely on me.'

It was obvious that Rafi was trying to convince her that the guy she'd seen wasn't Benny.

What Petra didn't know was why.

Part 3 – THE DELUDED

A delusion is something that people believe in despite a total lack of evidence.

Richard Dawkins

A nation is a society united by a delusion about its ancestry and by common hatred of its neighbours.

William Ralph Inge

35

The Israeli Embassy, Palace Gardens, London – The Next Day

'What do you want me to say?'

'Thank you, Rafi, for covering my ass. Thank you, Rafi, for saving the operation. Thank you, Rafi, for making me look a better intelligence officer than I am. How about that – just for starters?'

'You are an arrogant shit,' Eli said.

'Name calling isn't going to change the facts.'

'Which are that if you would have had better contact procedures with Trainer then she wouldn't have been tailing me around Bath while I was carrying a suicide belt in a sports bag. For God's sake, Rafi, once you got the text from Trainer saying that she was going to be in Bath, how hard would it have been to get a message to me?'

'By the time I found out that school woman was making Trainer go to Bath you were already there – and I phoned.'

'Too late,' Eli said.

They were sitting in the safe room at the embassy waiting for Yuval to arrive. Rafi was leaning against the wall while Eli tapped away at a laptop. There might have been more restraint between the two men if Yuval had been there but he was in the signals room battling to get a second surveillance team shipped in yesterday. Even though the pound was low, the Office was whining about budgets and the cost of accommodation in London.

Rafi's failure to warn him that Trainer was in Bath had been compounded by Eli's decision to put the surveillance team on to Red Cap for 24 hours; to see if there was anything in the agent's fears that he was being followed. They'd found nothing. As a result there'd been no one on the ground who might have warned Eli that he was being followed by Trainer. And, if it hadn't been for Rafi... if it hadn't been for Rafi...

Eli couldn't process the thought. The notion of having to be grateful to Rafi for his effective handling of a difficult situation was like swallowing shards of glass. Even worse, the incident had fuelled Yuval's skewed belief that the two intelligence officers made a good team. As for Eli's prospects of becoming the next station manager – Eli couldn't bear to even think about his hit wicket.

With effort Eli relaxed his face before he spoke, 'Besides making sure that when I see Trainer I never use my left arm, is there anything else I need to know?'

'No – it would be too obvious for you to bring up the accident you're supposed to have had.'

'It would be so much easier if we could take her out of the operation,' Eli said.

'I'm in full agreement,' Rafi said. 'Except for the school. After the operation she'll certainly be questioned by the police if not MI5 counter-terrorism and if she's already disappeared from the school it will look bad. We're stuck with her.'

'Some operations are just one problem after another; feels like they're cursed,' Eli said.

'That sounds like some crap you inherited from your grandparents. Speaking of family how's Sweetbait's brother.'

'Still whining about seeing her but his arm's healing up nicely.'

The hydraulic lock hissed open and Yuval stalked into the room. He threw his jacket on a chair and sat down on the seat next to it.

'Sometimes it's hard to believe we're on the same side. Anyway, I've got them; I've got the second team. I had to make all sorts of promises but we'll have a second team for two weeks by which time this will all be over. Where are we? Eli, summarise.'

'Rafi has advised me that he convinced Trainer that she didn't spot me – for which I am grateful.' That hurt but Eli said it. He went on, 'It shouldn't have happened with or without a team of watchers, I should have checked myself.' That hurt even more. 'In my defence, I had a limited amount of time with Sweetbait to show her the belt and fit her – '

Yuval interrupted, 'Rafi, how sure are you that Trainer is convinced?'

'As sure as I can be.'

'*Biddiook*,' Yuval waved his hand in dismissal. 'Very well, let's move on. The situation is that Eli has now had two meetings with Sweetbait. Do you think she's ready for the operation?'

'No. I need at least one more, two would be better.'

'You get one,' Yuval said. 'Next, we deal with Wasim. We have no choice; we've got to get him out of the UK before the operation. If this goes wrong the repercussions will be extensive to say the least; never mind our relationship with the UK/USA, we have more backdoor talks going on with Saudi as we speak and an embarrassing disaster would scupper them, never mind what it would do to our personal career prospects. One boy cannot be allowed to jeopardise this operation.'

'Crate?' Rafi said.

'Where to?' Yuval said. 'Home? We can't crate him up and put him in prison back home, at least not without a ton of paperwork and getting *Shabak* on our case. I have a much simpler idea.'

'Go on,' Eli noted the gleam in Yuval's eyes.

'I think we're overcomplicating the situation. The boy still believes that this is a Hamas operation; he's still whining about wanting to see his sister. Okay, what would happen if he did?'

'What?' Eli said. 'You're saying we engineer a meeting between the two of them?'

'I'm just thinking about it,' Yuval said. 'If the girl tells Wasim to go back to America, he might just do it. Honour satisfied. He's done his head of the family, man of authority, duty. His beloved sister has blessed him and he can go on his way. And more importantly, he can get out of our way.'

There was silence in the room. It was an inspired idea, audacious but inspired.

Eli spoke slowly, 'It's possible.'

'Think about it,' Yuval said. 'Think about how to make it work. We'll talk tomorrow but sometimes the simplest solutions are the best.'

Both men nodded. Yuval stood up, 'Anything else? How's Red Cap and his crazy wife?'

'I'm just going to see him now,' Eli stood up and tapped his jacket pocket where he kept his Moleskine notebook. 'I've got the detox clinic and a shrink lined up. Best in the UK. Hopefully we'll have the wife in there by tomorrow; the next day, latest.'

'Is there anything else we need to know? Eli? Rafi?'

The two men shook their heads like schoolboys before the head-master.

Yuval said, 'Good. No more fuck-ups, please.'

36

The Six Horseshoes Pub, Cheltenham – The Next Day

This certainly counted as a fuck-up, Eli thought as he sat in the Cheltenham pub where he was supposed to meet Red Cap. But please God, only a minor one. Agents missed meetings all the time. That's why there were fall-back arrangements, sometimes two or three with different times and locations. It was only because Red Cap was unfailingly precise and had always turned up at the right place, at the right time, that Eli had been lulled into a false sense of security.

Eli nursed his lager shandy and watched the stand-up comedian set up. As the man positioned his box of props, Eli almost had the sense that no time had passed in the pub since he'd last been there. Everything was the same; the scarred table, the ring spots, even down to the same stand-up comedian. He hadn't changed either. He still looked grizzled and lachrymose with untidy hair and scurfy beard. What sort of a life must it be standing up in front of drunk and uninterested people, trying to make them laugh? Mind you, what sort of a life was it sitting in a pub waiting for an agent to turn up?

Yet, it was good, Eli told himself. He had something concrete and positive to do. Something to stop him worrying about Sweetbait and whether or not he was losing his edge and was on the one-way trip to the benches and then the stands. Just some *altekakha* who talked about the good times, the glory days, and watched hungrier, clearer eyes glaze over when he told the same old story one more time.

But it was more than a game that he might have lost. London station and the chance to make a difference – that's what hurt the most. The bigger failure of a career in public service that achieved nothing except a pension.

Eli wished Red Cap would hurry up and they could get on with it. Eli felt his own beard. The bristles were itchy. He was letting it grow, and wondered what Gal would say when she saw it because it was now entirely grey. He glanced at his watch – again. Another fifteen minutes and he would make his way to the fall-back location, the café in Morrisons supermarket. He'd be tailed by the second team of watchers, fresh off the El Al flight.

Moving his hand from beard to ear, Eli felt for the small speaker. It was irritating especially as he was sure he could hear someone eating too near the mic. He'd have to find out who was doing that; if he had that noise going on all through the meeting he'd be the one who needed psychiatric help, not Red Cap's wife.

Now the stand-up comedian was walking around on the makeshift stage, he seemed to be doing some stretching exercises. Eli watched him take a swig from a glass of what might have been whisky and gargle before swallowing. Maybe Eli should do that. Maybe the bastard sitting in a car *fressing* on a Big Mac would start gargling also.

One more check of the watch and Eli would go, drive to Morrisons and take up position in the café. As he got up, the comedian caught his eye and gave Eli a sad smile as if to ask why he was going; why Eli, the only man in the audience, was abandoning the comic to the empty stage.

Morrisons café, with its bright lights, coffee choices and bank of doughnuts was similarly disappointing. No Red Cap. It was inconvenient but not necessarily a fuck-up. Eli sipped a bitter black coffee and felt it tussle with the lemonade shandy in his stomach. Watching the shoppers around him, he amused himself by memorising their features, and then recalled some of the spectacularly long waits he'd experienced in his career as an intelligence officer. And before that, in the army.

Waiting. You were no good as any type of intelligence officer if you couldn't wait and it was better to be sitting in a café with refreshments on tap than on street corners, station platforms, bus stops and car parks, in broiling sun and driving rain. While checking his watch he speculated, wondering whether he'd spent the same amount of time waiting as he had sleeping. Yet it could be worse. Somehow the watchers made an entire career out of waiting. For Eli there were, at least, breaks in the monotony.

When the thirty minutes were up and the coffee was too cold to drink Eli made his way to the car park where he knew that Segev, the lead watcher would be waiting for him. With his cropped hair and clear skin, the kid looked too young for the job but he seemed competent and it hadn't been him who'd been chomping on a sandwich that was for sure. The VW smelt of pine car freshener, not chips.

'I want you to drive me back to London,' Eli said.

Eli slipped into the seat beside Segev and admired his expert handling of the hire car. Hands at ten to two; negotiation of the traffic; checking mirrors; blind spots; it was all so precise that either he had just completed the training course or he thought that Eli had some clout that could further his career. The only conversation the kid had was with the other car.

It was unusual for Red Cap to miss a meeting without warning; it had never happened, but there were a hundred entirely logical reasons why the agent had been unable to meet Eli or leave a message. There was absolutely nothing for Eli to worry about.

37

M40 Motorway – One Hour Later

In the car on the way back to London Eli caught up with some of the peripheral business which included phoning the psychiatrist who was supervising Red Cap's wife into rehab. It was the first time the Office had used the Devonshire Street shrink who was supposed to be a leading light in substance abuse. She may have been an authority in her field but Eli hadn't warmed to her when they'd met. The stringy middle-aged woman was spikey, brittle and keen to talk about her academic achievements and standing in the psychiatric community. And she created obstacles. Although she readily agreed to make the referral to the specialist unit, she was hesitant about giving them all the medical records because of protocol and patient confidentiality. That was a big problem, because if Red Cap's wife continued to claim that her husband was a traitor during therapy suggestions, then the Office needed to know. But the shrink had been obdurate; it was like arguing with a child who didn't understand why something needed to be a certain way. The best Eli could get out of the woman was an agreement that she would think about giving them the medical records and they would speak.

She answered the phone on the second ring and after Eli announced himself the tone of her voice dramatically changed.

'I wondered when you were going to call,' she said, her voice high, accusing, as if he was an errant son making the weekly duty phone call.

'I'm sorry, if it's late, and if I'm disturbing you. Would there be a better time for me to call, say tomorrow?'

'Tomorrow? This can't possibly wait until tomorrow. I'm beside myself. I've been walking up and down waiting for you to call. And before you say another word, let me just tell you that this has put me in a very awkward position.'

'Doctor, we wouldn't be asking you to assist us in this way unless it was of the utmost importance. And let me just say that we are immensely grateful for your help,' Eli put his all into soothing the woman and keeping the irritation out of his voice. What did the woman think was going to happen when she was approached by an Israeli commercial attaché at a drinks party and asked if at some point she might assist the State of Israel in some undefined way? Maybe she thought she'd be going to more cocktail parties to meet dashing agents. Maybe she thought there'd be rendezvous in casinos in Caribbean resorts. Maybe she thought the phone would never ring and she could live with her fantasies. That was the most likely.

'All I agreed to do was write a referral to the clinic copying the woman's GP. But, now... this has implications for my professional integrity.'

'I'm very sorry, doctor, that you've been put in this position and please be assured I will pass on your thoughts but in the meantime, doctor...'

They were on the outskirts of London and had slowed at a traffic light. A gas station was on the corner and Eli had wanted to fill his body with junk. What was her problem? All she had to do was pass on the medical records. If he would have had her sitting opposite him in some coffee shop he would have laid on the noble cause she was serving, reference the Holocaust, Masada and if push came to shove the destruction of the second temple and exile to Babylon. But he had neither the time nor the patience. What's more he'd been on the phone long enough and comms signals to landlines needed to be in short bursts to avoid being picked up.

Eli's voice changed, 'Doctor, it's not enough to give the patient a referral; we need the patient's medical records.'

'There is no patient.'

'What?'

'Let me repeat, there is no patient,' she said. 'She was dead before admission to A&E and was taken to the mortuary.'

'What the hell are you talking about?' Eli said. 'Did she have an accident, car crash or something? What's happened to her husband?'

'Please do not make this appalling situation any worse.'

'I need to know what happened,' Eli said.

'Her husband found her, in the bath, dead. Wrist laceration and signs of substance abuse. There'll be a post-mortem but given her medical history and the input from her GP, cause looks to be suicide while the balance of her mind was disturbed.'

'Oh my God,' Eli said.

'Is that what you wanted to hear? That the police think it's suicide? That it doesn't look like foul play?' Her voice was shrill. She was frightened. Eli frowned and then the penny dropped. The stupid woman thought it was murder; she thought she was embroiled in an assassination.

Eli sighed, 'No. The patient's suicide is certainly not what I wanted to hear at all. It's a tragedy we were all too late to help her.'

'Oh,' the shrink said.

'I need to ask you,' Eli said, while she was on the back foot. 'Do you happen to know if a suicide note was found or have any way of finding out?'

'That's two questions and my answer is no to both. Please don't contact me again.'

She hung up.

Eli told Segev to pull in at the next fast food outlet or service station. He said he needed to take a piss and get a coffee and something to eat before they got to London. Truth was that he wanted to sit in a toilet stall with the door shut and compose himself.

Maybe Red Cap's wife wouldn't have killed herself if her husband hadn't betrayed his country. Maybe.

38

The Israeli Embassy, Palace Gardens, London – Three Hours Later

It was 2am and they were all tired and bad-tempered. Except for Rafi. He looked as if he could keep going till the sun came up and then do a run around the park. Perhaps, after all, there was something in those energy drinks he swallowed. The table in front of Eli was a mess of laptops and papers. Every half an hour, Yuval had been up and down the stairs, running in and out of the safe room; the reason was that Yuval didn't trust the kids in signals to bring up every message from home the second it arrived.

'The situation is that we are trying to make a decision with incomplete information,' Yuval said. 'Eli, are you sure you can't get the shrink to do any more for us?'

'If somebody else wants to try, fine, but she's fair-weather local help. She's not going to stick her neck out or do anything that might affect her fancy Devonshire Street practice. And that includes finding out if Red Cap's wife left a suicide note.'

'Have we got no one in the police or connected to the police in any way?' Yuval said.

'Not at the moment,' Rafi said looking at the laptop in front of him. 'There used to be someone who had access to the NPC, but he retired two years ago.'

Rafi pushed the swivel chair back and stood up. He paced the length of the room, 'Maybe the retired cop's still got some connections. They never let the job go, at least not at home they don't.'

'Retired cop or no retired cop, if she left a suicide note implicating us...' Eli said. 'It's daylight isn't it? We need to close everything down, and I mean everything, and go home before the knock on the door. And that won't go down well with the prime minister's office.'

'Would anyone believe her?' Yuval tapped his fingers on the table, beating out a roll of impatience. 'She's diagnosed as being crazy; for all anybody knows she could be paranoid and delusional. What if we're over-reacting? The hat burns on the thief's head.'

'Yes, and sometimes there's a reason, Yuval. The woman is lying in a hospital morgue. How long before HR at GCHQ talk to Red Cap? Don't you think it's hoping for too much luck to think that Red Cap will cope? He was unstable before, what's he going to be like now?'

'What about Sweetbait?' Rafi said. 'We're so close. We're days away from completing the operation. How can we walk away now? If Sweetbait works out – and it will – then no one's going to give a damn what some insane woman says in a suicide note. It won't matter. I think in the light of not having all the information we should take a chance. Come on. We've got everything else under control. Thanks to Eli, Sweetbait's ready to go, I've got Trainer under control, and for us to run away when there may be nothing to run away from is stupid.'

'Eli?' Yuval said.

I don't know. I don't know anything any more.

'Eli?' Yuval repeated.

Eli cleared his throat, as if he was clearing his mind, physically pushing aside the emotion that was stopping oxygen reaching his lungs. There was nothing he could do for Red Cap or Red Cap's wife. Not at the moment. There might come a time when Eli could comfort his friend – there would come a time. But it wasn't now. If they turned tail and ran, for Heathrow and the El Al cargo flight home – the shame plane – then Eli would find himself straight back to the UK desk in Tel Aviv at best. He'd certainly be at the back of the queue for an overseas posting. In other words, his career would be over.

Eli took a deep breath. 'I can see both sides, but overall, I'm with Rafi. I think we try to get a bit more intel. We speak to the shrink again and Rafi can contact the retired cop. We prepare and then we move.'

39

Marylebone High Street, London – The Next Day

Rafi and Eli worked the shrink meeting together in a tapas bar. To his chagrin Eli couldn't fault Rafi. He pitched it perfectly. Showing the right level of respect for the woman's professional accreditation – something she referred to in every other sentence – combined with a subdued but oleaginous charm that made Eli's stomach churn. Whatever the schmaltz did to Eli's digestive tract, it seemed to have the right effect on the spiky, nervous shrink. Under Rafi's overdone admiration the woman's shoulders dropped, the lines around her mouth softened and she agreed to make a phone call to Red Cap's wife's GP.

The shrink was briefed to check on the progress of the postmortem and ask about the presence of a suicide note explaining that it might help with diagnosis of the suicide's mental health if the coroner were to ask. The shrink even agreed to make the call outside on the street while they waited for her in the tapas bar. From their seat by the window, they watched her walk up and down as she talked into the phone and when she came back inside her eyes were shining.

'Sit,' Rafi said. 'Let me get you something else, perhaps a glass of champagne.' He'd stood up and was holding the chair for her to sit down. He certainly hadn't picked up that trick on the kibbutz.

'By the look of you, it went well,' Rafi said. 'Benny, see if you can find a waiter to get Jane a glass of champagne.'

'No, no, but thank you,' the doctor said. 'Very kind but I am delivering a paper a little later as part of The Tavistock's Weekend Seminar Series. It wouldn't be at all appropriate to arrive smelling of alcohol. Not when the subject is the psychopathology of alcohol abuse disorders.' She tittered as if she'd said something amusing.

'Then some other time,' Rafi said. 'I hope.'

'If you are due somewhere else, we certainly wouldn't want to delay you,' Eli said, wishing he'd left Rafi to do this on his own. 'After everything you've done for us that wouldn't be fair at all.'

She showed no sign of wanting to move.

'So, did you find out if there actually was a note?' Eli said.

'I certainly did,' the doctor said. 'In fact, I didn't have to ask because the GP asked the same question for the same reasons and according to him – there was no note.'

Together Rafi and Eli also met up with the retired cop. He was delighted to feel the sparkle of espionage fairy dust brighten up a dull day of retirement. Thrilled to swap the weekly shopping list and chores about the house for the shadowed doorways of the past. Even happier to have a proper reason to hang around at the pub with some cash in his pocket so he could play the big man with his old workmates and be generous with the drinks.

The end result was the same information: no suicide note. Just a text message with a single word: **Sorry**.

Eli thought it was a particularly bleak way to end a marriage and a life but knew better than to dwell on it.

With the spectre of the suicide note expunged, they could now focus on Sweetbait. Eli and Rafi set off in a hire car to drive to Oxford. Although it would have been inaccurate to say that Eli liked his colleague, or would, whatever the circumstances, he recognised in himself a nominal shift in his attitude to Rafi: a resentful respect for his abilities. The asshole had some operational talent.

'Are we clear about this afternoon?' Eli said. 'I need a full hour with Sweetbait and I don't want to be looking over my shoulder for Trainer.'

'Couldn't be easier.' Rafi swerved the hire car into the middle lane of the motorway forcing a driver in a blue BMW to brake.

During the next forty-five minutes they arranged the various rendezvous and with the operational logistics in place, Eli prepared for his meeting with Sahar. At the Beaconsfield service station on the M40, Rafi waited in the car park while Eli carried a plastic bag into the toilet where he changed into his gardener's outfit. The green shorts, tee shirt and blouson jacket with the name of the contract gardeners embroidered in yellow made him feel like a peasant. Outside he found Rafi leaning against the side of the car eating an apple.

'Nice legs,' Rafi successfully tossed the core into a nearby bin. 'You know, you should wear shorts more often.'

'Fuck off,' Eli said. He spent the rest of the journey with his earbuds in listening to texts from the Quran.

40

Watlingford Public School, Oxfordshire – Three Hours Later

The walled kitchen garden at the school was bathed in early evening light. As Eli knelt by his wheelbarrow making a show of weeding a patch of the chocolate-coloured loam he watched a worm undulate around a clod of earth. It was unfortunate. The worm made him think of decomposing bodies and Red Cap's wife.

These dark thoughts were disturbed by footsteps on the path and Eli was wrenched back to the present and the job in hand. Turning he glanced up to confirm that it was Sahar, and no one else. Eli composed his expression as he stood up.

'*Marhaba, shaheed al hay*,' he bowed and gestured with his arm towards the seat. The girl glided towards the wooden bench with careful dignity.

'*Marhaba*, Abu Marwan,' Sahar said.

'We have little time together,' Eli said. 'And I have much to tell you. I am sorry that we will not have the opportunity to pray this time, but I have much good news. Are you well?'

'Yes, I am well and full of resolve to carry out the will of Allah and the instructions of you, Abu.' She smiled at him.

'It's my honour to tell you that the day of your *shaheed* is approaching.'

She nodded, only the tightness around her eyes showed her fear that the time had come. Eli went on, 'But, before this great day you will have both a trial and a reward.'

'I do not need a reward in this realm, Abu.'

'Then it may be just a trial,' Eli smiled giving her the reassurance she needed. It had been agreed that if Sweetbait was distressed at the notion of seeing her brother then he would be crated, shipped out and they would deal with inquiry later. Everything hung on her response.

'If it could be arranged, would you like to see your brother?'

Her eyes filled with tears and she reached out to Eli, just stopping herself from touching his arm.

'Truly, is that possible?' she said.

'If that is what you wish. It is only because you are so admired that we would even consider this. But you would have to be strong, and prepared. If he loves you – and he is young – he might entreat you to change your mind. That is why I said that it would be a trial.'

'I am strong, Abu. Have no fear. It would give me great joy to say my farewell to my brother, if that is possible.'

'Very well,' Eli said. 'It will be done; soon. Tomorrow morning you will tell your teacher that you have a toothache and must see a dentist. Everything else will be arranged for you.'

'I understand.'

'There is something more. I need to talk to you about your day of martyrdom. As usual, the school will take you in a bus to a cultural location, but when you are there you will have the opportunity to meet me and I will give you the belt.'

How quickly her mood changed from joy to consternation. Now her brow creased between her eyebrows, 'What happens if it is difficult for me to leave the group? What do I do? Would it not be better if you gave me the belt before?' she said. 'I could hide it in my room at the school, or find somewhere in the grounds. There are many places.'

'The school is not secure. Your room might be searched when you're not there. And more importantly, the belt is delicate,' Eli said.

But the girl still looked worried. Her underlying concern was revealed in the shy way that she asked, 'Is it easy to use?'

'Yes,' Eli smiled. 'Very easy. Do not worry. That is the simple part. What might be difficult is for you to be in the right place.'

Eli took out of his pocket the map of the location. 'You need to memorise it so that you do not waste time when you are there. Understood?'

She nodded and moved closer to him on the bench. Eli pointed to the map. 'I will meet you here, The Vintage Village. You will follow me to a place where you will be prepared.'

Eli glanced over at her. She was silently repeating what he'd just said. He tapped another quadrant on the map. 'This is where you're going: the Techno Zone. Are you with me? Once inside, you will find the central point.'

'I know this; I understand where I must be.'

A suicide bomb that explodes at the central point of any space inflicts the most damage; it was another cruel fact in the lexicon of murder but it chilled Eli that Sahar was already aware of the requirement.

'Yes, Abu. I will count the steps across the diameter to be as precise as possible.'

'Very good.'

Judging by her expression the girl was mentally preparing for the operation. Another time and place this mindset would have been developed even further; if fate had made her Israeli and she'd been called up for military service. He glanced over at her thin hands and narrow shoulders. Who knows – if she'd worked out and built up some muscle she might even have got herself into one of the combat units that took women. She certainly had both the brains and the courage for it.

41

Watlingford Public School, Oxfordshire – The Same Evening

After Abu Marwan leaves, I've only got twenty minutes to get back to the dormitory to prepare for the evening. I'm so excited that I'll soon be seeing you, dear brother. I didn't ask where or how. I trust Abu Marwan; he has great wisdom.

The night's warm so I know that we'll be sitting outside the cricket pavilion, drinking lemonade, eating cookies and Petra will read to us. Sometimes she reads a short story, other times an article from a magazine. Afterwards she asks questions to see how much we understand.

I wish you could be here now, Wasim. Listening to Petra read reminds me of when *Mawmia* told me the stories from her childhood; the stories that she was told by her mother. And the stories I told you when you were a little boy. About the desert and the nomads and the hills and fountains; stories about the time before The Catastrophe.

Before I join the group at the pavilion I have to write down what Abu Marwan said; I'm going to draw the map he'd showed me, so that I can memorise it. You may think I'm fussing, brother, but I don't want to hesitate about where I should be when the time comes; I want to do it completely right and make Abu Marwan proud.

The dormitory block is empty; quiet because everybody has already gone to the cricket pavilion. As soon as I'm in my room, I pull the folder from my workbag and draw the map. Blue to turn left, red to turn right; I draw the lines that I remembered and then surveyed my work. There was something missing; a building on the left.

'Sahar? Are you still working?'

I turn around and there's Petra standing in the open doorway. I close the folder and my neck feels hot. She's leaning against the frame with her head to one side, did she see anything?

'Everyone's waiting at the cricket pavilion; we wondered where you were.'

'I... I was studying,' I say. 'Yes, and I also want to change my dress, I am sorry.'

Uninvited, Petra steps into the room. 'You're fine as you are,' she says.

'I want to wear a warm dress,' I say. 'The night is cold for me.'

I'm careful. I don't look at the folder with the drawing. I know better than that. I go to the wardrobe and pull out a blue wool dress. It's new, I haven't even worn it. I take it to the bed.

Petra glances at the dress and my other clothes hanging in the cupboard.

'Of course, Sahar, if you want to change, that's fine. I'll meet you down there, or I can wait outside for you.'

'Thank you,' I say.

'Sahar, forgive me for asking...'

Let her not ask to see what I'm studying. Dear God, please. She won't know what it is but I'll have to lie to her. I really don't want to do that, I like her.

Petra frowns, 'Are you okay?'

'Yes, yes, a little tired, and cold.'

'I forget our warm nights are not quite as warm as yours. Why don't I wait outside for you while you put on that nice warm dress?'

She goes out and closes the door behind her. Without wasting a second I tear the piece of paper with the drawing from the folder and tuck it into the ripped lining at the bottom of my workbag. It will be safe there. Then I undress and pull the wool dress over my head. My hands are shaking, I clench my fists and relax them concentrating on the soft wool. It's gentle on my skin and I smooth it over my hips but I feel cold all the way down to my soul.

The clothes I've just taken off are lying on the chair next to my workbag. Do I leave my bag behind? It might seem odd to take it with me; maybe I will tell Petra I have a headache and that I can't go. Yet, I really want to go. I want to sit by the pavilion with Aneeta and Li and Sergei and even Mfoniso and listen to Petra read a story. I want to hear Aneeta joke and make everyone laugh with her.

Whatever's going to happen next week is inevitable but tonight and the days ahead are mine. Is that selfish? Is that so wrong? Won't Allah forgive me as he forgives everything?

I pick up the workbag, put it over my shoulder and open the door. Petra is outside; she looks up from her phone and then tucks it into her jeans pocket.

'That is a lovely dress,' she says, 'such a pretty colour. Come on, let's join the others.'

Side by side we walk down the wide passage that leads to the main door. Petra is wearing black jeans and Converse trainers. She walks as if there are tiny springs on the balls of her feet, as if at any moment she might run, run for the joy of running. I feel small beside her, yet also, for the moment, somehow safe.

Petra opens the door to the quad and holds it for me. 'You know, Sahar, if there ever is something worrying you, something you don't want to talk to anybody about, you can always talk to me. That's why I'm here, it's not just to teach you English.'

'You are very kind,' I say. 'I am very well. Sometimes I am home-sick but I think that is the same for everyone.'

By now we're outside the dormitory block and walking down the path beside the quad. The green lawns spread out on either side of us and I hear the shoo-shoo sound of the sprinklers.

'Some people are more homesick than others,' Petra says. 'It's not easy being away from the people you love; your family. Do you have brothers and sisters? I forget.'

'A sister at home and a brother in America,' I say.

'Of course, I remember, America.'

'Yes, I am very proud. He is student. Engineer, very clever,' I say.

We turn past the quad down the path towards the cricket pavilion. On one side flowers grow up the side of the wall and as we pass the scent is sweet.

'What is that?' I say.

'Honeysuckle. Have you seen it before?'

I shake my head. Petra walks on the hallowed grass – we've been told this is forbidden – and tugs at two of the flowers. She hands me one and I hold it in my hand.

'Like this,' Petra tugs the green end at the base of the flower, 'Easy, gently,' she says and a silken thread comes out. Still attached there is a drop of moisture like a teardrop. 'Taste it. It's sweet; it's the nectar of the flower.'

I copy what she does; tug the thread and put the end of the flower into my mouth. The scent and flavour are amazing, it reminds me of the rosewater drink our mother made.

'That is delicious,' I say. 'I never see such a flower. It is called...' I struggle to remember the word. Petra helps me.

'Honeysuckle. The humming birds and the butterflies love it.'

'So do I.'

'I'm pleased,' Petra says.

In silence we continue our walk in the gathering night towards the pavilion. I really wish I might see Abu Marwan. I want to ask him if I can add Petra's name to the seventy who I can choose to join me in heaven when they die, even if she is a non-believer.

'Are you married?' I say. 'Do you have husband?' I wave over my shoulder to indicate the past.

'No, no.'

'I was with husband,' I struggle with the past tense. Petra doesn't correct me. It must be correct. 'He made a divorce. His mother does not like me. No babies.'

Petra looks down at me. 'And he agreed? Said yes to his mother and divorced you? Nice guy.' We walk for a few steps longer in silence. Petra goes on, 'I hope your mother and the women in your family were able to support you.'

'My mother is sick. My sister has babies and husband. They are busy. There's just my brother.'

'Well, I'm here. I mean it, Sahar, you can talk to me about anything and I will always try to help. I am difficult to shock, and I am on your side.'

By now the pavilion is in view and I can see the group sitting outside on the veranda. There are tiny lights strung above them, like stars and even from fifty metres away I can hear the laughter. I can just about make out Aneeta's silhouette; she seems to be dancing; Petra begins to walk faster. I struggle to keep up.

'Settle down everybody,' I hear Petra call out to the group. 'And make sure you've hidden anything you don't want me to see.'

When I reach the veranda, everyone is sitting in a circle. Petra is between the two Russian boys and Aneeta and Li, the Chinese girl are handing out the lemonade and cookies. Mfoniso has saved me a seat next to him; I love his sleepy smile.

Petra now speaks with her teacher voice. It is different to the warm voice she used when we walked here.

'Li, I'd like you to swap seats with Sergei who will attempt not to look like Romeo for the duration of this session. Alexei will put his phone away and stop checking his portfolio – or is it porn? And Mfoniso will stay awake. Just for tonight. Because this evening we're going to do something different. Instead of another Sherlock Holmes story, I'm going to read you the lyrics of a song. And then each of you is going to either give us a poem or tell us about a song from your culture. Or even, if you feel like it, sing.'

It's a happy evening. In my whole life I don't remember feeling so... I don't know what the right word is. Connected? I try to stay apart and be detached, but as I listen to Li sing a song about high mountains and flowing water I feel my eyes are wet. She says high mountains and flowing water mean cherished friendship.

When it comes to my turn everyone is silent, the air is still. I struggle to think of something and then remember a poem by Suad al-Sabah: *Be My Friend*. Afterwards, Petra looks it up on the internet and translates some of the words:

'How beautiful it would be if we remained friends

Every woman needs the hand of a friend

Be my friend.'

Aneeta stands up, crosses the veranda and hugs me. When she lets me go I see new respect in the eyes of Sergei and Alex. And Mfoniso winks at me and smiles even wider.

Afterwards we all walk back to the dormitory block together. I like these people. They are non-believers; they don't know the way, yet we have shared something. Maybe I feel like this because my time is coming.

'You're quiet,' Petra says as we climb the stairs to our rooms. 'Are you tired?'

'A little.'

'I liked your poem,' she says. 'It was beautiful.'

'There are many other poets,' I say.

'Really,' Petra says.

'Yes, I will write some names down for you.'

We're outside my room and she follows me inside.

'I'd like that,' she says. 'Do you have a pen in your bag?'

She reaches for my workbag and I step back, away from her hands, 'No... no, the pen is on the desk. Not in the bag.'

This isn't true but I'm terrified that she'll find the map. I feel her eyes on me. Desperate,

I find the pen and scrawl down some names on a scrap of paper and give it to her.

'Thanks.'

Petra tucks the piece of paper into the pocket of her jeans. She's standing in the doorway so I start to tidy, putting my clothes away.

'Can I ask you something, Sahar?' she says. 'I've been thinking about it all evening.'

I nod. I'm waiting for her to ask why I'm so nervous. I don't know what I'll say.

Petra says, 'Why do you hang your clothes on the hanger inside out?'

I follow her gaze. My wardrobe door is open. My dresses and trousers are hanging inside out. I'm confused for a moment. We always do that, don't we, brother? We do that so that when the bombs fall, the houses shake and the windows shatter; when the dust rises up and billows like clouds of sand in a storm; the dirt and debris doesn't cover our clothes.

'That is the way we do it at home,' I say.

'To keep them clean,' Petra says. 'Anyway, thank you for sharing your poem with us and don't forget what I said. If there is ever a time that I can help you, remember I am your friend.'

42

M40 Motorway – The Next Day

Spies love cars. That's what Alon had taught Petra: 'There's no better location than a moving car for getting into someone's head with the goal of rearranging it. The closed space invites confidences, the shared momentum suggests intimacy, and the controlled environment gives the spy the upper hand; far, far better than a restaurant where a waiter is guaranteed to interrupt at the most delicate time in a meeting; the moment when a spy is teasing out a tangled secret that makes the agent wince with remorse for his betrayal.

Well, a 90-minute run between Wallingford and central London wasn't exactly Land's End to John O'Groats but Petra reckoned it was good enough. It needed to be because that was all Petra was getting.

She'd got a call from Rafi at 1am that morning. He'd briefed her that if Sahar complained of a toothache at breakfast, Petra was to volunteer to drive her to London. There, Petra would drop off Sahar at a Harley Street address and leave her there. He was insistent about the last element; she had to leave Sahar in Harley Street and go to meet Rafi. That was clever of them; taking away her chance of lingering to see who was turning up to meet Sahar. After Bath, Benny and Rafi were being careful; but it was too late.

'Sure, understood,' Petra had said. Co-operative, obedient, a good soldier who didn't question orders.

Sitting by her side in the car as it bowled down the M40, Petra glanced over at Sahar, hunched in the seat, black rucksack planted between her feet as she stroked the seatbelt that crossed her narrow chest.

The night before, when Petra had gone to the girl's room and then walked her down to the pavilion, Petra had gone through every trick she knew to try to get the girl to open up to her, all to no avail. But the girl was certainly in trouble and it bothered Petra.

Ever since Petra had been at the street party where she'd saved Callum's life Petra had had flashbacks. Memories of the texture and summer meadow scent of the child's hair mixing with sour sweat and bile. These sensations ambushed idle moments and made Petra's heart race, notably when she was thinking about Sahar and the operational puzzle. Was it a premonition or maybe it was guilt? Whatever it was, Petra had a strong sense that Sahar needed protecting even if it was only from herself.

'Sahar, I really loved the poem you told last night, the one about friendship. You know, I've been thinking about it ever since.'

'Thank you. I like it too, there are many other poems, I like –'

'Do you know the word, "trust", Sahar?'

'I think I understand, yes.'

'I think that trust is the most important part of friendship. It is like belief. You trust that a friend will be kind and act in your best interests. Sahar, I want to be your friend, like in the poem, so I have to say what I feel; I am worried about you. I think there are events in your life that are troubling to you, that you are perhaps in a difficult situation.'

The girl was silent. Her eyes were looking straight ahead and when Petra glanced from windscreen to passenger she caught the rigid face, the glistening eyes that heralded tears.

'I have friends,' Sahar said 'and family.' She spoke with the conviction of the child who would clasp white-knuckled hands over ears and squeeze eyes shut.

'Of course you do. You have your friends here and your family back home and your brother in America,' Petra said with lightness, trying to ease Sahar back into a comfortable place, aware that she'd gone too far too quickly and needed to step back. Ahead the traffic had thinned out and Petra was able to accelerate, all the while framing a gentle question in her mind.

'Does your brother like America?'

'He's not there, America.' It was a whisper. Petra barely caught it.

'Not there? Is he here? On holiday?'

'I, yes, I do trust you, Petra and I know that you are my friend. There are things... I cannot say. But I do not go dentist. I am going to see my brother now.'

Petra felt her heart race and deliberately unclenched her hands around the steering wheel. She shouldn't be too eager, too interested, too concerned.

'Great, well, brilliant, and I don't blame you for telling a story. I'm not at all sure that Deanna would have let us out if you'd said you wanted to see your brother. Remember the fuss she made when Mfoniso's mother wanted to take him out for the weekend? I promise that you can trust me not to say what you're doing today. I hope you're going to have lunch with him somewhere nice? How long is he here for?'

'I don't know, not too long I think,' Sahar slumped back in her seat like a punctured balloon; the strain of telling the truth seemed to have deflated her. Petra could have banged her fists against the steering wheel; it felt like for every tantalising advance she made she got pushed back and now they were coming down the West Way on to the Marylebone Road. In minutes she'd be turning right into Harley Street and the opportunity would be over; the door would be slammed again.

Petra said, 'Even if he's only here for a little while, the important thing is that you're seeing him and that he knows you're among friends. I've got an idea. I want you to give him something from England. I was going to give one to all the students at the end of the course, but I've got a spare one in my bag and I want you to give it to your brother.'

'What is it?'

'Can you reach my bag, on the back seat?' Petra said. 'It's in the front right flap, in a plastic case.'

Sahar squirmed around and reached into Petra's bag, she pulled out the plastic box with the £2 Shakespeare commemorative coin. The gold glinted through the presentation case.

'Like it?' Petra said.

'It is beautiful,' Sahar said.

'That's Shakespeare, our greatest poet; there was an anniversary a few years ago and I bought the coins. Do you see the words on it? "All the world's a stage, and all the men and women merely players." I thought the students would like it.'

'Thank you, thank you. You are so kind, Petra. And I am so happy to have a gift for my brother. A special gift from England.'

'And I'm really happy to be able to give it to you,' Petra had turned into Harley Street and was reading the numbers on the houses. 'Thrilled. Do you have a special name for him?'

'Wasim Nadir, it means Wasim most loved. I tell him he is my favourite brother... I have only him.'

Petra glanced over at the girl as she began to manoeuvre the car into a parking place; Sahar's eyes were welling up again.

'That's so sweet,' Petra said. 'And now here we are, safe and sound. Text me when you're ready to be picked up, and don't forget to give your brother the present.'

43

West Hampstead, London – The Next Day

With his forehead pressed against the tiles of the shower, Eli felt the water run down his back. First under hot and then cold water, Eli tried to shake off the sleepless night wishing it would slough off as easily as the drops of water on his body. Watching the water swirl around his feet and listening to the drain swallow it away, Eli concentrated on what was positive; telling himself that, in spite of Red Cap, Sweetbait at least was okay. Sweetbait was on track. Sweetbait was near the finishing line. That's all he needed to remember.

And even if there were a couple of hurdles that they'd stumbled over – such as being spotted by Trainer in Bath and the brother – that was the nature of any operation. Rarely, if ever, did everything run according to plan. That's why the most important skill for an intelligence officer was to be flexible and able to adapt to changing circumstances. Yuval's unorthodox yet inspired idea for Sweetbait to meet Wasim had worked. The boy was still at the safe house but shortly he'd be on his way back to Kansas on an evening flight. Once there he'd be monitored by the Washington squad and gently recruited under a false flag.

Reasons to be cheerful.

By the time that Eli had dressed in his freshly dry-cleaned suit, he felt ready for the day and whatever it may bring.

That morning there was to be yet another meeting with Milne at The Travellers Club. If, and hopefully when, he became head of London station Eli had already decided that he'd ask Milne to put him forward for membership. It would be a fine thing to bring visiting heads of station there for drinks.

The purpose of this meeting was diplomatic; the Israelis were going to be introduced to the new CIA liaison officer, the replacement for Pen who had disappeared into the void where intelligence officers go when they no longer fit the culture of the organisation.

Still feeling the effects of sleeplessness Eli took a taxi and mused as it chugged along and morning London went to work. In spite of political changes, Eli observed a sense of order in the British capital, perhaps allied to the temperate weather or perhaps the phlegmatic nature of the British. Overhead, the sky was a soft grey; it was easy on the eye and soothing to the soul.

Eli wondered how Yuval was getting on in Paris where he was working a defection and debrief from an Iranian nuclear scientist. It was a volunteer operation, a walk-in with all the associated complications; among them was that the scientist wanted to live in France so that he could send his daughter to the Conservatoire in Paris. Trying to satisfy the scientist's resettlement requirements was causing a raft of problems hence the need for Yuval's expertise. The only way to get residency for the defector was to share intelligence product with the French Security Services. However, since the DGSE had more leaks than a colander and was devoutly and institutionally anti-Semitic, Yuval had his hands full.

With Yuval in Paris, Eli had no choice but to take Rafi to the meeting; as Yuval said, it was in the interests of protocol that two intelligence officers should meet one incoming CIA man. It was even more important to establish contact with only ten days to go to Sweetbait.

Standing on the corner of the Strand, Eli watched Rafi stride towards him. Wearing his new charcoal suit, he'd obviously struggled with the tie; the knot was too small and too tight but the suit fitted him well. Not quite the British gentleman or any gentleman come to that, but Rafi looked smart enough.

'*Yallah achi*, let's go, dude.' Rafi clapped Eli over the shoulders and he tried not to flinch.

'Do you want a couple of moments before we go in?' Eli said.

'No, I'm fine. All we're here to do is meet the new American,' Rafi said. 'And it's not the time to tell them that we know who the threat is because we're running her but *ein baayot*, no problem; we'll stop her before it happens.'

'Not funny, Rafi. And not secure, either.'

Rafi drew a slim black box out of his inside jacket pocket. It could have been an external drive; a white light blinked on it.

'Relax, I was just kidding,' Rafi said and put the sound buffer back in his pocket.

'I'd be grateful if you could try to keep your sense of humour under control for the duration of the meeting.' Eli stalked in the direction of the club.

Unlike previous meetings with Pen, this new American was early; they found her sitting on one of the sofas in the library engrossed in a copy of *Country Life*. She had a round face, almost cherubic and introduced herself with hearty hand pumping and eye twinkling. In her late thirties, she could have passed for younger and she spoke with the twang of the Deep South.

'Real good to meet you,' Charlene said. 'Call me Charlie, everybody else does. Helluva place this,' she said in a husky voice. 'There's so much history everywhere.'

Eli was on his guard. This level of bonhomie and wide-eyed wonderment was not to be trusted. There was no way that Charlie would have got a job at this level without both experience and a superior education.

'It's very good to meet you,' Eli said. 'But if you have a passion for history, some day you should come and visit us. I'd be delighted to show you around.'

'I'd love that,' the American smiled. She shook hands with Rafi, exchanged pleasantries and they sat down and waited for Milne.

'I'm still finding my way around.' Charlie laid a leather folder in front of her at right angles to her seat. She crossed one trousered leg over the other and fixed Eli with hard green eyes that were in contrast to her voice. 'There's a heck of a lot to take in so I hope you'll forgive me when we get started if I ask you to clarify issues already discussed with my predecessor.'

'Of course,' Eli said. 'How is Pen by the way?'

'Fine, as far as I know,' she said. 'Enjoying his career break in upstate New York.'

'Send him our best wishes,' Eli said.

'I sure will.'

By tacit agreement, the conversation stayed general while they waited for Milne to arrive. To Eli's profound relief, Rafi stuck to his brief and didn't treat Charlie to his usual gallantry; it seemed that he must have not only read and but also absorbed the diplomatic briefing manual that gave guidance on dealing with American women. They were comfortably discussing exercise regimes and health drink tips when Milne came into the room.

'Good morning, please accept my apologies for being so late. I had an early morning briefing and then hit appalling traffic even with a blue light on the car.' He looked flustered; there was a stiff set to his jaw but ever the consummate professional he recovered with speed. 'I see you've ordered coffee and have introduced yourselves. Excellent,' Milne said. 'Another cup please, and another pot I think.' Without looking at the man, Milne gestured to a hovering waiter.

'May I introduce my colleague, Rafi Shomer,' Eli said to Milne. Rafi stood up and shook hands and smiled.

'Delighted to meet you,' Milne said. 'No Yuval? Don't tell me he's been recalled?'

'No, he's responsible for the whole of Europe at the moment so we don't get his full attention.'

'In that case, let us begin,' Milne sighed. 'Just to recap for Charlene, our Israeli friends have advised us that there is a potential high-grade terrorist threat from a Hamas splinter group which is allegedly working with Al Qaeda. It's something that's going to take place on mainland UK – am I correct?' He looked to Eli for corroboration. 'And in order to evaluate it effectively, our Israeli partners want – if, indeed such intelligence exists – the raw data collected from the Qatar Embassy which is where Hamas have their European operations desk. Now, the problem for us is that even with the Five Eyes combined intelligence matrix, we haven't come up with anything that suggests that this threat actually might be real. So, what are we to do?'

'What about the Birmingham address we gave you?' Eli said.

'They were already on the MI5 watch list and were all low threat.'

There was a shape in the doorway. It was the retired soldier from the front desk. He came in, stood at Milne's elbow and passed a piece of paper to him. Milne read it and frowned as he looked up.

'It seems there is someone from your embassy at the front desk, Eli. You're needed.'

'What?' Eli said.

Eli looked at Rafi who was already on his feet.

'I'm sure it's nothing important,' Rafi said and was out of the room in swift strides.

'I'm so sorry,' Eli said, his mind racing through the likely disasters that would demand this interruption. 'Shall we go on?'

'Oh, why not wait till Rafi comes back?' Charlie said with a benign smile. 'Then we won't have to repeat ourselves.'

'Very sound,' Milne said, 'very sound indeed. How are you finding London, Charlene? Is your family here with you?'

'Call me Charlie, please, only my mother calls me Charlene,' the CIA woman said.

Milne kept up a stream of smooth chit-chat as if this was a social event, as if they weren't all wondering why the meeting had been interrupted. In response Eli mumbled comments about the scenic beauty of the Lake District and kept his eyes on the door. Just as Milne was reeling off a list of the best international schools in the capital, Rafi strode into the room.

'I'm afraid Eli has to go and you'll be left with me,' Rafi said with a relaxed smile that shared with the group the challenges of working to an exacting boss. 'We've just received an urgent message from Yuval about a European operation. He needs Eli's language skills.'

Feeling relieved, Eli allowed himself to be led out of the room by Rafi. As they were in the passage outside the wood panelled room Rafi took out of his pocket the sound buffer. He switched on the sleek black box and then spoke in rapid Hebrew, 'Red Cap's in the visa section at the embassy, drunk out of his mind.'

'What?' Eli's hand went to his scalp.

'Says he won't go away till he sees you. Says if you're not there in fifteen minutes he's going to piss against the gates and get himself arrested. What do you want to do?'

44

Hyde Park Corner, London – Five Minutes Later

The last time Eli had been on the back of a motorbike he'd been holding Gal around the waist and they were on holiday in the Peloponnese. Sitting behind Segev, the watcher, as they swung around London was a different experience.

Eli shut his eyes as the kid wove in front of a white Suzuki and yet another car blared its horn. Even though Eli was wearing the helmet that Segev had fished out of the back of the pizza delivery box on the back of the motorbike, he felt vulnerable. Riding through London traffic, swerving in and out lanes, perched behind a young man keen to demonstrate his advanced skills was not a good way for Eli to marshal his thoughts and work out how to handle Red Cap.

Drunks were unpredictable. Bereaved, angry, guilt-ridden drunks were liable to be explosive. Around St James's Square a delivery van pulled out and Segev had to brake. Eli was shunted against the young man's leather jacket and before he had the chance to rev up and mount the pavement, Eli said, 'Do not do that again; do not drive in a way that will get us arrested. This is not a film; you are not trying to escape from a POW camp. There are no Nazis chasing us.'

The kid looked over his shoulder at Eli, baffled.

'*Slicha*,' Segev said, 'Sorry.' The kid lifted his foot from the road and resumed driving, still fast, still weaving a sinuous route around the central London backstreets towards Kensington Gardens but at least now within acceptable margins of safety and discretion.

And in the end it wouldn't have made any difference if they had mounted pavements, driven down one-way streets and crossed Hyde Park on the green itself. When Eli walked into the visa section of the embassy, there was no sign of Red Cap sitting in the waiting area.

Sara, a redhead who ran the department with slick efficiency was waiting for Eli. She stood akimbo with her hands on her hips.

'Gone,' she said. 'That disgusting man left within five minutes of getting here. He said he needed a drink and you would know where to find him.'

'Shit,' Eli said. 'And you couldn't have stopped him?'

Her face became thunderous, 'You're joking, aren't you? There was a room full of people out there queuing up for visas and your madman was ranting about wanting to see, "his dear old chum". What were we supposed to do? Pin him down and bundle him in a crate? The queue had phones with cameras, Eli. You know your problem? Sometimes you people take too much on yourself and you ask too much of others.'

'Sorry,' Eli reached out and touched her forearm. 'I'm sorry. I wasn't getting at you. Okay? How did he look?'

'I have the footage from the CCTV lined up on the computer in my office,' she softened a fraction. 'It could have been worse. Much worse.'

She swivelled away from him and led the way into her office, her heels clipping against the floor. Sara's office, at the side of the visa section, was a windowless room that hummed from the air-filtering and air-conditioning unit; but she'd made it sweeter with a vase of freesias and pot of fresh coffee. Sarah placed a cup of coffee in front of Eli and stood behind her chair gesturing him to sit. He sat down and she leaned over his shoulder to key in her password. He was aware of her proximity but ignored it.

If Red Cap was picked up by police in the embassy area of Kensington, MI5 would certainly be informed that a distressed GCHQ employee was a long way from home. All it would take would be a few intelligent questions; an inappropriate response from Red Cap and the whole pile of operational cards would come tumbling down. It had happened before; one single drop of blood on a pillow in a

Dubai hotel, that's all it took. Instead of a verdict of accidental death on a Hamas official with heart problems, there was another passport scandal and subsequent diplomatic stink.

On the computer screen in front of Eli the frozen images on the screen began to move. They captured Red Cap from the moment that he approached the embassy and came into the visa section. Sara was right. It could have been worse. Red Cap might have been drunk and desperate but at least he'd been professional enough to cover his head with a Panama hat and was wearing sunglasses. That meant he might have looked odd but his face was shielded. What's more, since he had chosen to make a scene within the embassy, there would be no record of it. And judging from the images, Sara had managed to lead him away from the queue before he became too interesting to ignore.

Good. Eli picked up the coffee and sipped it.

If the camera outside had picked him up, Red Cap might be one of the many people seeking a work permit; they would have to be very unlucky if MI5 was examining outside footage frame by frame. Israel was hardly the main adversary and it also helped that the Brits didn't have the resources of the CIA.

The four minute and twenty-three second clip ended with Red Cap shoving Sara aside and weaving an uncertain route out of the waiting room.

'Thanks Sara, I really appreciate this,' Eli got up from the chair.

'What?' she had her hands back on her hips. 'What do you appreciate Eli: the coffee; me lining up the clip on my computer; or letting one of your disgusting agents push me out of his way?'

'All of it,' Eli said. 'All of it.'

Since there wasn't enough time to go back to the service flat, Eli used the security guards' changing rooms and borrowed some jeans, a tee shirt and a jacket. If he had to sit on the back of motorbike then he could at least be as comfortable as possible and get out of his suit. He also swapped his black Oxfords for trainers. Sitting in the cool basement on a metal bench, Eli tugged on his battered trainers. One of the security jocks came in fresh from the gym. The buffed warrior nodded at Eli but didn't engage; maybe it was locker room etiquette; or perhaps the unknown face had heard that the spooks had cocked-up and there'd been a scene in the visa section. Everybody learnt to step over shit on the pavement as quickly as possible. It was a national pastime.

Five minutes later Eli was pulling on his helmet, this time with a comms system hooked up not only to Segev but also to the rest of the surveillance team. As lead driver Segev was excited; he was bouncing on the balls of his feet, anxious to saddle up.

Eli swung a leg over the back of the bike, '*Yallah*, let's go. St John's Wood via the Westbourne safe house. And keep to the speed limit.'

It wasn't as if Eli was expecting Red Cap to be standing outside the safe house; or hovering at the end of the street; or sitting in any of the three pubs within five hundred yards of the safe house – but it would have been nice. Easy. Certainly easier than sifting through the 28,000 people at Lord's: all watching, milling around and drinking at the one-day Test match. At least Eli wasn't on his own for this herculean task. The surveillance teams were spread in classic formation and were working sector by sector.

The match had stopped for lunch and the afternoon had become hot and cloudy. It was oppressive and as Eli leaned against the rail at the top of the stairs of the north stand looking out over the grounds he realised the impossibility of finding Red Cap – even if he was there. Eli had banked on the idea that Red Cap would watch the action from one of the drinks tents before he passed out; but if he was actually watching the game, there was no chance.

'Excuse me.' What looked like an office party taking a day off bumped past Eli on the way down the stairs to their seats. Eli's earpiece buzzed.

'Zero Seven,'

'Zero Seven, go ahead,'

'Four Two has completed perimeter, no contact.'

'Roger, Four Two, one more pass.'

'Roger.'

The office party had settled back down in their seats. From her rucksack one of the young women had taken out a camera. With some skill she was looking through the viewfinder and fiddling around with lenses. She started to shoot off some pictures. He turned away out of habit. No photos – at least not without a scarf and a hat and glasses and anything else to conceal his identity.

That was when he felt a hand on the back pocket of his jeans. He spun round, there was no one there, the girl was still taking photographs and the office group were joshing and posing for her. No one was paying any attention to him or even trying to avoid his gaze. Eli brushed his hand against his jeans pocket and felt something; paper. He took it out. It was a receipt from an off license. What else would it be?

Eli smiled when he read the note, he recognised the writing:

The Spanish Bar, 1715. Without the wicket keepers, please.

Eli shoved the paper into his pocket. He'd have to explain in his report that he was going to meet Red Cap on his own because Red Cap had once again spotted the surveillance team. It was entirely logical that Eli went alone because if Red Cap could spot watchers then so could MI5.

'Four Two from Zero Seven,' Eli said into his phone. 'Stand down. Return to base. Without me. I'm going to wrap things up here.'

Eli went to the bar, bought a pint of lemonade shandy and spent the rest of the afternoon watching the match.

45

St John's Wood, London – Five Hours Later

After his afternoon at Lord's and on his way to the Spanish Bar Eli phoned Rafi. He was walking out of the cricket ground with a bustling crowd all heading towards St John's Wood tube station. The air was festive with people who'd had the day off work and who'd sat in the fresh air and watched the greatest game in the world.

Phone clamped to his ear, Eli didn't tell Rafi where he was meeting Red Cap, but he did say that contact had been made, he was going alone and why; the watchers had screwed up again.

Rafi said, 'It's too bad. They're all good kids from the best units.'

'I know that, but if we keep using the same methods we've used for the last fifty years, then anyone in the business can spot it. Don't forget Red Cap has done the British training course, he *knows* what he's looking for.'

Rafi said, 'We should have brought in a third team.'

'Yeah. Yuval tried but then he needed two teams for Paris. Have you heard how that's going?'

'Nothing official, but it's okay; he's due back tomorrow morning,' Rafi said.

Eli was at the turnstile about to go into the station where he would lose his signal. In his free hand he held his oyster card and shifting out of the way of the crowd around him, he hovered by a tree. There Eli stood, in front of a glassed-in poster of train timetables, staring at the arrivals and departures as if he was planning a journey; old habits are hard to break.

'How was the rest of the meeting? Were Milne and Charlene pissed off that I went?' Eli said.

'Would they say? Too polite, especially Milne. He's a cool one, so British; that guy's something else. But it was okay, fine, I just repeated our position: that we can't verify what we've got from our people on the ground without their data.'

'Good, perfect, I'll call you when I'm through with Red Cap,' Eli paused. 'And Rafi... thank you.'

Outside the Spanish Bar the early evening summer crowd had spread across the narrow street. Situated between Tottenham Court Road and lower Oxford Street, the bar was another excellent rendezvous for someone who wanted to check themselves. You could double up on yourself, slip into an open door around a curve in the street, or disappear completely into the melange of main streets that bordered the cut-through. The choice was yet another example of Red Cap's professional skills. Drunk and distressed though the agent may be, he was still the real deal.

Once inside, it took Eli a couple of moments for his eyes to adjust to the darkness, the cork-coloured floor tiles, wood slatted bar, the brass and wrought iron, the mahogany light stand set in the floor, black chipped stools and the deep red dralon banquettes. Ripped in places, worn down in others, but still functioning. Like the place itself. Like Eli and like Red Cap.

Red Cap was sitting in a corner with his back to the window and a clear view of the door. His Panama hat was on the seat beside him and his hair was squashed down into a flat cap of massed grey. In spite of the hat he had caught some sun from his day at the cricket and looked flushed, not just from alcohol.

When he reached the table Eli saw there were two untouched pints of beer in front of him.

Red Cap stood up and they shook hands. Their eyes met. It was the first time Eli had seen him since his wife's death. Eli tried to convey his compassion into the handshake, and a hand on his upper arm. And by waiting for Red Cap to talk about it – if that's what he wanted.

'Good work,' Eli said. 'Are you going to tell me how you got the note to me without me spotting you?'

Red Cap nodded, the wry smile curled his lips, 'No. You'll just have to work that one out. What did you think of the match?'

'Good, I particularly liked the look of their spinner. He has that rare mix of steady patience and concentration,' Eli said.

'I'm in total agreement, Benny. That young man is a real talent.'

As if they truly were friends, and not spy runner and agent, they slipped into the safe citadel of shared interests; two middle-aged, middle-class, well-educated men with diverse cultural interests, a shared sense of humour and passion for the great game – the other great game. But after the second beer the walls of that citadel were cracking. Eli placed the beer and shot on the table.

'What happened this morning, Derek?'

Red Cap's mouth worked before he said, 'What happened over the last fifteen years, Benny? What happened to me? What happened to my wife?' His voice cracked, he swallowed, but then Red Cap got it back under control. 'Look, I know Carole wasn't well, I recognise that. Fact is she wasn't well when I met her. It was at a party, she was the sister of somebody I was at school with. She used to tag along with him, we had a party at the flat we were all sharing in Kilburn, and she came and she stayed over. That's how I got to know her. She was ethereal – do you know what I mean? She seemed to float into a room, in her long dresses and shawls as if she was from another time. I never showed you a picture of her did I? She sang. On good days she would wake up and wander around the house singing. Soaring, joyful, songs; she'd have plans for doing so many things, and then on bad days...' the agent trailed off into silence.

'I can't imagine how you're feeling. It makes no difference to say this, and I don't know whether I'm saying this for me, or for you, but I'm sorry, Derek.'

'Thank you. I needed to talk to you; oh yes, they've given me compassionate leave and given me the option of counselling but I needed to talk to you – because, well... only you really know me.'

Red Cap sipped at the beer with unusual restraint.

'So, you see, I wasn't drunk this morning, or at least only from the night before, but I was in a rage. A total, fucking rage.'

'Had something happened?' In spite of Eli's compassion, his spy runner muscle was twitching.

Red Cap used a bony hand to brush off the idea, 'No, not at all. Nothing significant. I'm paranoid, imagine I'm being followed but that's not new. That goes with the job, doesn't it? No, why I flipped was the interview I had yesterday with a twat in HR – usual platitudes, usual crap people say when they don't give a shit. "Anything we can do? Take as much time off as you need. Deepest sympathy. Condolences." What the fuck do they know, Benny?'

He looked up at Eli who saw the despair in the agent's eyes.

'What makes it worse, Benny – if that was possible – is that they don't know how I feel because they haven't read the letter Carole left.'

Eli stiffened. He managed to keep his face neutral but he was rigid. This was exactly what they'd feared. Eli was still as Red Cap reached into the inside of his jacket and withdrew a stained white envelope. The agent placed it on the table between them.

Eli didn't want to touch it.

'Read it,' Red Cap said. 'Please.'

'Are you sure you want me to read this, Derek?'

'It's written to both of us.'

Eli took the envelope and opening it took out the two pages of fine lined paper. The note was handwritten, that was good. No copies. No back-up on a computer disk somewhere. The handwriting was mixed; some of it was bold, round letters, curled strokes below, some of it was a scrawl with underlining and capital letters.

Dearest Derek,

> *I hope you are reading this when I am dead. I hope I have, in this one thing at least, succeeded and done the job properly. It would be ironic if I failed at this as I have failed at everything else in my life.*

> *This is not a cry for help. There is nothing you can do, or anybody could have done to stop the unbearable ache I carry around with me day and night. Understand, it's not that I want to die; I just have to stop feeling like this.*

> *I hate myself. Nothing can change that. No stay in a fancy rehab joint is going to change that fact. And Derek, you will be better off without me.*

Eli glanced up from the page and saw Red Cap's already red eyes swelling with tears. 'This isn't your fault, Derek, she was ill.'

'Read it,' Red Cap said. 'I need you to read it.'

> *I saw you checking to see how much I'd drunk when you got back from work. I saw you cringe when you forced yourself to change my bed, soiled by my own shit. But you didn't understand, I deserved to lie in shit because I am worthless, entirely worthless.*

> *And I don't think you ever knew me. You thought I was someone else but it was a mask. All that singing I did, play-*

ing the piano, I was pretending. This is the real me, ugly in body and soul.

You always said I was creative Derek, that I should write my own songs. I'll tell you something, there's something very creative about planning to kill yourself. I thought about jumping off the side of the car park at Sainsbury's but I'd be too scared! Funny that.

This, what I've done, I hope, seems like the best option. It was easy getting the Valium, the GP was only too happy to give me the scrip and repeat it when I said I needed more. The aspirin and codeine I bought across the counter at the pharmacy and the knife at the kitchen shop where we bought the NutriBullet. It's serrated. That was a touch of my own. I thought that cutting the vein through the skin would be like cutting into a tomato.

You see, I told you it was creative.

Eli rubbed his scalp. He'd never known the woman but she was speaking to him now. He heard her voice, her sad, crazy voice. Why didn't they do more for God's sake? 'I'm sorry, Derek, I don't know what else I can say, or do.'

'Finish reading, please,' the agent said. 'I'll get you another beer.'

Eli nodded and went on reading:

... I told you it was creative. Only time will tell if I am right. There won't be a dress rehearsal.

I chose lavender to put in the diffuser. It's supposed to be a sedative. And as I write I can hear the bath running. It needs to be hot to bring my veins to the surface. I'm wearing the grey dress I bought online, the one you said made me look like a nun because it was so long. But I want to look respectable when I'm found just in case it's not you.

Forgive me.

The bath is ready and I've taken the first ten Valium. I have to be careful not to take too many at once in case I vomit. I've made a jug of dry martini, I hope you don't mind, I used the Waterford crystal jug we got as a wedding present from your godmother.

Don't blame yourself. You don't understand how I feel and would never understand. You've always had your passions, your chess, your crosswords, your cricket, your job and your secret life. I had nothing. No reasons to live. Only you.

One thing puzzles me: I don't know why if you had to break faith with work and be a traitor, you chose to do it for the Jews. Why them? What's the fascination? I never understood that. But I suppose it's just another Derek mystery. You didn't know me and I didn't know you. But I liked that about you, when we first got together, your reasoning, ideas, quirky, off the wall, bouncing, bouncing...

The handwriting was breaking up and Eli had to struggle to read the rest of the scrawl; the last sentence.

Derek, I'm feeling sleepy, I need to get into the bath and take the rest of the pills.

Eli kept his eyes down on the page for a couple of seconds longer before he looked up at Derek. He needed to process what he'd just read and work out some sort of way forward. More than anything he needed to get his agent runner hat back on his head, and not just for his own wellbeing: Derek was not jail sentence material; he wouldn't survive even a low security prison term, not for the length of time he'd go down if he was caught. Because if Derek were caught and the British knew that they already had some access to signals intelligence, then an angry British government would throw the book at Derek – in other words, twenty to thirty years.

'Derek, this...' Eli pushed the sheets towards Red Cap. 'This letter was not written by your wife. It wasn't written by the woman you fell in love with and married; it was written by her illness. I know that's hard –'

'How the hell do you know?' Red Cap growled.

'My wife...' Eli hesitated on the precipice of breaking protocol again; he jumped. 'Listen man, my wife is the leading PTSD psychologist in Israel. She knows a lot about depressive disorders.' Eli took back the sheets and pointed at the phrases; he stabbed at the words with his fingers as if they were the culprits. '"Failure"; "better off without me"; "the pain that's so bad that death is preferable". Those expressions are identifiable symptoms of the illness; they are not your wife.'

Derek was still for moments, his elbows were on the table and he covered his face with his bony hands.

Eli went on, talking to Red Cap's hands. 'If your wife had inoperable cancer would you be torturing yourself?' Eli said. 'If your wife was in a car crash would you blame yourself? What if your wife was in the queue to the gas chambers and you were sent to do forced labour? Would that be your fault? Derek, listen to me. Sometimes things happen. We deal with them and we endure them. That's just how it is.'

Red Cap moved his hands away from his face and Eli saw that the raddled face was dry.

'Benny, you are the only person I can talk to. I don't know what I'm thinking and feeling most of the time. But what terrifies me is that there are moments when I feel... relief. They're making me see the HR shrink tomorrow; how can I tell them you're the only person I trust?'

46

Hanway Street, London – One Hour Later

After another beer in the pub Eli was able to ease Red Cap up the stairs and out into the street. At 8pm it was still light and still warm. Some of the after-work drinkers had dispersed but the hardened sorts, set for a long night, were still in place. Deftly, Eli guided Red Cap around a group that sprawled from pavement to street. His plan was to take Red Cap to Chinatown for a meal. If Red Cap was seeing the HR shrink, it might just be standard procedure for a bereaved employee – or it might be more sinister.

Either way, this would be the last supper for a while; Eli also figured that the agent might react better if there was some food inside of him.

The restaurant was in a side road off Leicester Square and a brusque Chinese woman with a walkie-talkie shunted them up the narrow stairs. Once seated, they ordered rapidly; dim sum and duck; the black-clad waitress didn't blink when Red Cap ordered a bottle of Johnny Walker to go with the jasmine tea. They were sitting by an open window and street sounds floated up, cracks of laughter and shouts, the night coming alive.

'Here.' Using his chop sticks as he'd been taught by his diplomat father, Eli placed one of the choicest dim sum on Red Cap's plate.

'Thanks,' Red tossed another glass of whisky to the back of his throat but made no attempt to eat. His face had become contorted into a permanent grimace of anger as he approached the ugly-drunk phase. How far along he was down the path was hard to say. It felt like stepping out on to an icy pond trying to gauge when he would simply crack the surface and when it would break.

Eli ate a few mouthfuls of rice and then lay bowl and chop sticks on the table. 'Derek, we're going to have to break contact. You know that don't you?'

'I guessed it, I'm not stupid.'

'Never that,' Eli said. 'We also need to destroy the letter, don't we?'

'I should have done it there and then but I couldn't. I wanted you to see it and I'm pleased you did. I found what you said helpful. I'd like to keep it.'

'I don't think that's wise. Why don't I hold on to it until you feel better about all of this?'

'Better about all this? That's never go to happen.'

'I understand –'

'No you fucking don't,' Red Cap said. 'Don't pretend that you have any idea what I'm feeling at the moment. Don't pretend you had any idea how I felt when I read that letter.'

'It's not simply about feeling, Derek. We've got to think about security; you've got to think about security. Listen, the problem is it's not just the letter. With Carole, we're not entirely sure that she didn't talk to anybody else, we...'

'So, all you fucking care about is whether she blabbed and whether I will. That's it, isn't it?'

Eli poured out some jasmine tea into his cup; Red Cap's was untouched and had gone cold. 'Derek, you know the score; I'm not going to insult you by saying otherwise. There are security issues – you need to give me the letter.'

'Fuck that,' Red Cap sprang up from his chair and knocked over the bottle of whisky, the liquor spread across the table. Before Eli could react, the agent had darted for the door and disappeared leaving Eli holding his teacup.

Ever alert, the waitress approached as Eli tossed a fifty-pound note on the table and pounded down the stairs pushing aside some diners coming up.

'Which way?' Eli said to the woman at the front door. 'Which way did my friend go?' She pointed and Eli shifted along the street to the corner of Leicester Square. There he stood and scanned the crowd, looking for a single figure moving at a different pace to the rest of the heaving mass of people. Nothing. Shit. There was no point calling the watchers, by the time they got down there, Red Cap could be miles away. And Eli would have to explain why he'd gone to meet the agent alone in the first place.

He had to find him himself. He knew the man: Red Cap couldn't run fast or far because he wasn't fit. That meant a limited radius. His priority would be to get out of sight, maybe hide in an alley, or shop and then when he thought the coast was clear, he would find a bar and top up his alcohol levels.

He's near. I know he's near.

Eli reached for his phone and dialled Rafi. He answered on the second ring.

'Where are you?' Eli said. 'How fast can you get to Leicester Square?' He didn't wait for an answer. 'Make sure you've got a clean car.'

Eli put his phone away and concentrated on thinking into Red Cap's head. Anybody else would get as far away from the Chinese restaurant as possible; that would be the instinctive reaction, but the professional would circle and double back. The only question was how much of Red Cap's professional muscle was left and how much of it was pickled in a cocktail of grief, anger and alcohol. Whatever Red Cap had learnt on the British training course was hardwired into his brain; he wouldn't even have to think it through; it would be like swimming: instinctive.

But then, knowing how Eli thought, Red Cap just might double bluff.

Leicester Square was busy and as Eli walked past the Odeon, the ten o'clock show was coming out. Couples and groups fell out of the doors, stunned from their journey into a fictive world. There was no sign of Red Cap among the cinema goers or the tourists going into the casino on the square. Eli strode into an ersatz French bistro, looking left and right with the face of a man who was on a date, searching for the welcoming smile. No one challenged him. No one asked if he wanted a table. No one cared. And in the same way, he walked into every shop, casino, and bar working his way around the square and its tributary streets until he was back where he started; in the side street with the Chinese restaurant. There was a bar two doors down, a spit and sawdust relic of pre-gentrification. Too obvious. Much too obvious, but still Eli had to check.

On the point of pushing open the scuffed painted doors, Eli's phone buzzed. It was Rafi.

'Where are you?' Eli said.

'Adam Street... I got a van, just in case.'

'Thanks, nothing to put in it yet –' A shout from within the bar arrested whatever he was about to say next. Cutting the call, Eli pocketed the phone and pushed his way in.

He was there. Red Cap was at one end of the bar against a wall. A burly man with grey hair in a ponytail was standing over Red Cap. Nearby a small woman in a knitted skirt and boots was touching the man's elbow. Whether she was staff or relative or passer-by, Eli didn't wait to find out.

'What's going on?' Eli said trying to sound like authority which was just as well as the two kids behind the bar were cowering. He spoke to the big man, 'Is this man bothering you? This is supposed to be a quiet bar, not –'

'Keep out of it,' the ponytail said. 'I'm waiting for an apology from this creep here.'

'Benny, so pleased you could join me,' Red Cap slurred. 'Ever the faithful hound eh? This creature, this... this Caliban is an oaf. I was defending the honour of this lady and Caliban turned on me.'

'He don't mean no harm,' the woman said. Her face was even more lined than Red Cap's.

'Why don't we all calm down, okay?' Eli said, trying to edge round and take Red Cap's arm. 'Me and my friend will go and drink somewhere else. We'll get out of your way and leave you in peace. I'm sure he didn't mean any offence.'

'But I did, Benny. Truly, I did. I am deeply offended by this oaf and even more than that, disgusted by the rat tail at the back of the creature's head. It is a rat tail isn't it?'

There was a nervous laugh from the Goth girl behind the bar.

If it hadn't have been for the girl's laugh Eli might have got Red Cap out of there, but the loss of face was too much for the big guy who, judging by his face, was also drunk. He raised his fist. 'You deserve a good hiding and I'm the man gonna give it you; I'm gonna knock you all the way across this fucking room and enjoy it,' he said.

Before he could strike, Eli kicked him in the shin that was closest. With surprising speed, the man turned and before Eli could regain his balance he had his horny hands around Eli's throat.

Training kicked in. Without thinking Eli raised both hands, twisted round forty-five degrees, brought all his weight down on the big man's arms and broke the grip. Then he kneed him in the groin and when the oaf's head came down in agony, Eli head-butted him. The man crashed to the ground knocking over a table of drinks on the way.

'Oh bravo,' Red Cap said putting his hands together.

'Shut up.' Eli hauled him out of the bar, half carrying him when he stumbled. 'Derek, we have about two minutes before the police arrive.' Eli shoved Red Cap out of the door into the street, but the drunken agent's legs would no longer hold him upright. He lurched into the wall, hit his side and then slumped down like a sack.

'Get up, Derek,' Eli tugged at him. 'For God's sake get up.' His voice was rasping from his constricted throat.

A voice was at Eli's elbow. '*Bevakasha*,' Rafi said. 'May I?'

Without waiting for an answer Rafi knelt, put his hands under Red cap's armpits and hauled him upright in one fluid movement. 'You take his other side, your left arm round his waist and his arm over your shoulder. Right, now, lift and run.'

Carrying Red Cap between them they ran in the direction of Chinatown, away from Leicester Square. They charged through dawdling tourists and night-time revellers and it was only when they heard the sirens by Charing Cross Road that they slowed to a walk. Red Cap's head was lolling to the side but as they passed a patrolling pair of policemen, he still could have been any drunk being helped home by a couple of friends.

Five minutes later they had bundled Red Cap into the back of the Renault van and Rafi was nosing his way in the traffic while Eli sat back and massaged his throat. From the back of the car reverberated the sounds of Red Cap snoring.

'If we go A25 for two miles, past the Houses of Parliament, then out towards the M40 we should be in Cheltenham by 1 o'clock,' Eli said. 'Let's stop when we're out of London and patch up Red Cap. Did you bring your first aid kit?'

'What do you think? Never leave home without it.'

'Again, Rafi... thank you.'

'It was a pleasure. It was *keyf*, fun. I feel like I've been sitting in meetings for too long.'

'*Keyf*? That bastard nearly killed me,' Eli said.

'More like you nearly killed him, I watched you from the door, nice moves, Eli. Didn't think you had it in you. Come on, admit it, you enjoyed it.'

Eli thought for a moment, then turned to Rafi, 'Yeah, I did.'

Rafi and Eli patched up Red Cap in a service station on the M40; the agent's guardian angel must have been looking out for him because Red Cap had nothing worse than a few bruises and a hangover. After making sure that his house wasn't under surveillance, Eli decided to take the agent inside. He wanted a moment with him; he wanted to be sure, or as sure as he could be that Red Cap wasn't in any further danger.

Eli helped him up the path to the front door. Red Cap's hand was shaking as he tried to find the lock in the dark; gently Eli took the key from the man's cold hand.

'Good of you to take me all the way home,' Red Cap said. 'Come in for a coffee, before you go.' He sounded hopeful; it was almost a plea.

'We've got to get back to London, Derek, but some other time, I will.'

'Sure you will,' Red Cap said.

Inside the front door the hall had black and white tiles. Eli noted the dust balls nestling around the legs of a mahogany occasional table in the hallway. From the kitchen at the far end of the hallway he could smell a food bin that hadn't been emptied. The whole house had a sour scent.

'Let's get you upstairs,' Eli said. 'You've got to get some sleep if you're going to see the HR shrink tomorrow. Have you got a clean shirt?'

Eli was aware that it was the same conversation he had with his son before he took him to school in the morning. But Red Cap had no kids and no family.

'I'll be fine, I've been worse than this in my time. Run along Benny. Run along back to London and leave me to get on with it.' Red Cap waved his hand in the direction of Eli, dismissing him with a flick of his hand as he reached the first-floor landing. The action destabilised the agent and he wobbled, almost losing his balance. Eli put his arm over the man's shoulder and guided him into the nearest room where he sat the agent down on the unmade bed. The curtains were drawn, drooping in the middle where a ring was missing; piles of dirty and discarded clothing were buried under an armchair and the wardrobe was open showing more mess inside. From inside Eli's pocket he felt his phone vibrate, he reached in and saw a text message from Rafi: **How long?**

He texted back: **10**

By the time Eli had pocketed his phone again Red Cap had slumped over on to the pillow. 'Derek, I'm going to make you a coffee and bring you some water, okay?'

'What...' Red Cap's eyes were shut. 'I'll just sleep for a... for a...' A trickle of dribble was leaking out of the agent's mouth on to the pillow. One yellow eye opened, 'You still here?'

'Derek, sit up for a minute. I'm going to get your jacket and tie off, okay?'

'Tucking me up?' Red Cap slurred the words.

Eli hauled the drunk into a sitting position and eased the jacket over his shoulders. He undid the agent's tie and then eased him down on to the bed. Eli lifted Red Cap's legs, straightened the limbs out, removed the scuffed Oxfords and then covered him with a dressing gown he found lying on the floor.

'Derek, listen to me,' Eli said. He was hanging the jacket on the back of a chair the seat of which was piled high with clothes. With his back to Red Cap he felt inside the pocket and pulled out the envelope with Carole's letter. All the while he continued talking; his voice was soothing and firm. 'Derek, you have to get into work tomorrow. Even if you go in and say you feel too ill to talk to the shrink, you have to report in otherwise they will get interested in you and that won't be good.'

'I'm okay, Benny, I'll survive, I'm a survivor. Like you. Like the Jews. You know she asked, Carole asked why you, your people, why the Jews? I never had the chance to tell her... to tell her about Mrs Stein. I betrayed her, I betrayed Carole more than anyone else.'

Tears were in his eyes and they were trickling down his crinkled cheeks. 'What have I done?'

'What you needed to do, that's all any of us do. You did what you felt was right.'

'Is that what you do?'

'Yes, I do what I think is right. Listen Derek, I've got to go, it's nearly 4am and it's getting light. You have to get a couple of hours sleep before you go to work.' Eli took a step towards the door. 'I have to go Derek. But I'm not going to be far away.'

'You'll watch over me?' the agent said.

'Yes, I will watch over you.'

47

All Saints Road, Cheltenham – Early Next Morning

For the remainder of the night Eli and Rafi sat outside the house. At 7.30, they saw the curtains downstairs open and seven minutes later an unmarked minibus stopped outside the house to pick up Derek. From where they were sitting, a hundred metres down the road with the car facing in the opposite direction, Red Cap looked haggard. But judging by the bits of toilet paper stuck to his face, he'd made some attempt at shaving and he was wearing a different shirt from the one he'd worn the day before.

Only when the minibus had disappeared did Eli and Rafi start the drive back to London and the inevitable fallout from the night before. Orders from Yuval were to go straight to the embassy; there was no chance to go back to the serviced apartment to shower and shave: Yuval was waiting.

The tray of fresh coffee and platter of bagels on the table in the meeting room did not disguise Yuval's mood. He was sitting in front of a laptop frowning at the screen when the door swung open. He pushed the computer away and looked them up and down with clear disdain.

'At least you made good time,' Yuval said. 'The situation is like this – I've told HQ that Eli went to the meeting without the surveillance team because they'd been spotted by Red Cap. That's not going to make us popular with the watchers but it was the best explanation as to why you ended up in a fight in a pub.'

'But it's true,' Eli said.

'That's not the point.' Yuval held his thumb and forefinger together. 'We are this close from having Sweetbait closed down because of Red Cap; the ambassador heard about yesterday's scene in the visa section and he's furious. He is trying to get us sent home.'

Eli shrugged. His argument that Red Cap was unpredictable and should have been let go seemed to have been forgotten. Eli had too strong a sense of survival to remind Yuval. Maybe that's what Red Cap had meant when he talked about admiring the Jews with their ever-ready escape plans, passports and diamonds sewn into the lining of the clothes. Always ready to run – or always ready to strike back. Always alert. Always insecure. Survive, survive, whatever the cost.

'Eli? Are you listening?'

'Yes, yes of course, I'm listening. I'm thinking about what to do about Red Cap. We have limited options,' Eli said. 'But at least I got the suicide letter.'

'That's about the only good news there is,' Yuval said. 'How did you leave him?'

'Drunk, depressed.' Eli said.

'So, no change there,' Rafi had helped himself to a bagel and was eating it.

'Don't be cute,' Yuval growled. 'We need to make sure that Red Cap doesn't create any more upsets that might excite the attention of MI5. We don't want to get sent home. We are nine days away from zero hour on Sweetbait and we cannot afford any more problems.'

'There's one way of making sure there are no problems,' Rafi said with a full mouth. 'It's guaranteed. And since Sweetbait is the operation with the most important long-term benefits it could be deemed necessary. Yuval, if you give me a mandate, I'll work on a plan that would bring the risk levels within acceptable parameters –'

'Are you crazy?' Eli said. He turned to Yuval. 'Say something for God's sake. Or call security and get them to take Rafi away. What are you talking about?'

'Calm down, take a bath, Eli, this is an open forum, so let's not throw out ideas until we have better ones,' Yuval said. 'Rafi is extreme but he's approaching the problem logically. Besides the issues of legality, there is an argument that some action is necessary. Whether Rafi's suggestion is in proportion to the problem is one thing and also whether we can think of some other operational tactic.'

'Why don't we just take him on vacation for a few weeks?' Eli said. 'He must be owed some leave; if not, his wife just died, they couldn't begrudge him a holiday. We could take him to Cyprus, luxury hotel, buy some company for him; get him out the way until after we finish Sweetbait.'

'Except we never solved the problem of whether or not he's being watched by someone else or whether he's just a drunk paranoid,' Rafi said.

'And a convenient car crash isn't going to raise any awkward questions?' Eli said.

'It doesn't have to be a car crash,' Rafi said with the voice of someone considering a list of options.

'Assassinations are sanctioned and they have been ever since the Olympics disaster,' Eli said.

'I know that.'

'Do you? Do you really understand? It doesn't matter what method you come up with to kill Red Cap – it would be disproportionate and illegal. So whatever you may think of our prime minister, he's never going to sign off on that,' Eli said.

'You're probably right,' Rafi said.

'What's more it would be immoral and unethical but, of course, these concepts are completely alien to you, aren't they, Rafi? You have absolutely no idea what I'm talking about.'

'I'm starting to think you're the one who needs the vacation,' Yuval said. 'Red Cap is a tool; we do what is right for Mossad and Israel – don't forget it.'

'Okay, if we're not going to take him on holiday, we break all contact, close down the emergency contact lines, and we disappear. Red Cap goes back to work, keeps his nose clean, everybody's happy.'

'That's the whole problem,' Rafi said. 'Red Cap doesn't keep his nose clean.'

Eli forced himself to sound relaxed. Reaching for the thermos jug he poured some coffee into a cup, 'When all's said and done, Red Cap is a pro. When he sees the fallout from Sweetbait he'll get it immediately. He'll know why he has to keep his head down. And who knows, maybe down the line, we might even be able to make contact with him again.'

'What and go and have a cup of tea with him?' Rafi said. 'See the cricket and talk tweed jackets and draught beer. You live in a movie, Eli. This is the real world; he's an agent, a tool, an object. He's jeopardising the most important operation in the last five years and he's outlived his usefulness. You talk about me being irresponsible. If Red Cap kicks off again it will be on you. You don't take risks like that; it's irresponsible.'

'Me, irresponsible? I didn't break in to the teacher's house –'

Yuval interrupted, 'Eli, this is not taking us any further towards a decision about Red Cap and we're out of time. He's your agent, you know him better than anyone, he trusts you. How likely is it that he will create another problem?'

Rafi rolled his eyes, an expression that wasn't missed by Yuval who scowled at him.

'Well, Eli?' Yuval closed the laptop on the desk. 'There's risk in everything we do. What's the risk to Sweetbait, if we follow your suggestion and simply break all contact with Red Cap?'

'Ten percent,' Eli said. 'Fifteen maximum.'

'Then that's good enough for me.' Yuval glanced at his watch. 'Now, I've got to get to City Airport to sort out the mess in Paris. I'll see you two in a day or two.' Yuval pointed to the bagels on the table.

'Get this mess cleared up otherwise we'll have housekeeping on our backs.' Yuval stalked out of the room.

'You want one?' Eli said pointing at the platter.

'I've had enough. Smoked foods are full of carcinogens.'

'Okay, I'll take the platter down to visa section. I'm sure Sara will know what to do with the cancer food.' Eli started to gather up the used paper plates and put them in the bin. 'It's not personal,' Eli said.

'Of course it is, it's entirely personal. You don't like me, you think you're better than me but what you don't understand is that I'm the one who is going to help you.'

'Really,' Eli said. 'And how do you work that one out?'

'Because you're making a big mistake with Red Cap and I'm going to have to get you out of trouble... again.'

Part 4 – THE DEATH

Death may be the greatest of all human blessings.
  Socrates

Death is the solution to all problems. No man – no problem.
  Joseph Stalin

See, I have set before you this day life and good, death and evil...
I have set before you life and death, blessing and curse; therefore
choose life.
  Moses

48

Watlingford Public School, Oxfordshire, Classroom, The Next Day

My dearest brother,

I'm sitting in my English lesson thinking of you. We're supposed to be writing sentences with Sometimes, Often, Always. I've done mine.

Ever since I saw you last week I've been thinking about you, what you said, how you looked and how we parted. I know it wasn't easy for you.

I'm really pleased you liked the coin; keep it safe.

There were a lot of things I wanted to tell you and when we were there, in that room, and with so little time, I forgot. Among them was wanting to tell you how I remember when you were born. How excited I was; everybody was. I was ten, the oldest, and you were the first boy in our family. Dearest Wasim, you were such a prize, a treasure.

You won't remember – how could you – but *Mawmia* was ill after you were born. It was winter, wet and cold. The house was draughty even though we stuck newspaper in the window cracks and covered the cold floor tiles with sacking. *Mawmia* had bronchitis and pneumonia so she didn't have the strength to feed you. That became my duty and my joy.

I don't remember where our father was. Maybe that was the time he left us for good – all I remember was you. Our aunts came by every day with food and advice but when they went home it was my job to feed you and put you down at night. Poor *Mawmia* would be sleeping, fretful from the illness and I could pretend that you were mine, my own little boy. I loved you so much brother; I still do.

When I think of you and what you have achieved I'm crazy with pride for you. It makes my heart grow so large I feel it in my throat. You make light of it but I know just how hard you studied to win your place at the university in America. Uncle Fahed may have helped with your fees but he couldn't help you get the grades you needed – you did that. Night after night, when the other kids from your school were outside kicking a ball around in the dirt, playing their games, you were inside at our table doing your homework. Making sure there were no mistakes and there would be another A+ in your notebook. That's what gave you joy and me pride.

There was one year of particularly bad power cuts. I remember the candlelight on your face, how it glowed; how your mouth moved when you wrote and how you stuck your tongue out and it followed your hand across the page. We'd sit at the table together. You and me. I'd be working on my nursing studies and you would be doing homework. Everyone else was out visiting and it was just us, you and me, at the table studying.

Wasim, I'm truly sorry if you're upset about my decision to be *shaheeda*. Before I saw you in that room in London I knew it would be difficult and I was prepared for your arguments but not for your pain. I see that room now, as I write. I see the narrow stairs at the end of a carpeted passage. An empty doctor's room, just a desk and two chairs, more suited for a medical consultation than our last meeting place.

'Why?' you said. 'You were never devout when we were young. You liked movies. You had ambition, self-belief; you taught me that – you said to be proud of what I've got and to use it the best way I can.'

'It's my life, little brother, and I choose to use it as a weapon to free our people.'

'Sahar, it will make no difference, all you're doing is breaking my heart.'

You cried then little brother and I hugged you; I felt your tears on my cheek; I tried not to cry myself.

'Listen to me,' I said. 'I have no life without a husband and children. I'm our mother's carer and that will end one day; then I will have nothing.'

'You can live with me in America. I'll finish my studies, be an engineer or an academic. I'm good enough, sister.'

'I know you are.'

'I'll look after you,' you said.

'Would you deny me my chance to be a martyr?'

'Do you believe that? Do you believe you go to *Jennah* or maybe there is just nothing?'

'I believe Abu Marwan, he is wise, he knows this world and he knows the next. Don't forget he saved you from being arrested, didn't he? Brother, I have been chosen, I can be special – I can make a difference.'

And then little brother, you became angry. You turned from me and paced around the room, running your hands through your hair.

'I insist that you obey me,' you said. 'I'm the head of the family, your guardian and I forbid you to be *shaheeda*. Understand me, Sahar, you will go home from here and care for our mother.'

You also said many other things. Hurtful things. I won't write them down because I know you would want to forget them; it would make you sad if you remembered how cruel you were.

Dearest Wasim, I forgive you for what you said because always you were like that. When you were a little boy I remember you kicking the leg of the table in our kitchen, kicking it out of frustration, kicking it until you hurt your foot. But you never hurt the table, only yourself. I am the table, Wasim. I stand fixed, steady, scratched but unmoved. When we met and you were angry I did then what I did when you were a child; I sat quietly, my hands in my lap and I waited for you to finish.

At last you did.

I said, 'You will go back to America, to university where you will complete your studies and do the best you can. *Mawmia* will be fine; she will receive a pension because I am *shaheeda* and also help from the community. She will like that – you know she will. And you, you Wasim Nadir, will be brave and you will know that you are loved by me, for eternity.'

49

Watlingford Public School, Oxfordshire – At The Same Time

'*Sometimes*; *Often*; and *Always*. All describe the passage of time,' Petra said. She was standing in front of the whiteboard holding the blue marker with the words she'd printed behind her. She could smell the tang of the whiteboard pen; the special scent of 'school'. In front of her the students' faces gazed up. There was Sergei with a dark shadow on his upper lip that looked like dirt. As usual, Aneeta was next to him; today she'd tied up her wild curls exposing her neck where there was an angry love bite. Next to the Spanish girl, there was her friend: Sahar, head down, diligently copying the words into her notebook, her mouth working with concentration.

It had been two days since Petra had driven Sahar to London and back and Petra had been busy. Taking matters into her own hands was not something to be done lightly but given that she'd certainly seen Sahar with Benny in Bath and Rafi had tried to convince her otherwise, Petra felt she had little choice. The final straw was realising that a meeting had been arranged between Sahar and her so-called dangerous brother. Petra was now surer than ever that it was Sahar who was in danger and that she, Petra, was the naive girl's only hope of safe passage out of the maze. But now she had a plan; she was going to get something that she could barter for Sahar's safety.

Turning back to the board Petra pointed to the first word: *Sometimes*.

'Sometimes, when you have a problem the very best thing you can do is to find someone you trust and talk about it,' Petra said. 'Did everyone understand that?'

There were nods. Mfoniso scribbled in his notebook with industry.

'In that case, would anyone like to try to construct a sentence with *Sometimes*? Li?' The Chinese girl shook her head. 'Okay, how about Aneeta? No? Sahar can you construct a sentence with *Sometimes*?'

'Sometimes I am happy,' Sahar said. 'Sometimes I am sad. But always I like to be here.'

Led by Aneeta the class erupted into applause.

'That was very good,' Petra said. 'Sahar has raised the bar, given us a good example, and now I'm going to give you all the chance to write sentences using *Sometimes*, *Often* and *Always*. Okay? You have ten minutes.'

Petra noted the time on her watch and took a sip from the water bottle on the desk. The classroom became silent. There was just the scratching of pen against paper. A few of the students were sucking the ends of their writing instruments or looking around vacantly for inspiration. Petra ignored them and stared out of the window at the quad. The weather had turned oppressively hot; it felt as if the bricks of the old building sucked up the heat during the day and then radiated it into the rooms to suffocate her.

Turning away from the window and the students, Petra looked up at the whiteboard: *Sometimes. Always. Often.*

Besides her frustration about getting Sahar to confide in her, Petra had been musing about the past. All her memories of the time with Rafi were blurred; the chronology jumbled into a kaleidoscope of images and sound. Flights all over Europe; departure gates; loading laundry into the washing machine and dryer before repacking and lulling herself to sleep in run-down city hotels by reciting her cover names. Exhausted she'd come back to London and have a coffee with Alon and he'd remind her why she was working round the clock: she was a Jew; she was making a difference; she was keeping people safe. And she was doing something that would have made her father proud. Somewhere between the work grind and the pep talks there were a few high-octane moments with Rafi but it was mostly relentless work.

Petra's eyes rested on the parquet floor and she noticed the rubber scuff marks and ground dirt at the base of the desk's legs. But her mind was in Geneva again, where her early career had come to an end. They were staying at the Beau Rivage Hotel on the lake within sight of the Jet d'Eau; the hotel was a welcome change from the side street guest houses and motels of most operations. It was elegant and grand. She was playing the role of a British businesswoman; a science expert trying to buy data for an industrial plant in Kuwait to enhance the oil industry. The seller was a Pakistani scientist. It seemed like a straightforward job; all she had to do was keep her eyes out for the Swiss authorities who were famously intolerant of clandestine activities.

It was one of the rare times that she was in the field with Alon who was by then largely deskbound. It was a treat to be with the older man. When they arrived in Geneva they had dinner at L'Entrecôte. They'd even spent an afternoon by the side of the lake while they waited for the Pakistani to peel off from his meetings at the UN Environmental Programme.

It was all standard; everything was usual; a nice easy job. The last thing Petra remembered before it all went wrong was how pleased she was with the pashmina she'd bought at the Duty Free boutique in the hotel; she was arranging it around her shoulders on the ground floor of the Beau Rivage.

'We have to get out of here,' Alon appeared by her side. 'Malik's been followed and they're dangerous.'

'What?'

Alon's face was non-committal but he was sweating. He went on, 'Leave everything; we have to get to the car and drive to France.'

Matching Alon's pace Petra walked briskly to the exit and down the street towards the public car park.

'How dangerous, for God's sake,' she said. 'This is Switzerland. No one carries here; that's the arrangement with them; everyone knows that.'

'Freelancers don't,' Alon said. 'They're not civil servants, so they don't play by the rules.'

Former KGB officers with skills but inflation-hit pensions were offering themselves as guns for hire. Often to be found in hotel bars trying to pick up work, any work, they were generally vicious and the bane of the international intelligence community.

Petra lengthened her stride, wishing that she wasn't wearing heels. The air was whipping up cold from Lake Leman and she clutched the pashmina closer around her as they crossed the street at a trot into the car park.

They found the Pakistani scientist on the second floor by their VW. In a foetal position he was being kicked by two shaven-headed middle-aged men who looked more like backroom desk men than entrepreneurial muscle.

'Play straight,' Alon whispered.

'*Qu'est-ce que vous faites?*' Petra held up her phone. 'What are you doing? Leave that man alone. I've called the police and they are on their way.'

One of the men paused in his rhythmic kicking of Malik's ribs. She never forgot the man's expression; she never would. Looking up from his task, his head was to one side and he grinned at her, like a kid caught doing something naughty but who knew he would be forgiven. Meanwhile, Malik was on the cement floor of the car park, he'd stopped moving. She didn't know if he was dead or just playing dead.

Petra took two steps forward and drew herself up to her full height. '*Hors d'ici!*' she said.

The smiling goon tapped his colleague on the arm and they both started walking towards Petra and Alon. What did they look like?

A woman in a business suit and an old man. No matter how fit he kept himself, Alon was more than sixty with a shock of white hair and narrow shoulders. As if they were terrified, Petra and Alon stood still.

'You must be the British woman our friend here speaks of,' he said in a thick accent.

'Pardon?' Petra twisted her pashmina shawl between her hand as if she was anxious. *Je comprends pas; que voulez-vous dire?*

She caught a glint of steel at his wrist and then spotted the knife. In her peripheral vision, she saw Alon. His arms were open in supplication; he appeared to be the frail older man who was trying to make peace. Not the practised Krav Maga black belt.

In tandem, they went for the goons. Using one of his open arms, Alon grabbed the Russian freelancer, pulled him towards him and kicked his groin; fast, quick and repeated. Meanwhile, Petra tossed the pashmina over the head of the grinning bastard, slipped off her shoe and used the heel like a hammer to whack the knife from her attacker's hand.

But she was off-balance. With a roar the man ripped the pashmina off his head and lashed out; he punched her; she toppled down and hit the cement shoulder first and felt the excruciating pain of dislocation. The knife skittered on the cement and with her good arm she lunged for it, grabbed it and held the knife upwards as the Russian threw himself on top of Petra pinning her down.

His hands were at her throat and she was moving from side to side, struggling to breathe, feeling sick from the pain, trying to free her good hand. On top of her the Russian had his hands around her throat and he was banging her head against the ground. Petra got her arm free and with all her force she plunged the knife into the man's neck.

He sat up, sat back on his heels and felt his wound. His face showed shock. Petra wrenched out the knife and stabbed him again and again and again, until Alon pulled the dead Russian away.

The scratching pens of the students on paper became the sounds of Petra and Alon dragging the bodies of the two men into the boot of the car. Between them they picked up Malik and gently lay him on the back seat where he whimpered with pain from the attack. But Malik was lucky – a thick coat over a heavy suit meant he only suffered bruised and broken ribs.

She remembered the blank grey sky and the blizzard that was their friend; Geneva was plunged into swirling mist and snow and they reached France without incident. There Malik was cared for and Petra's shoulder was pushed back into its socket. It took weeks for all the bruises to come and to go; months for the physio to get her movement range back to near normal; but no matter how many years passed, Petra never forgot the fear and rage that made her kill.

Petra watched the students as the last seconds ticked away on her phone. The alarm rang. Her voice sounded flat, even to her own ears. 'Okay people, you've had enough time to write *War and Peace*. Let's hear some of those sentences. Who wants to go first?'

But before the teaching could resume the classroom opened and Deanna came in with the spaniel trotting behind her, its claws clicking across the parquet. The dog scampered up to Petra and tried to climb on to her lap.

'Good afternoon Deanna, welcome. You're just in time to hear the group's sentences.'

'That sounds marvellous, can't wait. If the class will forgive us, I'll be back in a few moments to hear those sentences,' Deanna said.

Petra stood up and followed Deanna out of the classroom into the corridor where they stood under a depleted noticeboard. There was a sheet of exam results, a poster for the drama club; torn pinpricks in the cork and ragged remnants of blue tack. Past times. Forgotten events. Best let go.

'Is there anything I need to know,' Deanna said.

'No, they're reading out their sentences and then I was going to show them another episode of *Downton Abbey*.'

'Very good,' Deanna said but she didn't look happy.

'I truly appreciate this, Deanna, I promise to get back as quickly as I can but if I don't take my godfather to his hospital appointment it won't happen and the poor chap is all on his own. The hospital have called him in for a procedure he's been waiting for for months because there was a cancellation and he's really got no one but me to help him.'

'Of course, Petra. I understand; anything to help.'

Petra put her hand on Deanna's arm. 'Thank you. You could be saving a life.'

50

Watlingford Public School,
Oxfordshire – One Hour Later

Eli paced up and down the gravel path in the kitchen garden and kicked at the boundary stone that neatly contained the vegetable beds. 'Where the hell is Trainer?' Eli said into his phone. 'I'm standing here waiting and there's no sign of Sweetbait; if anyone ought to know where the girl is then Trainer should.'

'Trainer left a message,' Rafi said. 'I've only just picked it up. She had to go to the airport to pick up a kid; some job she had to do for the school.'

'Just what we need. Trainer off site and no idea where Sweetbait is.'

'Where's your fall-back? Go there, give Sweetbait half an hour and then I'll pick you up. *Savlanut*, patience, Eli.'

'*Ein li savlanut*,' Eli said. 'I don't have any patience, I need –' Eli turned around to see Sahar standing a metre away with a puzzled expression on her face. He held his finger to his lips and continued to speak in Hebrew. '*Ken, mevin*,' Eli said. 'Yes, understood. Make sure everything is in place. Be safe.' Eli ended the call, pocketed the phone and with an open-handed gesture towards Sweetbait showed her the wooden bench. She hovered, hesitant.

'*Ahlan bik*. Welcome, welcome, you are well?' Eli said in Arabic. 'I have something for you. Something very important from home,' he added.

She was frowning. 'Abu Marwan, I thought... you speak the language of the Zionist monkeys?'

'Of course I do,' Eli said. 'How else do you think we pass unnoticed among them? I am proud of my accent, I have studied hard to make it authentic, and I believe it to be convincing, *inshallah*. When we walk among the wolves we must not look like sheep. Now, come, please. Time is short and I want to be certain that you understand the plan because it's possible I won't see you again until the day of your martyrdom.'

Eli reckoned his confident explanation had quelled the obvious doubts that she'd had. It was the first rule of deceit. Own and acknowledge and then move on. If he explained any further, then it would raise even more questions in the girl's mind.

Eli started by testing Sweetbait on the layout of the operational location.

'To the right is the red entrance,' her eyes were half shut as she visualised the map. 'Across the main concourse is the area where there are stalls with clothes. I... I... turn left towards the control tower but before I get there I turn left towards the pavilions. When I see the Techno Zone I go down the path and find the central point in the space. That is correct?'

'*Mumtaz*,' Eli said. 'Excellent. And this is all in your memory? You are remarkable; it's as if you are seeing the map in front of your eyes. How Allah has blessed us. Do you have a photographic memory?'

She blushed, her fine skin was rosy, 'I work hard, Abu Marwan. I want all to be well with my *Shahada*, and I am nervous that I may make a mistake. That is why I work so hard. I worry –'

'Don't worry, never worry,' Eli said. 'You are blessed and God will guide you. Now, I want you to give me the phone you have been using and I am going to give you a fresh phone.'

Her hands clenched and Eli saw in her frown and eyes that look again. The one he always saw on agents whenever the schedule was changed, whenever they had to grasp a new set of instructions, whenever the tenuous hold they had on events by routine was tugged away from them. It was the look he'd seen on every single agent he'd ever worked with – apart from Red Cap.

Faced with Sweetbait's anxious eyes Eli used a voice that would soothe her anxiety. 'It's the exact same phone as the other one so there will be nothing new for you to learn. *Aiwa*? You will carry it with you at all times but will only use it on your day of *Shahada*. Do you understand?'

'Yes.'

'Only use on day of martyrdom,' she said. And then repeated the words to herself without sound. He saw her lips move as if she was trying to imprint them on her brain or perhaps trying to calm herself with another ritual.

It might have been nice to tell her that the fresh phone had no blue tooth connection. To have let her know that, although she was at the heart of a complex covert operation, on her day of martyrdom she wasn't going to blow herself to kingdom come. To have comforted her with the knowledge that she didn't have to steel herself for death, but that when she pressed the sequence of buttons – nothing would happen. At least, not in any final sense. But then, agents never got to learn the full story.

51

Watlingford Public School, Oxfordshire – The Next Day

Since it was a small group and a local trip Petra was the sole leader. Standing in the aisle of the minibus, Petra spotted an empty seat next to Sahar. As soon as the diesel engine had powered up, she swayed down the aisle and sat next to the girl who looked pale.

'How are you this morning, Sahar?' Petra beamed. 'You're going to love the outing today. It's everything that makes England special at this time of year.'

'Thank you. I know that I will like... it,' Sahar said.

'Bravo! Future tense!' Petra said.

There was a flush of pleasure in the girl's face. 'I want to thank you, Petra. You are all the time kind to me.'

Petra smiled back, 'It's very easy to be kind to you.'

Although she smiled, that morning Petra was tired. She hadn't got to bed till 3am. The 150-mile round trip, the nervous anticipation and what she had to do had been taxing. Yet she felt good; much had been accomplished. In spite of her worry that the tracker wouldn't work for some reason, it had been absolutely accurate. Now Petra needed her lucky streak to hold.

The minibus with students rumbled along and after fifteen minutes it drew up at the riverside dock where they were to board their punts and meet their punting guides.

Standing on the dock by the punts, the excursion leader addressed the group. 'Just a couple of health and safety issues. Do not stand up in the punt please, unless your guide has explained to you how to do it safely. We don't want any accidents. And there's just one other thing, we'd like you to leave your bags and rucksacks and what-not in the minibus. There's room for cameras on the punts but no bags.'

'That's fine,' Petra said. 'Mick will be here and he'll look after the bags.'

Petra noticed that Sahar was grasping her black rucksack with both hands.

'I cannot go,' Sahar said. 'I do not leave my bag with Mick.'

A picture flashed into Petra's mind; an image she'd missed during her tunnel-vision attempts to get Sahar to talk to her; to trust her; to spill out everything to her. The image was Sahar, in her room, talking about changing into a warm dress – and eyeing her bag; guarding it like a dog.

'What's the problem?' Petra said her voice was reassuring and calm. 'Is there something you need on the punt?'

'No, no.' The girl's eyes darted around in panic.

'You can absolutely trust Mick,' Petra said. 'Truly. He's entirely honest and reliable. He's just going to sit in the minibus until we all come back.'

'I do not know him. I won't go. I stay here. It is okay, you go. I stay.'

'Please come,' Aneeta said. 'Sahar, you are my friend, I want you to share.'

Petra looked from one girl to the other and said, 'Listen, Sahar, you cannot take the bag on the punt but I've got an idea. Do you think you can trust me to look after it? If I promise to sit on the bus with all the bags and keep them safe?'

Petra looked into Sahar's eyes and she saw the girl was cornered by Aneeta's plea and her own solution to the problem.

Five minutes later, Petra stood by the riverside as the class set off on the three punts; only one small face turned back and a hand was raised to wave back at her.

Petra strode back to the bus aware that she was being watched by Mick the driver. Too bad. If he hadn't been staring out of the window keen for the company she'd have been able to go straight into the boathouse toilets to search Sahar's bag.

Petra climbed back into the bus.

'What was that all about?'

'Don't ask me,' Petra yawned and sat on the front seat tossing Sahar's bag carelessly next to her. 'They all have issues of one sort or another. Do you have kids, Mick?'

'Two. Girls. You're right. There's always something going on with them. How about you?'

'No, I just teach them. That's quite enough for me,' Petra was focused on Sahar's bag next to her on the seat; how was she supposed to search with Mick sitting two feet away?

'You know, I'd really love a coffee,' Petra said. 'Do you know anywhere round here we could get one? I'm happy to stay here if you go. My shout, Mick.'

'Oh, we don't have to go to all that trouble,' Mick reached under his seat and took out a box. 'My wife says I'm a proper boy scout.' He took out a flask and a cup.

'She's right,' Petra said. 'I bet you've even got some biscuits.'

'Hobnobs,' Mick said with pride.

'My favourite. I'll just pop to the loo and wash my hands.'

Petra was still holding on to Sahar's bag ready to take it with her. She stepped out of the minibus.

'Isn't that the little girl's bag?' Mick called after her, 'The one who was making all that fuss about leaving it behind?'

Petra looked down at the bag. 'So it is – I forgot I was holding it.'

'It'll be all right with me,' Mick said.

Petra had no choice; it would have aroused his suspicions if she'd insisted on taking it. She picked up her own bag.

In the toilet Petra stooped down and loosened the shoelaces of one of her high-top trainers and slipped the nail scissors from her make-up bag into her back pocket. Emerging from the boathouse into the sunshine, conscious of Mick watching her in his side windows, she approached the minibus from the rear. Just when she was abreast of the rear tyre she knelt on the ground to tie her shoelace. But before she stood up, she slid her hand into her back pocket and neatly knifed the tyre near the hubcap where a tear wouldn't be immediately visible. Standing up Petra slid the scissors into her jeans and ambled towards the door of the minibus.

Mick had poured out the coffees and laid the biscuits out on a piece of kitchen towel.

'Mick, I'm no car mechanic but...'

'What?'

'Could be nothing, probably is nothing but I think your rear left tyre looks a little flat...'

'Shouldn't be. I check them before every outing; religious like, it's what I learnt to do when I did my HGV course. It takes five minutes and can save a lot of grief.'

'I'm sure you're right,' Petra said.

'But it's a good idea to check,' he hauled himself up and using the handle to steady himself, climbed down from the bus. Petra followed Mick round to the back of the bus where he was leaning over the tyre.

'That's funny' he said. 'You're right, it does look a bit flat.'

'We can't have a flat tyre on the way back to the school. Deanna will go nuts. She says it's just the sort of thing that upsets the parents and it'll be my fault.'

'And mine.' With one hand Mick squeezed his jowls together. 'You stay here and wait for the kids. I'll go to a KwikFit and get it sorted. It'll be faster than calling out a garage.'

'What about the bags? You can't take the bags, Mick, not if you're going to a garage. Or at least you can't take the bag that belongs to my over-anxious student. She'll be hysterical if she comes back and it's not here.'

'You're right. You'd better keep it with you.'

Petra had barely alighted from the minibus when it was moving off. Striding back to the toilets Petra grabbed a handful of paper towels from the dispenser and locked herself into the cubicle. There, she lay the paper towels on the floor to make a mat and tipped the contents of the bag on to it. Out tumbled a notebook; two pens; a roll of sweets; lip balm; a purse.

As she looked at the objects on the grey paper towels, one of Alon's phrases came to mind; vinyl tradecraft he called it. Chalk; paper; invisible ink and public phone boxes.

Petra did the search as he'd taught her on a tray in her sitting room. He'd smoke as he sat watching her, eyes narrowed as he glanced down at the timer to see how quickly and efficiently she could find what was hidden, and then make assumptions about what she was examining.

First she examined the pens to see if they were what they seemed to be or whether they had any other function. She twisted and twiddled, held the pen up to the skylight looking for scratches and tapped the barrel. Nothing. After that she unwrapped the sweets, carefully unpeeling the paper at the top. Crouched in the toilet cubicle, her hands started to get sweaty and she glanced at her watch. She needed to get a spurt on; they would be back in fifteen minutes.

There was nothing in the sweet packet. By the time she'd ripped the tube of mints apart there was no way she could get them back again so she had no choice but to bin them in the sanitary towel container and hope for the best.

The lip balm was what it appeared to be, as was the purse that only contained UK money. There was no photo, no credit card and nothing personal in it all. If ever there was proof of guilty intent, it was the identity-free purse. Next, Petra leafed through the red workbook; she saw pages of Arabic, beautiful script that she couldn't read. She also saw pages of verbs in columns with presumably the Arabic translation. There was nothing there. Deflated, Petra slid back on her heels against the wall of the cubicle. The whole hassle of getting rid of Mick had been for nothing.

Petra lifted the empty rucksack up and shook it; she pressed it on the outside; down the seams; she felt inside; eyes closed; her finger tips examined each section of the lining as she'd been taught. The lining was true at the bottom; at the front; at the side... but... not at the back. The edge was slightly raised; it had some texture. With care, as if she was peeling back a grape skin, Petra lifted a corner of the lining and stuck her finger inside. She felt paper. A sheet of folded paper.

As she eased out the sheet, Petra was aware of her heart hammering. It was a good feeling: she'd been right.

But when she unfolded the sheet of paper her exhilaration ceased; on the paper was a hand-drawn diagram; or maybe it was a map. The drawing was annotated in what looked like Arabic and it was certainly Sahar's handwriting. That was as much as Petra could work out. Again, she looked at her watch; laying the paper out flat, Petra photographed it with her phone. Then quickly and efficiently, Petra repacked the bag, slid the paper into its hiding place and exited the toilets and the boathouse at a trot.

Only when Petra was sitting by the side of the river with her feet tucked under her did her heart rate slow. Inhaling deeply and slowly, Petra willed herself into a place of calm thought. She focused on the murky green water, a plastic bottle trapped in some weeds on the bank and a dragonfly dying moment by moment.

Petra heard the punts approaching before she saw them: Aneeta's laugh; some splashing; the hollow sound of the oar against the punt and shouts of warning. But it was all good-natured; they weren't shouts of fear and terror or pain. Turning towards the boathouse, Petra saw that Mick had completed the round trip and the minibus was in position to pick up the students.

Petra stood up to greet the arriving punts, but before they arrived she pulled out her phone and texted Rafi.

Call me. 1 hour.

52

The Ironworkers Pub, Cowley, Oxfordshire – The Next Day

'It's a map,' Petra said. 'It can't be anything else. It's a map that she's drawn because it's in her writing. It's a map of somewhere she's going to go. And there's a clandestine element to it because she hid it.'

She was sitting in a pub on the outskirts of Oxford with Benny and Rafi. It was off the student and tourist beat, closer to the old manufacturing side of Oxford where cars and light industry were the other side of the city's prosperity. Long gone, the area was ripe for re-generation.

At 3pm in the afternoon the pub was between-times; in the dismal zone between the pensioner lunchers who'd consumed sad salads and the after-work drinkers yet to come. Their only witness was a solitary drunk woman perched on a bar stool, fist around a glass of whisky.

Rafi said, 'We've forwarded the images to headquarters and our analysts are already on it.'

'So, you have absolutely no idea what it is?' Petra said.

Rafi shook his head.

'Well, I'll tell you what I think needs to be done. Since she's here in the UK, we bypass your analysts in Tel Aviv and call the police.' Petra said. 'I can do that; you don't have to be involved. And then let them deal with it and also deal with her.'

'No, no,' Benny said. 'That won't work. That won't work at all. We will do it but we have to go through official channels.'

'Why?'

Petra watched Benny with the detachment of a scientist. This was his chance to explain why he had met Sahar in Bath; his opportunity to get her to trust them again and she wondered in the most dispassionate manner if he would.

'Because that's how it's done, Petra. There are diplomatic issues here that I can't explain at the moment, but that's how it's done.'

She said nothing, deliberately waiting for him to fill the silence. He did. 'And, the other element to consider is that if we inform the authorities then we can't keep you out of it.'

'Out of what? I'm working the gig under my own name. I am within my rights as a British citizen; no, I am impelled as a British citizen to phone the police and say I am concerned about a student.'

Rafi's brow creased into lines of sincerity. 'Petra, you have to trust us; we are on top of this. We will make sure that the people who need to know do know, at the right time. You have my word on that.'

Petra was laying out red carpet for them; all they had to do was walk up it and she'd be applauding them. She gave the men one final opportunity to do the right thing; it was more than they deserved but she was being generous. 'So what about that guy in Bath I saw her meeting? Did you get any further with that?'

Benny said, 'Rafi, why don't you see if there's a decent bottle of wine in this establishment.'

Rafi got up from the table and ambled towards the bar where a dull-looking blonde with a tattoo dancing down her right arm was drying glasses. When she saw Rafi approach she tucked away her cloth and leaned across the burnished bar.

'You've done a terrific job, Petra,' Benny said. 'When you followed the girl in Bath, that gave us valuable information. You are right, she is involved in something but if you raise the alarm at a low level, then we won't get to the people who are behind her. Such as her brother.'

'Her brother, you say?'

'Yes, him. And that's the objective we want to achieve. That's the objective that will make a difference and save lives. So, hard though it is, what we want you to do is... nothing. Carry on, observe her, and finish the job here. That's all you have to do. You have one more cultural excursion to do, then there's the graduation party and that's it.'

'Benny, or whatever your name is, I'm a reasonable person. Honourable, trustworthy, the kind of woman who tries to do right even in a dirty job like this. But I have limited patience with insincerity.'

Petra felt the tension in the pit of her stomach, she raised her finger in warning and went on, 'Would it surprise you to hear that the girl is planning to be a martyr; and that's the reason why she's in the UK. Be very careful how you answer, I'm warning you.'

'What makes you say that?' Benny said.

'You didn't answer my question,' Petra said with gentle reason. 'Are you surprised to hear that the girl is planning to be a martyr; I believe the correct term is *shaheeda*?'

If she'd needed any further confirmation on what she knew to be true, Benny's determined shrug of dismissal, shaking head and frown was it.

'Shame on you,' Petra said.

'How about this?' Rafi was standing over the table holding a tray with a bottle of champagne and three glasses. 'Marianne says this is the best in the house. Shall we try it?'

'Sit down,' Benny said without looking up. He kept his grey-eyed gaze on Petra. 'Did Sahar tell you?'

Petra chuckled. 'No, she's right under your thumb. I made no headway with her; she'll do whatever you tell her to do and thank you for it. No, she didn't tell me that she's hoping to commit suicide for whatever half-baked reason she's been fed; she didn't say that this miserable act of self-destruction is the best future she can hope for. And she didn't tell me that she believes her death will help liberate her people. Her brother did.'

53

The Ironworkers Pub, Cowley, Oxfordshire – Continuous

'I said she was smart,' Rafi said pouring out the foaming champagne into flutes as if Petra had just announced successfully completing a crossword puzzle.

'*Sheket*,' Benny said. 'Shut up. Have you spoken to the girl's brother? Did you meet him when you brought her to London? This is all much more complicated than you realise, you know. I'm telling you for your own good because there are a lot of other interests that you don't know about.'

'Don't threaten me, don't even obliquely threaten me,' Petra said. 'You had your chance to come clean when I saw you in Bath and I gave you another chance just now and you blew it. So whatever you say, including your crappy attempts to scare me have about as much currency as a politician's promise. You want to know if I've spoken to the girl's brother? As a matter of fact I have, at length. What's more he's not in Kansas attending lectures and hanging out on the campus – he's here.'

'What have you done?' Benny covered his face with his hands.

'Let's all calm down,' Rafi said. 'Let's hear what Petra has to say. I'm sure she had her reasons for doing what she did and if we'd just shown her a little more respect by giving her the bigger picture this would never have happened.'

'Need to know,' Benny said.

'Need to share,' Rafi responded. 'Petra, let's start at the beginning – where is Wasim at the moment and how did he get there?'

Petra was impressed by Rafi's equanimity. Not that she trusted him an iota but it made it easier to have a dialogue. Briefly she described how she had used a tracking device to locate Wasim and how she found him at Heathrow, eating a burger before he went through security. She'd barely needed the tracking device, he was so much like his sister; the same slight build, wiry hair and worried expression. Petra had slipped Wasim a ready prepared note that used the special name Sahar had for her brother; the note said he was to trust Petra and go with her.

'What's this special name she has for him?' Benny said.

'Do you really think I'm going to tell you?' Petra said.

'It was worth asking.'

'Fuck you. He's now safe,' Petra said.

'How do you know that? MI5 could be all over him and he could be picked up at any time,' Benny said.

'I know he's safe because I'm good at what I do.' No more details. She would give them no more information that might help them find Wasim. He was safe. Her neighbour Bob had said he'd do anything for her after she saved his grandson and Petra had taken him up on the offer. Wasim was staying in one of Bob's empty flats after she told him that one of her students had missed his flight and was nervous about immigration controls. The bastards had absolutely no hope of finding Wasim; the kid was safe.

Flow is what it was. Petra recognised that making contact with Wasim and getting him to safety was one of the few times in her life and career when she'd been entirely in the moment and supremely confident about both her abilities and her understanding. The sensation was neither cognitive nor rational; it was a sense of flow, a sense of glowing confidence and clarity as she'd glided into Terminal 3 at Heathrow.

Knowing that she'd outsmarted the bastards, Petra was in no doubt that not only would she find Wasim at Heathrow but that she'd be able to use him to save Sahar from both the Office's dirty operation and the girl's own naivety.

Once inside the terminal Petra had made an easy 180-degree sweep of her surroundings; she had the look of someone searching for check-in; drop-off; departure board or travelling companion. Meanwhile, she scoped space, cameras, police – both uniformed and plain clothes – as well as entrances and exit. Her observational senses had tingled while around her people moved in fits and starts, burst towards gates, stumbled over luggage and shifted around her island of calm acuity.

Petra had been in no hurry; by her feet there was a small black suitcase on four wheels and in her hand she'd held her phone and watched Wasim's tracker's approach, its green throbbing pulse signalling the steady advance to its ultimate rendezvous.

At 250 metres away, the airport bus would be close to the terminal and there was no doubt he was on the bus because Petra had overtaken it on the M40; she'd even glimpsed the boy. In his window seat, he'd been gazing out, looking at the traffic flow, consumed with whatever thoughts he might have about his journey back to Kansas.

Yes, Wasim was hers as certainly as the sun would set and darkness would follow.

Positioning herself to the right of the door nearest to the coach drop off, Petra had placed the case by her side and using the long handle slid it around on the four wheels. Satisfied, Petra had taken a seed bar out of her pocket and munched on it with deliberation; she was a passenger waiting to meet a friend. She checked her phone as if looking for a message; she was a passenger waiting to meet a friend. No one would think otherwise.

One hundred and fifty metres now. He was close. The bus must be pulling up into the parking bay and Wasim would climb down. Petra was ready. If he had luggage there would be a delay of four minutes and the green pulse on her phone would rest.

One hundred metres. There was obviously no luggage. Petra had felt for the handle on her case rolling it back and forth, testing its range, feeling the hard flooring and the shiver of excitement in her hands.

Fifty metres. Petra had felt in her pocket for the note she'd prepared; the evidence to give her credence; the proof that she was friend and not foe. Glancing at her phone again, she'd seen the green dot flashing; the boy was drawing closer.

Twenty metres, he was walking towards the door.

Just then a family from the Indian subcontinent came through the door. A winsome toddler perched on a suitcase on top of a trolley; behind, a white-haired matriarch was pushed in her wheelchair; two young men hauled oversized suitcases with their wives following on, burdened with carry-on bags and neck cushions and a baby in carrycot. They were crowding the entrance, blocking Petra's view, they could kill her plan. Yet they wouldn't; Petra had been certain.

Ten metres. The family had passed. Wasim came through the door and Petra inhaled deeply with satisfaction. Even without the tracker, she'd have known him for his resemblance to Sahar, he was darker but had the same slight build and air of intensity; the same fine eyes, albeit behind glasses and the same unruly hair.

He was alone, the space between them was empty; he was hers. Petra took a step forward and seemed, if she'd been observed, to have slipped. The suitcase left her hand and slammed into Wasim's legs then it careened at an angle and hit the floor where the weakened lock burst open and clothes and shoes and books tumbled out.

'I am so sorry,' Petra blocked his progress.

Wasim had stumbled and almost lost his balance; stability regained he shifted from leg to leg, unsure for a moment and then he knelt to help Petra stuff jeans and jumpers back into the case.

'Thank you so much, I'm such an idiot,' Petra said. 'This is incredibly kind of you, I'm totally embarrassed.'

'You're welcome, ma'am,' she heard the American twang in his accent.

Now close to Wasim, close enough to see his nascent beard, Petra reached into her pocket and slipped the note towards the boy. She dropped her dizzy passenger in distress voice. 'Men's room is on the first floor. Read this in private, okay? I'll be in the car park, second floor, bay 22. I'll wait here; you can trust me, Wasim Nadir.'

She'd looked into his eyes and gave him a long steady gaze. He was hers; of course he followed her to the car park and the safety of Bob's flat.

Sipping her champagne Petra smiled at Rafi and Benny.

'Like I said, the boy's safe and I'm listening.'

Rafi said, 'Benny, do you want to explain our side of the story?'

'Not particularly, but since we have no choice, I will. Sahar may think she's going to be a martyr to her cause and make a difference but she's completely wrong. Before there's the slightest chance of this happening, she will be stopped and a grateful British government will reward us with a specific piece of intelligence that they are withholding. It's as simple as that; that's what this entire operation is about. And for what it's worth, Petra, I am appalled that you would think for one single moment that we, Mossad, Israel, Jews, would actually let this happen. Truly. Life is sacred to us. All life. Why do you think we take soldiers up to Masada when they pass out of the army? You know what happened there – the biggest mass suicide in the Bible based on historical fact. We go there to remember that this must never, ever happen again. Because suicide is an aberration, an obscenity, it's a sickness, a terrible, terrible sickness. And to use suicide for political gain is perverse.'

There was silence at the table and Petra had the sense that Benny was talking about something else. Or somebody else. For that moment, he wasn't with them. Then he seemed to become aware and reacquainted with the conversation.

He smiled weakly, 'You see, Wasim isn't going to lose his precious big sister, everything is going to be just fine.'

Petra said nothing as she tried to absorb what Benny had just said; even though it was an astonishing idea for an operation, what Benny said had the ring of truth.

He said, 'I presume you didn't tell him we were involved.'

'You presume correct. It would have only terrified him and he's scared enough as it is.'

'Where is he?' Rafi said.

'I told you, he's safe. And now I want to know more. How does this all work?'

'I can't give you all the details, I'm not going to,' Benny said. 'Not without someone else signing off on this; there's too much at stake and I simply don't have that authority. What I will say is that when the girl's arrested you'll be interviewed by MI5 which is the other reason we wanted you at the school under your real name; a fake story wouldn't have stood up for ten minutes. And also, to be fair on us, that's why we kept you in the dark – we were trying to protect you.'

'Thanks a lot. What about her? Trial? Prison?'

'Don't get sentimental about her,' Rafi said. 'She's a tool; she may not know her part in all this but she was ready to kill innocent people. Don't forget that.'

Benny broke in, 'And if she knew you were a Jew all her hate education would kick in. She gets out of this okay. This is the UK. There will be no trial and no conviction. We will request her extradition on the grounds that we need to source her contacts and then will be in a position to secure her future, a much better future than she could ever have hoped for if she hadn't been unwittingly involved in this operation.'

Petra folded her arms and studied him, he seemed genuine; yes, she was pretty sure that he was genuine. For want of a better word, he had that smell; that special, impossible to define smell that he believed what he was saying.

'I really need to think about this,' Petra said. 'And you need to get authorisation to give me the rest of the details about location and timing that will prove to me that you aren't lying. Can you do that by tomorrow?'

'No, I need a couple of days to get this signed off at quite a high level,' Benny said.

Petra thought about the week ahead, 'I've got to take the students on a cultural excursion on Friday, so let's meet Sunday or Monday.'

'Okay.'

'Where's the boy?' Rafi said.

'Safe. I told you, how many times do you want me to repeat what I said? And understand this, I told him I would bring his sister to him safely and that's exactly what I'm going to do.'

Eli and Rafi dropped off Petra at the bottom of the school's drive and watched her walk through the security gates into the grounds of the school. Before she disappeared, Eli watched her in his wing mirror. She was talking to the security man at the gate, exchanging some pleasantry and the man was laughing.

'Given the circumstances, that went okay,' Rafi said.

'You think so?' Eli flicked on the ignition and moved away from the parking spot. 'I think this whole thing is falling down around our ears.'

'Well, by Sunday it will all be over,' Rafi said. 'Problem solved.'

'I hope you're right,' Eli drove in silence for a while. 'It's too bad you didn't stay over. Take Trainer out for dinner or something, find out what she really thinks, what she's going to do. Find out where the boy is.'

'I thought she made that pretty clear,' Rafi said. 'Don't worry, Eli, it will all be fine, I'm certain of it. This time next week we'll be back home; the heroes of the hour.'

Eli didn't respond. He drove into a petrol station and up to a vacant pump. Once outside he started to fill the car. A dribble of petrol went down the side; it glistened in the evening light, it smelt sharp to his nostrils, reminded him of petrol fires on the West Bank and kids throwing home-made Molotov bombs. It was all so incendiary, and filling the car with fuel made him think about throwing petrol on the flames of his paranoia. Even though Rafi was saying that everything would be fine, Eli wasn't convinced. It wasn't that he was superstitious but sometimes operations were dogged with bad luck. Or maybe he was simply losing his confidence and Rafi was right; everything would sort itself out and he would emerge from the operation as the man most likely to take over London station.

54

The Israeli Embassy, Palace Gardens, London – The Next Day

For the final preparations of Sweetbait the safe room at the embassy was busy. Yuval led the briefings, witnessed by the government minister and the deputy ambassador who were also in the room as they would be in the front line of the media. Mia, the government minister, was a former regional director of the organisation; she'd left to go into politics and retained a fondness for the old team. Yossi, the deputy ambassador, was a different matter; the ferret-faced suit was the ambassador's hatchet man. Formerly known as Joe Rappaport, he was a British businessman who had made *aliyah*, some said, for the tax benefits. Two seats down from Eli, he looked upon the proceedings with apparent disdain. Or maybe he simply didn't understand the Byzantine workings of the operation. Whatever his problem was, he looked like he'd rather be somewhere else. Anywhere else.

Rafi and Eli sat either side of Yuval at the top of the table. In front of them was a spread of coffee, water, sandwiches and fruit to fuel the meeting. It hadn't been Yuval's choice but it was in deference to the bigwigs who were used to kinder care on the diplomatic circuit than Yuval's tent in the desert approach.

On one side of the room the screens showed a series of images: Sweetbait herself, the diagram of the operation location and the order of events including fall-back plans. Contact details had been circulated and by noon everybody knew what they needed to know.

'This is all very well,' Yossi sighed as if in pain, 'but the ambassador needs an assurance that there will be no more episodes such as the incident in the visa section.'

'That was something entirely different,' Eli said. 'Regretable, but an isolated incident.'

'The ambassador does not want to have to face media pressure because of any more *regrettable* incidents. The affair of the passports left in the phone box is still very fresh in the public's consciousness and handicaps our diplomatic initiatives. Yet another *regrettable* incident would be supremely embarrassing for the ambassador.'

'Yossi, we are not here to mull over the past; this is a pre-op briefing,' Yuval said. 'We can discuss this later. The purpose of the briefing is to make sure that everyone knows what to do and when to do it thus minimising the possibility of error.'

Yossi looked as if a lemon had been shoved down his throat but at least he shut up.

'Thank you, Yuval,' Mia filled the gap; she smoothed down her skirt before she stood up. 'This all seems clear. I'll report back to the prime minister that we are in safe hands and that while, as I know, outcomes are sometimes subject to change, we have all signed off on the operation.'

She came around the table and held out her hand to Yuval, 'On behalf of the prime minister's office, good luck and God go with you.'

The room slowly emptied leaving Eli alone with Rafi and Yuval.

'Besides Yossi's flounce, that went okay,' Rafi said. 'It's great having Mia in our camp.'

'She's a politician,' Yuval said. 'Always has been, very good at backing the winning team and better at not being around when the shit flies. So be warned, she'll only be in our camp as long as it suits her.'

He got up from the table and helped himself to one of the sandwiches that were by now curling at the edges. He took a mouthful and continued talking.

'We've still got a couple of loose threads. Where are we with Trainer?'

'I spoke to her this morning and arranged to meet on Sunday when it's all over,' Rafi said. 'It will be a simple matter of diverting her at the operation location. She'll tell us where the brother is when she realises it's too late. She's not stupid; she knows she's going to have MI5 on her arse so her only hope of helping the brother is to stay away from him. She'll have to trust us.'

'Are you sure about that?' Yuval said.

'I can be very persuasive,' Rafi said.

'I suppose that's as good as it could be,' Yuval brushed his fringe away from his forehead. 'So that just leaves Sweetbait. Do you need to see her again, Eli? Ask her why she gave her brother a tracking device and while you're at it, you can ask why she drew a copy of the fucking map for Trainer to find.'

Eli put down his water bottle and did up the cap. 'Yuval, I know why she made the map. She's a worrier; she didn't want to make mistakes. Of course, I told Sweetbait to memorise the location and not write it down but she's anxious; that's part of her personality.'

Yuval leaned back in his chair and used both hands to brush his hair off his forehead. 'Okay, here's what we're going to do over the next twenty-four hours. I am going to make nice with Mia, take her out for dinner, probably with that miserable Yossi; make sure that we are in good odour with the prime minister's office. Rafi is going to have a meeting with our friends at MI6; he needs to tell Milne that we have a location so he can pass on the information to MI5. We want to make sure that all the wheels are oiled for tomorrow, and that they have people in place to arrest Sweetbait.'

Eli said, 'I thought I was talking to Milne.'

'You'll see him afterwards; after the girl's arrested. Rafi is quite capable of passing on the details. What I want you to do, Eli, is to go to Oxford and try to see Sweetbait again. Just to make sure everything is okay and she doesn't run off with Trainer. Okay? Take the surveillance teams, stay over in the area tonight and meet at the operational location. Consider it checking our equipment before the op.'

'Speaking of equipment, what about the belt?' Rafi said. 'Eli can't keep it overnight in some hotel near the oploc.'

'*Lama lo?*' Eli said. 'Why not? I'll have the surveillance team with me. They can sit up all night and look at it.'

Rafi stood up, stretched across the table and poured some hot water on to his green tea bag. 'It's not secure. That's why. Let's leave as little to chance as possible. I can check it out of the armoury at dawn and drive up.'

'Okay,' Yuval said. 'I'll make sure that you have access. I want all equipment – human or otherwise – checked and rechecked and rechecked. We leave as little to chance as possible.'

Yuval stood up and shrugged himself into his crushed linen jacket. He felt in the patch pockets and jiggled some change.

'Next time I see you both it will all be over. Be lucky and be safe.'

55

Watlingford Public School, Oxfordshire – The Next Day

Dearest brother, dearest Wasim, I'm ready. I prayed through the night, watched night turn to dawn and this morning I'll fast. I'm at peace and in a state of grace. Any regrets are now gone, like chaff before the wind. I promise you, there's no sorrow. I feel only joy because I know that when the time comes, I'll be comforted in the arms of Allah. And later, all the people that I love, all the people I'll miss will be among the seventy chosen ones who will join me in the afterlife.

I've been racking my brains trying to work out how to give you this notebook because I can't tell Abu Marwan that I've been keeping a diary. I'm going to give it to Petra to give to you. I really trust her. She's the teacher who drove me to London when we met; she gave me the commemoration coin that I gave you. I know you'll like her.

I've got one small regret, brother. Something I can admit to you. I really wish that I could include two non-believers among the seventy: Aneeta and Petra. When I see the angel I'll ask to put them on the list in the hope that at some point they will be guided towards Allah and we can all be together again.

I'm sitting at my desk in this room, my last home on my last morning, writing in my notebook to you. Quite soon I'll go down to the study block where I'll join my fellow students for the last lesson before we go on the cultural excursion. That's where I'll meet Abu Marwan, my commander. This is where he'll give me the belt, I'll say the *Shahada*. Then I'll be ready. I'll detonate the belt and my soul will be carried aloft by the sacred birds.

I'm scared, Wasim. I'm scared of the pain before the end, but I'm not going to think of that.

Yesterday evening I was blessed with a wonderful surprise. I was not expecting to see Abu Marwan; that's what he said the last time I saw him. But then I got a text from him to say that he was waiting for me in the kitchen garden and I had five precious minutes with him. During that time he blessed me and he gave me some beautiful amber prayer beads; he told me what I must do; he repeated the instructions – as if he needed to. I've rehearsed them over and over again. Recited them like the *Fatihah*, five times a day. I've studied the map of the location, learned where every single building is, until I can draw it with my left hand.

Abu Marwan told me something else; he warned me. He said that if anyone approaches me and tells me not to go ahead, even if it's someone that I know and trust, it would be a representative of the devil. He said that sometimes *Shaytan* tempts martyrs in their last moments. He said that *Shaytan* might appear in many forms to stop me from my mission. 'Be warned,' Abu Marwan said, 'be alert.' The devil likes to play on the *shaheeda*'s fears during the last hours but only by ignoring the devil will I achieve martyrdom. Only by spurning fear will I make a difference. Only by shunning doubt will I strike a blow against the Zionist monkeys and in some small way help the fight forward.

Dearest brother, I am truly happy. I am blessed. *Allah Akbar*.

56

Watlingford Public School, Oxfordshire – The Same Day

With Wasim safe in Bob's empty flat, there was nothing for Petra to do until Sunday. Then she'd meet Rafi and Benny and find out about the operational location so she could negotiate safe passage for Sahar out of this situation, whether the girl liked it or not. Wasim was the key and Petra was certain that the threat of full disclosure to the British authorities would secure a neat solution to the problem. But it was a threat she would only carry out as a very last resort because for sure, MI6 would be as self-serving as any other intelligence service; that's just the way it was.

Today Mick's minibus was picking the group up at 12pm to take them to the Air Tattoo at RAF Fairborough. It wasn't a cultural event; there was no English language, literature or historical aspect to it; however, it fitted the brief because they'd received free tickets – Deanna's husband Rod had done some PR for one of the aviation companies.

'Rod has to meet with the clients,' Deanna said. 'So we won't be travelling with you and the students on the minibus.'

'That's fine,' Petra said.

'Let me know if there are any problems, but we go every year and the students seem to absolutely love it.'

By 11.50, Petra was in the café rounding up the kids who were still lingering.

'Come on,' Petra said. 'Don't you want to go and see the Red Arrows? It's very exciting. And we're not going to wait.'

The students gathered up their bags and headed for the door but at one table for two there was no movement. Both Aneeta and Sergei had long faces; it looked as if they'd had a row.

Lingering by their table, Petra affected a breezy manner, 'If you two don't want to go...'

In answer Aneeta stood up and stalked past Petra to the door. 'I go. I care not if he goes.'

Sergei flushed, got slowly to his feet and lumbered after her out of the café.

The last person in the café was Sahar who had been sitting alone sipping a plastic cup of water. She was fingering some amber beads. As Petra approached she packed them away. Neatly. With gentle fingers. Sahar placed the beads in a green velvet bag, zipped it up and tucked it in her rucksack. Petra went towards the girl, 'Ready?'

'I am,' Sahar smiled at Petra.

Together they walked out of the café and into the corridor that led to the exit.

'Do you know what's going on with Aneeta and Sergei?' Petra said. 'Have they had some sort of fight?'

'A small one, I think. Aneeta wants Sergei to come to Spain with her when the course is finished but Sergei's father is in London.'

'It doesn't seem like a big problem, is it?' Petra said.

'I think Sergei is worried that his father may not like Aneeta.'

'How could anyone not like Aneeta?'

'Yes. That is true,' Sahar said. 'Petra, may I ask you a favour?'

'Of course,'

'I am not taking my bag today, it is heavy, but I have my writing book with me with all my work. Will you take it and look after it?'

'Sure, I'll keep it safe.'

Petra held out her hand for the dusky pink notebook, there were loose sheets and a post card of London slipped out. She picked it up from the floor and put the book in her shoulder bag.

'Okay?'

'Yes,' Sahar said. 'Okay.'

Outside the front door of the school the bus door was open, Mick was at the wheel and the rest of the class were already in their seats. Petra guided Sahar to go in front of her then climbed aboard.

Standing in the aisle she counted the students. Aneeta was sitting with Sahar leaving Sergei on his own concentrating on his phone and avoiding contact. The bus started to move off.

'Seat belts, please,' Petra said. From the bag on her seat, Petra pulled out the promotional material that went with the tickets and handed them around. There were folders for each of the students with their passes on lanyards, information about the various events at the Tattoo, the programme and a map.

Ignoring her own seat belt directive, Petra knelt on the seat looking at the students over the top of the headrest.

'Has everyone got a pack?' Petra said. They nodded. 'You need the pack to get in and you need your pass which you have to wear at all times. It's got your photograph on so check it. When we get there Mick will drop us off at one of the gates. It is VERY important that you remember which gate it is because that's the gate where we will leave from. There are thousands of people there; if you get lost, find the information tent or text me. Okay?'

There were more nods, although Aneeta was whispering to Sahar and no doubt telling her what the row was about.

'Aneeta, please. Just give me five minutes. Could everyone check that you have your passes and maps. And my mobile number.'

There was a rustle while the students went through the process that they'd carried out on each cultural excursion giving it about the same attention as frequent flyer air passengers give to safety instructions. While they were leafing through the plastic folders Petra took out her own pass and put the lanyard around her head.

'Has everyone checked?' Petra said. There were more nods. 'Then enjoy the rest of the journey.'

Petra turned around and slumped down on the seat. As soon as she got to the Tattoo she would find the nearest café and grab some thinking time. Having laid out her cards on the table and admitted that she had Wasim in a safe place – risky enough in itself – Petra had to keep him that way. That meant second guessing and third guessing in this human chess game, anticipating the moves that her opponents might make. It was lowering to consider that Benny and Rafi were opponents but that's how it was.

To locate a café quickly Petra slid the map out of the plastic folder and opened it out on her lap.

The image jumped out at her; it blurred and then came back into focus. She was gaping at a full-colour version of the drawing she'd found in Sahar's bag.

It took Petra a full minute to calm her breathing to the point where she could think rationally. In an almost detached way she noticed that her right hand – the hand that held the map – was trembling. She used her left hand to still the tremor.

'Christ,' Petra said aloud.

They were at traffic lights and Mick turned and smiled at her.

'Everything okay?'

'Yes,' Petra said. Her voice was tight and didn't invite further conversation. Disappointed, Mick turned back to the road.

If Sahar had hidden in her bag a hand-drawn map of the Tattoo grounds then the location must have significance for her. Either she was meeting someone there or worse.

'Operations do not always run smoothly. In fact they rarely do and you will have to be quick thinking and adaptable to changes in the situation.' That's what Alon had told her; he liked to quote Von Clausewitz and talk about war. He preferred to sit in her flat where he could smoke. Over endless cups of tea and coffee, Alon would smoke cigarette after cigarette; narrowing his eyes; waving the smoke away and coughing – even then.

'If there is a problem, you need to think slow and act fast,' Alon said. 'Use waiting time to analyse the situation and work out your tactics.'

Petra felt dizzy for a few seconds; around her there was the chatter and laughter of the students and she was desperate to tell them to shut up so she could think.

Then she saw it – as clearly as a plunge in icy water. No wonder the bastards were happy to agree to a meeting on Sunday; all that crap about getting higher authority to sign off; citing organisational bureaucracy. Sahar was going to be arrested at the Tattoo and once that happened there wasn't much Petra could do.

Petra cast her mind back to Bath; Sahar guided along the street by Benny – carrying a sports bag. A sports bag. Any equipment she might use would be in the bag. That was it. Petra felt the logic of her conclusion in a sense of horrified satisfaction that was visceral.

If they'd deliberately duped Petra about the time and location of this operation, there was no reason to believe that they weren't going to let the girl blow herself up. And how likely was it that Petra would be allowed to roam free with that information, Jew or no Jew. She wouldn't be the first whistle-blower who'd disappeared, and for all Benny's assurances events could escalate out of his control. What had she done?

Petra took out her mobile phone and held it in her hand. Her finger hovered over the keys trying to work out her next step.

The police? Forget it. She was in too deep with Wasim stashed away.

Through the front of the minibus she had a clear view of the road ahead. The steady progression down the dual carriageway had changed as they joined other cars and transport heading to the airfield.

'How far away are we, Mick?' Petra called over the chugging of the diesel engine.

He looked at the satnav, 'Another five minutes and we should be there.'

'Thanks.'

Five minutes. Not much time to think.

57

RAF Fairborough, Oxfordshire – Ten Minutes Later

Eli tucked the microphone into his ear and tried to shift it into a more comfortable position. Satisfied that its location was about as good as it could be he got out of the car and started to set up the picnic table on the grassy field that was being used for parking. Nearby, Segev and his crew, dressed for the occasion in cut-offs, tee shirts and open sandals, unloaded a picnic. There were plastic containers, a hamper, and a crate of beer. They looked like tourists. Once they'd unloaded and the trestle table was set up the squad lounged against the side of the car and seemed to be using their binoculars to look at the fly past overhead. There was nothing in their manner to suggest that they were anything other than a bunch of kids with their older relative – him – having a day out.

'Zero Seven,' Eli said into his tee shirt. 'We're in position, with a good view of the event. Copy.'

There was a crackle in his ear that made him want to take the microphone out but then the volume was adjusted and he heard clearly.

'Tango 28 copy. We have the other entrance.'

'Good. Any sign of Alpha Four.' That was Rafi's call sign. 'He has the product.'

'I'm here, Zero Seven,' Eli heard in his ear. 'I have the product.'

'Okay Alpha Four.'

Segev was nudging Eli. It might have looked as if he was offering him his binoculars to look at the fly past of the P149 American bi-plane that was overhead, but in fact he was pointing Eli towards the track at the main entrance. There, a minibus was being guided by the parking marshals into the section for larger vehicles.

'We have visual,' Eli said. '70621 coordinates. Heading that way now. Contact at 55209 coordinates. Go.'

Leaving one lad by the picnic table the surveillance team separated into two pairs and two singles and ambled in the direction of the minibus – as if their only interest was to get a good position to watch the next fly past and enjoy the day.

Having been there since the gates had opened, the team had scoped the best positions to survey the grounds. It was an almighty task as the event was spread over twenty-five acres.

The plan was for Sweetbait to separate as quickly as possible from the student group and make her way to the Vintage Village. There Eli would find her and take her to one of the exhibitors' caravans where she would be given the belt. Then she would walk towards the Techno Zone and long before she reached there she'd be stopped by primed MI5 and police officers.

Even though there was hardly any explosive in the belt and the detonator was set to malfunction Eli had planned the shortest possible distance between picking up the belt and being arrested.

Once Rafi had delivered the belt to the caravan, he was tasked with diverting Trainer if necessary to keep her away from the arrest.

The problems began the moment that Sahar stepped down from the minibus. She was supposed to get through the customer point and then walk along the main concourse on her own – trusting that she would be picked up by a contact who would be holding amber beads like her own.

But that wasn't happening.

From his vantage point standing on a ladder in the car park, Eli saw Petra take the girl's arm. She was talking to her intently. Another girl came up to the pair. Dark flowing hair. Animated, Petra seemed to be telling them what they were supposed to do. The dark girl went off leaving Trainer with Sweetbait.

'Has anyone got a fix on what they're saying?' Eli said into his mike.

There was a howl and boom of an overhead jet, then the crackle in his ear. 'We keep losing it, but Trainer is trying to persuade Sweet-bait to do something.'

58

RAF Fairborough, Oxfordshire – Five Minutes Later

'Sahar, I know why you are here. I know what you're planning and you have to trust me, you have to get out of here. Now.'

The girl's eyes opened so wide that they were bulging.

'I... I do not understand. Why, what are you saying this thing? I have to go. I must go.'

She turned and tried to move off. Petra grabbed the girl's forearm and was surprised how slight it was. There was nothing on her. No muscle, no fat; she was fragile, like a bird.

'I know that you met someone in Bath because I followed you. You must not trust him, Sahar. He doesn't want to help you. If you do what he says you will be in trouble – big trouble. Do you understand?'

'You followed me? You saw me with... Who are you? You are the one I cannot trust.'

She started muttering in Arabic. Petra couldn't understand what she was saying but the girl looked wild. Crazed. Like an animal who was trapped and needed to fight her way out.

'He told to me that you, someone like you would be... you come and you are not true. I know that. You are not true and it is wrong. I must go. You must go. I think you are my friend. I think you are good, but –'

'I am good. I am true, Sahar. I might not be a Moslem but I want to help and protect you. I understand that this is difficult but they have lied to you so that you do what they want. It is not to help your people. It is to help the Israelis.'

'The Israelis? I not believe – who are they? Who are *you*?'

'Later; now I have to get you out of here before the police get to you. You have to trust me, Sahar. I will protect you. Do you understand?'

The girl was crying and shaking. Petra put her hand on her shoulder to try to steady her. 'Listen to me, I promise I will look after you. Nothing bad will happen. But do not go with whatever the man called himself. If you see him, stay away. Okay? See that stall there, the one with the vintage hats – stay there for one minute. Where I can see you.'

Petra took two steps away from the shaking girl and took out her phone. She dialled, she waited. She called again, the phone was answered.

'Deanna, where are you? I need to borrow your car. There's been an accident and I need to get one of the students –'

'Which one?' Deanna said.

Petra could hear clinking glasses in the background. 'Sahar. Serious enough for the St John Ambulance people. Yeah, she's in the tent with them now. No, no, you don't need to come over.' Petra looked over at Sahar quivering by the vintage hat stand. The girl's face was grey with fear. Petra smiled at her as she continued talking to Deanna. 'If you tell me where you are I'll pick up your keys and get her out of here.'

Transport arranged Petra took Sahar's arm, 'I'm going to take you somewhere safe but we must go quickly. Come.'

Sahar took five steps, tripped and then seemed to buckle at the knee. 'I'm sorry, I... I cannot go fast. I am not good. I am sick.'

Petra looked her over, could she carry her? No. Drag her along, hardly. And if Sahar went slowly, at the pace her quivering limbs could manage, then the chances of being picked up by Benny and the gang were multiplied. Regrettably Petra had no choice; it would be faster to leave the girl and come back with the keys. Petra could run;

the girl couldn't and at the moment Sahar looked as if she would collapse to the ground.

Petra eased Sahar back towards the vintage hat stand and smiled down at the shaking girl. 'Don't worry, it's all arranged. I'm going to get some transport. Okay? You stay here, wait for me, keep out of sight at the back of the stall. I promise I'll protect you. Nothing bad will happen. Do you understand?'

'Yes... yes... I understand.'

The deep frown line splitting Sahar's brows softened, 'You are true. I know that you are true.'

59

RAF Fairborough, Oxfordshire – Three Minutes Later

'Zero Seven to Alpha Four. Trainer has left the perimeter. Tail her and detain her.'

'Alpha Four to Zero Seven,' Rafi said. 'Negative. I am just fixing the product.' He sounded preternaturally calm. 'One thing at a time, Zero Seven.'

'Alpha Four – it's daylight with Trainer.'

'What?' Rafi said. 'I can't leave this, really not... not even for a few minutes.'

'Understood.'

Eli walked across the decking that had been laid across the ground between the stalls. People were all over the place, right and left and straight ahead. Breaking into a jog, Eli realised how out of condition he was, but there was Sweetbait ahead of him; standing by a hat stand looking lost and out of place. Before he drew up to her Eli wiped the sweat off his face on his shirt and schooled his features into one of calm and reassurance. As if everything was normal and everything was going to proceed as planned.

'*Maha'ba, shaheeda,*' Eli said softly.

The girl was holding a green felt hat in her hands; she dropped it as if it was on fire.

'It is normal for martyrs to feel fear before *Shihada*,' Eli said. 'But the fears will go when we pray together. We have a sacred place set aside to do this. It will be my honour to lead you there.'

She looked panicked and confused to the point of being speechless.

'Allah, hear us, hear your humble servants,' Eli said. 'Most blessed *shaheeda*, I must ask, were you spared, or did the devil come to you?

How often that happens. How cunning are the forces against us. I wish I might have been here to face the devil by your side and we could have sent it on its way standing together.'

'She is... she is not; she said the people I will help are –'

'She? The devil in the form of a woman? Ah *habibti*, that is the cruellest form that *Iblis* can take. I see it now – maybe she was like a mother to you. Someone you thought you could trust, someone honourable and true. But they wouldn't be devils if they were not cunning, would they? Come, come with me; I will protect you. I am here now and I will stay by your side until the end; until the final moments. How blessed we are that today you will be taken aloft to the arms of Allah.'

60

RAF Fairborough, Oxfordshire – 11 Minutes Later

Petra found Deanna waiting for her outside the hospitality tent. She was chatting animatedly to a tall man. Hovering, Petra allowed Deanna to disentangle herself; aware that she was sweaty and dusty and stank from the run. After a few moments, Deanna gave her empty glass to the man and looking pleased with herself strolled over towards Petra.

'There's always one, every course, there's always one problem student,' Deanna said. 'Where is she?'

'I left her with the St John Ambulance people,' Petra said.

'What on earth happened? You said accident?'

'Not exactly accident. She had a panic attack when she heard the first supersonic boom from the F16 fighter plane display. Luckily St John Ambulance was right next to us but they can't prescribe. They just said the best thing would be to get her away from the Tattoo as quickly as possible.'

Deanna sighed, 'This is all very awkward, but on the other hand Rod won't feel like driving back after lunch so it might all be for the best. I'm sure I can shepherd the rest of them back on the minibus. Very well.' Deanna fished into her tiny bag and handed Petra the keys to the Mercedes Estate.

'Thanks,' Petra said. 'I'll get Sahar back to the school and make sure she's settled. If she is all right, then I can come back and get you and Rod.'

'That would be terribly kind,' Deanna said.

Now that Petra had the keys she was keen to get away but Deanna was expounding with the conviction of a drunk. She put her hand on Petra's forearm. 'The student must come first; that's what I promise the parents and that's what we deliver. And, Petra, we cannot complain; we've been so lucky with this group – no upsets, no drugs. One has to be so careful. I didn't tell you what happened when we checked the references of that other chap who applied for the job at the same time as you. Shocking, absolutely shocking. He was some sort of pervert.'

Petra looked overhead as a flight display trailed red smoke. 'I've got to get back to the St John tent.'

'I'm terribly grateful for your help Petra. Oh, Andrew, how lovely – you're spoiling me.'

Andrew, the man in tweed, had returned, not just with a glass but a bottle.

'Andrew, allow me to introduce you to Petra. She's my most trusted teacher, my secret weapon.'

'Delighted to meet you, shall I get another glass?'

'I'm afraid I'm on duty,' Petra said striding away.

Now, all she had to do was get the girl. It took Petra another seven minutes to reach the stalls where she'd left Sahar. The area was now crowded with shoppers so she was forced to slow her pace as she passed a stall selling NASA mugs and air force memorabilia from the Second World War. Next to it was a stand that only sold flying jackets. People were spilling out on to the space in between the stalls, trying on jackets, posing in front of a mirror, taking pictures. Petra pushed her way around them until she reached the end of the row; the retro hat stall where she'd left the girl.

Drawing closer, Petra squinted, trying to see Sahar who would surely be on the lookout for her. Perhaps she was deeper, perhaps she was inside the stall. Maybe the girl had been far-sighted enough to take herself to the darkest corner of the stall.

Yet as she reached the stall, before she peered into the back, and even ahead of stepping inside of the murk and gloom of the hat stall, Petra already knew; the girl wasn't there.

Turning on her toes and ignoring the stall-holder's question as to whether she was looking for anything special, Petra walked out on to the main concourse. Here, crowds of people were walking from one end of the site to the other. Petra looked up and down, trying to catch a glimpse of the girl among the bobbing heads of the mass. Desperate, Petra felt in her pocket for her school phone to see if there was a message from Sahar; a text to say she was somewhere else; somewhere safer. But as she keyed in the numeric password, she knew that there would be nothing.

Petra stood on the spot, not knowing what to do or where to go. For no logical reason she checked the work phone; the one the bastards had given her. Here, there was one message. From Rafi. No words, just an emoji winking.

61

RAF Fairborough, Oxfordshire – Three Minutes Later

Eli walked a few paces in front of the girl to give himself some cover so he could mutter into his microphone. Overhead the Red Arrows screamed through the sky leaving a trail of red, white and blue; the fly past was accompanied by a booming commentary and the combined decibels were playing havoc not only with comms but also Eli's own hearing. He pressed his earpiece into his ear to try to shut out the racket and kept his message short.

'Zero Seven approaching 258 with SB.'

As he drew closer to their stallholder's caravan, Eli felt his heart rate slow and spirits lighten. Once Sweetbait had the belt around her waist and was headed in the direction where Special Branch were waiting, they'd be on the home run.

The squad would remove all traces of their presence and like ghosts at dawn they would slip away from the Tattoo as if they'd never been there.

Next – within days, if not hours – they would be summoned by Milne. Eli pondered where the audience would take place; it would need to be somewhere appropriate; somewhere where the MI6 man – on behalf of Her Majesty's Government – could express his grateful thanks for their discreet and effective help with a potential terrorist threat. In return, they would receive the prize: the raw data from the Qatar Embassy RAT. Job done. Operation Sweetbait would be good for Eli; good for Mossad, good for Israel and long term, good for the region.

Step by step they crossed the grass towards the camping ground where the trade exhibitors had set up their motorhomes and caravans. As they drew closer to a big caravan, Eli glanced behind to make sure that Sweetbait was keeping up with him.

'Be strong, *habibti*,' Eli said.

'I follow you with joy,' the girl said.

Ahead Eli saw the caravan with its half-open window and half-drawn curtain on the right. This indicated the all-clear. He slowed to allow the girl to catch up and they were jostled by a stallholder coming in the other direction, 'Great crowd today,' the bleached blonde woman said. 'Don't remember when we've had such a good morning. Second time we've restocked.' She was carrying a black plastic bag that bulged in different directions. She gestured upwards, 'Gotta be the weather. You?'

'Very good,' Eli bent his head away from her.

Satisfied, she shifted back towards the grounds.

Indeed, the sky *was* clear and there was a break in the display and the incessant commentary. This meant that the crowds would be lowering their gaze from the heavens and seeing where they could eat and what they could buy. The timing was perfect.

Eli reached the aluminium fold-down steps of the caravan and rapped.

'Who is it?' the voice said in English.

Standard procedure. Never open any door without asking who is on the other side even if there is a camera.

'Beloved of the Lord,' Eli said.

The door opened out and Eli stood aside so that Sweetbait could go first. Her hand trembled and he reached out to guide her up the steps. Standing at the door was Niorah; she was smiling with warmth and respect.

Perfect choice. Niorah was much in demand throughout the organisation; it had been hard to prise her away from other operations but Yuval had insisted. It was even better that Sweetbait seemed to recognise Niorah as the girl who had helped with the clothes swap after she was picked up from the airport.

'Welcome,' Niorah said in English. 'I am honoured to be able to assist you again.' She bowed in deference to the *shaheeda*.

As soon as she was inside the caravan, Eli climbed the stairs and looked around. At the small table there was an unwelcome sight: Rafi. Spread out, with the big black sports bag on the table in front of him; he was fiddling with his phone.

Rafi put the phone away and stood up and bent so as not to hit his head on the low ceiling. For the occasion, he had covered his head with a *taqyiah* and with his black beard, he looked the part. Uncoiling himself from the small seat, he came out and bowed towards Sweetbait with deference and solemnity.

'Blessings be with you *shaheeda*,' he said. 'I am honoured.'

Eli glanced around. The room dressing was good. At one end of the caravan they'd set up prayer mats; light from the Perspex window shed a shaft across the rich red pattern. For any weary soul it would be a welcome spot to rest and pray.

Gently and with respect, Niorah guided Sweetbait towards the small shower cubicle where the girl would bathe before prayers and before she put on the belt. With soft words Niorah moved the girl step by step to the other end of the caravan.

When the door was safely shut behind and he could hear the spattering sound of the shower and the whine of the pump, Eli glared at Rafi. He hissed, in English, just to be safe, 'Where is Trainer? You were supposed to find her and contain her.'

'Relax, she's got the second surveillance team on her tail.' Rafi tapped his ear to indicate the microphone. 'Resourceful as ever, she phoned the school owner, said the girl had been in an accident and asked to borrow their car. She got the key, went back to the stall.' He looked at his watch. 'And she's just realised the girl's gone.'

'Go and intercept her,' Eli said.

'I can't. I need to fit the belt. It's really delicate, Eli. Why don't we just tell the surveillance team to grab Trainer?'

Beyond the curtain that divided the caravan Eli heard the door to the shower cubicle open followed by the hushed voices of the women. Eli switched to Arabic and recited the *Fatihah*, the first chapter of the Quran.

From the rustling and murmurs behind the curtain, Niorah was helping Sahar dress in the white *abaya*.

There was nothing else for it. After prayers, Eli would have to leave Rafi and Niorah to fit the belt. And also leave Rafi to guide Sweetbait in the direction of the hospitality tents where she'd be arrested.

It would be Eli's task to convince Trainer that although she might not have been told everything, there were good reasons and, most importantly, it was for the greater good.

Above the caravan there was the scream of a jet fighter ripping the air. Eli flinched at the noise. At the same moment, Niorah drew back the curtain and Sahar stood before them in her *abaya*. Another time and place she would have looked like a communion bride of God. Eli swallowed and donned the *taqyiah* he had in his pocket. He stepped towards the girl. 'It is an honour to pray with you, *shaheeda*.'

Eli led the prayers. He found it oddly soothing to mouth the words of respect to Allah. It was meditative and gave him the chance to detach from the maelstrom of the operation. It was like being in the eye of a storm. Forehead to the carpet, he turned to his right and opened an eye; Rafi was deep in prayer; he looked like an old picture Eli had seen of a family of Sephardi Jews from Turkey; he had the strong profile, the dark eyes. And the devotion of a believer. Eli would never understand that guy. A self-serving adulterer, yet a patriot. An uncultured oaf, yet a sophisticated spy. And, it seemed to Eli as he watched Rafi at prayer, in some way that Eli didn't understand at all, Rafi was devout.

Prayers over, Eli held his hands a few centimetres above Sahar's head and blessed her.

'And now, *shahida*, I entrust you to Abu Shemon's care; he is a fellow warrior; he will assist with the belt and guide you in the direction of the sacred point. There he will give you final instructions and leave you. Allah will bless you and take you swiftly to his arms.'

Eli turned quickly and stepped out of the caravan. Even though he knew that the girl was not going to blow herself up and in twenty minutes would be on her way to be interrogated, he still didn't want to meet her eyes. As he walked towards the grounds and the Techno Zone where he was going to intercept Trainer, he wondered why it was so hard for him to look at the girl. Perhaps it was because there was something particularly obscene about committing suicide for a religious or political cause.

Anyway, at least he'd be able to assure Trainer that this wasn't going to happen today.

62

RAF Fairborough, Oxfordshire – Five Minutes Later

Another motorbike trip: Segev dropped off Eli at the Blue Entrance to the Air Tattoo. The second surveillance team had texted Eli the coordinates of Petra's phone; she was now walking along the main concourse between the RAF Village and the Autodrome; no doubt looking for the girl. Fortunately, her pace had slowed; fortunate because Eli didn't much feel like jogging.

Overhead, a display of US helicopter troopships flew in formation pounding the air with their blades; ugly and mighty. Nearby some school kids clamped their hands over their ears in a pathetic attempt at shutting out some of the decibels. Eli walked past aircrew, members of the display teams, swaggering in their overalls. That same swagger; that same look; Eli remembered it from the anniversary paratrooper jumps. All the old guys coming out of their hardware shops and law firms; their vegetable plots and their banks; for one more jump, just like the old days. Same swagger, the whole world over; same swagger of the big swinging dicks.

Halfway down the main concourse Eli saw a sign for the Techno Zone – simultaneously the GPS in his pocket buzzed; Trainer was close. Pushing open the door of the temporary construction, Eli felt the give of portable flooring laid over the grass. The place was packed and Eli was jostled as he stepped inside. The Techno Zone was an education centre with different stalls and demonstrations; kids milled around at the Boeing stand and on the Rolls-Royce stand a man in overalls was showing a group around the full-size jet engines.

Eli's earpiece crackled into life, 'Zero Seven, T1 is at your location.'

'Roger, heading in the direction,' Eli said.

He saw Petra before the surveillance team had given him a firm fix. She was standing next to a girl with wild dark hair and even wilder eyes. The girl was talking with great animation, waving hands and tossing her hair.

Petra was nodding, unable to interject and when the girl's face crumpled into tears, Petra held the girl by the shoulders to steady her. She herself looked drained; her eyes darting over the girl's shoulders and as she scanned the crowd her gaze fell on Eli.

He raised his hand to his forehead in mock salute and smiled.

Irritating and indeed dangerous though her actions had been, she was acting out of the best intentions. Having got Petra's attention he nodded in the direction of the main door, tapped on his watch and held up his palm with five outstretched fingers. Five minutes.

She nodded. She also scowled her agreement. He couldn't blame her for that either.

Confident that she would follow him out of the area, Eli walked towards the main door. There was enough time for him to put her right as to the operation and get her back on board before Sweetbait's arrest. He respected Trainer. It was a difficult situation for her exacerbated by Rafi using his so-called connection with her; these things always ended badly. Yet once Trainer was back in the box, Eli would be free to find a good observation point to watch the MI5 people do their job.

So far the British security had kept their presence well concealed. They weren't clod-hopping all over the place in any obvious way; they obviously knew their stuff.

Standing outside the Techno Zone, Eli scanned the crowd to see if he could spot any MI5 or Special Branch guys doing the circuit while he waited for Petra to emerge.

'Benny?' A voice said behind him. 'My avenging angel? Is it really you?'

Eli swivelled round to where the voice was coming from; that languorous familiar voice.

'My good man, I'm delighted to see you but...' Red Cap was holding out his hand to shake Eli's. He was smiling. 'What the devil are you doing here?' Red Cap said.

63

Techno Zone, RAF Fairborough –
Three Minutes Later

'Aneeta, listen to me for a moment, please,' Petra said. In front of her the girl's face was ugly with anguish.

'I understand this is difficult –' Petra began.

'Not difficult, no, not difficult. Bad. Very bad. I love Sergei and no Sergei, my life – finish.'

'Shut up and listen to me – this is important. Have you seen Sahar?'

'I love him,' Aneeta said.

'I need to find Sahar. It's important – DO YOU UNDERSTAND? Have you seen her?'

Aneeta wasn't listening. Petra had a déjà vu moment of realising how surreal this situation was. It wasn't the first time that real life had spilled over into an operation. Alon called it the alternative reality moment when operational black holes opened up and stories entangled missions in grisly webs.

Petra needed to plug this particular black hole as fast as possible. She continued to hold the girl's shoulder, hoping that steady and calm pressure might bring her down. 'Forget about Sergei, he loves you. Do you understand?'

Something seemed to have penetrated the wall of outrage. Her face relaxed. Petra became aware her throat was aching; she had been shouting over the noise of machinery demonstrations, children's clattering and the hubbub of the show.

'I have not see Sahar after we are off the bus,' Aneeta said.

'Okay. Right, there's a coffee place at the end of the tent. Go there, sit down, and keep phoning Sahar and sending her text messages. If you see her, keep her with you, make her stay with you and call me. Okay? It's important, really important.'

Petra's reward was a teary smile but she couldn't relish it because she was already striding towards the exit.

64

Techno Zone, RAF Fairborough – The Same Time

'What am *I* doing here?' Eli said. 'What are *you* doing here, Derek? You look well.'

For once Eli wasn't lying. Red Cap was wearing an obviously new jacket and a clean shirt. His eyes weren't puffy and yellow and his hair wasn't greasy and long; the agent looked ten years younger.

'Have you been to a spa or something?' Eli said.

'Something,' Red Cap looked at his watch and then at the door. 'Dammit, I've got to get back to the desk, I'm already late.'

'Desk?'

Red Cap rolled his eyes with rueful embarrassment. 'I'm on the GCHQ education desk... I have a champion in HR.'

Eli ran his eyes over the new outfit, 'Looks like more than a champion to me. Lady is she? Just a guess.'

'She's just a friend. I'm on half-day compassionate leave for another three weeks and she got me this gig on the education desk. Kids come up and we give them GCHQ quizzes so they get a taste of cyber security.'

'Cute,' Eli said.

'And I don't want to let her down. It's not a romance but she's stuck her neck out for me. Are you around later?' Red Cap said.

'No,' Eli said. 'Today I am not here.'

'Understood... Listen. This... this seeing you is serendipity. I wanted to thank you for that night, for listening. I was angry and I still am; but I knew when I married Carole; I suppose I always knew it. And now I'm feeling... well, I'm not feeling paranoid for one thing. I've stopped imagining I'm being followed. My friend in HR has a lot to do with it.'

Eli pumped the agent's hand, trying to convey warmth by squeezing his palm, knowing that even now a hug would not be welcome.

'It's so good to see you... like this,' Eli said. 'Not now, but one day, Derek, I don't know when, but one day... Until then, good luck, Derek. You're a good man.'

'So are you.'

Red Cap dived through the double doors leaving Eli with the sense of unreality. Wondering if he had imagined what had happened. Eli straightened up. It was hopeful. In spite of everything, in spite of all the dirt that Eli churned up in the wake of his career, sometimes there was hope; sometimes life moved forward in a positive way. If Derek could move on after being on a certain trajectory to disaster then anything was possible.

While Eli waited for Petra he studied the map of the site to make sure that he had found the best observation point. There, he would demonstrate to Trainer that he'd told her the truth. That Sweetbait, far from blowing herself up, or being shot by a sniper, was going to be gently and courteously led away. And within days, admittedly unpleasant days for her, Sweetbait would be released as part of a back-door arrangement with a grateful British government. After that, she would be on her way to a new life in the US, Canada – or New Zealand if she preferred.

The door swung open and Petra burst out of the Techno Zone among a group of teens who were clutching bits of paper they had picked up at the stands.

'Let's get away from here,' she said to Eli. 'All right, Benny? I am so close to calling the police, MI5 and every media outlet I can think of. Whatever you've got to say had better be good.'

'It's better than good,' Eli said. 'Now we are going to the Aviation Club where we will be able to see what happens. The girl is going to be arrested but think of it as an unpleasant interlude before things improve for her.'

'How sure are you?'

'One hundred per cent. Listen, we've told MI6 what's going to happen, they're professionals. I promise you, they will stop her before anything happens.'

'It's sickening; she has no idea who you are and then she's going to be arrested. That's unacceptable. Why in God's name does Sahar have to suffer?'

They were walking along the concourse in the direction of the Aviation Club. It was perched on a rise in the ground and leading up to it the path narrowed and the gradient increased.

Eli stopped and looked Petra full in the face. 'Sahar has to suffer because she was in the wrong place at the wrong time. Like many people all over the world; Syrian refugees, disabled women in Boko Haram, even, if you like, Jews in 1940s Europe. And do not forget, she was prepared to kill innocent people along with herself.'

'She's a brainwashed idiot.'

'So be it, but we just took advantage of the brainwashing, we didn't invent it. Her people did that as well as feeding the international anti-Semitism monster with lies about Holocaust denial and global Jewish conspiracies. That's part of Hamas strategy. This is ours. And Petra, you will be pleased to know, that the girl's suffering is coming to an end. Since this is all being done under the radar, after a brief interrogation here, we will ask to interview her back home. Then she will be relocated somewhere of her choice. She may even believe that it is Allah's will that she survived. And she and her family will never know that we, the "Zionist monkeys", had anything to do with the changes in her life – the positive changes. As for her brother, hopefully he'll feel that his trust in you led to her being saved and that's also a positive outcome.'

'You're never going to try to recruit him?'

'Who knows? It'll be a wasted opportunity if we don't. Meanwhile, the only people who are aware that we are behind all these positive changes to this family's future are those whose life depends on their silence. You might even consider that your part in this has actually been to improve her and her brother's life; to make a positive difference. And how many times can we truly say that?'

By this time, they were at the top of the slight hill outside the Aviation Club. The small green in front of the private club was packed with tables and chairs. The clink of glasses mingled with chatter as wine was quaffed and the Club members and their ladies were entertained.

'We can't go in there,' Petra said.

'I know. But we can see from the path.' He handed her his binoculars. 'Focus on the concourse; she should be coming from the left to the right. Then she will turn towards the Techno Zone; that's when we'll get the best view because she will be stopped... right over there.' Eli put his hand on Petra's shoulders to point her in the right direction. 'Now you can see down there; about a hundred metres to the left of the control tower; two guys. My guess is that they're the ones waiting for her. And possibly the group on the other side to the left. See that woman in the green dress? So you can see the route is well covered.'

'Oh God – there she is,' Petra said.

65

The Aviation Club, RAF Fairborough – Two Minutes Later

She looked so small from the top of the hill. So alone.

Petra watched the girl, imagining what was going through her head, hoping that the prayers that she was no doubt saying to herself would in some way quell the terror. Maybe the interrogation that would follow her arrest would be a relief after the fear of her own death. What could possibly make her think that dying by her own hand would change anything? What desperation had taken her to that point?

Step after step the girl moved forward and Petra was only dimly aware of Benny by her side. He had his phone out and seemed to be talking on it but she guessed it was just cover for the microphone.

'Yes,' he said, 'very good news,' in a bland voice. 'They should be appearing any second now.'

Petra went back to the binoculars, watching Sahar walk towards her destiny. She indulged the thought that once resettled and with decent enough English, she'd find a community where she was valued for herself; not as daughter, wife, mother or martyr. Through the binoculars Petra thought she saw Sahar's lips moving. But whatever she was feeling, the girl's pace was steady. She had such courage – or was it belief?

At the cross roads to the intersection, Sahar stopped and Petra watched her stop. Even as her heart pounded, she smiled; typical Sahar; she was looking at the map before she made the turn. Always careful; always precise; always keen to be correct. As Petra watched, Sahar tucked the map in her pocket and with clear resolve she turned left towards the Techno Zone.

Petra took the binoculars away from her eyes and saw Benny staring; his face was contorted as he watched Sahar.

'I don't know,' Petra heard Benny say into his phone. 'I don't fucking know where they are. Get over there now.'

Ignoring her, Benny ran towards the concourse. She saw him shift fast; dodge around slower groups of people and shove others out of his way. A woman stumbled, lost her balance and had to be helped to her feet. Another man yelled after Benny, angry at being pushed – but he was gone.

Petra switched her gaze to the concourse. Rapt, she followed Sahar's course; watched her move steadily, saw the resolution and the certainty as she approached the Techno Zone.

No one had stepped out of the crowd to stop her.

66

Techno Zone, RAF Fairborough – Ten Seconds Later

Black.

Before I walk through the door, I close my eyes. I know what I've got to do and I want to be in the dark and rest. Just for a moment. No longer. I've done everything that's been asked of me. It's now time and I crave one second of peace before the end.

Although I know it's not the end and I'm going to *Jennah* it's the end of this time and this place. I swallow and as I open the door the clamour of the noise fills my mind. People shout over thudding machinery and children squeal with excitement. Although I try, Allah knows how hard I try, I lose my place in the final prayer. He, who is almighty and merciful, he will forgive me.

Ahead of me I try to see the way I need to go through the mass of people; this place, for a mad second it reminds me of the old covered souk where I used to go early to buy the *Jibnah Biladi* cheese my mother likes. The same atmosphere; everyone standing; everyone crying for attention.

So many people are around me. They jostle; I see someone ahead fifty metres away. She smiles.

Oh Allah, no, no, be merciful, please, not more tests. I beg of you. Let me do what I must do for your glory. Let me go into your arms with only the blood of strangers on me.

I turn, I go back the way I came towards the door, I go behind a stand and hide; trying to avoid her; trying to avoid Aneeta.

I succeed, she's gone. Slowly I make a circuit of the zone, go past the stands with their machines and people, children and their teachers until I reach the stand with the man and the desk. This is the place

Abu Marwan has told me to be; the centre of the pavilion. I'm standing in front of the man at the desk. He smiles.

My fingers rest on the keypad of the phone, ready to tap the sequence. That's when I feel a hand on my shoulder; an arm; a scent.

'Sahar, my friend, I look for you. I need you –' Aneeta grips my arm.

'Go, this no good, go,' I cannot speak.

'Why?'

The man at the desk stands up, he smiles, he has bad teeth but he looks kind.

'Good afternoon ladies,' he says. 'Let me tell you everything about GCHQ. My name is Derek and I'm a project manager in cryptography. Allow me to explain what we do –'

There is a noise at the end of the tent, by the door. A crash, someone is shouting. I turn. I see Abu Marwan running towards me; he pushes people out of the way.

I know.

He is there to tell me what I must do; he is there to tell me not to hesitate, not to falter.

I tap the keys on the phone.

Black.

67

The Aviation Club, RAF Fairborough – Three Seconds Later

There was a crash from the Techno Zone, immediately followed by screams. Behind Petra, on the green, clinking glasses and tinkling lunch chatter paused. People nudged each other and gaped at people streaming out of the Techno Zone crying. A boy with a bloody arm was being half carried by a woman. Petra froze. She could hear the terror in the cries that carried up the hill. A siren went off. But the commentary on the fly past went on and on until it stopped mid-sentence.

'What happened? What the hell's going on?' A man with white hair and moustache said to no one in particular. 'Was that an explosion?'

'Petra... Petra... listen,' he was by her side. Rafi. He was standing right next to her.

'Where's Benny?' Petra croaked. Her voice didn't sound like her own. 'He ran down the... Rafi, what –'

'Come here a minute,' he guided her around the corner away from the gawping crowd and opened his arms and held her to him, hugging her. In shock, she stood there for a second; she allowed his warmth to soothe her.

She put her hands on his chest and pushed at him. 'Get away from me; this is you. Your doing.'

Rafi took a step back; his expression was neutral. 'Sometimes things work out in different ways,' he said with quiet certainty.

'What's that's supposed to mean?'

'Petra, we don't have time to discuss this. I need your work phone and I'm also taking the tracker phone. I presume it's in your bag. You can't be caught with it on you. We're going to have to take care of Wasim, now. Where is he?'

'I'm not telling you,' she was crying; tears and snot were making it hard to speak.

'Do you want his arrest on your conscience as well as what's just happened here? Listen, we're the boy's only hope of getting out of here before anyone realises that he's connected. Do it, Petra. It's best for everyone. You can't help the girl now. Where is he?'

'He's safe, in a flat near...'

Before she had time to protest he reached into her bag, into the section where she kept her phones, and pocketed them. Rafi went on, 'Prepare – you're going to be questioned and there isn't anything you need to say; you're completely clean, you worked at the school, it was a summer gig, that's it.'

'Except I'm going to tell anybody who asks that it's on you,' Petra said.

'That won't make any difference to what's just happened. Think about it for a minute. The girl did what she wanted to do for something she believed in. And you did what you wanted to do for something you believed in. Same thing, isn't it?'

'No. It isn't.'

Again, Rafi shrugged. 'If you want my advice, don't make your life more complicated than it already is. If you make a big thing out of it then you will be the one that suffers. That's how the world works.'

'And what about you? What have you done?'

'I did what was right,' Rafi said. 'I did what needed to be done.'

68

RAF Fairborough, Exhibitors' Caravan Site – 10 Minutes Later

The caravan looked like the backroom of a butcher's. Blood was pouring from Eli's forehead into his eyes which was hampering the phone conversation he was trying to have with Yuval. Worse, he was half deaf from the aftershock of the blast compounded by the activity around him. In the end Eli handed the phone to Rafi while Niorah did an emergency clean of the wound and stuck closure strips over it. The rest of the crew packed up and cleaned up, spraying cleaner, wiping down, then putting the disposable wipes in plastic bags and the plastic bags in picnic baskets. Given the circumstances the squad was as calm as possible; they'd all been under fire before and they'd all rehearsed exit operations many times.

Rafi was now speaking and Eli half heard and half read his lips. 'First priority is Wasim. You, me and Segev will drive. Everybody else goes straight to the airport. There's a cargo plane waiting for us.'

Rafi checked the contents of his black rucksack before helping Eli up to his feet, out of the caravan and into the car.

Getting away from the airfield was surreal; the traffic marshals were trying to get people away from the airfield as quickly as possible in case there was another bomb, and police, ambulances and fire engines were pushing in the other direction. It helped. Neighbouring farms had opened up their gates to facilitate the evacuation and the car bumped across uneven fields, through cow pats and long grass before reaching the main road and the steady crawl to the motorway. Once they picked up speed Eli was barely aware of Segev's driving; sitting in the back seat he was only aware of blurred scenery flashing past and his ringing ears. This was no time to think; like everybody on the squad, Eli had to act and his first challenge was to hear what Rafi was saying.

'Here, this is flavinoid candy. It might help the tinnitus,' Rafi had turned and was thrusting a wrapped bar at him. Eli chewed what tasted like citric cardboard and swallowed it down with water.

'I'm okay,' Eli said.

'We've got the boy's location from Trainer's phone. Even if we considered her reliable, she'll be among the first people to be interviewed so she needs to be available. That just leaves you as the only person who knows Wasim. We've got to get to him before Five does and we're going to get him out of here one way or another.'

'Meaning?' Eli said.

'Meaning, this is your chance to show us all how much of a spy runner you really are.'

'What about what happened back there. Where the fuck was MI5?'

'I don't know,' Rafi looked away. 'Really. What I do know is that if Wasim gets picked up the situation will be even worse than it already is, so what are you going to do, Eli? Make a big thing about it now when we're in the middle of all this shit or are you going to be on the team? Simple choice, man.'

It took ninety minutes to get to Tilton and the flat where Wasim's commemorative coin was sending out its steady homing signal. With Segev's driving they'd have been there earlier but had to spend an extra fifteen minutes in the toilet cubicle of a service station where Eli submitted to Rafi cleaning and stitching his wound on his forehead. Sitting on the toilet, Rafi standing over him, Eli held the unrolled sterilised medi-pack on his lap while Rafi cleaned, probed, then sewed. For a big-handed man, he was surprisingly deft.

'You're very lucky,' Rafi said puffing antibiotic powder on to his work. 'It's clean and neat. More than you deserve.'

When they came out of the cubicle together they kept their heads down but they still got a look from a man at the urinals. Rafi kept his arm around Eli to try to hide the blood that had dripped down his tee shirt. Casual homosexual sex might be ignored; an obvious wound would be harder. Back in the car Eli changed into the clean tee shirt that Segev had just bought and by the time they'd located the ground-floor flat where Wasim's tracker was signalling Eli was about as ready as he ever would be. He'd show Rafi what sort of spy runner he was.

The peripheral location was clean – a conversion in a Victorian terrace at the end of a quiet street near a park. No stray cars with occupants, no white vans with dark windows, no workman digging up cables. At 3.30pm on a Friday afternoon in suburbia the only sign of life on the street was a pensioner picking up dead leaves and a woman walking an old white dog that shuffled along at the same pace as its owner.

Segev pulled up 50 metres away from the house and the two men got out of the car, Rafi with his hand in his rucksack ready to locate the appropriate tool for the job.

At the shabby front door Rafi smiled. 'About time we had some luck; we won't even need to break a window.'

He withdrew a 5x5 centimetre key pad with a small screen and two plastic-coated wires coming out of the base. Sliding the wires in the gap between door and door frame, he keyed in the details from the reading, pressed enter and there was a click as the latch slipped back.

The men stepped inside and closed the door behind them.

In spite of summer the flat smelt damp; there were brown stains on the ceiling from a leak, old wallpaper that was ripped by a cat or dog, and the bare wooden boards were scuffed. A door to the right was the bathroom, further along a galley kitchen, and ahead the bedroom door was open.

Wasim was under a duvet, curled up in a foetal position. He was sobbing quietly. On the floor there was the detritus of a teenager; Eli recognised it from his own son – the pizza boxes and the cola cans. A chair in the corner was camouflaged by the kid's dirty clothes and Eli lifted them up and moved them to the chest of drawers, smelling the sweaty, scared young man in the bundle. Then Eli placed the chair by the side of the bed in a position that a visiting doctor might use. Rafi was still standing in the doorway but with a hand gesture, Eli waved him away.

'I am so very sorry, *habibti*,' Eli said softly. 'But you must be brave now, braver than ever.'

The top of the duvet moved and Wasim's pointed face appeared. He was blinking like a mole, in this case a red-eyed mole. Eli handed the boy the spectacles that were on the bedside table.

'I saw it on my feed, I knew it was her.'

'Listen, listen,' Eli said. 'You have to believe, it will make it easier. Allah took her into his arms and she is in *Jennah*. She died well and with great courage, and with love for you. It's what she wanted. There was nothing you could have done. Wasim, you must live well to honour her.'

The kid looked more like a boy than a man and Eli couldn't help think of his own son. How would Doron have coped in this situation of being in the wrong place at the wrong time? He had already seen combat and the ugly side of occupation. Was he hardened, could he still weep?

'What about Petra? She promised...' the kid's face gurned into an ugly sob of loss.

'Dead. Or nearly dead. Badly injured anyway,' Eli said. They needed to plug that particular hole fast. Eli went on, 'She tried to save your sister from *shaheeda*; she didn't understand, she wanted to save you too.' At least that part was true.

Eli felt in his jacket pocket for the syringe that Rafi had prepared in the car. He was close enough if need be.

'You now have a choice to make, *habibti*, you can either stay here and wait for the police and MI5 to come for you, or you can come with us and we will get you back to America safely, *inshallah*. If you come with us you will go back to school, finish your studies and when the time comes we will be there – if you want. If you stay here... if you decide to stay here, we cannot help you.'

Wasim pulled himself up to a sitting position and Eli got a clear view of the boy's bare chest and arms. One swift move and he'd be able to press the plunger on the syringe into the boy's arm.

'I don't want to pressure you,' Eli said.

But he did. If Wasim wasn't immediately recruitable then he would be tranquilised and crated; shipped back to Israel and imprisoned under the terrorist act because of his connection with Sahar. At best he'd get a short sentence and his potential career would be ruined. At worst wasn't good at all.

Eli smiled, 'We haven't got much time, maybe a couple of hours, maybe less. Shall I find the kitchen and make you some coffee?' Eli stood up; it would be easier to use the syringe from a standing position. If the kid agreed to go back to the US he'd have a different life. He'd be recruited as an agent for Mossad. He might never know who he was working for but he'd be a tool, just like his sister, because he was in the wrong place at the wrong time.

'Well, *habibti*?' Eli said. 'Coffee, America, what do you want to do?'

'I want to go home. I want to go back to Kansas.'

'*Mumtaz*, excellent, you have made a good choice.'

69

Ramat Gan, Tel Aviv – A Month Later

'Thanks for the lift,' Yuval said as he strapped himself into the passenger seat of the Toyota hybrid. It wasn't as if Eli had much choice; Yuval had told him that he wanted Eli to drive him to Ben Gurion airport for his flight to Washington.

'I wanted to talk to you away from the Office.' Yuval said. His small hands tapped at his carry-on bag. 'There's too much going on there at the moment with the inquiry; too much talk; too much speculation. What we need to do is take a step away from it, consolidate our situation, and look forward.'

The evidence was still being given to the inquiry and the atmosphere was uncertain to say the least. It was what Eli imagined a Medici court would have been like; in every corner and meeting room, by every plant and desk, there'd be one or two or three people talking, stopping talking, sharing what they'd heard or thought they'd heard, and postulating the outcome of the inquiry.

'The situation is like this,' Yuval said. 'First we need to tie up all loose ends. What's the status on Wasim, any further contact logged?'

'None direct since he went back; but we're maintaining a regular check,' Eli said. 'It's too early to be absolutely certain, but he seems okay, he's attending lectures, behaving normally. The FBI paid him a visit but the duplicate passport we gave him did the rest. We can probably start developing him in six months or so.'

'Good,' Yuval said. 'Like my grandmother used to say, you can always make a meal out of the leftovers, they're often the best part. It would have been a pity if Wasim is wasted.'

Eli fingered the four-centimetre scar on his forehead. It was healing faster than the rest of him. They'd just come off the Ayalon and were close to the airport.

'Once you're in the UK your first priority will be rebuilding our relationship with the British,' Yuval said.

'*Mevin*.' Eli indicated and turned towards the airport. 'Understood. I've been thinking about that; we've already given them the product from the Iranian scientist as a peace offering. That should help particularly as I doubt that the French shared it.'

Ahead of Eli, the security gate to the airport opened. He slowed down at the checkpoint and was waved through.

'We also need to monitor Trainer,' Yuval said. 'Regularly. Make sure she's on track.'

'*Tov*. Anything else?' Eli said.

'No, that should do for starters. I'm coming through in October and I'll make sure we have time to catch up.' Yuval said.

'What about Rafi?' Eli blurted out.

'We wait and see,' Yuval said. 'He insists that he gave all the details to Milne but it seems impossible to believe given what he said about Red Cap. In the meantime we have to keep everything running smoothly and not allow any leaks about the inquiry to get into the press. That's why I need you to go to London as acting station manager.'

'I don't care about the outcome of the inquiry; if Rafi isn't jailed I'll resign.'

Yuval gave a short, hard laugh, 'You can't resign. I'm sorry Eli but that's how it is.'

Eli shook his head in frustration, '*We* protected Rafi... We should have thrown the book at him; that's what he deserved.'

Yuval said nothing.

Eli pulled up at the passenger drop-off spot, switched off the engine and turned to Yuval. 'How could we have someone in the organisation who deliberately disobeyed direct orders? It's completely wrong. He murdered Red Cap.'

Yuval had his hand on the door handle; Eli could hear him breathing. Eventually he said, 'We don't know that. The only way we can corroborate Rafi's claim that he gave Milne the information about the attack is by asking Milne; and that's the one thing we can't do. Like this, we keep everything under control and that's why you can't resign. Eli, all the time we must ask ourselves, is it good for Mossad and is it good for Israel?'

'Is it good for Israel?' Eli said.

'This is our burden and we have to live with it. I know it's dirty, but that's the work.'

Throughout the drive back home, Eli thought about Yuval's parting words. He pulled up at a roadside kiosk and bought a pretzel and a coke from a scrawny lad by the till. Leaning against the car, feeling the heat of the metal on his butt he ate and drank and watched the planes take off over the freeway and bank towards Cyprus and the north.

Superficially Eli was fine; he'd seen the medics; talked to the shrink; and passed the necessary medicals. He knew the answers to the questions; he knew how to dance around any suggestion that he wasn't fit for purpose. But the truth was that Eli was still in shock; still sick to his stomach.

Eli screwed up the paper that had held the pretzel and got back into the car. He was disheartened; everything that Yuval had said on the drive to the airport was true. He couldn't resign; he had to go to London and hope that the inquiry would recommend criminal proceedings against Rafi. Meanwhile, the collateral damage was outweighed by the flow of product. It was a balancing act and on balance, they were ahead. Yet Red Cap wasn't ahead; neither was Sweetbait nor the Spanish student who was in the wrong place at the wrong time. And as for Trainer who knew what she was suffering or how she might react.

70

Thames End Village, Surrey – Two Weeks Later

That morning Petra drifted around the house in the heavy daze of the sleep deprived. She showered and ate; she neither noticed what she wore nor what she swallowed. The malaise had been going on for weeks. At least once a day Petra went to her wardrobe safe and took out Sahar's notebook. She'd run her fingers over the beautiful script, wondering what it said, what the girl had written about and was so important that she'd begged her to keep it safe. Looking at the book was a ritual that Petra recognised as being dysfunctional but the act was still helping her deal with her state of mind.

Fortunately, Matt was still away but as she sat at the kitchen table drinking tea and the doorbell rang, she hoped that he would be there and not Sandie or anybody else to whom she would have to pretend that everything was okay.

Petra looked through the spy hole, hesitated for a second, and then pulled open the front door.

'What do you want?' Petra said.

'I want to come in.'

Benny was holding a bunch of autumn flowers. 'I want to see you, find out how you are, and I want to explain what happened.'

'I know what happened, I was there.' Yet she still turned around and let him follow her into the kitchen. He didn't sit down, but lay the flowers gently on the table. She didn't offer him anything.

'What's going to happen to Rafi? Is he going to prison? I'd be happy to testify if that's the case,' Petra said.

'May I have some water please,' Benny said.

She took a glass from the draining board and filled it with tap water. She didn't hand it to him; she placed it on the table with the rust-coloured chrysanthemums.

'Be assured that you won't see Rafi again,' Benny said.

'That's not enough, I want to know what's going to happen to him and I want to be satisfied that he's been punished,' Petra said. 'I don't think that's too much to ask for keeping my side of the bargain and keeping quiet when I was interviewed by Special Branch.'

'The inquiry is ongoing,' Benny said. 'Believe me, I'm as sick about it as you are, but I've got a job to do. What happened with Deanna? How did she cope with the interviews?'

'She was hysterical, kept crying about the school's reputation. And when they tried to trace the source of payments they found she hadn't filed her annual accounts for five years; I think it was supposed to have been her husband's responsibility. Anyway, I spoke to her last week, she's still in a bad way and I think the business will go bust.'

'Are you sorry for her?'

'No. What happened to Wasim? Did you kill him too?'

Benny shook his head as if he was weary. 'He's back home in Kansas, in school, but we told him you were dead, injured in the blast, just to tidy everything up.'

'Expected. Is he okay?'

'He's been interviewed by the FBI if that's what you mean but he's as good as he could be given the circumstances. Listen, he could be in a British jail or worse.'

She saw Benny blink and shift his head to one side; it was a recognisable tell. He was going to try to soothe her and say whatever was necessary to get her back on the team. The sight of it made Petra feel weary all the way down to the cells within the marrow of her bones; she was exhausted to death. She was sick of the lies; the prevarication; the massaging and the manipulation.

'You told me that the end result of this sick operation was that Sahar would be arrested and relocated to some idyll. And now she's dead. Did you know all along? Are you really so disgusting as to use a human being in this way?'

Benny sighed. 'Something went very wrong, that's why there's an inquiry. That's all I can say except we take this seriously; if Rafi is guilty he'll be punished. You have my word on that.'

'Sure,' Petra said without emotion.

'Is there anything you need? Anything we can help you with? I'd like to pop by from time to time, have a coffee –'

'And check up on me,' she interrupted in a flat voice. 'Just tell me one thing, Benny. Why the hell should I keep the faith? How can I possibly trust you? You lie, you cheat, you kill.'

There was a painful silence in the kitchen. At last Benny spoke, 'You can trust me because I trust you. Because we're both trying to make a difference and we both made mistakes; bad mistakes. It's as simple as that. I'll be in touch.'

He pushed the seat back, stood up and walked to the door. He turned around before he left the kitchen. 'By the way, my real name is Eli Amiram.'

71

Queen's Park, London – Two Weeks Later

On the TV screen the birds took off from the African river in massed panic desperate to evade the prowling cheetah on the dry riverbank. They soared higher and higher into the parched blue sky swirling away from danger. Eli leaned back into Gal's arms; she loved the wildlife programmes.

For Eli, the flapping birds only made him think about the organisation's reaction to Sweetbait. Officially, it was deemed a success; the intelligence conduits between MI6 and Mossad were wide open and raw data from the Qatar embassies in both London and Washington was now spewing like blood from a carotid artery. Survival was success. Product was success. Avoiding the prowling cheetah was success.

And now Eli was in London, on the sofa with Gal.

'Do you think I should resign?' Eli said.

'If that's what you want to do,' Gal sipped her green tea.

'Or we could just go away, run away, live somewhere else.'

'I don't think that would work; you're not that kind of guy. You stick at things.'

'Maybe they're the wrong things.'

'Eli, you're entitled to be depressed; but you will come to terms with the situation and it will not blight your life,' she kissed his eyebrow.

'That's very kind of you to say so, but I made mistakes, bad mistakes, errors of judgement. People got hurt who didn't deserve to.'

'Nobody deserves to get hurt,' Gal said.

'I'm not so sure about that,' Eli said. He sat up and moved away from Gal. 'I spoke to Asher today –'

'Asher?'

'Doesn't matter. He knows someone in the secretariat who read all the witness statements.'

'Should you be telling me this?'

'I don't care; I have to speak to someone. Rafi insists that he did everything correctly and that it was impossible for the detonator to go off. At the very least he fucked up; in my opinion it was deliberate but if he sticks to his story he gets himself off the hook; no criminal proceedings. It hurts, Gal, it hurts.'

'What do you want to happen?' Gal said.

Eli got up from the sofa and paced to the floor-to-ceiling window where he looked out over the green grass and grey sky of the park beyond their north-west London flat. 'He should have gone to prison.'

'Why didn't you say that when you talked to the inquiry? Why didn't you tell Yuval that you couldn't keep quiet about what you think happened?'

Eli said nothing.

For the first time since the blast Gal's voice showed exasperation. 'Okay, so you made mistakes; you misjudged situations; people got hurt. How many times does that happen in battle? How many times does that happen in life? People make mistakes when they're driving; they're on the phone; a bike pulls out.'

Eli's eyes followed a squirrel that was scampering across the wet grass, trying to get to safety before the foxes came out. Behind him he was aware that Gal had picked up the remote and paused the TV. The room was quiet.

Eli sensed Gal rise from the sofa and come towards him. She put her hand on his shoulder and her touch was comforting.

She said, 'Eli how much of your anguish is to do with your self-perceived mistakes and regret about the people who got hurt? And how much is it guilt that you've got the London job?'

72

The Travellers Club – Next Day

The lunch was billed as a welcome back but Eli was in no doubt that the welcome element would be seasoned with bitter herbs. Since the explosion, communication with Milne had been through official channels; no intimate chit chat over coffee or meals with fine wine. Today's meeting would be the first time the two men had sat across the table breaking bread and Eli assumed that after the explosion Milne must have been flayed for mishandling the situation. If so, he would be in no mood to be pleasant.

But Eli was wrong.

'Sherry I seem to remember,' Milne said. 'The club has changed the wine list since you were here last and I must recommend the Manzanilla Solear; they serve it ice cold and it's really quite delicious.'

'Thank you,' Eli said.' I've been looking forward to this lunch. Perhaps some day I'll be able to entertain you in Tel Aviv – we have some very fine restaurants.'

'So I hear.' Milne didn't look up from the menu.

As far as Eli was concerned the purpose of the lunch was entirely conciliatory; he was there to make no point other than to assure Milne of his respect and commitment to working well together in the future.

'It really has to be the grouse,' Milne said. 'There's nothing like it.'

'Great choice, I'll have the same; we see a lot of different foods in Tel Aviv but not grouse.'

Milne laid the menu down and glanced at the waiter who took their order with swiftness and efficiency.

'I believe the grouse is shot on an estate in Scotland where the club has shooting rights,' Milne said. 'I never read the newsletters they send out, maybe I should start. Do you shoot?'

'Not for fun,' Eli said. 'That's for amateurs.'

The comment cracked the ice; Milne looked up and smiled. His expression was surprisingly warm on his smoothly shaved face.

'How's your wife settling in?' Milne said.

'Quite well, thank you – there's a lot to do with the move, getting things organised. We're now waiting for our son to join us so she'll be busy with him. Once that's done, knowing her, she'll be looking for something to do.' Eli broke up the warm roll, careful to keep the crumbs on the plate.

He went on, 'Overseas postings have advantages and disadvantages for a family.'

'I know all about that,' Milne said. 'I had three years in Singapore at the High Commission, then three in Basra which was dreadful, then two in Istanbul; the last posting with three children under the age of eight. That nearly ended my marriage. I was never there – always travelling.'

'It happens,' Eli said. 'If my wife can work we'll be fine but that's not going to be so easy. She's a child psychologist, very senior, a specialist in PTSD; she could teach or do research but that may not be possible... Of course, you already knew that, didn't you?' Eli smiled.

'There's so much product flying around at any one time, who's got time to read the personal background of... friends.'

The starters came; the asparagus gleamed under a coating of butter and to Eli, the atmosphere seemed promising. In spite of what must have been considered to be a serious intelligence failure, Milne was relaxed. Perhaps this was the famous British sangfroid that had stimulated Kipling to write *If*. Eli's father loved to recite it when he was a child and talk about triumph and disaster as the same imposters.

Talk at the table turned from social and sport to the CIA and Charlene, the American head of station.

'I'll invite her to join us next time,' Milne said surveying with satisfaction his grouse carcass; he'd picked it bare with the efficiency of a vulture. Milne looked up. 'By the way, I understand you've got their Qatar Embassy product as well as ours. Happy now?'

'Yes, but I'm told the British raw data is the more valuable. Even though there's certainly Hamas activity in Washington buying arms, and activity with drug cartels in South America, this is still the jumping-off point for operations. The UK is nearer to Switzerland for finance and offshore laundering, not to mention Africa. How is Charlene doing?'

Eli was due to see the American for lunch the following week and an impression, even a skewed impression, would be helpful.

'She's an extremely clever woman,' Milne said.

'That's the feeling I got.'

'She does an absolutely magnificent imitation of a Deep South cheerleader; meanwhile she's got a PhD in international affairs and intelligence studies; she literally wrote the book on covert operation efficacy analysis.'

'I heard about that, Yuval said he'd send me a copy. How about in the field? Academic prowess doesn't necessarily go with street smarts.'

'She's got that too,' Milne said. 'Iraq, Afghanistan. And she speaks Egyptian Arabic and Dari. She's the new wave.'

'Dari? That's impressive. If she's that smart she might not survive.'

Like old colleagues from different companies in the same industry the two men gossiped over the port and stilton. Eli told Milne that Yuval was now station head in Washington. They speculated about the most recent changes at the Russian rezidentura and, after what Eli believed to be a most satisfactory, relationship-building lunch, Milne signalled for the bill.

Yet... yet there was something in Eli's peripheral awareness that niggled him. It was like a note in a piano concerto that was almost but not quite flat. Milne was looking over his glasses at the bill and signed with a flourish.

'Next time I hope you'll allow me to entertain you,' Eli said.

'That would be delightful,' Milne said. 'But this one really is on me.' He replaced the fancy writing instrument in his inner pocket and looked up. 'By the way, I didn't ask you how your charming colleague Rafi was faring.'

That's what it was, the whole way through the damn lunch. Through the sherry, the grouse, the plate of English cheese, Rafi had been the miasma.

'How is Rafi?' Milne said. 'Did he also get an overseas posting?'

'No, not this time. He's on attachment to a special unit,' Eli said hoping the bland response didn't seem like the curtness of a slammed door.

Milne leaned across the table and made a steeple with his hands. He said, 'I owe Rafi an apology; perhaps you'd be good enough to convey it to him.'

'Apology?'

'Rafi gave me some information about the location and timing of the terrorist attack at RAF Fairborough. I'm afraid we decided not to act on it in quite the way you expected.'

Eli felt lunch churning in his gut. He reached for the crystal glass of water that was still on the table and sipped.

'Why... why was that?' Eli said.

Milne lowered his voice and leaned a little closer, 'The fact is we had a problem at GCHQ. One of our section deputy managers had been downloading data on to a chip at regular intervals. Poor chap had some personal problems too, drink and an alcoholic wife. You know the type of thing; absolutely tragic. Anyway, Five had surveillance on him on and off, and although we weren't absolutely 100 per cent certain where the data was going, we needed to stop the flow. Happily you, via Rafi, gave us enough information so our people were able to, as it were, orchestrate events to our advantage. These remote administrative tools are quite remarkable.'

Eli felt his heart pound against his ribs; he used all his strength to maintain a calm expression. Milne went on in the same collaborative tone, 'Eli, I don't have to tell you how much we'd have disliked having to go through an arrest, trial and conviction. When that happens we're always the losers; haranguing press, the minister out to get us, questions in Parliament.'

The mask dropped and Milne seemed genuinely uncomfortable. 'Eli, given the prevailing instability where we really don't know who our friends or who our enemies are going to be, we simply could not be seen to be have had such an egregious breach of our security. It was too good an opportunity to let slip. I'm afraid we had to think about what's good for SIS and what's good for the UK.'

73

Queen's Park, London – A Week Later

It was the least he could do.

It was the night before *Rosh Hashana* and for the last few days Gal had been making lists, ordering food and cutlery, and getting the flat ready to host the entire security department of the embassy and their families. It was one of the duties of the head of station and his wife to host high days and holidays for the section; to suggest that they were one big family.

'We don't have enough chairs,' Gal said. 'And I'm not sure we have enough space for everyone. The kids are going to have to sit on the floor.'

'I'm sure everything will be perfect.' Eli picked up the keys from the hall table and went to work. He spent the morning doing paperwork in his office at the embassy and at midday he cleared his desk and told his bag girl that he was going home to help Gal prepare for the party like the good husband he was. He noted the look of approval in the youngster's eyes; the blonde twenty-year-old seemed like a nice girl with decent values.

Clear of the embassy Eli caught the tube to the car hire company and signed out a silver Honda.

The drive was easy. There wasn't much traffic about and he was able to play some music and enjoy the smooth road and the newly tuned vehicle. After an hour he felt hungry and stopped at a service station where he ate a sandwich standing in the car park, listening to the roar of the motorway, watching the people around him, all on journeys, all going somewhere. No one was tailing him, not that it would matter that much if they did; as station manager, he was an accredited diplomat; a commercial attaché.

Sandwich and coffee consumed, Eli binned the packaging and before he resumed the journey he patted his pockets to check he'd got what was necessary.

It started to rain just as he was parking the car. The afternoon was dank and the rain dripped off the tapestry coloured trees and pattered to the ground. Opposite where he'd parked there was a school and a clutch of parents, unfurling their umbrellas as they stood like sentries, waiting for their children to come out. For a moment Eli watched them at the school gate; chatting, sharing, living. It seemed odd that the end of life should be juxtaposed with the beginning of life, or maybe not, Eli thought as he walked through the gates into the municipal cemetery.

Eli found the grave easily; there was a grave marker in lieu of the stone that would be erected once the ground had settled. As he walked along the path Eli considered that of all the subjects they'd discussed, they'd never talked about mortality. It would have been a lively discussion; Eli regretted that it was now too late to do so.

With his feet slightly apart Eli closed his eyes and composed himself. He knew the words by heart; how could he not? He'd said them often enough; at the graveside of fallen friends, family and colleagues. Most recently he'd said them at Alon's funeral in the high-rise cemetery that was like a car park. That had also been a dark day.

But today Eli said *kaddish* for Red Cap; for Derek; for his friend.

As Eli mouthed the words quietly in this English cemetery with trees dripping rain on to sodden leaves and the distant hush of a motorway in the distance, Eli pictured the agent as he'd last seen him: whole; strong and smiling. No doubt Derek would say that what Eli was doing was foolish sentimentality but just the same he'd still be happy Eli was there. He wished Derek would have been there; Eli wished he could have shared the information he'd got from Milne. Nobody but the dead agent, with his charm and humanity and devilish humour would have truly appreciated the ridiculous irony of his own death.

Eli was tearful but he went on, nodding his head as he recited the ancient prayer. 'Have mercy upon him; pardon all his transgressions... shelter his soul in the shadow of Thy wings. Make known to him the path of life. *Oseh shalom bimrovav*,' Eli sang softly. 'He who makes peace in high places, shall make peace upon us.'

From his pocket Eli took out the stone he'd brought with him to place on the grave. He knelt and the scent of damp earth filled his nostrils. His eyes were moist and he brushed his sleeve across them. The stone was smooth and oval and using his left hand he placed it next to the grave marker.

There was one final task for Eli to complete; reaching into his right-hand pocket, Eli took out a piece of yellow chalk and nicked the base of the grave marker with a tick: it was the signal to Red Cap that all was well.

The End

Author's Notes

Although I've written and script edited in different genres and media, I've never written a spy novel until now. I love reading them and I studied the genre as part of an MA in Crime Fiction at the University of East Anglia, but it wasn't until I got stuck into the research that I found my story.

None of the characters or events in the novel are based on real people or real events but the narrative is based on real types of people and the sorts of activities that the intelligence professions pursue.

Whether they are British, Israeli, Russian, American, North Korean, Chinese or any other nationality, intelligence organisations have the same objectives: they collect intelligence about other countries; they try to identify other countries' espionage activities. And, they try to influence other countries in a way that is beneficial to their own country's interests.

During the Cold War, the Soviet Union helped the CND movement and the Greenham Common Protest. On the other side, the CIA supported the church and religion in the Soviet bloc. Both these activities were aimed at undermining the opposing regimes as part of the respective governments' foreign policies.

It's what intelligence organisations do: regime change; election fixing; blackmail; propaganda (aka fake news); kidnapping, targeted assassination (aka murder) – and so on.

We can throw up our hands in despair about the immorality of these actions, the notion of the KGB manipulating well-meaning, peaceable people to support Soviet aims while the CIA uses religious beliefs to try to destabilise the Soviet bloc, but it's the nature of the profession.

What intrigues me, as a writer, is that these transgressive acts are being planned and carried out by mostly decent, intelligent people with the very best of intentions.

THE RIGHTEOUS SPY

These are some of the books I read:-

Gideon's Spies, Gordon Thomas

The Mitrokhin Archive, Christopher Andrew and Vasili Mitrokhin

Memoirs of a Spymaster, Markus Wolf with Anne McElvoy

Spycatcher, Peter Wright

The Oxford Handbook of National Security Intelligence, Ed. Loch K Johnson

National Security Intelligence, Loch K Johnson

Intercept, Gordon Corera

By Way of Deception, Victor Ostrovsky and Claire Hoy

GCHQ, Richard J Aldrich

Spy Handler, Victor Cherkashin with Gregory Peter

On Intelligence, John Hughes-Wilson

Disrupt and Deny, Rory Cormac

Book Club Questions

Who do you think is the Righteous Spy? In other words, which character is morally right?

What does the book say about the world of espionage?

Which other writers would you compare Merle Nygate to and would you read another book by her?

Which parts of the book stood out for you? What did you think of Nygate's writing style?

Did you learn anything that you weren't aware of before?

Who was the character that you identified with the most?

Were you satisfied with the ending? What feeling did you take away?

Please feel free to send your thoughts to the publisher at

info@vervebooks.co.uk

Acknowledgements

There may only be one person's name on the front of the book and one person tapping away at the keyboard but many people have helped me.

I'd like to thank everybody who talked to me, read drafts and gave me feedback. As well as reading, Isabelle Grey has been a great friend and a constant support. Also, Martin Fletcher, John Corry, Theresa Boden, Tika Cope, Joe Millis and a special big thank you and hug to Loni Arditi. I'd also like to thank those people who don't want to be name checked. Your input has made it a stronger and more convincing book.

As well as those who helped for love, I'd also like to thank the professionals. Arzu Tahsin for her thoughtful and incisive notes; Jon Elek and Rosa Schierenberg at United Agents for representing me; and the tutors and my cohort on the MA Crime Fiction at UEA, especially Suzanne Mustacich. Thank you also to Clare Smith at Little Brown for giving me the UEA/Little Brown prize. And Clare Quinlivan and Katherine Sunderland at Verve for publishing the novel.

Finally, I'd like to thank my beloved husband, James, for listening to my endless conversations about the book. I know it's been hell, but it'll be worth it. I think.

To be the first to hear about new books and exclusive deals
from Verve Books, sign up to our newsletters:
vervebooks.co.uk/signup

VERVE
BOOKS